LEGENDS

Emily West

For Peggy.

1

The dry, barren land is rough against my knees as I bend down and hide behind a pile of large boulders, shading myself from the sun. My breathing is even; I've been in hiding for so long from the evil who took our homes, and the mindless henchmen that came with it, I've learnt how to control my shallow, scared gasps, and make myself as silent as I can. Pulling out my flask and unscrewing the lid, I hold it up to my mouth feeling the small drops of water instantly refresh my cracked lips, before holding the flask up and letting the cool water fill my mouth and run down my throat. I make myself stop, knowing I'll need to save it until I can get access to the river to refill. I don't know how long that will be.

I freeze when a dark figure steps in front of the sun. I

see the shadows cast over the boulders behind me and stretch out in front of me. From the shape I know it is one of the henchmen, referred to as Ghost Men throughout the lands, for their impractical white coloured uniform that defies the laws of nature and never seems to dirty. They have broad builds and large helmets that cover their faces; no one has ever seen a Ghost without the head armour. They're always looking for rogues. I've come across them before, and just made it out several times. They'll imprison you, injure you, or kill you. I stop a chill threatening to run up my spine and keep calm, sinking further into the crevices of the rocks to conceal myself. Even in the hot desert sun, the presence the Ghost brings with it while it's around is cold and dark.

When the shadow doesn't leave, I fear it knows I am here, so I push back against the pile. The boulders scratch against my bare skin, as I will myself to press further out of sight. I don't utter a sound and eventually the shadow moves, retreating away. I find the guts to peer around and just catch a glimpse of two Ghosts' white capes being whipped around by a breeze before they vanish into thin air. I have to make sure the coast is clear; I was unaware there was more than one Ghost here. I have to get back to my usual camping spot before night comes or I will freeze. The dry lands get very cold at night.

As I poke my head out further from my hiding place and

look out at the scene behind the boulders I see just what I expected. Empty, dry land that spreads for miles. The air above the ground wavers and flickers, indicating the heat radiating from the dirt. Just as I stand up and have a clearer view, I notice something unfamiliar and black lying to the side, not far from where I am. Ducking my head in fear, I wait a moment before realizing there's no way they couldn't have seen me and if whatever it is hasn't come after me, it can't be a threat. I gingerly rise to a standing stance again and get a better look at what it is.

I see a person. It's a man lying on the ground. He is decked out in black denim with many belts and pockets, holding knives and a flask, much like my own. He is scruffy and his leather jacket lies open, showing me his wound in full view. My eyes widen and in a moment of instinct I run out to the man and kneel by his side, conscious that I am now in open land and vulnerable. But I put that thought to the back of my mind, knowing this area had just been patrolled, by not one but two Ghosts, and think only of the man in front of me who must have just been injured by one of them as the wound is fresh, and blood drips over his hip.

He has not been severely injured, though he is unconscious, and with no supplies, left lying here wounded he would most likely develop infection and die, and I assume that was the Ghost's intention. I drop some water over his wound and over my rag, washing off dust and dirt before I ball it up and press it to his hip, applying pressure and hoping to stop the blood flow quickly, so I can move him to a safer place.

A moan escapes the man's lips as I make contact with his body. He coughs and splutters for a moment, trying to raise his head to get a glimpse of the person kneeling beside him.

"Shh," I coo. He blinks at me and settles back down. He must have taken a blow to the head too which has left him woozy. To be left only injured, and not dead, means he must have put up a fight. I think I can make out some swelling around his eye, which will most likely form into a bruise. It is then that I finally get a good look at his face.

As he lays back down, in a gesture that says he trusts me, I hope, I have a chance to inspect him more closely. His skin radiates beauty, despite the scuff marks and dirt across his neck and cheeks. His lips are dark pink and cracked, so I hold one hand on my rag over his hip, and with the other slowly pour some more water from my flask into his mouth. I encourage him to drink by putting the rim of the flask to his lips, to which he responds and I sigh with relief.

His eyes open briefly again and I almost forget my name when his blue eyes look straight at me. They shine bright, full of life, despite how his form may say otherwise.

Regardless, he is beautiful. I have to tell myself to stay focused and remind myself of my name. Kayin Sesay, you can do this. Help this man, I think, urging myself on. I gently put my hand across his forehead.

"How do you feel?" I whisper. You never know if you are being watched.

His eyes twinkle in the fading sunlight, searching mine, like he's trying to figure me out.

"Winded," he croaks. I take his answer into consideration, knowing it will probably be best for him to sit or stand up if he feels winded. However, I'm not sure how easy that would be given his hip wound, and I'm not certain of the condition his head is in.

"I'm going to slowly sit you up. Is that okay?" I keep my voice calm, hoping to reassure him. He doesn't look scared; he seems to be dealing well. In fact, I would say he looks like a seasoned warrior, even if his face tells me he is no older than early twenties.

I slide my arm under his body and across his upper back, sharing his weight as he pulls himself up. Once straight I immediately put pressure back on his wound and he winces.

"I need to clean it," I say, feeling shy suddenly. Even sitting down his body seems to tower over mine.

"I understand."

"Do you need more water?" I ask. He shakes his head,

and closes his eyes. He lifts a hand to his face, probably feeling the damage around his left eye. I go back to surveying his cut.

I lift away my rag, which is covered in his blood, but I am glad to see the blood flowing from his skin is no longer a major threat. I look at the deep cut carefully, surrounded by sore, bloodstained skin, and ponder. It is nowhere near as bad as it should be. Either the Ghost Men are getting sloppy or this man put up quite a fight indeed. I suspect it is the latter.

I find a clean part of the rag and soak it in water, then go to work dabbing and softly rubbing at his skin and anything around the area that looks dirty and could lead to infection.

After a short while I am able to coax him up and get him to safety. I find a discarded building and take shelter there. I can tell it was once part of quite a large village because I notice a small stream running parallel to us. Having a stream or small river running through the middle of civilisations was common in the bigger villages.

Settling the man down in a corner, I shiver as a breeze blows in. The sun has almost set so I know we are lucky to have found shelter when we did. We will have to brave the cold tonight. I'm sure I can find some old blankets or rags to block the chill of the night. But before that, we need water, so I take his flask out of his belt and hold it with mine, telling him to keep pressure on his wound still and not to make any sudden movements. I tell him I'll be back shortly.

As I venture out of the building and towards the stream, constantly looking for any enemies, I think about what has just happened. It's not often I run into other rogues like me; unless I find some much like that man, who have been left injured or on their deathbed. And I'm always happy to help. It's run in my family for years, centuries, being a healer. It's a special title handed down from my ancestors, to each first born in the Sesay family, and down to me. When the Ghosts captured my family, I found my chance to flee after two years of imprisonment. My parents had begged me to get out. When we found an opening, a slight opportunity for me to make it out of the prison, they had pushed me, quite literally. So I had to keep moving forward to freedom, or risk hesitating or going back and getting caught.

Obviously freedom is a relative term. But I would still pick being out here to being in there. I constantly think of my parents, how they might be coping…if they are still alive. It's not a thought I like to dwell on, so before I can let it run any further through my mind, I screw on the lids of the flasks and start making my way back, shaking those thoughts away.

As I near, I hear voices floating across the breeze on the other side of the building. I panic and freeze. Who could that be? Surely not more Ghost Men now? I hear the man I had helped groan and the voices head that way. For a moment I wonder whether I should run in and help him, but I'd be no use. I'm a healer, not a fighter. And I would bet that this man was a better fighter than me even in his state.

"Oh there you are!" I hear a relieved, feminine voice say. I look around the arch entrance and see a man and a woman, both handsome and beautiful, respectively. They approach the man with no caution and kneel by his side. I wonder if they are working for the Ghost Men. When the Ghosts first invaded our people, we were given the choice by a loud booming voice that echoed into our cells, as if by magic, to work for them and serve their people, whoever they may be, integrate with their society, or stay in prison to rot. If you chose to work, and be one of them, betrayal is a crime punishable by death, so deciding to work for them was not a decision taken lightly. Those who take the offer are considered to be betraying their own people, and are often referred to as traitors. I wonder if these people here are traitors and have come to collect the man, but their affectionate attitude towards him strikes those thoughts down.

"We must get him back to the rest of the group," the other man tells the woman, and then turns to his friend. "We've been worried about you," he says with more tenderness.

I catch a glimpse of the new man's jacket, which has white writing on the back. It is worn down a bit, but even from this distance it's not hard to miss the word 'Cryptic'. I gasp, and then duck my head away, not wanting to be seen. Cryptic? As in one of the Four? Surely they're not real? I thought they were myths, stories my mother Gracine Sesay used to tell me. Uplifting tales of four people; a fearless and clever leader, a caring and enchanting medium, an alluring and mystic sorcerer, and a passionate and strong fighter. The Oracle, the Divine, the Cryptic and the Vehement. They would rule the rogues when our land was taken from us by evil. The Rogue Resistance, they were called.

True, in reality our land has been taken away, and over the years the evil has grown stronger, however I still believed they were just stories. I never thought the myth was true; four people who would rise up to leadership and carry out a rebellion.

Still in shock and now confused, I look back and see the man and woman helping the other man out of the ruins and away from me. He seems to have blacked out again. I watch them turn their backs to me. I'm still staring longingly at the Cryptic, wondering if it is true, when I see another name scrawled across the leather jacket of the man I helped. I can practically feel my eyes pop out of my head.

A seasoned warrior, indeed, I think to myself. I just helped another supposed man of legend, the Oracle.

I am alone once again. I have taken my place for the night in the corner that once held a man. But not just any man. The Oracle. I relish in the feeling that maybe, just maybe, I was sitting in the faint presence of a legend.

The sudden talk of rebellions and the Four make me think back to when I was told those stories. I remember my mother tucking me into bed. She'd lean over and kiss my forehead, ask if I was comfortable, then launch into another gripping tale of how four people found the power within them to unite. It always started with 'Many moons ago...' evil would control our lands, humans would be in danger, but the Four would be skilled in many areas. They'd be quick, smart, nimble, powerful and above all heroes. They would guide the rogues, lead the Resistance, and start a rebellion. My mother kept the stories child friendly, but I knew the full myths and legends included gory battles on the desert land. People like us, healers, would work behind the front line, helping injured soldiers, bringing life back into their eyes. And history was to repeat itself; every few centuries another Four would rise to fulfil their destiny. I'd fall asleep filled with hope that I was safe.

When I was older, 11 or 12, it was like realising there was no tooth fairy. In your adolescent mind you decide that the myths were just that; myths. Or if you were more naïve minded, you would maybe believe that it just wouldn't happen in your lifetime. They were not true tales of long ago, just stories; that's what I believed. At 20, I didn't think I'd ever change my mind, but now I am having doubts.

Maybe they were frauds. People who believed they could be great and forged the names on their jackets. They seemed young, how could they know they were part of a prophecy, and already know which character they were supposed to play? I suppose having great power would mean they had a sense all along. No, I'm not possibly thinking this is true, am I? I can't rest my faith in people that I haven't formerly met who claim to be legends. In fact I've never seen them around before. And where the hell is this Rogue Resistance, then?

Maybe they're just that good, my subconscious whispers to me. I squint my eyes shut and stop thinking about it. I can't let myself get distracted of what could and could not be, when I have to survive out here on my own.

I bring a flask up to my lips and take a swig, knowing I have two to last me through the night and morning. Wait, two? I look at my hand, holding a sleek black flask that was thicker than mine. He didn't take it back when he left. I screw the lid back on and let my thumb trace over the engraved letter on the top. O...O for Oracle... I think dreamily. I give in. I let my mind fill of old stories and memories and tales of the Rogues and thoughts of rebellion as I drift off to sleep.

In the morning, I awake feeling warm and comforted. I blink my eyes open and know I have to move soon. The light streams through the holes in the roof of the run down building and I can infer that it is at least 10am. I can't stay in the same place for too long, for fear of being caught. I stand up and brush myself down. I shake down the blanket I had found, getting what dirt that I could off of it, and drop it over my right shoulder, tying it at my left hip, like a sash. I can use it later tonight when I am back at my camp and it will keep the strong sun off of my skin for a while.

I secure both the flasks to my belts and keep a ready hand at my right, ready to pull my blade out of its place at a moment's notice; a habit of mine that has now saved me once or twice.

I creep along the old stone floor and then leave the building, flitting from boulder to boulder, finding the safest, most hidden route to scavenge food, until...

"Oof," I run into something unexpectedly and it knocks me back for a moment. Even as I stumble back I grab for the handle of my knife. I hold it out in front of me and catch my bearings, looking up into the face of the handsome man I saw last night; the so-called Cryptic. I am still on guard, not knowing whether he is in fact who he thinks he is.

"What's your name?" he speaks calmly, not even flinching at my ready-to-fight stance, or the blade that is inches from him. It is a small blade, but a blade all the same, it can do some damage with the right know-how.

"Who's asking?" I counter, with a step back, but I push my shoulders back in a show of confidence. I may be backing away but I'm not (completely) scared. A soft deep chuckle escapes his lips and he looks at the floor, then back up to me. This show of comfortableness he has around me makes me lower my blade a little. I suppose he isn't an immediate threat.

"I've come to retrieve you, and take you back with me," he steps towards me slowly.

I furrow my eyebrows and watch him carefully. He doesn't look necessarily like a strong warrior, not to say he doesn't look strong. He has a lean body and is also wearing a leather jacket, though his is more of a vest. I wonder where I can get one myself, and whether it is worth it. I shake my head and focus again.

"Take me back where?"

"To our camp. I know you have something of ours," he says it kindly, like he means no harm. I wonder what I have that shouldn't be mine. My blanket? No, I found that abandoned. The flask? Of course, it must be, what else?

I finally lower my knife back to my belt and swap it for the flask.

"Is this what you mean?" I ask, knowing the answer. The man steps forward and holds the flask, placing his hand over mine, inspecting it. I feel a tingling sensation running under his skin, I can feel it against my own. What is that feeling? He particularly eyes the lid, and then seems satisfied.

"Could you not just take it, and let me be?" I ask. I have to go back to finding food, I am running low on my usual berries that I snack on during the day, kept in a pouch on my belt.

"No worries, you can come back with me too. I was told you would make a good ally to our group."

This strikes a chord in me. Group? I would be a good ally? What does that mean, and who is this group? Then something else occurs to me. Most of my time being out here, I have been on my own, finding seldom others like me, but I knew they existed - individuals surviving out here in our old homelands. But I didn't think...there were enough to form groups? Together? How many people in a group? How many groups? Why was I alone...?

"There are more of us?" I whisper, my voice hoarse as my mind runs over time. When no answer comes I look up and watch the man survey the area.

"Maybe it's best to talk when we're back at camp. I promise to provide answers then."

I like the way he is looking at me. It is serious, but kind. He is telling the truth. I tuck the flask away again, and then pop a berry into my mouth as I finally nod. He smiles at my action and steps close to me.

"This is for protection," he tells me. I wonder how close proximity could be protection as I look down at our bodies, when in my experience I need space to fight. I am about to voice my thought when I look up, but catch my sentence back as I watch what is happening.

All around us, in what looks to be a bubble, the air is fizzing. It is like we have just been enclosed in a see through dome. I lift my free hand out to feel the fizzing air and watch it ripple around my touch. We are most definitely enclosed. It feels like time has slowed around us and we are isolated.

"It's an invisibility shield," the man whispers, before I even ask.

"An invisibility shield," I hear myself repeat quietly. I also hear the astonishment in my voice. What kind of power is this? Shadow work? Is that how the Ghosts disappear into thin air? By just turning invisible?

"It's not an evil power," he says, as if reading my mind, as we start to walk. I wonder for a moment if he actually is reading my mind, and what else he can do. "The Ghost Men actually disappear. Their forms dissipate into atoms and they travel where they want to, showing up anywhere else. I, however, can bend and refract light and air around me and make it seem like we don't exist."

I take his words in. I don't know what to make of it. Should I be scared? Happy? Should I try to kill this man that seems to have extraordinary powers? After a long silent moment, where we continue walking, I finally speak again.

"Who are you?" I ask once more. He looks around for any company. "I suppose just because we're invisible, doesn't mean we still can't be heard?" I lower my voice more.

He looks down at me with a smile, almost a proud smile. I've mostly forgotten what that's like.

"You're smart," he pauses and looks straight ahead.

"Right, we'll talk at camp," I say quietly again, hiding a small eye roll as I look away and into the distance. Why do I trust this stranger? Better yet, why do I feel so okay in trusting this stranger?

We come to what looks like a ditch to an untrained eye, but I notice the small telltale signs that someone has been here and lives here. The fuzzy feeling around us vanishes and I know we are visible again. I follow the Cryptic's lead as he jumps into the ditch, silently hitting the side and sliding down the sandy walls to the floor. I come up behind him and wait for him to make the first move.

He lifts two fingers up to his mouth and lets out a high pitched whistle. It isn't very loud, but the pitch is enough to sting your ears and let people know you are here. I wonder whether this sound was chosen specifically, because Ghost Men can't hear sounds that high.

In a second the ditch comes to life. Flaps that were camouflaged into the walls of the ditch lift up and reveal tunnels and large underground rooms behind them. People started filing out, one by one, out of the secret entrances. I notice a few smaller children, many people in their late teens and those my age. With more people filtering in, I spot some older people as well, though not many. They surround us with looks of respect for the man standing next to me, and looks of intrigue at the stranger that is me. I feel shy, vulnerable, out of place, an outcast to begin with. But it has been so long since I have been around so many people I have forgotten how to react. Timidly, I look around at the different faces. Some are covered in black mud, others have rags around their heads, and some have black rings around their eyes or war paint across their cheeks. I am stunned. Another fuzzy dome ripples over the top of the ditch, concealing us all. I look to the Cryptic, who is staring proudly and the people in front of him.

"This," he pauses and glances at me, then holds up his hands and looks up again, "is the Rogue Resistance."

2

I am stunned to silence. I'm sure my mouth is hanging open as I gape at the mass of people. Sure, there's a crowd of people standing in front of me, who supposedly call themselves the Rogue Resistance, but that doesn't mean they're the rebellion group from the myth, right? I mean, they are a rebellion group; otherwise they wouldn't be here, but...but...

Before I can doubt myself further, another final flap lifts up behind the crowd, and they part like the red sea. I see two women followed by a man emerge and walk through slowly, heading towards me. They look gratefully at the crowd who openly seem to adore them. I catch eyes with the man I had spent time with yesterday. It is a quick glance and then he looks straight ahead, at his friend who has brought me to him. They greet each other by gripping each other's forearm and patting backs.

"Brother," says the man I helped, smiling at the Cryptic.

I feel even more out of place now standing in front of the crowd, beside the four people who seem to be the leaders here, as if I am one of them. I am not a leader; I am a loner. I long to edge to the back of the crowd, but a firm hand on my shoulder keeps me in place. I gulp.

"Resistance, we have a new ally!"

I look to my right where the man I helped is standing and notice his wound is patched up. I look up to his face and do indeed see a black and purple bruise across his left cheekbone, faintly leading up to his temple and around his eye. I wince. He continues.

"She helped me yesterday, she brought me to safety," he speaks, no need to raise his voice much over the silent audience. Which is good since the invisibility dome isn't sound proof. I feel like I am being sacrificed as I feel many pairs of eyes fall on me because of this man's admittance.

"She is a healer!" the Cryptic speaks up, and smiles at me. "I felt it in your hand," he says, more to only me when I raise an eyebrow questioningly.

The man turns to me, but still speaks loud enough for others to hear. "Will you join our rebellion?" he asks. I hear shuffling and quiet murmuring from the hushed crowd when the question is asked. They await my answer.

I don't know what I am walking in to. I have been alone for 4 years now. I didn't think anything like this was out there. An actual legion of rebels. Of rogues. Though this is new territory and it feels strange, there is a longing in my heart to be a part of something. Something on a scale of this size too. I have forgotten what it is like to have friends or allies, or even just human contact. I so desperately want to be a part of the rebellion. I scan the faces of the crowd, some hopeful, some smiling, and some passive. I don't care; I want to be in that crowd even though it scares me. I will have to start trusting again.

When I look to the four people that surround me, their faces glowing and radiating kindness, I feel accepted and ready to trust. It feels right.

"Yes," I breathe. "Of course," I confirm, a little louder. Cheers come from the crowd and several yells of congratulations. As the crowd moves and mingles, the Cryptic catches me and makes me face him.

"What do I call you?" I ask.

"My real name is Abeo, but I'm known as the Cryptic to the Resistance," he tells me. He doesn't give me a chance to reply, just gives my hand a squeeze before walking away, and as I watch him go, I see the familiar word written across the back of his leather jacket.

I have so many emotions running through me. This is it. I am in the Resistance, and this is my new home. I am confused and thrilled. Where do I stay, what happens now? Is it the real Rogue Resistance? I am still not sure. I have my suspicions. How can I not when I feel as if the old tales I knew so well in my youth are replaying right in front of my eyes? I feel a pang of sadness that my parents aren't here. I can't tell them, show them the Resistance. I can't prove to them that maybe it wasn't all tales. But as much as I feel sad, a bright new hope flares inside of me. If this is real, if I am with the Four, am an actual member of the legendary Rogue Resistance, then that means rebellion. And that means the freedom of our people, which hopefully includes my parents.

"Kayin?" I spin to see one of the women I haven't run into yet. "I felt your sorrow."

I don't know how to respond. I dangle my mouth open expecting her to continue.

"The Divine," she says, as an introduction. She holds her hand out and I reciprocate the action, ready to shake, but she lifts my knuckles to her mouth and kisses my hand instead.

"I don't mean to pry, but I feel negativity in your aura. Is there something troubling you, healer?"

She seems to be very formal with the names, apart from when she first caught my attention. The Cryptic had told me his name was Abeo; the Divine has left that bit out. Will everyone call me Healer from now on?

I sigh. "Is this real? I mean is this...is this what I think it is? The actual Rogue Resistance, the stuff of legend?" I come straight out with it. There's no use in wasting my time with hope if down the line I find out this isn't history repeating itself, but just a group of rebels doomed to fail. I earn a deep chuckle from the Divine.

"I believe it is," she says. I can't tell if she is confirming my questions or simply just telling me her beliefs, but it makes me feel better regardless.

"Is there going to be a rebellion?" I say, daring to ask, my voice is barely audible above the noise of the crowd, but she hears it anyway. She gives me a meaningful look, which I can't quite decipher.

"You've suffered a loss, haven't you?" she says, skipping on to new conversation.

"I was separated from my parents when I escaped from the prison." I feel myself telling her the truth no matter what. She places her hand on my shoulder comfortingly.

"You must never give up faith."

I want to tell her that I won't, but I don't feel any words coming out of my mouth. She smiles and walks away. I see the other woman, the last of the Four that I have not come across yet. Her eyes catch mine and hold them and I can't resist watching her as she strolls through the crowd then finally stops in front of me.

Much like the Divine, she brings my hand up to her lips and kisses it, though this is more sultry than the Divine's greeting. She looks up at me through her long dark eyelashes as she is bent forward with her gesture, and then stands back up straight.

"I'm Imara, the Vehement," she says with a grin. "I hope Orisa hasn't set the tone as too serious. It's great to meet you."

"Pleasure," I return with a smile. Orisa. So that's the Divine's name.

"Tell me something," I continue, feeling a little rejuvenated.

"Yes, dear?"

"Where do I sleep, how does this work?" I ask, finding myself scanning the ditch and its secret entrances again, wondering if behind one of those flaps there is room for me and my blanket.

"It's not up to me, I'm sorry," she says, but doesn't sound sorry. There is a gleam in her eye. "But my door is always open."

I glance back at where they had entered. "Am I even allowed in there?" I guess it is safe to assume for now that these two men and two women are the Four, and they are the true legends. Despite my pessimistic instinct, I know that negativity will not help me, so I should be as positive as I can. I try not to think about their status too much for I worry that I might become bashful in their presence, and I have to remain strong and confident in the Resistance.

"Oh no, no, darling, you aren't allowed in there, but that isn't our room. Think of it as...our office. Maybe I'll show you to my room another time," she teases. She has a positively electric energy about her, and I love it.

"I thought it was all a myth, you know? I thought you guys were just..." I trail off as I look at her. It is unusual to be eye level with another woman; I am particularly tall, always have been, but she is just as tall.

"Just mythical Gods?" she says, obnoxiously flexing a muscle in front of me in jest. "Yeah," she laughs. "I use to get told those stories too, and now look at me," she says with a bit more humility. She looks around at her own surroundings with an expression of adoration, taking it in.

"It's not always like this. We're usually a lot quieter; keep to ourselves but always looking out for each other. However it's not every day we get to welcome a new rogue. We don't come across a lot of rebels nowadays because most of them are already here."

Hearing her call me a rogue makes me smile. Maybe I can believe it. When she notices I am caught up in my own thoughts she shoots me another smile and a small wave and slips away.

I consider talking to the other Resistance members, wondering what happens now. How everything will go down. I think I am done with introductions when I remember I haven't officially been introduced to the Oracle. His name gives me shivers, only because I hadn't realised I had worked so close to such a powerful being yesterday, when trying to heal him. I look around, wondering if he's realised the same thing and wants to talk or whether it doesn't bother him that we haven't spoken. When I can't spot him, I decide to explore.

I make my way to the edge of the ditch and trail my hand along the rough wall. My fingers drop into indents that people use to climb out. I feel the raised edge of a flap that could be misconstrued as just another bump in the rock. I circle round for a minute or so, not even making a full lap of the ditch, until I have to stop. My eyes fall to the floor where I see a pair of black boots facing my own, but his are bigger. I track my eyes up his legs that are long like my own, but his are stronger. I let my eyes linger on his torso, looking at the bandage taped to his hip before I meet his face.

I want to ask how he is feeling, but the smile on his face as he looks at me makes me speechless. The hot sun and long day yesterday had not faltered my vision; this man is just as beautiful as I remember. He has his fingers locked behind his back, watching me. And then he leans forward. I expect him to stop, to make it some kind of bow, but he keeps leaning, right up to and passed my face, stopping finally when his lips are next to my ear, so much so that his breath tickles me.

"Thanks for bringing it back," he whispers. He keeps his mouth there, while I feel a tug on my belt. I don't need to look to know he is pulling his flask out of its place, so I keep my eyes looking forward over his shoulder, unprepared for this close proximity. When he has taken back his flask and leans back, I feel a chill on my neck.

"H-how's the hip?" I ask. He glances down at it and smirks.

"It's doing fine, thank you," he says with a genuine smile. I can't help but mirror his actions.

"So..." I begin. I just have to ask. "You're the real life Oracle." It comes out as more of a statement.

"Yes, I am," he replies with a shrug. He doesn't elaborate any further. The way each of the Four reacted when I confirmed their status was different. It intrigues me. I look down at the floor now there's a lull in the conversation. Should I walk away now?

"Why don't I show you around, so you get a feel of the land? Where do you usually camp?" he asks, beginning to move, so I have to follow him.

Instead of walking around the ditch like I think he is going to, he climbs out of it, out of the invisibility dome, and holds his hand out to help me when he is at the top. I am nimble and make it up by myself fine, but I take his hand at the end out of politeness.

"On the edge of Dead Man's Desert," I respond, referring to the vast land parallel to the Ervon Gorge. I look over my shoulder and find it weird to see an empty ditch, when I know underneath an invisible shield, there is a crowd of people. I can hear their faint chatter. So the dome does block out some noise, I think.

"By the old capital? Crasmere city?" the Oracle questions, with a sideways glance at me. For a moment I think he looks impressed.

"Even after all this time, since it has been abandoned, there are still scraps and rubbish that wild animals come to find, many of them take shelter in the old buildings too...And I'm good with a slingshot," I pat my weapon of choice which is secured in my belt next to my little blade.

"So you're a good hunter?"

"I wouldn't call it hunting, more waiting than anything. In the meantime, I'll eat berries and chew mint leaves, whatever I can find that won't kill me," I tell him. He nods quietly.

"Show me your aim," he instructs. I hesitate. "Let's see what you've got," he encourages. I look around the bare land and find a sizeable rock, which will fit nicely into the seat of my slingshot. I set it up and look for prey.

I feel thrilled to be showing my skill to the Oracle, it still feels surreal that he is...real. But I am also nervous because I know what talents he holds according to the legends and I want this to be good. I want to impress him.

I spot a bird in the sky. I note which way it is flying and aim farther in front of it, making sure the sun is behind me and won't tamper with my vision. I quickly make an estimate of speed, distance and time, and when the bird is in position I launch the rock high into the air. It soars up until it looks no bigger than a fly. The Oracle and I wait with anticipation for a hit. We can't hear it, but watching the sky we see the bird fly off course a little, like a stutter in its flight. Then suddenly it drops a few feet. It struggles to fly on and with a last flap of its wings it gives up and spirals to the ground. I put my hand on the Oracle's stomach, and push him back a few steps without even thinking, while watching the sky.

A few seconds later both our gazes follow the bird as it finally hits the floor between us. I let out a sigh of relief and timidly looked up. I meet his eyes and am happy to see an approving smile.

I realise the Oracle hasn't actually shown me any land; we've just been walking and now we've come to a cluster of buildings. It must have been one of the more recent town desertions because the buildings are still in tact mostly. Tin sheets cover holes in walls, and make up their own huts on the ground, with large sheets of cloth acting as curtains everywhere. They are hung from building to building; in front of the tin huts, squaring off other sheets to create makeshift tents. It feels as if the small town is joined together, like patchwork, but still looks deserted enough to appear uninhabited. A few fellow rogues are already here, wandering back and forth to each other's rooms.

"This is mostly where we live." I notice the current of the stream still going strong through the town as we corner a building. The Oracle looks up, so I follow his gaze. It is just one of the taller buildings, that hasn't crumbled in an attack. The Oracle seems to consider something, and then shakes his head.

"What is it?" I ask.

"I was going to ask if you'd ever seen the Shadow Lands, where the Ghosts reside, but I assume seeing a prison would be enough of their world for you," he replies truthfully.

"How did you know I was-"

"I...see things" he cut me off.

Of course. Legend says the Oracle can see your memories. It's how he deciphers his enemies' weaknesses and makes such good strategies to defeat them. I don't question it further.

There is a pause between us and he glances up at the building again.

"I want to see it," I whisper daintily. He of course hears. He looks at me, and I can feel him trying to figure me out, much like yesterday when he opened his eyes and looked right at me for the first time. I had the same feeling then. But I keep my eyes glued up, watching the building like a hawk, until I finally feel his gaze leave my face and he walks away.

"This way," he nods with his chin and I follow silently. We go back around the building and enter it, climbing up four flights of stairs and then a ladder. I try to keep as close to the Oracle as possible but I am right in thinking he is much fitter than I am and moves quicker. He goes up the ladder first and climbs onto the roof, then looks back at me to make sure I am getting up okay, once again helping me at the top. Instead of letting my hand go, he continues to hold it and leads me to the other side of the roof, where a telescope and a pair of binoculars are set up. He separates from me and goes to the telescope. I instinctively go to pick up the binoculars.

"Hang on," he says, holding a finger up, but not taking

his eye away from the telescope. "Here."

I take his place and bend over to peer through. The Oracle picks up the binoculars beside me to view what I'm seeing at the same time. I concentrate on my view and let out a small gasp. A huge, tall black building, visible above a congregation of trees, towers in the distance. Even with the powerful telescope it still looks far away. I can only imagine how far it really is. There are tall black columns at the front. I wonder then where we are, relative to the prison.

When you're taken there, you're chained to the people in front and behind you, like a long link of slaves, and you're blindfolded. Being only sixteen and dazed when I escaped, I just remember running and hiding, and running some more. I soon found a routine and piece of land where I was comfortable, on the edge of the desert by the old capital. I only ventured out further if I needed to. But to this day I still don't know where the prison is.

I don't realise I have taken my eye away from the telescope, but I have. I am looking into the distance with my normal sight, a snarl etched on my face. But I can see nothing. I feel the Oracle's presence beside me, probably reading my mind and watching my memory as I relive it, but before he can say anything, a high pitched whistle rings out three times. I think it's the Cryptic, but it is different from when he did it last time.

The Oracle's face falls blank and hard as he listens intently. Then he puts his fingers to his mouth and relays a whistle back. I wince and cover my ears briefly.

"Can everyone do that?"

He looks at me, deciding something. For the tiniest of moments I see the corner of his mouth twitch. "Only some. Maybe you'll learn." But then he gets serious again. "Run." And he was off.

I figure whatever that whistle meant it can't be good as it suddenly changed the Oracle's demeanour. He's become stern and serious, which only makes this more real. Running in front of me as we make our way back to the ditch, is a leader in his element. This is the man I've been told about. I am finally witnessing him doing what he was born to, taking control. Not that I don't like how he just was, it's a nice change of pace from my lonely days to suddenly have that kind of interaction and conversation with someone. But I can't help thinking that, as I run behind him now, this is where my journey begins.

We sink into the invisibility dome and find a commotion playing out in front of us. The Oracle takes on a deep, controlling voice.

"What's happened?" He looks down at the remaining three of the Four crowding over something. As I get closer I realise it is someone. A girl. The Vehement has one hand on the back of her neck as she lays there, holding her head up more, and the other is gripping her hand desperately.

"Why did you go out there?!" she says through gritted teeth, straining her voice. The girl coughs and splutters trying to speak, just as another girl breaks through the crowd. They must both be at least 17 or 18.

"Selene!" she cries, kneeling by the wounded girl's side, next to the Vehement. "Imara, is she okay? Shall I..." she addresses her directly, not finishing her sentence but Imara knows how it finishes.

"No, only as a last resort, Mari" she tells her. Mari looks down to Selene, who seems to be fighting to stay conscious. I realise then that they are twins, or at least close resembling sisters. Selene has blood pouring from her head, oozing into her sand coloured hair.

"Head wound," I whisper to myself. Think. "Let me through," I say, my voice mostly hushing the people around me. I squeeze between the Vehement and Divine. I know Orisa would lead her peacefully into the Underworld and look after her there if she were to die; she is a medium to the afterlife and can enter the edge of the underworld, according to the old stories. I give her a look as if to say 'not today'. She nods solemnly.

I look down at Selene, observing her as quickly as I can. It looks like she has received quite a hard blow to her head.

It is possible that there is a small crack in her skull on the hairline, and the bleeding indicates it is a compound skull fracture. Knowing I can't waste any time, I stand straight and yell orders.

"I'm going to need hot water! Clean rags and cloths, a sterilised needle and thread, hurry!" I bark at no one in particular, but they seem to trust my judgement and several people run off in different directions. I suppose since the Cryptic announced I am a healer they have no reason to not trust me.

"Do we have any pain numbing medication?" I ask any of the Four. The Cryptic shoots up.

"I'll see what I can find." I mutter a thank you as he walks away. If the skull fracture is anything worse than a linear fracture it won't heal on its own. I need to clean the wound, stitch and bandage it up.

"Selene, I'm Kayin. Talk to me," I tell her in a calming voice. I look up at the Vehement who has worry written all over her face.

"Hold her neck securely, make sure she doesn't fall asleep yet, she could have a concussion." She nods.

"Selene, where did you go?" the Vehement asks her.

"I...I was out," she has to stop for a moment. "Picking berries, d-down by the o-old Oak"

I absent-mindedly let my hand trail over her cheek, as

supplies start coming back to me. Thankfully it is the towels and clean water.

"Keep talking to her Vehement," I gently remind her.

"What else?" she urges. We are all dying to know how she was injured, and I need her distracted because cleaning will probably hurt.

I go about cleaning as I would with any other wound, but make sure to press more gently so I won't damage the skull any further. Selene flinches at the first touch. The water runs down her face, mixing with the blood.

"And t-they, they were...they came," she stutters helplessly. Mari winces and holds her sister's hand tighter, as does the Vehement.

"Who did, Sel?" Mari asks cautiously, but we know the answer.

"G-G…Ghosts." She groans, as I have to finish cleaning the wound a bit rougher than before. Finally a pot of hot water with a sterilised needle and thread is brought in. I thread the needle quickly, tie a knot in the end and lean over.

"I-I was hidden, and they were, uh," she pauses, thinking, and I take the opportunity to pierce her skin. She freezes as I pull the length of the thread through, but she softens.

"They were talking," she whispers.

"About what?" the Vehement prompts.

"Ambush," Selene replies quietly. The people surrounding her go silent and exchange glances. No more needs to be said. I feel the pressure as everyone has now turned their attention fully on me. Four stitches later, I am taping a bandage over it.

"Make sure she takes that pain medicine twice a day. The wound should subside in less than two weeks, but it won't fully heal for months. She'll need lots of rest." The Four are gathered around me, Selene is in a bed and Mari, short for Marisol, who is in fact her twin, is watching over her.

When I finish my orders, and my duty is done, I feel the rush of adrenaline seep out of me and suddenly I'm exhausted and very aware that I have four powerful people hovering over me, listening intently to me. This is intense.

The Vehement disperses first, going back to Selene. As I watch her leave, the Divine tells me the twins are her cousins, which explains why her concern runs deeper than the others'. She then leaves to give her the first dose of medication.

"I admire your control back there," the Oracle speaks. The Cryptic leaves us as he starts speaking.

"Thank you," I say, feeling the blood rush to my cheeks. This man born to be one of the greatest leaders ever admires my control.

"You handled the situation well. We've lost many rogues through injury that we lacked the knowledge to handle. You have no idea how beneficial your contributions and assets will be to the Resistance. We're lucky to have found you," he tells me. He is still in leader mode, speaking authoritatively, but there is a lighter tone to his words, like how we spoke before the incident. As I'm about to mutter another thank you and drop my eyes to the floor, his movement catches my attention again. He stands like he did when I ran into him earlier, hands behind his back and he leans forward, just a fraction this time, to signal he is only talking to me. "I was lucky you found me."

His words mean a lot and if I wasn't blushing before I definitely am now. Though I don't quite believe him; it wasn't a life-threatening wound and he had people out looking for him anyway, but I am grateful for the sentiment.

He straightens up and looks into the distance. "You should go and get some rest," he tells me, keeping his eyes up.

It is just bordering late afternoon, but I have done a lot today. Compared to my usual lonesome days of moving from one place to another.

He calls over a boy a few years younger than me. "Would you show Kayin to the empty room north of the stream, please?"

The boy is happy to oblige and smiles at me as he turns, gesturing for me to follow him.

The Oracle watches Kayin walk away. He strides over to the Cryptic, still watching her back.

"You said you felt that Kayin was a healer in her hands," the Oracle says. The Cryptic ponders it and nods.

"I could feel strong currents of power in her skin." The Cryptic pauses, glancing around. Then he puts his hand on the Oracle's arm, watching it as he feels for the surges of power within him. "Very strong, much like ours."

He drops his hand and the Oracle crosses his arms, nodding at his friend.

"I guessed she is a healer as it makes sense considering her instinct to help you when you were injured and to take control just now. They are healer instincts she possesses. I just don't think she's aware of her abilities yet."

As I follow the boy through the door, I see the room isn't very big, but it is enough for a bed and I am very grateful. The boy leaves me then. I take off my belts and shoes, crawl into the bed and pull the blanket over my lap. The sun is beginning to set and there's a gorgeous collision of orange and pink and purple across the sky. Today has been a blur, and I'm still not sure how I feel about everything. But since the morning, I can feel a glimmer of hope in my chest that wasn't there before and I hope from now on it will only grow as the days go by.

I sigh contentedly, but then I think seriously. I need to trust in this system and these people, that it's real; it's the only way to potentially save my people, specifically my parents. I am thrilled at the thought of seeing them again, but I can't get my hopes up too much; I just have to have faith. I swear from this moment to put my all into whatever is thrown at me.

3

I wake up to Marisol gently shaking me the next morning. I blink my eyes up at her and roll onto my back.

"Hey," she whispers. "I just wanted to say thanks again for yesterday. You stayed really calm, it helped."

"It was no problem," I reply, sitting up and rubbing my eyes. When I look up she is still watching me, smiling.

"We've never had a healer before," she tells me, as though I am something extraordinary. "Sure, we've had people who know what they're doing, but never a titled healer."

I'm not naïve enough to assume my family is the only healer bloodline out there, but maybe we are just less common nowadays. "I'm glad to help."

"Does anyone in your family have the special healer

powers?" she asks me, her eyes lighting up.

"My Nana. On my Mother's side. She was amazing, she had a true gift." I tell her. I know exactly what she is talking about. There are rumours that healers can possess powers that aid them in helping others; I have seen it first hand in my Nana, she was magical.

Marisol suddenly realises something and her eyes go wide with a smile.

"Is your Nana Diola Sesay? I met her, a long time ago," she says quietly, a sad smile hanging on her face. I nod; Diola was my Nana. She was old and wise and plump, and one of the best healers I knew.

"She knew and helped many people. How did you meet her?" I ask.

"When my mother became ill, and Selene and I were only 6, we sent for help. We got every one we knew to pass on messages for us, while we stayed at our mother's side. Then one day Diola came along. Her eyes flashed and her hands glowed and golden streaks of light jump in and out of our mother like fish in a lake. It was incredible. I'll never forget it."

Marisol looks down at her hands, and plays with her fingers. I don't need any special powers to sense heaviness in her heart.

"My mother lived for another 2 years, and it was

definitely all down to your Nana's work...But I guess not even a great healer can avoid an inevitable death. I'm just glad she did what she did and gave us more time with her."

"I'm so sorry, Marisol," I say quietly.

"Thanks. It's okay though, it was a long time ago, we've learnt to remember the good times," she replies with a bittersweet smile. "You can call me Mari," she adds. After a moment, something strikes me.

"Hey," I say, grabbing her attention. "What did you mean yesterday when you ran over to us and asked the Vehement 'should I...' but didn't finish your sentence?"

"Oh, Selene and I share a gift. If I were an only child I would possess the full talent, but as twins we share it. I can induce comas, and Selene can wake people up from comas."

I don't say anything; I nod, hoping she continues.

"Well, you know, sometimes it can be hard, deciding whether to induce a coma, whether it's safe for the person in their condition. Sometimes when people are injured, I'll put them under because they're in so much pain. When I saw Sel yesterday...she looked like she was in so much agony, I thought if I put her under...I wondered if she'd be able to wake herself up, if it worked like that," she pauses for a moment, thinking. "But I am glad I didn't need to do it," she gives me a genuine smile then.

She tilts her head, like something else has occurred to

her. "And by keeping her awake we know...about the supposed ambush," she looks at me warily.

We don't say a lot after that, both caught up in our own thoughts. I appreciate Mari's kindness, since I am new to the Resistance. I watch her, thinking about what she has said. She and her sister are very pretty, both with deep golden skin, and big round amber eyes. Mari has a fringe that falls straight above her eyebrows and the rest of her dark blonde hair is messily pushed back at the sides behind her ears.

I think about how she described my Nana at work. What she'd seen. I look to my hands. Do I have the potential to make my hands glow? And to have gold streams of light swimming in and out of my patient? Flashing eyes, too. I'd never considered that maybe I could be a magical healer. I almost become excited at the thought of being able to do these things, and it is the first time I let myself enjoy my situation fully, before strong ripples in the land shake the room and cause me to almost fall out of bed. Mari pulls me back up and stays firmly planted in place, matching the rocking of the bed and staying balanced, like she's experienced this before. When it is over, she looks at me with big eyes.

"Imara's up."

I dress quickly, mirroring Mari's speedy movements. I wonder why she is eager to get outside. I pull on my tight black jeans that have scuffmarks and holes in them, particularly at the knees. I brush my feet off and pulled on my boots, that are worn and not as sturdy as they used to be, but it's what I'm comfortable with; I've become accustomed to them. I slip my short black top over my head. It used to be full length, making it all the way down to my hips, until I caught it on a branch when falling out of a tree (a story for another time maybe) and got a tear from the waist to the end, so I ripped the bottom off. My limited access to food means I'm slimmer than I used to be before the Ghosts came, but I'm fitter than I used to be, due to the running and climbing I get up to.

I clip my belts around my hips, jump a few times to test the security of them and then walk out with Mari. The sun is hot on my face as soon as we walk out of my room. I'm surprised at how cool the rooms stay in the stone houses. At night you have enough shelter and blankets to fight the chill of the night, but in the day the buildings seem to hang on to the cold air and stop the rooms getting too hot.

I pop a berry into my mouth as we walk. I discreetly offer Mari one, which she accepts. I don't want everyone to see because I now have only two left after not following through on my plans to top up yesterday, after the Cryptic came to collect me.

Mari knows the routes around here like the back of her

hand and we are soon back at the ditch. A few metres away from it is the Vehement, standing beside a hole, with crumbling dirt and rocks. It is fresh.

"Imara?!" Mari calls. I admire how casual they are with each other, and how Mari doesn't bat an eyelid at everyone else calling her the Vehement.

She looks our way and momentarily smiles, but it doesn't last long. The Divine and Cryptic are with her, talking her down, calmingly resting their hands on her shoulder and patting her back. Though she is nice when she's calm, I know the Vehement can have quite the temper, for obvious reasons. Looking at the pile of rubble beside them and the mini quake we felt just moments ago, I deduce that it was because of her. She is upset about something. I follow Mari over to them.

"What's happening?" she asks, with more solemnity in her voice than when she had commonly called Imara's name moments ago. I guess she understands whom she is talking to. There's a time and a place, as they say.

"Selene was awake long enough to talk this morning," Orisa tells us, as if that explains everything.

"She spoke more of her experience yesterday," the Cryptic adds.

"She told us what we already expected; they are planning an ambush. She said the Ghost Men are going to hunt for three days straight and whatever they find they will kill. But it's not a case of just sitting back and hiding," the Vehement tells us, raising her voice a little as she turns to her friends. "We must fight too!"

Before she can stomp on the ground in frustration, the Divine speaks.

"We must gather together and discuss the situation," she tells her firmly. "We need to talk about strategy and find a game plan."

The Vehement nods reluctantly. Then she glances at me. "We may need you more than ever," she says quietly, but her low voice rattles my bones. I swallow hard.

They walk away then. I watch Mari staring at their backs as they leave us.

"Do you want to go see Selene?"

We step silently into the room where injured people stay. I notice two others in there, in the beds farthest away from us. But to our left is where Selene lays, eyes closed.

"Is she sleeping?" I whisper to Mari, but to no avail. She has already left my side and is holding Selene's hand, shaking gently and squeezing.

"Selly?"

"Oh, Mari," she sighs, as she opens her eyes.

"I was so worried," Mari admits. I wonder whether to leave them alone for a moment, but Selene speaks again.

"I know," she replies with a small, meaningful smile at Marisol. "But listen, you two must prepare for the Ghosts," she says; now addressing me too.

"What do you mean?" Mari asks her, never letting go of her hand.

"We must make sure we're hidden. Leave no sign of life around these parts. They will come and they will destroy it all, including us. We can't let them find us," she tells us seriously. "I don't know how many there will be of them. But I do know it isn't enough to just hide. We should fight back."

I see a glimpse on the Vehement in her then. You can tell they are related.

"You two should be ready. We'll need people out there. Skilled people. If we can take them out before they take out us we'll have the advantage," Selene now whispers. "We'll need our healer," she says looking at me. "We'll rely on the Four. And they'll need back up. I don't know what they'll plan but they must do it soon so we are ready and prepared for when they come."

Selene leaves us thinking when she stops talking. Mari and I share a glance and look back to Selene. Before we leave, Mari asks, "when are they supposed to come?"

I am afraid of this question. Everyone speaks with such urgency, and I know it is serious. I wonder how much time I have to prepare, to ready myself like everyone says to. Am I ready for this so soon after joining the Resistance? I hold my breath.

"Sometime in the next week."

In the days that follow, the desert becomes a training ground. I still have little knowledge of our plan, if there is one, but everyone is ready and willing to fight, train and prepare behind the battlegrounds.

Those in the Resistance that are training are good. I mean really good. Their combat skills range from amateur to skilled to almost expert. I wonder where they could have learnt this, or whether they've been in the Resistance long enough to learn it all here. Makeshift weapons are made to accompany the many knives people already have. Staffs made of sharpened branches and the like. I keep my slingshot close by at all times.

Then there are also those who work best supporting the fighters and helping in other areas. Some people are good with medical situations, injuries and illnesses. They weren't completely helpless when I wasn't here; these guys are excellent. I'm glad all the pressure to keep people fit and healthy isn't solely resting on me. War paint is made and shared around, different patterns and masks are being adorned on the faces of almost all members.

I've since been taken care of. I have two small braids at the front of my long dark hair, and I have war paint across my eyes and nose and left to drip down my cheeks. I've been given new clothes. I have a new pair of jeans which must have more elastic in because they are much more versatile than my old pair. And I've received a new tank top. It is tight and supportive and long enough to tuck it into my jeans. It is better to do this because it would never obstruct my belt this way; my belts and chains lie on top. To finish off my new Resistance persona, as I like to think of it, I have a pair of fingerless, black leather gloves. They're comfy and soft and help me when I use my slingshot. I will no longer get hurt when I accidentally catch my palm on the rubber band.

The best part about training is watching the Four at work. Sometimes you will catch them standing around together, plotting, planning. Most of the time you'll catch them up and working though. They fight well with and without weapons. They have such speed and skill it's hard to keep up sometimes. I watch them longingly, like they have stepped right out of a storybook. I hope to one-day fight like that. It's amazing to see all of their powers. They practice safely together, and I have finally figured out who can do what.

The Vehement is immensely strong, as I know. She

doesn't have bulging muscles or even a particularly large build; she has an athletic body and stands tall at 5'10" like myself. Her dark skin has a natural glow and she wears her hair in braids, away from her face, which accentuates her impressive bone structure. Her supernatural strength seems to materialise from nowhere when you watch her. She can push down trees, create ditches by stamping and cause earthquakes on a variety of scales if she wants to.

As I have experienced, the Cryptic can conjure invisibility by fracturing the light particles around him or something like that, I'm still not quite sure of the science behind it, if it is science at all. Watching him the other day was extraordinary. He has some kind of control over fire, and can also create fireballs from his hands. It is surreal to watch him throw fireballs at a target 100 feet away and juggle them in his hands. He practices with different sizes and his skill doesn't falter. I know he also has some kind of sense as to whether you have powers and what they are; he can feel it in your skin somehow.

The Divine also has power over light particles. She can deflect and bend them in a way that will unfocus her body. When you're looking at her it becomes hard to concentrate because her image confuses your brain and your eyes slide right off of her, as if you're not interested. In addition to this she can enhance the light around her to make it look like she's shining, and create an almost blinding light that forces you to look away. Both of these can work very effectively if dealing with enemies, as you can imagine. The Divine is also a medium for the afterlife, which I was already aware of. She can sense people's auras as well and aid people in their journey to the underworld.

The word Oracle gives the impression of one who can see the future. However, while the Oracle can read minds, he can't see the future. His excellent skills in deduction and leadership, as well as a sharp mind, allow him to calculate your next moves, giving the impression of knowing what will happen next. He can counter his enemies' attacks and disable them before they can understand what's happening. He also has a scary power, in which he can manipulate others thoughts and temporarily control minds. I saw him use it against the Divine while they were sparring one day. Mid fight, I watched the Divine straighten up and turn away, literally walking away from the battle. She went quite far until she shook it off and bent the light around her so the Oracle could no longer concentrate on controlling her.

I'm not sure of my skills at the moment. I haven't been brave enough to take part in combat training yet, so I stay in the shadows, working on my own powers. Or trying to - I have given myself the task of finding out if I have any powers like my Nana had. I have the chance to talk to

Marisol and Selene (when she is feeling up to it) more about what they had seen. They were only young but they give me vivid details of how my Nana worked and what she did. I'm not sure how to go about finding them or controlling them. Finally, I decide to take part in combat training, wondering whether I'll be better up front or behind battle. I think I should try out all angles. If I've ventured well enough on my own, then I'm sure if I focus on working in a team that it can only be better. Two heads are better than one. Working in the Resistance means that I want to be in the best place possible for the rest of the group and need to know where that is.

I surprise myself with the use of my fists; I'm fairly fast and can read the battle and block most of my partners' shots. Though that doesn't mean I haven't taken a few blows either. I'm most certainly not the best fighter, but I'm not bad.

We pick up our weapons next. I'm training against a boy called Rhyland. He is bigger than me, but about the same age I think. He picks up his make shift spear in his big hands and I hold my knife tightly in my fist. We battle generously back and forth for a while until we're ready to pick up the pace and intensity. The more we develop our tactics, the more we feel comfortable to move around as we spar. I dodge one of Rhyland's swings and press my back to a tree, finding ammo and quickly putting it in my slingshot. I turn around the tree and shoot the few berries I have found on the floor at him. They hit him in the chest, like quick small pellets and I see him flinch and falter. This as a good sign to me as a few old, soft berries shouldn't have much impact, but it's good enough to make a man flinch with the help of my slingshot, so I like the idea of having hard ammo to launch at prospective enemies.

As I make my way passed others who are fighting and training, I turn to the left around a group of people and see a spear coming towards me. It isn't intentional; it isn't aimed at me purposefully. It's a rogue throw that's gone off target, and I just happen to be in its flight path. Unprepared, I scream as it closes in. It goes quiet as the sudden noise catches the attention of others. They gasp and I can vaguely see people moving towards me, but I don't think there is any hope of moving now, I'm scared and frozen in place. A hard blow to my stomach propels me backwards. I land on my back and lose my breath, winded, desperately trying to gasp in some air, but it only makes me light headed. My stomach feels numb where the spear collided with me and I don't dare look down at my wound. I blink and open my eyes wide and see the crowd around me. When I focus my eyes, I realise they look stunned. I must be bleeding badly. Oh no, I can't even feel it, so it must be awful. What does this mean for me?

Rhyland kneels by my side, having seen the whole thing, looking as pale as his tanned skin can possibly look. He gingerly lifts his hand. I shake my head slowly, objecting to him touching me, but he ignores me and continues to lower his hand to my stomach. First he lifts away the spear. I don't feel a thing so I assume it wasn't piercing through me and he didn't pull it out as I thought might have happened. At least that's something. I continue to watch the shocked expression locked on his face as he finally touches my tummy. I wince instinctively, still winded, and when he takes his hand away I swear I feel all the air left in me leave my lungs.

There is no blood on his hand. In fact, I recall there being no blood on the spear. What? It certainly wasn't blunt, how could it not have broken any skin with such an impact? The crowd breaks and I see the Four walk through the gap and look down on me just as I have the courage to finally lift my head and look at myself.

I am fine. I am clean. There is no sign of damage apart from the winded feeling I feel and a small scuff across my top. I fear pain will suddenly kick in if I move, so I very slowly sit up, leaning back on my elbows, waiting for the inevitable hurt to come, but it doesn't. I look to Rhyland and the rest of the crowd. They are as shocked as me, so I know I'm not crazy. They saw the weapon hurtling towards me. I inspect the spear now by my side. It is sharp enough. It should have pierced me, left at least a scratch. I glance up to the Four. They have mixed expressions of worry, confusion and admiration. I see the look of potential reflect in the Cryptic's eyes.

Rhyland helps me sit straighter, and then the Oracle holds a hand out for me to take. I feel the crowd look to him and then back at me; they are all definitely as confused as I am, and also looking to the Four for some answers. I take his hand and he pulls me up to my feet. I look down at my stomach again, wondering if now that I am upright blood would start dripping, but it still doesn't. I feel bold enough to lift up my top, only to find a slight red mark on my skin where it had hit me. This is so strange.

Without so much as a word, the Oracle nods his head, gesturing behind him and turns around. The Four begin walking away so I follow them after the Vehement calls to the crowd, warning them to control their weapons. I leave the shell-shocked crowd and follow the Four back to our town and into a private room. I suddenly feel trapped as they all stop and turn to me, half circling me. The Vehement speaks first.

"What was that?" She isn't mad, or shocked, she is mostly intrigued. As one of great physical power I guess she is mostly interested in how I was able to withstand the blow.

"I-I'm not sure what happened," I say slowly. I'm still

cradling my tummy in my hand; scared to let go as if I might fall apart, but I know that won't happen. I'm just in shock.

"Has that ever happened before?" the Cryptic cuts in. I shake my head, no, and the Four exchange a glance.

"We should test it," the Oracle says. I am confused.

"We can't. What if she gets hurt?" the Divine counters. What are they thinking of?

"But what if she doesn't?" the Oracle replies. "We all saw it. How the spear bounced off of her."

Did it really? I can't even imagine a sight like that.

"She should be severely wounded..." he looks at me. "But she's not."

"I thought I was done for," I admit. They each take my comment into consideration. After a long pause the Oracle speaks again.

"I'm not saying we toss a dagger at her," he says, without taking his eyes off me. It makes me nervous. "Let's not throw anything at her. Just find something sharp," he tells them. Orisa picks up a knife on the counter.

I'm too scared to speak; I trust the Four and all their wisdom, but I have no idea what they are talking about or what they are about to do. My mouth is scared shut, not wanting to talk and voice my doubts, and just because I'm afraid of what is in store for me.

"Kayin, we're not going to hurt you." It sends a shiver

up my spine when the Oracle says my name, for more than one reason I suspect.

The Divine walks towards me with the knife. She takes my hand in hers and looks into my eyes. I trust her, I do, but I let my eyes drop back to my arm, which she is about to poke with a knife. The tip touches my skin, and then she slowly presses harder. I feel a pinch but it isn't much, not like I expect it to be. At this point the blade is making a considerable indent in my skin but it has not pierced me. She sends a glance at the Oracle, who nods solemnly, and then she straightens the knife horizontally against my skin, so the sharp blade drags across my arm. But still there is no cut.

"It's a power," the Cryptic states. My head snaps up at his voice. "That's it. Perhaps a healer, it is no use her being injured when she needs to heal those who are. She's impervious to weapons," he says, his eyes sparkling. I feel my jaw hit the ground. What? But I've been hurt before. I've bled before. How could this be?

"What is defined as a weapon though? Does it have any limits?" the Vehement asks the rest of them.

"I've bled and been injured before, it can't be?" I interject. They watch me for a moment while they think.

"Then help us figure this out," the Cryptic continues. "When you've been hurt, what was the cause of it?"

I try to think back to the times I've been hurt. "I

remember falling out of a tree...once or twice" I begin telling them. They nod and look at me patiently, as I aim to figure it out in my head. Being on my own for so long and hiding well means I haven't come across a lot of combat and weapons. But I've come face to face with the Ghosts. How did they hurt me? I remember once, one of them knocked me across the ground with their white staff. Then it punched me while I was on the ground. I had been knocked out but when I woke up I had dried blood on my cheek, and found the cut on my cheekbone.

"I can be hit," I tell them. "A Ghost once knocked me across the ground and hit me with his fist," I continue. Then think of something. "Why didn't he just stab me? I suppose I know now it wouldn't have worked but...but why didn't he try?"

"He must have known," the Cryptic answers without missing a beat.

"Do they...know about me?" This makes me angry. They know what I am, what powers I have, before me?! I've been kept in the dark for so long. I am mad at myself mostly for not venturing out and experimenting. Maybe I could have found the Resistance and discovered my powers sooner. I'm just confused.

"I think they must do, somehow. Maybe they, too, have powers like mine and sense talent in others," the Cryptic suggests.

"Does this mean I can't die?" The thought suddenly occurs to me.

"No. You can still die. Your skin just can't be broken with weapons," the Divine takes over.

"But we still don't know what counts as a weapon," the Vehement reminds them, looking at them and back at me.

"Hand me that pencil." The Vehement picks up the pencil and hands it to the Oracle as asked. He does just as the Divine did; he takes my hand and slowly pushes the pencil into my arm. When that has no affect, he suddenly lifts it and jabs it back into my skin. I'm shocked at the sudden action, surprised at his confidence in the action. But it seems to have come from a genuine hunch as my arm does not bleed, and it scarcely hurt, just a tingling sensation that I'm not too fond of experiencing, but I can handle.

"Objects with the intent of hurting you." We decide this after several trials, including a test where I graze passed a nail left on the edge of the table, which does scratch my skin. The Divine then tries to harm me with the same nail, with no result.

"The pencil is not considered a weapon, but still should have hurt you. When used as a weapon, with the intent of injury, you were unaffected by it," the Oracle says.

I know my Nana had three visible powers, but she may

well have been impervious to weapons too. I have doubt in my mind as to why she would have never mentioned it. I know it's not a conventional healer power despite the Cryptic's confidence that it must be linked. Maybe it is a healer power that isn't guaranteed, just like powers as a whole aren't guaranteed to every healer but I still have my suspicions.

I assume I will have the same powers as my Nana, so, now that I know I'm capable of powers, in theory I have three more to discover. I'm fascinated and excited. The Four leave me alone to my thoughts but not before the Oracle holds back and speaks in a low voice.

"You've faced the Ghosts before?" he is about to walk out with the others but has stopped at my side, facing me and leaning down to keep our talk private. I nod.

"How many times?"

"When I was sent to prison," I answer, checking the area for anyone who might hear. I don't want everyone knowing I have experienced the prison. "And maybe seven times since I've escaped? That's physical contact; I've seen them around a lot. That's in the space of four years, since I've been a rogue," I tell him. Was that right? I think I'm correct. The Oracle nods but doesn't move. I let my mind slip back to my two-year sentence at the prison, and then think to where I am now. I let out a breath I didn't realise I'd been holding, in relief to be in such a better place. I feel safe.

"We won't let that happen to you again," the Oracle tells me, his voice rough and low, reading my thoughts. He is so close now I can feel his breath on my face. "The only reason we'll ever enter the prison is to free our people. And we'll keep you safe. I won't let anything happen to you."

My breath hitches at his change from 'we' to 'I'. I look up into his eyes, which are shining with the truth he is speaking. He means it; he is completely serious. This rebellion is real and he promises to keep me safe.

4

"Kayin? Kay?" I hear Mari whisper.

She shakes me gently at first, as I blink the sleep from my eyes, and then she roughly jogs me out of slumber. I sit up quickly and look at her. She has a finger up to her lips, urging me to be quiet. Then she curls her finger, motioning for me to get up and follow her.

I had a tiring day yesterday. It was the day after I found out I can't be severely harmed by weapons, so after the initial shock, I had become what I could only describe as excited. When others found out, I let them things thrown at me all day. At first it was just Rhyland, who skipped up to me and threw a small rock at me. It bounced off just as expected with a little tickle and then the game branched out from there. I felt a part of something as I joined in with training and practice. At one point I was helping people with their aim; I would run back and forth and dodge throws, while they practised throwing at a moving object. Getting hit a few times here and there wasn't bad, and it only meant I was helping them get better, so I didn't mind. Though as soon as I retreated to my room, I took off my jeans, boots and belts and fell asleep as soon as my head hit the pillow.

I quickly and silently redress and follow Mari, who I notice is already ready for the day, out of my room. It is still dark out, but not as dark as the middle of the night. I can see the horizon slowly beginning to get lighter.

"Quickly," she says as we run across the land and to the medical room. We go to the other end of the room and Mari pulls a curtain aside and standing round the bed behind it I see the Four and Selene surrounding a man. Selene has her hand on his forehead and the other on his chest. Her eyes are closed, eyebrows furrowed and it looks like she is concentrating hard.

"She's trying to wake him up," Mari leans over and whispers to me. At the sound of her voice, the Four glance around and see me. They usher me closer and I stand at the bedside. I recognise the man unconscious in bed, I've seen him around.

"The attack has begun," the Oracle says solemnly, watching Selene working. She scrunches her face up, putting more pressure on his head and chest, until she finally lets go. She looks up at us with sad eyes.

"I can't wake him up," she tells us sadly. She spots me. "Kayin, you need to help him."

I can feel eyes on me and without hesitating, I move forward, inspecting his body. I can make out probably several fractures in his left wrist due to swelling and rapid bruising, and heavy damage to his ribs. I tell the others what I think and they respond immediately, tending to his fractures. The main problem is the wound to his head. A bandage has already been tied around his temple but it is soaked with blood. His lip is swollen and the skin has broken, not to mention the blood that is oozing from his mouth. He has a worrying amount of bruising peaking out from beneath his bandage.

We work together to do all we can. Mari and I clean him up and the Divine stands by his head, telling us that she can't make a connection with his soul yet so he is still mostly with us. I become frustrated when my methods seem to be useless. I feel useless. The man isn't doing very well and I desperately want to help him. It is in my blood. I want to scream because I don't have the powers to help. My Nana prolonged the life of a woman with a fatal illness, and I can't help this wounded man?! What else am I good for if I can't heal?! He has awful injuries and won't wake up even with the help of Selene. After stitching his wounds, supporting his fractures and cleaning him, all we can do is hope that time will eventually heal him on his own. It is out of my hands.

I can feel his pulse slowing down under my fingers as I hold them to his neck.

"No...no, no, no," I quietly whine. I'm aware I'm putting a lot of the responsibility on myself, and it isn't helping at all. I need to concentrate.

"No!" I cry. I feel his life slip away under my touch. I can't bear to open my eyes and face the others. After a long moment of silence, a tear falls down my cheek and I look at the man. He is still. He will never move again. I couldn't help.

As I blink another tear rolls down my face and I finally turn my head to look at the others. "I'm sorry," I whisper.

My voice is hoarse and my breath catches in my throat, so my apology is barely audible, but I see them give me a small nod. Nothing is said. We remain like that for a while, until I feel Orisa's presence beside me. She takes the man's hand and closes her eyes. I know she is taking him down to the Underworld to make sure he is safe on his new journey. I can feel it.

"Who is he?" I ask quietly. The Four have left and taken the man with them, Selene is back in her bed and now sleeping from exhaustion of being injured herself still and trying to wake up the man, and Mari and I sit beside her. I'm still upset; I let my head hang low, and play with my hands.

"His name was Maynard. He was on lookout, North of here. They're closing in." Mari replies. She watches me for a moment when I don't speak again. "You can't blame yourself," she whispers to me.

"Why couldn't I help him?" I ask, knowing she doesn't have the answer. I feel Mari rest her arm around my shoulders. "Is it going to be like this now? Now the Ghosts are coming? This isn't the last fatality."

Mari doesn't reply, which gives me all the answers I need. I stand up and pace, making my first full movements since I walked in here. I catch my reflection in an old mirror that hangs on the wall. It is dirty and scratched, but I can still make out my red, bloodshot eyes, the faded, smudged war paint across my face and the trail of a tear that cuts through the dirt.

The sun has almost fully risen now. I know the Ghosts are close. The Oracle has said the attack has begun and they'll ambush us any moment now.

"We need to get ready," I tell Mari, turning back to her. She nods in understanding and we leave Selene, making our way to the ditch. As we pass through the invisibility shield, we see the Four already here. The ditch is decorated with weapons and supplies, lying around everywhere, ready for the rogues to equip themselves. My knife and slingshot are strapped to my sides, but I know I won't be battling. I'll be stationed in the medical room, helping the others fix as many people as we can. Though I've taken a blow to my confidence, I know I can't dwell on it; there will be more that I need to help and I can't be distracted.

The Cryptic whistles, the high pitch tone that resonates throughout your whole body, and within minutes the Resistance is joining us; collecting weapons, stocking up on supplies, and beginning to move out to their allocated areas.

Five sharp whistles are heard in the distance, and whoever is left in the ditch moves; we know it is the signal to tell us they are here. I run back to the medical room and wait, making sure I have everything we will need. Myself, and the others who are situated in the medical room with me are barely in there ten minutes before I can feel myself going crazy in anticipation. The whole idea of being useless until someone gets injured is maddening and I make the decision to scope out the situation. I hear the clink of blades and the moans of the battlefield. I have a good aim, I can help out somehow.

Poking my head out of the window of the medical room, I see people in the distance fighting. There are at least seven Ghosts that I can see. I look to my side and up, and realise I can probably make my way up onto the roof by climbing the wall.

"Call me if someone comes in," I tell the others over my shoulder. Mari and Selene, another girl and two boys who I don't know yet, who are also looking unsure about what to do with themselves, nod back at me and promise to yell if they need me back. I then climb out of the window and latch on to the bricks. Slowly I make my way up and jump over the ledge and haul myself onto the roof. It is littered with stones and rocks and debris, which is perfect. I quickly load my slingshot with one of the heftier rocks, and look out at the fight again. It is surreal to finally be a part of something. This isn't just me hiding and defending myself alone from the Ghost Men, this is a full-blown battle. I wonder if we hadn't got a warning about it, how well we would have faced them.

I lift my slingshot and take aim at a Ghost. I aim for his helmet, and then take into consideration the wind and distance, and launch the rock. Thankfully I make a hit, and I can almost hear the crack of his mask from here. He stumbles back and I look on, satisfied. I crouch down so no one will spot me if they look up to the roof, but I do peek over and see some people looking around for the source of the shot.

My eyes widen in wonderment as I watch a black figure bound up to the Ghost while he is distracted. The woman jumps high and with both feet kicks the Ghost in the chest, pushing him to the ground. The impact leaves a hole in the desert land as they both skid across the floor. Then with a punch where I had hit him, she cracks the remainder of the Ghost's helmet. There is only one person to have the power to make a strike like that. I smile at the skill of the Vehement, as she leaps off and begins fighting again.

I continue to propel rocks and ammo at the battle. Some of the shots don't quite make an impact; some don't hit a target at all. But I like to think I am helping. Someone yells for me, so I climb back down as quickly as I can. I have one leg in the window and I'm about to jump back in when I see a Ghost emerge from thin air below us. He appears on the edge of our town, away from the battle and begins striding in to our land.

My breathing stops as I stare at him. Everyone is hidden but I know he is searching to destroy. My attention is stolen when I hear a groan and glance into the room where I see a girl lying on the bed.

"What's her status?" I ask quickly.

"Possible shoulder dislocation," one of the boys answers. The girl cries out again, and I see Mari and Selene nod, before Mari holds the injured girl's hand and slowly she slips under, away from the pain she feels.

I shoot a look back at the Ghost and see he is getting

closer to our buildings and camps. I can't just leave him. I need to stop him.

"You can handle it. I'm sorry I need to go. I'll be back!"

As I look to the floor I wonder if my experience of jumping out of trees will cover me for jumping from a second story window. Doubtfully, I wonder if this is the best idea, to head in to combat. I am better helping rather than fighting, so I have learnt. But I can't let him walk into our homes when there are people unguarded and unaware of his presence. So I jump.

I land with a thud and roll across the ground. Instantly, I catch the attention of the Ghost as I turn over onto my back in front of him. On seeing me, he runs forward, white staff raised and ready to strike. When he gets close enough I kick my legs out and hit him, which sends him stumbling backwards, giving me enough time to get to my feet before he comes back for another hit, where he strikes me in my stomach before I can dodge out of his way. He can't have had the intention of stabbing me, because he followed through with his swing, as if he knew it would just bounce off, so he keeps up the momentum and throws me across the ground.

It isn't the first time I've experienced a winding like this, from one of the Ghost Men. I squint up towards the sky as he towers over me. He lifts his fist, ready to blow, and I narrowly miss his punch by turning to the side and letting him hit the ground. I feel it vibrate underneath me, and know that would have done some damage to my head. While he is straightening up I swing my leg round and kick up into the back of his knee. His leg buckles and he falls to his knees and I take the opportunity to get up onto my own knees and for a moment I feel like time stands still. We are face to face. I've never been this intimately close with a Ghost. I stare into the black holes that are his eyes and I can see no emotion. He is a robot, nothing more than a machine for all I care.

In an overwhelming feeling of anger, I quickly jump to my feet and kick him hard in the head. He falls backwards from his knees onto his back while I ignore the throbbing pain in my foot, and stomp on his helmet. It cracks underneath my boot and it feels good. I feel white-hot rage coursing through me as I look at the black demon. He is much larger than me, and I have brought him down. I stand over him waiting for him to move again. Eyeing his white uniform, long cloak and gleaming, slick mask, I am reminded of all the pain the Ghosts have brought upon me. My family. My people. It is all coming out on this lone Ghost.

Suddenly I feel myself being slung against a wall. The Ghost has used some kind of telekinesis and picks me up with only a move of his hand. I struggle against the force that keeps me pinned back, frustrated with the sudden exchange of power and hold my hand out to grasp the air, in hopes to free myself, while I watch the Ghost stand up. He reclaims his staff and walks towards me.

I know he can't make me bleed with that staff. He knows it too. But it doesn't mean it doesn't pack a punch when he swings it round the side of my head. I know it would have been a lot worse if I wasn't somewhat protected because of my power.

A scream erupts from the battlefield. An all-consuming feeling of déjà vu takes over then. Back when I was 14, and my town had come under attack, there were kids screaming, people fighting, Ghosts plagued the streets. The dreaded feeling that it was happening again pushes me forward. My life, my home, my family and friends were torn away from me when the Ghosts came the first time and I have only just got that feeling of having somewhere to belong and friends to rely on back. I can't shake the sensation that it's being taken away again.

I find myself breaking free of the force that binds me and I hold up my hand to the Ghost. I think of the only thing I can that could possibly slow the Ghost down, so I curl my fingers and feel a hot sensation running through my veins. And then my hand starts glowing.

The Ghost slows down. One step after the other he tries

to pull away from whatever hold I have on him. He is struggling and I'm not sure right away if it is my doing, but I have to believe it is.

"You ruined my life!" I scream. "You took everything from me!"

"Our people are superior," he speaks. My jaw almost hits the floor, but I have to keep my cool. I've never heard a Ghost speak before and it spooks me. His voice is low, dark and menacing. It seems to echo behind his mask and ring through my body. "Our civilisation rules and we could not mix with the likes of filth like you."

I raise my hand higher and clench my fingers, the golden light shining brighter from my hand. I keep replaying the images of my Nana using this power over and over in my head. I can't afford to lose this power now, whatever it is; it seems to be helping me.

"My people are better than you will ever be. We will rebel and destroy you. You cannot defeat this Resistance." I can almost feel my own voice echoing with the power I speak of. I have a funny feeling like the rest of the world is blurred out and all I can see or hear is the Ghost who gives the impression of growing weaker by the second. I am a healer; my powers should be used for good, how is this happening?

I am somewhat disappointed in myself to be using a

healing power to create such a negative impact on the Ghost. It almost scares me enough that I am prepared to stop myself, but I know I can't give in just yet. I'll face the consequences later.

"You haven't faced the worst of us yet," he tells me. His voice is still deep and steady, despite the fact he is struggling to stand now. "We have an ultimate being who leads us and our lord. Our Supreme," he laughs darkly as he divulges this new information to me. But he can do no more, as he then collapses.

I fall backwards, dropping my hand, shaking with what I have just done. Have I killed him? Who is the Supreme? What do they have to do with anything?

Suddenly a dark figure is running towards me, and in a smooth movement has bent down and picked me up from my fragile position and carries me away. I see the Vehement approach the Ghost I have...well, I don't know what I have done to him. I feel my eyes falling shut. No, I must stay awake. I must help! But I can't fight the overwhelming feeling of fatigue that suddenly hits me, and I let myself fall limp in the arms of the man carrying me.

"Did I kill him?" is the first thing I mumble when consciousness finds me again. When I open my eyes I realise

I am alone.

Well, alone in the sense that no one is crowded around my bed. I sit up and see I am in the medical room; the one I'm supposed to be working in, not sleeping in, and all attention is on other patients. Immediately I hop out of the bed, ignoring the dizziness I feel and go to the nearest huddle.

"What's going on?" I ask.

"Broken ankle, we think," a boy tells me. I nod and gently feel for signs of breakage, and the ankle is indeed broken. I give them instructions to handle it, ask the patient if she is okay to which she shakily replies yes, and then I move on. I continue on to five other people in the room, all with varying degrees of injuries. I have to fight the reflex to gag when I approach a bloodstained bed where a man has a large gash down the side of his stomach. Once I have given advice and do what I can for each of them, I go round to them all again. I keep repeating this, adding new patients to the cycle as they come in, accounting for people who have left to go back to fighting with minor injuries, until I have a steady rhythm.

Eventually more people stop coming in. The night finally comes and people begin drifting off in peace and leaving and I am left alone in the medical room with seven sleeping patients. The battle is over.

I look over the soundless bodies in the beds around me. Not including Selene, I have six casualties bad enough which means they are staying in here in case they need my assistance. I wonder how many others are out there injured, but not enough that they feel they need help. And I wonder how many fatalities there have been, if any at all since the case this morning. I hope for the latter.

I end up falling asleep in the medical bed I had woken up in hours before. Just before lying down I remember how I got there in the first place. The Ghost that I had killed. Or had I? I still don't know the answer. Did the Vehement finish him off? I roll my eyes at my worry – they are evil, they don't think twice about killing us off, what does it matter if they are injured or dead? I quickly regret the eye rolling when I feel a pain in my temples. I put my hand up to my forehead, to steady myself, even though I'm not moving. I feel dizzy again. Slowly, I lie back down and feel my whole world tip backwards with me.

It feels like I only blinked, but I must have dozed off because when my eyes open again, the room is lighter than before. Only by a few shades of grey. I still have to focus to see very far in front of me, but I can tell an hour or two has passed.

I swing my legs out of bed silently and sit on the edge, stretching. I don't feel like sleeping. All that is on my mind is my patients. So I stand up, ready to check on them and make sure they are all still comfortably sleeping, when as I turn I spot a dark figure in a chair, that wasn't here before. In the short hours I had blacked out, they had come in.

"You should be resting," the Oracle whispers. His voice is heavy with exhaustion.

"I could say the same to you," I say just as quietly, but still not as confidently as I would have liked. My voice slips out of my mouth clumsily as I wonder why he is here.

"Couldn't sleep," he replies, and I think I can hear a slight strain in his voice.

"Me neither." I feel myself smile. I can still only see a dark outline, so I inch closer to the chair by the wall at the end of my bed. I see him better then. He has no shirt on and he is leaning forward, resting his elbows on his knees, his head hanging as he speaks.

"How are you?" he asks sincerely. When he lifts his head I see his blue eyes sparkle in the moonlight. It would have taken my breath away if my breath weren't already caught in my throat. I finally exhale and take one more step towards him.

"I've been better," I reply honestly. "Does that hurt?" I ask, noticing the blood across his stomach as he sits up straighter. It is dry, but it may still need assistance.

He groans softly as a yes, and tries to shift his body so I

can get a better look in the dim light. I wonder whether it will be much of a disturbance if I switch on the small lamp by the bed I'm using tonight.

"Come here," I say. I help him walk over to the bed and he flops down, hand holding his hip. I shut the curtains around the bed and then turn on the small light. His face is suddenly illuminated and I catch him staring at me, but he doesn't look away as I come closer to inspect his wound. I finally see the dirt and blood on his face, and I wonder if it is his own.

In fact, there are marks of blood all over his body, mixed with dust, mud and war paint. I motion for him to sit back and he obliges, while I tip toe away. My feet pad across the floor as I go to get a sponge, fill a cup with warm water and grab some bandages.

I can't help being thrown back to the day I first found him and had no idea who he was. I gently clean the cuts down his side and the grazes across his torso. I dab them dry and put a bandage over the worst ones. As he lies there, half sat up against the pillows, I decide I should just give the rest of him a clean, because I have to stay here tonight with the other patients, which means I'll just crawl back into this bed when I'm done, and I don't want it getting dirtier than it already is. Plus it's just unhygienic.

He doesn't object as I dip the sponge back into the

warm water and drag it down his arms. I gently hold his wrist and don't rub too hard, just enough to get the layer of dirt off. He slips his arm back so instead of holding his wrist I am holding his hand. It was a simple gesture but if I think about it too much, I will get flustered. So I ask some questions that have been playing on my mind all day.

"Did you see the Ghost that came into town?" I whisper. His eyes are closed as he relaxes back into the pillows. He almost looks like a normal guy. Then he smiles and I feel my heart waver.

"Of course. I saw you fight. I carried you back here," he tells me. I didn't know it was him. The memory of being held close to someone's chest, and letting myself relax into their arms seems all the more strange now I know it was him. A good strange.

"What happened to the Ghost Man? Did I kill him?"

He opens his eyes and lets his head drop to the side to look at me. As I make eye contact with him I drop his hand and hesitate, before leaning forward and cleaning the rest of his torso and chest. He gives me a small smile. "The Ghost was taken care of."

I don't want to ask any more of that. So I concentrate on cleaning him.

"You don't have to do this," he lifts his hand and puts it on my forearm as I hold the sponge across his body. He leaves it there, as if in polite protest, but he closes his eyes and lets his hand follow the movement of my arm, and I know he likes it.

"I like taking care of people," is all I whisper back. The sponge gently brushes over the small cuts I haven't patched up, and I think about him sitting in the chair by my bed, waiting.

"Did you come here tonight for my help with this..." I ask, gently brushing a cut with the sponge, "or just to watch me sleep?"

His eyes open and he watches me, but I don't falter this time. I feel confident in this; I'm only teasing but I have valid reasons to suspect wanting help with his injuries isn't the only reason he is here. And I'm not going to deny my romantic side the chance to imagine that.

"I needed some work done, of course," he says kindly, and then graciously smiles as he looks between my face and the bandages.

"Really? Why didn't you wake me up sooner?" I question. I want to smirk, but I restrain myself.

"You woke up anyway."

"But how long were you sitting there by my bed?" I ask. The only place I have left to clean is his neck and face, so I slowly move the sponge to his neck while I wait for an answer. He is just watching me, watching when I dampen the sponge, how I pay close attention to his skin. He brings his hand up and places it over mine, making me stop my movement. I freeze at the contact, my hands still holding the sponge that is delicately placed on his neck.

I absent-mindedly let my fingers slip from the sponge and the tips rest on his jaw line. I graze his skin finely, my movements restricted from the hand he has over mine.

"I didn't want to disturb your rest." When he speaks again I retract my fingers immediately and wipe his neck despite his hand still being there. What do I think I'm doing?

Holding my breath, I finally get to his face and wipe his cheeks, and across his forehead. I avoid his gaze as he continues to watch me. He makes me so nervy and I'm not fully sure why. Well, I can take a few guesses. Maybe because he's one of the most beautiful men I've ever seen. Maybe I am in awe of how powerful he is. I'm pretty sure I am still star struck, in a sense, at finding out he, the Oracle, is real and all this is not a myth. He just makes me nervous, and makes my heart flutter, and I want to smile every time he says my name. But I can't allow myself to ever develop feelings, and let myself believe he would reciprocate those feelings. There will never be anything between us. In blunt terms, I am a lowly rogue girl, and he is a man of legend. I am not special, or worthy enough, to be with him in that sense.

A shaky breath escapes me as I realise all this. Why am I thinking about this? I know the answer. Because, though I have just said not to allow myself to develop feelings, I think they had started growing the minute I found him in the desert and he laid his eyes on me for the first time. He was a beautiful stranger, something new and someone I could help. I won't be able to extinguish the feelings I've felt for him since that moment, but I can't let it go any further. I'd only set myself up for disappointment.

I realise the Oracle has fallen asleep, for when I finally let myself look at him properly again, his eyes are closed, but not just resting; they are closed for the rest of the night. I feel my lack of sleep catching up with me, so I put my supplies down and am about to trudge over to another bed, but the idea of sliding up next to the Oracle and switching off the light just seems so much more appealing. I don't know if it is the slight head wound, or fatigue, but nothing tells me it is a bad idea, so I climb up, scoot in next to him and lay on my side, facing him. I breathe in his scent and close my eyes. Clumsily, I reach over to turn the lamp off, and when I pull my arm back, the Oracle catches it and brings it down to his body. In the new darkness, I'm not sure if he is awake or subconsciously grabbing my arm, but I don't argue with the action and let my arm lie across his chest as I finally fall asleep again.

5

I wake up alone, curled up in bed. The Oracle has already left, as I expected him to. The thought doesn't stay in my mind for long; I make myself busy. Before I leave the medical room I check on the patients. They are stable, healing, and all sleeping, as it is still fairly early. The sun is warm on my skin as I make my way to my room. I walk slowly, arms crossed, peering around at our town.

It's pretty, as pretty as it can be since being deserted and then re-inhabited by the rogues. I wonder where exactly we are, what town this is. It's one of the larger towns with a stream running through it, that large cube stone houses sit on either side of. Most of the buildings in this town are still whole, so I can why the Resistance made camp here. Thankfully I do not seeing a lot of damage. There is discarded ammo and some litter lying around, but that can easily be taken care of. I see a few large cloths, which were once tent-like structures on the edge of our camp, strewn across the land, some ripped. I wonder what the actual battleground looks like, where the majority of fighting had been done. I expect there are several dents in the floor due to the Vehement, maybe skids and burns and broken weapons and rags.

I enter my room and change into my extra pair of jeans and top. I clean my face and arms, and tie my hair up. Feeling a little more refreshed I walk across the stream to Mari's room. When I enter smiling, she looks up and grins at me.

"How are you feeling?" she asks straight away, walking over to me.

"My heads a little cloudy, I got a blow from one of the Ghosts," I tell her, and she nods sympathetically. "What happened? How was the fight?" I ask her.

"Well, after you jumped out of the window..." she gives me a stern look that tells me I will have to explain myself soon, "we had injuries come and go. Selene and I worked hard helping people and knocking people out to work on them and waking them back up again. It was tiring for me, but even more of a strain on Sel. She's still recovering from her little head injury, but she held up really well," she smiles to herself.

"I haven't heard a lot about the fighting though, I

suspect we'll find out eventually, probably today at some point. Everyone will be talking about it," she stares at me for a moment as I take in what she's said. "Now what happened to you?"

I begin with climbing up on to the roof to fire rocks at the battle. Which leads on to how I'd spotted the Ghost as he entered our town. Then how I jumped and we fought, how I used all I had to fight him and what he had said to me. I briefly mention how he spoke of his civilisation and the Supreme. I skip over his words because I don't want to dwell on the memory and the sick feeling I get in my stomach when I think about it; besides, I know I would have to go into detail about it later, most likely with one of the Four, so I can avoid it for now. I tell her about my glowing hands and how he reacted to them, and she nods along unfazed. Just as I suspected she would. I'm on the homestretch of my story, telling her how the Oracle had taken me to the medical room, and that's when I started helping again. And then I casually slip in that he had come back in the night. I don't go in to detail about that bit though.

We are silent for a moment as Mari processes what I have told her. Sitting face to face on her bed, we're both caught in our own thoughts. I replay the moment I discovered my power in my head, staring at the white wall behind Mari, and then I finally let myself acknowledge what

I did.

"I controlled his heart."

She looks up, waiting for me to continue. Now I've said it out loud I realise it must be true. "My hands were glowing; just like my Nana's. I begged and begged my body to make it happen, told myself how it was supposed to work, thought about everything you had told me too from when you saw her use it. And I controlled the Ghost's heart."

"I remember when Diola used it on my mother." Mari's voice is dreamy thinking about the memory. "Delicately hovering her glowing hand over her," she says, mimicking the action and holding her hand aloft as if there is a body lying in front of her. "She calmed my mother and it allowed her to work on her safely."

I sigh heavily, and unintentionally snap Mari out of her memory.

"What's wrong?"

"It feels wrong. I'm meant to be a healer. The way you talk about my Nana, I almost feel ashamed that I could have taken a power she used so wholesomely and use it negatively. The exact opposite of healing," I admit. "How do I control it?"

"Why don't we find out and go see the Four? I'm sure they all want an update of yesterday and will be willing to help you figure this out. It definitely has good and bad effects. So we can work on it from there," she tells me, full of optimism. Though she is a few years younger than me at 17, I admire her calmness in all situations, and the light-hearted attitude she always has. She is very mature, and I know that comes from experience and years of being in the Resistance.

We have some food first. We eat the breakfast that is available to us in the communal kitchen of the house she lives in. Her and Selene share a bedroom, which would in fact be the living room if a family were to live here. I haven't met the people who live in the two bedrooms upstairs yet. The house is quite bare and only contains the necessities such as beds and chairs, a refrigerator and an electric grill; all that was left intact from the attack of Ghosts all those many years ago, I assume. When we've had our fix of food, Mari then gets dressed. It feels good to be in a clean set of my sturdy, daily clothes rather than the clothes I had worn repeatedly the last few days, training and fighting. We wash up more thoroughly by the stream and I rinse the remaining dirt and war paint off of my skin, and the feeling of battle away with it. We are safe, for now.

I find some left over berries in the pouch of my belt so Mari and I snack on them as we look for the Four. Along the way we come across people talking and overhear conversations of the ambush, what had gone down.

Apparently at least 21 Ghost Men had been here in total, continuously fighting and roaming the land. It was hard to track them down and make sure there were no stragglers that could attack while we were off guard, but evidently it worked out for the best. Some were killed, but most had been so terribly injured that they had to retreat, and vanished.

"No word of a lie, his helmet cracked, his mask broke completely and fell off. I did it; I made the final blow. And to see what was underneath...boy, you wouldn't believe it. He didn't look human. It was like a skeleton, bug, and human mix. Sharp, shadowed cheekbones, deep set eyes, red iris's! It was unreal," we hear one man telling his friends. They are hanging on his every word as he recalls the event. I don't doubt a word he says, and it sends a shiver up my spine.

When we come to the ditch but can't find any of the Four, we consider heading back to our town, but decide not.

"What if we check out the land?" Mari suggests. I agree and we head further away from the Resistance and roam the desert. Not too far, we both still feel a little on edge and we don't want to run into trouble. But we inspect the battlegrounds, which look nothing like the smooth, dry, flat surfaces of the desert that can be seen for miles. These pieces of land consist of turned up rocks, dirt piles and ditches. Mud skids, blood patches, and the works. Mari and I share a grimace, and continue looking.

"Look, I think I see someone," I point as I see the bodies up ahead. We stop when we saw a Ghost with the Four, deciding to stay back in case they are battling, but when it is evident that the Ghost Man is of no threat, we slowly approach.

The Oracle is using his power and making the Ghost Man collect broken weapons from the floor. It is strange to see him act like this, almost domestic, when we all know he is anything but that.

"Marisol, Kayin," the Divine addresses us. She has her arms crossed over her chest and is putting most of her weight on one leg as she watches the Ghost work apprehensively, giving us only a small glance when we join them. Her dark frizzy hair is being blown about gently in the breeze, but she doesn't make a move to push it away from her face.

"Is this an okay time?" Mari asks, aiming her question at the Vehement mostly. I've figured out from my time here so far that Mari is much more comfortable approaching and talking to the Four when Imara is around. Being cousins, I guess it is more natural to act around her than the others, even though all four of them are said to be legends.

I turn my head and look across the land to see how far we have come, and as I expect I can't see the town or ditch, just desert. I look back to the people in front of me, who are watching the Ghost Man with hard-set eyes. I don't say anything. I scan the people. I watch them. They all have powers too. I wonder how they came to terms with it and how they discovered them all and when.

I think about my own powers. Not wanting to disrupt the situation at the moment, I stay silent. Mari said my Nana had calmed her mother. I seemed to destroy the Ghost. He grew weak and struggled; he was not calm. It goes against everything I have been taught.

"I control hearts," I say. All heads snap up at my voice. I don't mean to say it out loud, but it slipped out straight away when I decided that I want to talk about it. "I think," I add a little more quietly.

The Cryptic brings his hands up and puts his index fingers to his lips in thought, watching me. I feel exposed under his stare so I look at the others. The Divine looks intrigued, a ghost of a smile playing on her face. At least she doesn't look worried about the Ghost anymore. The Oracle shares a look with the others, and then turns to me.

"We're done here." He holds his hand up and the Ghost Man stops instantly. He is frozen. "And how do you feel?" he asks, never taking his eyes off me.

"I feel bad about how I used it," I tell him honestly. It makes me feel good when no one doubts me or questions my power, and then I realise it's because it makes me feel validated, something I didn't realise I craved.

"Would you like to practice?" he asks, glancing at the Ghost pointedly. The thought almost makes my own heart stop. Ghost Man or not, I do not like the idea of controlling heartbeats negatively, and I'm not sure if I could control the power. I suppose that's the exact reason I need practice, however.

"H-how will we know if it's working?" I reply. Would the Ghost reveal if I were controlling his heart? Or would he stay silent until he collapsed. I suspect he wouldn't reveal anything.

"We have no use for him, regardless," the Cryptic chips in. "You may as well try."

I have to remind myself for a moment that these men and women are soldiers, warriors. The Ghost Man is their enemy and they are going to destroy him one way or another. I may as well try, as the Cryptic says, especially if I may get answers. I suck in a shaky breath and raise my hand.

I try hard to muster up the power I felt yesterday but I can't do it. It's like teaching myself a new trick and I haven't quite mastered the technique. I drop my hand and sigh, then shrug as I look at the others.

"Think," the Oracle says softly. "What were you feeling when you summoned the power before?" He is thinking tactics. I turn back to the Ghost Man. They all looked the same. I think of the one I had weakened. He called our people filth; he said their civilisation ruled. Suddenly I feel the anger rising in me again.

I lift my hand and tense my muscles, aiming at the Ghost as I feel the same rush of heat through my veins and see my hand start glowing. The others take a step back; I see them do it in the corner of my eye. I would have too if I were in their position.

"I don't know what to do now!" I admit shakily, suppressing the feeling of fear creeping through me.

"It's okay. Stay calm and think of nothing but your actions," the Cryptic assures me.

I remind myself of the talk about the Supreme. Of the battle I witnessed. The memories of the ambush yesterday and the one in my town all those years ago surface in my mind. The imprisonment of my people and the desperate looks my parents had on their faces when they pushed me forward, the last look I got of them before I escaped the prison.

I curl my fingertips and the Ghost Man doubles over, gloved hand up to his chest. The Oracle is no longer controlling him; I know it, I can feel it. Keeping him in place now is all on me. I bite my lip, trying to concentrate. Then I close my eyes, no more distractions. I am focused, but also avoiding having to watch what I am doing.

I hear his heart beat in my head; it ripples through the angry emotions clouding my mind. They mix as the heat in my veins grows stronger, and then I hear a thump on the ground. Silence in my head. I drop my arm by my side and dare myself to open my eyes. Slowly, the scene appears in front of me again. The Ghost is crumpled on the ground, and the others are surveying the situation. There is no doubt in my mind that I have killed the Ghost this time.

A flash of light materialises as the Cryptic shoots a small ball of fire at the Ghost, and we leave his body to burn alone. I follow the others away. I don't want to be the first one to speak, lacking the words to say really, and I know we are all lost in our own thoughts.

We walk all the way back to the town and back into the same room where we had tested if I could be cut with weapons. Mari takes my hand and squeezes it affectionately, giving me a comforting smile, and then lets go, sitting down at the side of the room. Finally I break the silence before anyone else can talk.

"Apart from confirming that I do indeed have this power now, that little exercise back there didn't help me," I realise with sadness. I am mad at myself for doing again what I did yesterday, which caused me all this self doubt in the first place.

"I just practiced it negatively, and I still don't know if I can control it or if I can use it for good, the way it is intended for a healer. And I have to get angry before I can use it. I was livid. I can't do that every time I use it. For whatever I use it for," I continue, emptying all the thoughts in me head. There is a pause and the Oracle steps forward.

"Try it on me," he instructs me. I widen my eyes in horror and look at him as if he is crazy.

"Are you serious?"

"You're right, the power needs to be controlled therefore you need to test your power on someone who will give you feedback, so use it on me, someone who doesn't make you livid," he says very matter-of-factly. "At least I hope I don't," he adds with a small smirk when I don't respond straight away, in a successful attempt to lighten the mood. I hesitate still, shaking my head lightly.

"I don't want to hurt you," I admit. Though he is much more powerful, I am essentially controlling his beating heart, what if I accidentally stop it? He takes another larger step towards me. He looks so tall in this not so big room, the closer he gets the more of my vision he dominates.

"I trust you to stop when I say so."

I look up at him, still unsure. But he just waits; he knows I will give in. I close my eyes and sigh, an action I feel like I'm doing a lot lately, and then lift my hand in resignation. I don't want to get angry. I don't want to channel such awful thoughts and memories to use the power. In all honesty I don't know whether I want to use the power at all, specifically because I don't know what good I can do with it yet.

I think of the Oracle, standing in front of my closed eyes and force myself to open them and look at him, bracing himself for what could potentially happen. I want to make him proud, make him look at me with respect and astonishment. Most importantly I want his trust in me to not be in vain. So I try to use that to my advantage. I think about it, how he will react if I can do this well.

When my hand starts glowing he stiffens, but I continue to think about the positive emotions and feelings I have in mind. I can't take my eyes off his face as I do this, in fear I will lose my train of thought. Instead of wanting to hurt him, I want to help. I want to relax him, take the stiffness away from him. And as I think of that, my Nana pops into my mind, how Mari told me she had relaxed and calmed her mother. That's what I must do. I hear the Oracle's heartbeat in my head and focus on slowing it to the point of relaxation and enjoyment, rather than pain.

He looks down at his chest, then up to me with a small smile and heavy eyelids. I see his shoulders drop and the smile gets bigger. He is visibly relaxing and it makes me happy. He gives me a meaningful nod, so I close my eyes and concentrate on stopping the flow in my veins and lowering my arm without disrupting his heart. Then I open my eyes with a grin

"I can control the speed of a heart beat," I say excitedly. The Oracle smiles at my reaction. Just what I wanted. Then the Cryptic speaks up again.

"I admit, I can see the benefits for a healer to have this power, and I hate to put a dampener the situation, but I think it's best you still don't use the power until you've mastered it more. It can still be very dangerous and depending on your state of mind could have different effects."

I take in his words, and slowly nod along with him. I want to argue that this could really help me with my patients now, but I understand. I can't get too ambitious when I've only used the power three times, and only once for good intentions. Only because I was thinking about the Oracle was I able to use it safely. This is a tough power, and he has every right to tell me that it was not fully safe to use it yet.

The next day, I find myself climbing up through the tall building in town and hopping on to the roof where you can see the Shadow Lands. I'm hoping that maybe by looking and examining it, what's available to see, it will put into perspective what the Ghost had said, and I can make some sense of it. I've mostly just come up here to think and reflect.

I considered going to the Four. But I don't know how to approach them about it. Whether to just speak to one, or all of them, or where to talk. So I decided to let them find me, whichever one makes contact with me first, accidental or not, I will tell. I've given myself to the end of the day as a deadline, otherwise it will get to the point where they will wonder why I hadn't told them sooner.

But the deadline doesn't matter. As I sit leaning against the brick ledge of the roof, picking at the berries I had collected early this morning, I see the hatch open across the roof and the Oracle emerges. I hold my breath as he stands straight and turns around, spotting me. Without any sign to show me how he is feeling, he begins walking over to me. I scramble to my feet and stand up beside him, quickly swallowing the berry I have in my mouth.

"What are you doing up here?" he asks, his voice smooth. It doesn't bother him that I am up here, he is just asking. He peers into the distance at the horizon, resting his hands on the ledge. The view makes you appreciate how strong the telescope is; from here we can't even see Ervon Gorge, let alone the civilisation that lives miles on the other side of it.

"I was hoping someone would find me," I tell him honestly. He lowers himself onto his elbows as he leans on the ledge, one foot crossed over the other as he stands there, and turns his head to me with an interested look.

"And why is that?"

"I wanted to know how much you guys knew about the Ghosts, and who they live with, who they might work for? If anyone. And…well, the Ghost Man said some things, when I was…slowing his heart…the first one, I mean." It feels weird to say. I wait for him to say something in reply, but then think it will be best to ask the questions myself.

"What is their civilisation like? How did this all happen?" I ask. I have never thought about what their people are like. I have never given them much of a second thought. All I think of are the Ghost Men and their intentions, and who they might be working for. I never stopped to consider the people in between.

"They come from another land," he tells me, looking out at into the distance again. "Over there, it may as well be another world. They thrive in the shadows; a dense forest shrouds their buildings. We don't know much more than that because we've never been over there," he shrugs.

"We're not sure what inspired the sudden attack, since our people have been living on each side of Ervon Gorge so peacefully for centuries. But slowly, each town was evacuated by them. When word got out of other towns being ambushed some farther East packed up their things and headed away. I don't know where the next populated land is, or if those who ran ever made it to anywhere safe. But I know those here who refused to cooperate were sent to prison. Our land was cleared of our people piece by piece. They have towns and homes on the other side of the building we can see through the telescope, what we think is their headquarters. They live where we can't see, on large expanses of land we suspect."

I listen silently, completely enthralled by his story. It is different hearing it from him, rather than as a vague story when I was younger. He is speaking of facts.

"And who are the Ghosts? Do they have a leader?" I ask after a moment.

"From what we can tell, there's a Ghost with a higher status than the rest who seems to be in charge and make the orders, and whoever is in that position no longer takes part in tasks that the soldier Ghosts do. Then, of course, below him is the generation of Ghost Men. Under them is the human-like civilisation, but they aren't human, don't be fooled if you ever see them. They're called shilo and, other than looks, they begin lacking similarities to us humans."

I close my eyes and turn my face into the wind, letting it blow the stray hairs out of my eyes as I take in this information. I can't understand their intentions any more than anyone else, especially after the Oracle has just told me we've lived peacefully for so long, which I was vaguely aware of due to hearing my parents and Nana mention another kind of people who lived far away. I wonder whether this higher status Ghost is the same as the Supreme.

"What's on your mind?" he questions. It takes me a second to remember he can read minds, but he asked me out of politeness.

"The Ghost Man I fought said we hadn't faced the worst of them yet...and there is a Supreme," I speak cautiously, watching his reaction. He stiffens slightly when I mention it.

"He said that?" the Oracle asks to confirm. When he looks at me I nod, and then he faces forward again. The early sun illuminates his profile beautifully and a light breeze causes him to squint his eyes and turn his face towards me slightly so I have a clear view. And I dare to inch closer.

"Do you know what the Supreme is? I've got no idea..." I tell him, looking forward also. The view is extraordinary but the knowledge of the Ghosts living out there somewhere is enough to ruin it.

"There's an old legend, older than the legend of us and the Resistance, a legend from another land, known around the world. An ultimate being. The Supreme," he says with a subtle head nod and a stony expression. "The Supreme is said to be almost undefeatable, but no one has found its weakness to this day. They're meant to be on the scale of a God, like Zeus or similar. I always assumed it was an over exaggeration; that no one person could have so much power. I never doubted the existence of the Supreme; I just didn't expect the Ghosts to bring it with them. The Supreme hasn't been mentioned in decades."

I don't feel like there is much to say after that. Honestly I don't know how to reply either. This new discovery, an ultimate being, it somewhat scares me. Can we battle something like that? What if it doesn't have a weakness at all? What if this is the difference between freeing our people and me seeing my parents again or losing? Can figuring out all my powers and where they come from be any help to this situation? I suddenly have a lot on my mind.

When I snap back to my senses, I feel the presence of the Oracle a lot closer than before. He stands beside me, his body slightly angled to face me.

"So, tell me about you" I say. I want to keep him talking so I can concentrate on not letting my brain turn to mush at this close proximity.

"What do you want to know?" he replies openly. I am glad he sounds so forthcoming, because I am really interested in his story

"When did you realise you were part of a prophecy?" I

ask.

He chuckles and leans down, once again resting on his elbows, and his arm brushes against mine.

He tells me how it is in his family; his great, great, great grandfather had been the last Oracle. He says he used to believe his mother was lying, when she told him that it was in their bloodline.

"And even if I had believed her, what were the odds it would stay in our family? Anyone can be the Oracle. I can't even say I have an exciting origin story of my powers. I heard my mother say my father's shirt was awful, and when I called her out on it, she was astonished," he continues to tell the story, pausing only to laugh lightly.

"She hadn't actually said it out loud. That's when we learnt I had the power to read minds. It was as simple as that. I was 10 then; school was fun after that. Sometimes it was such a pain. All those kids with non-stop thoughts and I had no idea how to control the power and block it out when I needed to. After a year or two of messing around with it, I then got serious. I practiced and worked on my power, until I developed it into being able to see people's past thoughts and memories. When I was 15 I figured out I could move things, like telekinesis, that kind of thing," he tells me.

This is new information to me, I hadn't realised he could do that. I've never seen him do it. I thought I had picked up on all the powers the Four have. I guess not.

I'm distracted when he puts his hand on my forearm. I look up and see his smile, showing his straight white teeth. It makes my heart melt.

"I don't use it," he informs me, obviously knowing that I was wondering why I don't know about it. I feel myself blush.

"But why? Y-you could be even greater, it could help, surely?" I ask nervously.

"I don't need it. Don't get me wrong, when I was 15 and at the peak of my lazy teen years, it came in very useful. I know how to use it well. But I always figured that the day I start relying on my powers to get me through tasks and battles, or anything, then I'll ultimately be failing. I don't need it to fight. I'm highly trained in combat. I'm skilled with weapons. That's not to say I won't have to use it one day, maybe. But I haven't needed it yet," he explains. I respect that.

We both keep to ourselves for a moment, in our own thoughts. I'm idly thinking about a young Oracle; unaware of his skills yet. What he was like. And I hope he is caught up in his own thoughts so as not be reading mine.

"What's your name?" I ask, desperate to know suddenly.

"You mean other than the Oracle?" he asks with a smirk in my direction. I nod shyly. He looks away and stays silent. I don't prompt him, telling myself he'll answer in his own time if he wants to. And he does.

"Olon," he says. His voice is low and his name rolls off his tongue with ease, smooth as honey. I close my eyes. Kayin and Olon. Olon and Kayin. Whoa, stop thinking of that. Stop. Inappropriate thoughts are not okay in front of a mind reader.

I hear him laugh gently. Oh God, he caught me.

"Are you happy here?" he asks unexpectedly, surprising me. He stands up straight and turns his whole body to me, looking down on me with his full attention. So I mirror his actions and look up at him.

"More than anything," I reply, my voice more quiet than I intend it to be.

Slowly he lifts his right hand and holds my chin between his thumb and index finger.

"Good," his voice is soft, almost a whisper like mine. He has such a deep voice and it sounds so good against my ears. I muster enough courage to raise my own left hand and hold onto his wrist lightly, as his thumb caresses my skin. A breeze blows by and I close my eyes, thoroughly enjoying the moment and drinking it all in; the warm sun, cool breeze, Olon's contact.

His hand falls away as the breeze drops and I open my eyes again. He is still standing close, possibly closer, and his eyes won't leave mine. I could look into those eyes all day.

"I'll still call you Oracle," I say, my voice hoarse and my throat dry suddenly.

"Probably best when people are around," he replies. Does that mean I can call him Olon when we are alone? I let the idea of more moments like this cross my mind briefly before I dismiss it, in case he reads my thoughts.

He smiles then and turns away, striding back to the hatch across the roof.

"Kayin and Olon," he chuckles under his breath as he walks away, loud enough for me to hear. "It sounds better that way."

I feel the colour drain from my face, realising I had indeed been caught out. He doesn't look back though. He climbs off of the roof and leaves me feeling flustered.

6

"Hey."

I jump slightly at the voice, and stop washing my clothes in the stream. I spin around in my crouched position and look up at the girl in front of me. I can't remember seeing her around before, I feel like I would have remembered that curly, orange hair. She has freckles splashed across her face and dark blue eyes. I haven't seen anyone around with skin as light as hers in a while. She smiles down at me with straight, white teeth.

"I didn't mean to startle you," she says with a soft drawl of an accent I don't quite recognise, so I assume she was raised in one of the towns further south than mine.

"That's alright," I say, rising to a standing position.

"I'm Ailin, I'm kind of new," she tells me.

"No kidding? I'm Kayin."

"Oh good, you are Kayin. They uh, this guy told me to come find you."

I look at her inquisitively, drying off my hands. "Really? What can I do for you?" I ask kindly, slightly taken aback but glad that someone thought of me when this girl asked for help. She looks down and then back up at me, gingerly lifting her arm up.

"I think I've done something to my wrist? I don't mean to bother you, I'm not quite sure why they told me to find you, but I suppose you can help, maybe?"

"I sure can," I smile back, to make her feel comfortable. I lightly hold her wrist, turning it over in my hands and gently examining it. "I'd say you almost fractured it, but not quite. You'll be fine. If you head up to the medical room, they'll fix you up with a splint and some bandages," I tell her. I look up at her and she is watching me, a grin growing on her soft face.

"That was impressive! How can you tell so quickly?" she asks. I chuckle.

"I'm a healer," I tell her with a friendly laugh, as an explanation. She still looks bewildered. "If you come find me later, I'd be happy to exchange stories, but you should sort your wrist out first."

She shakes her head vigorously, as if shaking away her surprise, and then nods at me gratefully, and walks away. I watch her go. She doesn't seem much older than me, and I wonder where she came from. Shrugging to myself, I turn around and finish up my washing.

I go to find Mari after that, carrying my wet clothes over my shoulder. I walk towards her room and see her reading outside the front door, so I jog over to where she's sitting.

"Can I use your washing line to hang out my clothes to dry?" I ask after we say hello. She nods her consent and I grin a thanks. Between Mari's house and the one next to it, there are several lines pinned up between the walls for hanging clothes on. I don't have that on my side of the stream. When I'm finished I sit down beside Mari and tell her about the new girl.

"No, I haven't heard of any Ailin girl," she says with a shrug when I ask her if she's heard about anyone new joining us. I lean back on my hands and face forward. Hm. It does strike me as odd that there wasn't an announcement of a new rogue, like there was for me.

"I'm going to go for a walk," I announced, pulling myself up to my feet. "Want to come?" When I look down, Mari is already opening her book again and flattening out the folded corner of the page she's on.

"Not this time. Don't go far," Mari replies, before burying her face back in her book.

I leave her there and make my way to the centre of the

town where I am about to set off in my usual direction, but then I notice the stream at my feet. I realise I always turn left, follow it upstream when I go for walks. And everything that I need is up that direction. What if I turn right? Went downstream?

So I do exactly that. The dry land crunches under my boots, I rest my thumbs in my belt loops and stroll away from the town. The buildings dissipate and the chatter of rogues and sounds of living get quieter behind me. Following the river I come across open land where I know I have officially left the town and consider turning back, but up ahead of me I can see a pile of rocks and the land beyond suddenly drops in front of me. Curiosity gets the better of me and I approach the rocks, stepping slower until I can see what is on the other side.

Water from the stream runs down through the rocks and into a pool below, and the look of the clear, crisp splashing water causes dryness in my mouth. I lick my lips and run down the hill at the side of the rocks. I want to jump straight in but find myself pausing by the edge. I survey the area. The rocks hide the pool from anyone behind me, back in the town, unless they walk out as far as I have. And I can see else nothing downstream, just the river that disappears over the horizon, so I am alone.

I slip off my boots, and my belts follow. Then I take off

my jeans, and finally pull off my top. In only my underwear, I dip a toe into the water and am gladly surprised to feel it's warm, but still cool enough to feel satisfying in this desert heat. And then I jump in. It is such a glorious feeling; I haven't had a good swim in years, and this is the closest I'll come to having one. I paddle over to the rocks and let the water drop on top of my head, soaking my hair, and I scrub my face.

"Kayin?"

For the second time I jump as I hear the voice. I am submerged in the blue water up to my neck, but I still cross my arms over my body to try and cover up.

And then I see Ailin standing awkwardly on the edge of the pool, nervously looking down at me.

"Did I scare you again?"

"Yeah, a little," I laugh. I ease forward, towards where I have left my clothes.

"I saw you head this way after I got my wrist wrapped up," she holds up her bandaged arm. "Was I not supposed to follow you? I thought we could talk," she says hopefully.

I smile to myself because I had indeed offered to swap stories. And of course this area isn't private. I mean I assume it isn't, I have just stumbled across this part of the land myself. I realise it would be useless to dress again since I am soaked, but because it is only another girl, just Ailin, I feel comfortable enough to pull my body out of the water and sit on the edge, hanging my feet in the pool.

"Sure, let's talk." I smile.

"So, if it's okay to ask..." she sits beside me, "what's a healer?"

I tell her. Explaining how it runs in my bloodline, and passes on to each first born in the family, she looks fascinated all the way through. It leads on to how I joined the Resistance, discovering that maybe I have healer powers like my Nana and how I've come across my current powers, for example the control I have of hearts.

"What's your story?" I ask, after I feel like I have been talking forever. I feel my skin drying in the sun so I slip my top and jeans back on, but roll them up to my knees and keep my toes dangling in the water.

Ailin drops her head and tucks her hair behind her ear, even though the volume of her frizz just makes it fall back in her face. I wait patiently.

"Well, I don't have powers or anything like that. I'd never really come across anything like that until the Ghost Men came to my town. I'm from Aramore, by the way."

I nod in recognition, my suspicions confirmed; Aramore is one of the farthest towns heading south.

"Um, it was just me and my dad when, when they did come." She speaks slowly, choosing her words carefully. "It was about 5 years ago, when I was 16. My town is quite far out in the land, so I guess we were one of the last places to be captured. I don't remember much, up until my escape last year. It was all a blur, I think I've blocked it out."

I decide not to push it further, knowing how she feels. I haven't exactly revealed anything very personal about myself, apart from my powers, but she has, so I don't want to force her into telling me more. She seems to perk up after a short silence.

"So tell me about the Resistance. What's it all about, what are the secrets?"

"Secrets?" I laugh. "I don't know about that. But..." I look for anyone who could possibly be listening in. "We're the people who are going to fight the Ghosts. We don't agree with their methods or intentions. This is the place to be if you don't believe in what they stand for. And for that, we're of course their number one enemy," I tell her.

"So what's the plan? The schemes?"

I study her carefully for a moment. "Our main aim is rebellion," I say slowly, my voice low.

"But there must be something happening now? Something in the works?"

"Nothing I can think of." I am a little hesitant in answering her persistent questions. "We're just trying to survive."

I think she catches on to the fact I am feeling a little uncomfortable, so she stops pressing. I stand up and shake the water off my feet, and put the rest of my clothes and accessories on. I feel completely refreshed, more than I have felt in a while. I give Ailin a hand to help her stand up and suggest we head back. I don't know how long it has been, probably not that long, but usually my walks are quicker than this, just to get some air, and I don't want Mari to wonder where I am. So we head back downstream to the town. I tell Ailin that I am just going to let Mari know I am back.

I poke my head through the door of her room when I don't see her sitting outside. She spots me and smiles, I tell her to wait one second and I'll be in. When I back out of the room to ask Ailin if she wants to meet Mari, she is gone. She must have gone back to wherever she is staying. I'm sure I'll see her later.

As I stroll around the town aimlessly for a while, I wonder whether or not Ailin could become a good friend of mine, like Mari. I am still getting accustomed to the feeling of having a friend, or friends, at all, after being alone for years, but I like the prospect of it. I absentmindedly make my way over to the ditch where I see the Four talking. I feel comfortable enough to approach them; after all they've done for me and how they've helped me, I like to think they think nicely enough of me that I can talk to them when I see them.

"Which one of you found Ailin, then?" I ask when I reach them and notice they are sitting quietly, sipping their drinks.

"Ailin?" the Vehement questions. I can't tell if she is making small talk or is genuinely interested in the arrival of a new girl, which I assume she would be.

"She's got red hair, quite small. She found me today, earlier. And that's how it works isn't it? One of you guys find someone and bring them to the Resistance?" I ask, sitting down beside them, feeling comfortable and happy; until I see their expressions.

"That's right, but..." the Cryptic begins speaking. All Four share looks, silently asking each other which one of them found the girl. After a pause, they come to the same conclusion. "None of us found her."

"Well then who is she? Could she have just walked in?" I ask, wondering how many people are in the Resistance because they stumbled upon it, which can't be that safe or whether they were actually brought to it, like me.

"I doubt it," the Oracle looks sceptical. "Unless..."

He trails off and doesn't make a noise for another moment. None of them do. I can't take it any more and have to prompt them.

"Unless what?"

"She could be a traitor."

I am suspicious with the idea that a traitor is among us. I find Mari and we go back to my room where I tell her. She listens intently.

"I don't think we should jump to any conclusions yet, you know? It could just be a misunderstanding," she says. There she goes again, always the rational mind.

"I guess that's fair. I mean, she seemed pretty harmless, but I guess we shouldn't judge her on that yet either." I pause, wondering whether to continue. "...Do you think we should go find her?"

Mari chews this over in her mind, and then shakes her head.

"Let her come to us if she wants to."

"But what if she is dangerous? Or if she's snooping around right now, can we let her do that?" I ask. I don't know what to think.

"I don't think she'd try anything on the same day she gets here. If anything, she would try to gain our trust first, right? If she is smart. If I was a traitor, that's what I'd do."

I settle down on my bed, cross my legs and put my hands in my lap. "Do we have any secrets?" I ask, my voice lower now. "You know, like anything a traitor would want to get their hands on?"

"I'm not sure personally. But I know a traitor is bad news, and I wouldn't be surprised if the Four have something hidden, or there are secrets within our history. You know like when the previous Four have come about, it's all written and recorded and all the files are stored in the chapel. There must be some information to get out of that," she tells me. I take in her words.

"There's a chapel?" I ask. I had no idea. I haven't seen one about, and I didn't know there was information held about the previous wars and battles. All our history...Well, I'd like to read up on that.

"Sure, have you not been?" she replies. I shake my head. "Do you want to go? I want to pick up another book from the chapel library anyway," she says, lifting her book to show me she's finished it.

"Now?"

"You got anything better to do?" she says with a smirk. I smile and get up, following her out.

We walk for what feels like miles. Out of the town, passed the ditch, in a new direction. I tell myself that I should venture out a bit more, since only this morning I found a rock pool by just walking a different way, and now I'm on my way to a chapel I didn't know existed either. Although in the back of my mind I know I probably don't explore much any more because I feel safe within the Resistance and don't want to lose that feeling by going too far.

After another few minutes a long, thin building comes into sight. It has a steeple with a black circle on the top. It is white stone, with black beams outlining it. The windows are boarded up with black wood and a big, arch shaped door is at the front. I walk up behind Mari and stand there, while she pushe the old, creaking door open.

We walk passed the rows of pews, to the front of the chapel and up some steps. I follow Mari round a corner, where you'd be unseen by those sitting in the pews. The ceilings are high and beautifully painted. Or rather you could tell they were once beautifully painted. They are faded, chipped and cracking now. We pass a gorgeous stain glass window that is concealed from the front of the church outside, but here you can see it in all its glory as the sun shines through it, beaming different colours of light across the alcove where we stand.

I look down to Mari and she is standing by a small brown door, watching me with a smile, as I take in all the sights.

"You know, I used to go to church every Sunday," I tell her, with another glance at the window. That was many years ago now.

"Really?"

I smile to myself. "I never was the religious type though. I was the kid in the back who would screw up all the hymns.

But I liked it, the community aspect of it."

Mari doesn't say another word. She pushes open the door and reveals a small room. It looks more modern than the rest of the chapel, but is definitely not new. The walls are lined with bookcases after bookcases, and the shelves are jam packed with papers and books and files. I let my mouth fall open as I take in the enormity of information there must be here. Mari was right when she said there was probably something here that could be useful to a traitor.

"Do you want to look up some stuff?" she asks.

"I wouldn't know where to begin," I reply. Mari takes this into consideration, and then walks towards the bookcase at the back of the room. She pulls a chair up from the small table in the corner and stands on it, still struggling to reach a shelf high above her. She reaches for a hefty file, and drops it on to the fragile wooden table. A cloud of dust rises as it hits the surface, then she climbs back down.

"This is interesting to me, specifically," she says, opening the front of the file, and flicking through some papers. The paper is old and yellow, the further back the paper was the cleaner it got, signalling that the newer stuff went to the back, but she stops looking about 6 pages in to the thick file.

"Isoken Dorra" she states. I look at her questioningly, and then let my gaze drop to the sheets she holds out to me. An old picture, faded and wrinkly, is attached to the paper. It is such bad quality and looks so old I suspect it must have been a picture of a painting. It is the bust of a woman, sitting very stiffly. She has thick black hair that droops around her face.

"She is the first recorded Oracle," she tells me. "And she's also my ancestor."

"You mean...wait, that's so interesting, Mari!" I exclaim, careful to turn over the page, as I browse more information.

"Our Oracle may descend from his great, great, great grandfather, but it's not exclusive to one bloodline. Oracle's, or rather any of the Four, can emerge from any family, and any gender, when the time is right." She smiles at me, proud of her memorised facts and takes my silence as an okay to launch into a story.

"It is said that Isoken Dorra was insane," she begins. She turns her back on me and looks for something else. "It could be anywhere in here," she murmurs to herself before turning back to me for a moment.

"Basically, Isoken was a storybook Oracle, down to the last detail. She could actually see the future, but not very clearly, only bursts of things and puzzling visions. You know how in Greek mythology, Cassandra the Prophet was believed to be insane because Apollo cursed her when she turned down his advances. All her visions were true but nobody believed her. Isoken was in a similar situation to that, except she wasn't cursed, but the 'Apollo' in her generation was a man called Otto Thorne, a highly respected man of the church. Isoken rejected his marriage proposal and then began having visions years later that Otto's nephew was evil, and would turn on them all. Otto dismissed these claims and made everyone believe that she was insane and there was no such thing as 'future-seeing'. Mostly because he was a man in a respected job and she was a woman, everyone took his side immediately." she explains. "You still with me?" she asks.

I had taken a seat on top of the table and up until then I had been staring at the floor, concentrating on what she was telling me.

"You're quite the book worm, aren't you?" I grin at her. "That's such a great origin story."

"I spend a lot of my time reading," she replies with a nervous chuckle.

"So Isoken had real, future-seeing visions, not just mind reading and seeing memories like Olon?"

Mari raises an eyebrow and smirks at me. "First name basis now, are we?"

I feel myself blush. She rolls her eyes playfully and continues. "She could see the future, yes. Eventually, even though no one was believing her, she could decipher her visions, but by then it was too late to prevent Otto's nephew from wandering into the Tarid mountains that are very far south, at the end of Ervon Gorge, and recruiting the mountain people, basically giants, to come and crush his people, for reasons that are still unknown. Perhaps he was the crazy one.

"Because of the presumed insanity, Isoken Dorra never married as she was seen unfit. When war commenced she took on her destined role as Oracle and after defeating the evil, she died several days after due to injuries. Her brother Obi Dorra carried on the family name and future generations all know the story of Isoken," Mari reads the last bit from a page in front of her with difficulty, pausing often to decipher the faded scripture.

"They locked Isoken up in an asylum. Until the Vehement broke down the walls. The Four have a connection, and once the others came to realise their powers they believed Isoken. And that's when it's believed the first Resistance came about. The first group of Rogues who rebelled against evil." She finally concludes.

"There's a whole big book, telling the story of the first Four in detail, but who knows where that is," she half laughs, half scoffs, looking up at the masses of information around us.

"That's a lot to take in," I breathe. She smiles at me.

"I feel like I've been speaking for years," she tells me,

and we laugh. We decide to head back then, to grab a drink and snacks, so Mari grabs a new book and we leave the room and close the door behind us. We traipse back through the alcove, pass the window and walk into the main chapel, where we head to the big arch door.

The sun is lower in the sky than it was when we arrived, and though it is still very warm, dusk is setting in and it's good that we are heading back now.

Mari is a few paces in front of me, and I am about to jog to catch her up, after closing the door behind me, but a figure falls from the sky and knocks Mari to the floor. Instantaneously I am running towards her, but taken aback when the figure straightens up and Ailin turns to face me. I guess I shouldn't be totally surprised, there was speculation, but I agreed with Mari when she said that she didn't think a traitor would attack the same day they arrived.

Suddenly a knife is hurtling towards my face. As an instinct, I duck to dodge it, but I'm not quick enough and it bounces off my face. I notice the shock and hesitation in Ailin's expression. I failed to mention before that weapons couldn't hurt me, so I guess she wasn't anticipating this. I take this chance to run towards her and knock her in the chest, bringing her down to the floor with me and away from Mari who is lying on the floor, struggling to get up with injuries.

Ailin doesn't miss a beat and flips over, landing on top of me, straddling my neck and pinning my hands down under her knees. I try to knee and kick her in the back, but she takes each blow in her stride. She tightly grips my neck, digging her fingers in to my skin and making it hard to breathe.

"So when you said you escaped a year ago..." I struggle to speak. I have to keep my game face on; I can't succumb to the lack of oxygen.

"Did I say escape? I meant to say walked out freely...After I agreed to work with the Ghosts," she says, her voice dripping with fake sweetness. I slip my right arm out from under her knee and whack her hard across the face, knocking her to my side.

"You're a traitor! We're of the same people, why are we fighting?!" I say, gasping for breath and struggling to get up.

"Because I need to survive! Why should I have to rot in prison any longer when I can live a good life on the winning side? Have you seen their lands? They're beautiful and luxurious. The shilo are just misunderstood, they help me live a better life."

We are standing now, facing each other and ready to pounce.

"They're evil!" I rasp, just as she lunges for me. I'm not the best fighter, so I rely on my powers. I try my hardest to control her heart, slow it down while she lands blow after blow on my face. Her fists are tight and precise as they come into contact with my body. It begins hurting, I am getting dizzy after continuous blows to my head and I can't concentrate anymore. I am angry, I am not focused, I have no idea how to stop her and soon enough I black out.

7

All I can see is the inside of my eyelids as I regain consciousness. When I slowly open my eyes it's not much of an improvement. Darkness consumes me. I blink, trying to focus my eyes and see anything in front of me, but the only light is the glow coming through the crack of a door about 15 feet away from me.

I wonder what's beyond that door, where I am. I struggle to move but my wrists are tied together behind the chair I'm strapped to. The rope cuts across my sore skin and I wonder how long I've been here, possibly fighting against the restraints.

I'm fairly appreciative of the darkness because I can feel a pounding in my head and know any bright light would contribute to the pain. I ache all over. I can feel my limbs badly bruised and I know my face must look awful, after the beating my head took from Ailin.

Ailin. She beat me. Did she kidnap me? Where has she brought me? It's starting to come back to me. Did she leave Mari alone? I hope for her sake she did. If she hurt Mari, I swear on the stars above she won't live to see another night once I make it out of here. Would she risk letting Mari go, letting her get back to the others? Surely they would launch a rescue plan, infiltrating wherever I am. The Resistance is smart; they would figure it out. Something tells me that Ailin wouldn't let Mari get away.

Why am I here? Was I just in the wrong place at the wrong time? Did they want me specifically? That would explain why Ailin was there when she was ready to attack us.

I can't ponder it any more. The door across the distance in front of me opens, and the soft glow that surrounds it's edges expands into a bright light coming from the room on the other side, illuminating the space I'm in a certain amount. I see high shelves, even higher ceilings. Concrete walls, solid floors. It looks like some kind of storage place, a warehouse of sorts. They've stored me in their warehouse.

Piercing through the source of light comes a large silhouette. The blinding white light around them prevents me seeing them properly. I want to shield my eyes, cover my face with my arms to block the light, but I can't raise my arms so I have to settle for squinting, trying to watch but desperately trying to keep away the pain in my head that's threatening to spill over.

Suddenly the light vanishes with a loud bang of the door slamming behind the person who has just entered. I can see them no longer, but I hear their footsteps, slowly etching towards me across the stone floor. And then a clap. A loud clap that echoes through the warehouse, followed by another, and another until they acquire a slow rhythm. I feel a small gush of air as their hands stop right in front of my face.

"Congratulations, healer, you got yourself caught," comes a deep manly voice, mocking me. Spitting my title like it is venom on his tongue. A dark laugh escapes his lips. "Healer," he scoffs. "You're proud of that? Oh, child..."

I want to lash out at whoever this man is. Insulting me is one thing, but insulting the title of a healer means he's attacking every generation of my family.

"Oh, how you've been misled. What a dull existence. Humans live such pathetic lives. What you are...What you can become..." he continues, adding a tone of boredom to his voice.

I writhe against my restraints, shaking the shackles around my ankles and only aggravating the sore skin around my wrists against the rope more, but I don't care.

"Shut up! You don't know me! Let me go, or I swear..." I cry out.

"Oh, no, no," the man says smoothly, tutting. His callous fingers gently graze my cheek, and I feel my blood boil. "This won't do. You must preserve your strength if you want to be of any use to us."

I gather a ball of saliva in my mouth and spit it in what I hope is his direction. Who does he think he is? He must be a shilo, and think he's better than us.

"Why would I want to be of use to you?" I say. My voice is hoarse and broken. I haven't spoken in a while.

Warm breath fans out across my face and I feel his hands brush against my arms as he leans forward and rests them on the arms of the chair, inching his face closer to mine. "Because otherwise," he begins, his voice lower and practically growling as he speaks, "we'll kill every one you love. Point blank."

I don't say anything else. The promise in his words is enough to shut me up. I have few people left in my life that I truly love, but I care for the whole Resistance and will do what I can to keep everyone safe.

"Who are you?" I speak slowly, grimacing as I can still feel his presence close to me.

He sniffs me loudly, leaning in against my neck. His touch makes my skin crawl, but I can't move away. I bite my lip, resisting the urge to yell, holding my eyes shut tight. I can feel tears threatening as a deep-throated sigh escapes his mouth and covers my skin.

"Baby, I'm your worst nightmare," he growls, grazing his teeth from my neck up to my jaw. I let my head drop to the side away from him, but he takes this chance to bite my earlobe.

"I'll kill you, I swear." I can't hide the emotion in my shaky voice. He's got me riled up, threatening me with the lives of my loved ones, touching me without consent. But he just laughs at my empty threat. He sees no harm when I'm tied to this chair.

"Keep talking dirty," he replies, unfazed. He hooks a finger on the neckline of my vest, yanking me forward slightly and no doubt trying to get a glimpse down my top. The thought of how old this man could be makes me gag. He could be a vile, creepy old man. He could be my age. He could be mid age. I don't know what one feels worse. He steps away and a cold breeze replaces where he stood.

In the dark, my mind clouded with thoughts and emotions, it's hard to concentrate on this man. I don't know where he stands, where his body is, so I can't concentrate on his heart to use that power. My mind starts running over time wondering how I can use my imperviousness to weapons against him, but there's no use. I haven't come across a power yet that can help me. All I need is to be able to figure out where he is. Just to see him in the dark, briefly even.

Something like…of course! My Nana used it all the time; bone vision! It was the power that made her eyes flash. I was never sure of what it was, but it makes sense now. It must have been bone vision. She used it the most, to see fractures and breaks of her patients. If only I could work out how to summon it. I could use it to work out where he is. He's been awfully quiet and I can't help but get nervous. What is he planning?

I close my eyes and think about what to do. In theory, I know what the power does and I know how it's noticeable. Repeating the memory in my mind, I keep thinking what it should feel like. A sensation in the back of my mind or a tingling in my eyes, maybe? I open my eyes and concentrate on the darkness around me. A flash from my eyes briefly lights a small area in front of me, but it hasn't worked. The man, wherever he is, has not noticed what I'm doing yet thankfully, so I try again. In another burst of light, a little brighter this time, his skeleton shows itself to me in the dim light. His bones glow through his body and I see exactly where he stands, healthy. I try not to get my hopes up, although I'm thrilled to have pulled off the power. But I now use his position to my advantage. Though I can't see him standing here, I saw his position, stance, and structure. I hope this is enough to concentrate on to control his heart. I quickly decide that the way he's acted and the circumstances I'm in means he can be of no good, so his death won't be a loss. Still, I'm not happy about what I try to do.

"It's useless, sweetheart!" he laughs. I'm finally connecting to his heartbeat in my head. It's strong and feels like a bigger heart than usual. Bigger than a human heart. My skin is ravished in goose bumps and disgust when his hands grip at my shoulders from behind, and I'm suddenly wishing I don't know where he is again.

My head is banging again and he seems unaffected by my futile attempts to hurt him. If anything I have only calmed him, which surely only puts him in a better position. I couldn't work hard enough to slow his heart to anything close to painful.

"You're so weak. So pathetic."

He continues to insult me, and for a moment I let myself become what he says. I'm weak. Why do I have no affect on him? Is he too powerful? Does he have powers at all? Is it me? I've been beaten and bruised, and who knows how long I've been here at this point. I'm no use. I let a tear fall from my eyes in the darkness. I feel a hand across my face and I gasp as my head is jolted to the side.

"Listen to me when I'm degrading you!" he yells, trying to sound fierce, but I can tell he's loving every minute of having power over me. I can detect humour in his voice. I'm sure he's thrilled to have my body to do what he wants with.

I hang my head and let my shoulders fall. There's no point trying to fight right now. I may as well cooperate as much as I can until I'm no longer so injured and powerless. I wonder again why I'm here. What they want with me. Who wants me here? How long have I been tied to this chair? I'm so tired. I'm done.

I think of something else. Somewhere I'd rather be. And my thoughts drift to Olon. The Oracle. I want him to save me. To come and rescue me and tell me that we'll work on my powers and I'll get strong and no one can hurt my loved ones. He said he wouldn't let anything happen to me. Up until this point I hadn't let myself indulge in thoughts of Olon, but I let myself now. I want him to hold me. I want to feel his arms around me.

My eyes squeeze tighter shut as another hand smacks me, slapping my head to the side. I concentrate harder on being with Olon as the man's profanities towards me continue. Another slap sends my head flying the other way, but instead of hitting the back of the chair, my face falls against something hard. I feel warmth on my skin but I daren't open my eyes. I block out the sensations. My hair falls in front of my face; I'm on my side, he must have knocked over my chair.

"Kayin?"

I assume that I have imagined it so desperately, that in my delirious state it feels lifelike. It's Olon's voice. He's surprised. I feel the presence of others around us, but I'm preoccupied. It's not real. I struggle against my restraints when I feel hands on me, picking up the chair and putting it upright again. I want so much for this to be real, to be in the ditch with the Four and the rest of the Resistance. I don't want to open my eyes again, knowing I'll find myself back in the warehouse, under the abuse of the mysterious man.

I hear quiet murmuring around me, my head is dizzy, but eventually I look around; my eyes flutter open slowly as the sudden light hurts. There are several pairs of hands working around me; I'm being untied.

It's real?

The tears from my eyes fall into my lap as I look around at the familiar friendly faces. I look up to see the Oracle looking down at me, his expression laced with confusion, anger, worry, and concern.

"Kayin, what happened?"

I ignore the question and turn in a circle as I spring up out of the chair, my sore body and joints arguing with my sudden movements, finding myself truly in the ditch with the Resistance. They're gathered together, had clearly been discussing something before I popped up. The hot sun is a nice change from the cool air of the warehouse. It just confuses me more. I must have blacked out. I must be dreaming. The man has knocked me out, or I'm hallucinating. Vividly. The faces of the Resistance are all looking the same. Worried and confused, staring straight at me.

"What happened?" I throw the question back at them. "How am I here? Are you real?!" I hiccup and feel myself bordering hysterics and I can't stop myself when I lurch forward onto my knees. Everything's happened so fast. Twenty minutes ago I found myself in a warehouse being reduced to tears by a man I didn't know. Now Olon is kneeling by my side and gripping my shoulders protectively, shielding me.

No answer is given straight away. I lift my hand gingerly to my face and inspect the damage with the top of my finger. I wipe at the blood on my lip and shiver at the amount that is smeared across the back of my hand. Olon just holds me, sharing a cautious look with the Four.

Olon helps me stand up again and holds me at arms length. I tuck my arms against my chest. I feel so small; I never feel small. I suddenly don't want all these eyes on me, seeing me so vulnerable. I am still trying to catch my breath. Olon leans down face to face with me, and makes me look him in the eye.

"Calm down," he says gently. He puts a steady hand up and makes me focus. I took a deep breath, imitating his actions, and nod.

"Tell me I was dreaming," I beg, closing my eyes, continuing my deep breaths.

"Dreaming what? What happened to you?" he asks again softly. I know then that dreaming was a possibility out of the question. I scrunch up my face, knowing it is all real and even more confusing.

"I...I was in a warehouse..." I almost let the sentence end as a question. I open my eyes, and see the Oracle has all the patience in the world for me. He waits for me to continue. "I think it belonged to the Ghosts. It was Ailin, she knocked me out, and she hurt Mari. That girl I told you about earlier. She is a traitor!"

"That was..." I hear a voice behind the Oracle. "That was 2 days ago."

I look over his shoulder and spot Mari, standing with Selene. She looks tired. Everyone does in all fairness. Olon lets go of me as I run towards her, throwing my shaky arms around her neck.

"Mari, I thought she took you!" I mumble against her shoulder. She hugs me back tightly.

"I got up and ran while you two were fighting. I sw-I

swear I was going to come back with help, but by the time I got anyone's attention..." she squeezes me even tighter, "by the time we got back there you were both gone. I didn't mean to let her get away with you."

I chuckle a little, sniffing as I step back. "I believe you." Then I turn back to the Four. "Two days?" I ask.

"Let's sit you down first." Orisa says, taking me under her arm. "Thank you everyone, greatly, for your help." She announces and turns with me to leave the ditch. The rest of the Four, and Mari who catches up to hold my hand as we walk, follow us.

They take me back to my room and let me get comfortable on my bed, bringing me some water. Mari sits beside me and delicately cleans my face with a sponge while the four stand around my bed, ready to discuss the events.

"Mari came to us in a panic..." The Vehement begins speaking.

Apparently when Mari ran off she had gone straight to the ditch, which was the closest place to find anyone. She yelled traitor to anyone who could hear and turned on her heel again. People were already up and following her, including the Vehement and the Cryptic. They ran back to the Chapel but Ailin and I were gone. I fill in the blanks as she tells the story. I say that must have been just after Ailin knocked me out. I don't know where she went or how she got me away so fast though. Assuming it was her acting alone. The Cryptic tells me he whistled, alerting the others of a possible kidnapping. A search party was issued around the Resistance land, and when there was no sign of us, the Four came together with others to hastily plan a larger search party, as I expected.

The next day, groups went out further to search for signs and clues of Ailin's or my whereabouts, but to no avail. And it was still before noon today, just as they were regrouping in the ditch, listening intently to the Oracle's new plan that I literally appeared out of thin air, strapped to a chair on my side.

Which of course confused the hell out of everyone.

So when I'm caught up, I let them in on my side of the story. Waking up sore and alone, tied to a chair. The strange, horrid man who came in and threw abuse at me, physically and verbally, touching me while I couldn't do anything about it. I feel a shiver run up my spine as I recount the events that happened not long ago, but it feels like I'm in another world, another life, now I'm back with the Resistance. How am I back here, come to think of it?

"So you're saying I literally materialised out of thin air?" I ask, trying to wrap my head around it. "There is no way I could have snuck in?" I'm hoping I can come up with a crazy yet believable story that maybe I had blacked out and subconsciously made my way to the ditch and broke through the crowd, before becoming aware of my actions. But of course that is ludicrous given that I was tied up…to a chair.

"He was literally standing in the middle of the ditch, surrounded by the rest of us," Mari tells me. "Then you just appeared, right at his feet. Like you teleported or something," she says as if the idea is preposterous. I scoff too.

"Let's just go over the last moments of your capture. Right before you came here. What was happening to you?" the Cryptic asks, catching everyone's attention. They all wait for my answer.

"Um," I try to think of where to start, suddenly feeling everyone's eyes on me again. I take another sip of water and collect my thoughts. "Well the man, he was yelling insults at me, profanities. I closed my eyes and tried to ignore it, think of something else, you know?" I pause, looking around. The Oracle has situated himself in the chair at the end of my bed, elbows on knees and hands clasped together, looking down at the floor while I speak. I become aware, as I am talking, that the last thing I was doing was thinking of Olon and his embrace, trying to tune out the man. Would it really be appropriate to admit that to him, especially with everyone else around?

The Cryptic gives me a nod as if to say go on, so I drop

my head and continue. Let's just get it over with, so we can move on and figure this out.

"The man hit me then, slapped me side to side. But I kept my thoughts on the Resistance; eyes shut so tight it almost hurt. And I kept thinking about, about the Oracle, my thoughts were mostly centred on the four of you. And how much I wanted to be back here…anywhere but in that warehouse. And then suddenly…I was."

I slowly lift my gaze, and watch everyone catch on to what I was insinuating. That I was picturing myself here, and then it happened. I didn't dare meet the Oracle's eyes for myself, hoping to have saved my dignity somewhat by mentioning the others too, but I see his shoulders are stiff in the corner of my eye before he, too, raises his head to look at everyone else. I wonder if he felt it necessary to read my mind, and knows more than what I was saying.

"I wouldn't rule out teleportation just yet," the Cryptic says after a moments pause, claiming my full attention back, and the Four solemnly nod in agreement, while I almost choke on the air.

"Is that sentence serious?!" I exclaim, looking at them all in shock, before trying to regain some composure. "I mean, are we going to consider that as a seriously possibility? Me? Teleporting?"

"I was only joking when I said that," Mari chips in,

sponge held mid air near my face, frozen with shock.

"We know it's possible, just think of the Ghost Men-"

"My point exactly," I cut him off, regretting my rudeness instantly. I start again more calmly. "I'm a healer. At best I have the powers to help me heal, and even then I find it hard to use them, the powers that run in my family. Teleporting is so off the scale in regards to my life."

"As you've described the events, they all match to the possibility of it though," the Divine contributes. I don't know how to argue back. I try to form a sentence but I just find myself stuttering and struggling for coherent words. I am too confused and shocked they are seriously considering it.

After a long moment of everyone thinking his or her own thoughts, I speak again.

"Let's just say, hypothetically," I begin, emphasising the word, "that I did teleport. How? Why me? As you just said yourself it's what the Ghost Men do. Can our people do it? Humans? Has that ever been...a thing?"

The Four ponder on this for a moment. Then the Oracle speaks, standing up.

"It's never been documented. And in all honesty it seems unlikely. But we can't deny what we all saw today, and how your story lines up with the idea of it."

I finally look up and catch his eyes for the first time

since I've sat down. I desperately want to know what he is thinking, how he is reacting to the news that while tied up and being abused, my thoughts fell to him, which he obviously caught on to. And I can only hope that he isn't reading my thoughts right now.

I suddenly feel embarrassed by it. That in my moment of weakness I thought of Olon and, in front of everyone, had to half admit it. How was I to know I would make those thoughts a reality? I was just indulging in those thoughts to distract myself.

But I can't think about that right now. My more important thoughts now consist of who that man is. Why me? And is it possible that I teleported? And if the answer to that last question is no, then the question 'how did I get out?' comes to mind.

8

I spend the rest of the day alone in the chapel. It is weird coming back here when I feel like it was only yesterday that Ailin jumped us here, but it was two days ago. I sit in the small room filled with information in the back of the chapel, at the table on the wonky wooden chair and read through Isoken Dorra's file.

I was hoping for something along the lines of 'Isoken Dorra was the first recorded Oracle. She could tell the future. People thought she was insane. And hey she could also teleport'. My justifications were that I thought if there is any documentation of humans teleporting, it would be here, and it would probably be by one of the powerful humans of history.

Something like that, just so I could try and believe that,

if this whole teleporting thing is true, that it wasn't just me. But no such luck. With nothing to go on, I just scan over the files and books and papers around the room, pulling out things that catch my eye. An old red leather bound book that has information on all things foliage and berry related and how to survive in the woods and what was poisonous and what you could eat, dating back to who knows when. A file of listed legends; the names of all the people who rose to power to become the Four throughout the ages. Anything I could find on possible family members of mine, but that is a limited search. I become stuck.

Honestly I don't know what I'm looking for. Something to confirm that teleporting is possible for our people. Something to confirm that it has actually happened before. Or just something that can explain how I escaped the warehouse – teleporting related or not.

I resort to sitting on top of the table, put my feet up on the chair next to it, and rock it back and forth. I put my elbows on my knees, drop my head into my hands and let myself go numb.

It is so quiet that I even hear the usually silent step of the Oracle's boot as he enters. I don't move. I feel his presence as he stands by the door behind me. Watching me. I will my mind to be blank, hoping there is nothing for him to read and potentially embarrass me.

Even with my eyes closed, my breath hitches when I feel him come closer. Unexpectedly, he pushes my feet off the chair. My legs fall from beneath my elbows and I almost topple forwards, but just catch my balance. I have to look up then, as Olon sits down where my feet have just been. My legs dangle to the side of him, he stretches his out under the table. Suddenly feeling shy I look up at the shelves, but keep him in my peripheral vision. I make it seem like I am truly interested in what lies on the shelves behind him, and truthfully I was only moments ago, but now I am tired and distracted.

"I don't have any answers for you," he breaks the silence first. I let my gaze drop to him. He sits in the chair calmly, leaning back, arms crossed gently over his chest. It is in scenarios like this that I remember he's a man in his early 20's, still young, thrown into greatness. And subconsciously I think I rely on him a lot. The stories I heard growing up, though not necessarily about him, were about the legend that is The Oracle; a great leader, wise and talented. And that is him; sitting in front of me now, pulling on his vest idly, tapping his foot on the floor. Without meaning to, I still think of him as an untouchable character in old myths. But he is here, he is with me, he is smiling at me and he...he is reading my mind.

He chuckles as I drop my head, but I can't help but let a

small smile creep onto my face too. He leans forward then, resting his elbows on his knees, looking up at me through the curtain of hair that fell around my face when I looked down. With that lopsided smile of his aimed at me I feel the blood rush to my cheeks.

In the continuing silence that follows, I think about how I came to be here, sitting in this chapel, and my happy expression falls. He notices my sudden change in demeanour; I see it on his face as his smile fades to slight concern.

"All thoughts of my escape aside...was it me they wanted to capture in the first place?" I ask the question that has been on my mind since I got back. I don't know which answer makes me feel worse; that I was just in the wrong place at the wrong time, or that I was specifically targeted.

"We think so," Olon replies quietly, his deep voice charming me, despite what he is telling me. "We suspect it was a kidnapping ploy all along, a quick mission. Which is why Ailin didn't hang around too long. She was sent in to get you and retrieve you as quick as she could."

"What do they want me for?" I ask, my voice dropping lower.

He is silent for a moment. "We're not sure, but we're working on it."

I lay back on the table, looking up at the ceiling. Not so

long ago, I was alone in the desert, surviving by myself. Now I am potentially developing feelings for a man I've been told stories about and being specifically targeted by the evil that he is supposed to defeat. It was so much easier to hear the stories and believe how good always won over evil, but when you're living it, it's hard. I trust the Four and the Rogues more than I've trusted most, but that nagging in the back of my mind that maybe, what if we can't do it? What if this time it doesn't work out? It's getting on my nerves. We are no doubt heading towards war; it's inevitable.

There can't be a group of rebels without a forthcoming rebellion, which will result in battle.

"That man said I had been misled. And he talked a lot of how I am useful to them, but didn't mention how," I find myself admitting. I have my arm over my face now as I lay back, feet still dangling off the edge of the table. I try to relax as I close my eyes and recall what I can.

"What are you saying, Kayin?"

"He scoffed at the idea of me being a healer. Or healer's in general, maybe. But I am. I know I am. It's just..." I take my arm away and stare upward, wondering how to phrase my next sentence. "What if I'm not? Or what if there's something more to this? I don't know how but I escaped, literally appearing out of thin air. I'm impervious to weapons, is that normal? What if I'm different? What if I'm a freak? I feel like there's something else going on."

I involuntarily gasp, gulping in air as my breath catches in my throat. I desperately don't want to cry, but I feel a small tear slip down the side of my face. I have to stop, so I quickly wipe it away as I sit up and keep my cool. I don't want this man to get to me. I delicately trace the bruising around my face, and gently prod my still puffy lip.

"Who am I?" I whisper delicately.

Olon stands in front of me, sensing my confusion and worry. I keep my eyes straight and blur the world around me, not focusing on Olon, or his torso, which now is right in front of my face as he stands there.

Surprisingly his hand cups my face, and he lifts my chin making me look at him, so I focus my eyes again. His expression is soft which comforts me, and he gently grazes his thumb over my cheek, feeling the faint trail of the single tear. But he soon cleans any trace of it.

"I told you I would keep you safe, and that I wouldn't let anything happen to you. I intend to keep that promise," he says, hushing any doubt in my mind that I am unsafe. "As for being a freak...who cares? Aren't we all? So what if there's something we can't explain right now? And who knows, maybe there is something more to you, but it's okay. It's all right. You're not a bad person. And you're safe."

He speaks so softly, so gently, it soothes me completely.

He's very good at this. My eyelids fall shut and I allow myself a moment to lean my face into his hand and relax.

I wonder if he ever acts like this with anyone else. Does he cup anyone else's face? And if not, why just me? I think about our chance meeting, finding him wounded in the desert that day, and the next thing I know he's told everyone about me and now I'm part of the Rogue Resistance. I wonder if he felt the connection I did on that first day.

I allow myself a small chuckle. "I never know when you might read my mind, that kind of makes me nervous," I admit, though I'm still smiling.

I open my eyes and look at him when he finally takes his hand away. Since he caught me out when I was thinking about how our names sounded together, I've tried to be careful with my thoughts around him, but they usually get away from me. I feel embarrassed at all the times he could have potentially been reading my mind and seen my thoughts about the two of us. And it's certainly no secret now that I have thoughts like that, especially since I subtly admitted that those exact kinds of thoughts got me out of the warehouse.

"I try to pick a time and place," he replies.

"What kind of time and place do you usually read my mind?" I inquire. I am still in a relaxed trance after how he calmed me.

"When you're alone. Sometimes when you think I'm not around, sometimes when I'm with you. Like now."

Oh, that catches my attention. So he knows that I was wondering if he does this with anyone else. Oh, no.

"It's when I can get your most honest thoughts. You let your guard down," he continues. "People try and fool me with fake thoughts if they know I might read their mind, but they never come through quite right and just get muddled up. When people are thinking honest thoughts, then it comes through clearly."

"So..." I wonder how to bring it up. Is it worth bringing up? Shall I mention it? He cuts me off before I can continue.

"So...you're right," he lets out a single laugh, raises the hand he was just touching my face with, and looks at it. "I guess I don't do this with others," then he looks up to me with a smirk. "I wonder why that is."

I can't reply because he starts walking out then, taking two steps backwards facing me, and then turns away.

I hear the door shut gently behind him and I let out a huge sigh. I feel the nerves in my body calm down. Damn, I wish I could read his mind.

I sit there a few minutes more before deciding any more reading would be futile today because I am already exhausted, and when I leave that small room I can see the sky is darkening through a window of the chapel, so it is time to go anyway. The adrenaline rush that I had after making it back here due to somewhat unexplainable circumstances has faded. I make the walk back to our town in quick time, still a little paranoid of being in open land on my own. Knowing that others are still going about their business and using up what little light of the day we have left doesn't stop me from crawling into my own bed in the early evening and falling asleep.

In the morning I sit up right away. The sudden movement coming out of sleep makes my head a little fuzzy. I wait for it to go away as I rub my eyes, glad to feel that my face isn't so delicate today. Not sure of the time but with a rumbling stomach, I swing my legs out of bed and stand up. My body just goes through the motions of going outside to get some fresh water, washing and freshening up, getting dressed, brushing my hair and braiding it out of my face. My mind is elsewhere however. I haven't been able to think straight since yesterday morning when I got back. My thoughts are jumbled and I jump from one idea to the next, one question after the other. Powers aside, I currently have my thoughts on Ailin; where she took me, how she got there so quick, and overall just a big fat why?

I leave my room and jump across the small stream with a leap instead of crossing where the plank is. I open the door to Marisol and Selene's room gently in case I wake anyone. I turn to my left where Selene sleeps. She is allowed to sleep in her own room now, no longer needing to sleep in the medical room, but she still has a bandage around her head and a bottle of pills by her bed for her injury. It won't be long now before she's totally healed. I turn back to my right where Mari is sat up, reading her book as usual, but she stops and looks up when she realises I am here.

"Want to get some breakfast?" she whispers, reading my mind.

We sit outside with our bowls of fruit and nuts, and some oats too. We eat slowly, watching the town come to life. More people begin walking passed as everyone starts waking up and getting on with the day. It is all pretty routine until Elias, one of the smartest people I know, runs passed, stumbling over things and almost bumping in to people, bag swaying side to side on his back. Mari and I share a look as his dark figure flies by, and then we decide to get up and follow him, see what the rush is.

Elias is at least 26 from what I can tell, darker skin than most of the people here, and very nice. And he is impressively intelligent. He wears thick, black-framed glasses that just magnify his eyes, which are always looking at the world around him with wonder and endless possibilities. I've never had a proper conversation with him, but we smile at each other in passing.

Mari and I race over the stream and catch up to Elias, jogging along behind him. Mari calls his name but he doesn't give us more than a quick glance and a wave over his shoulder, which almost knocks him off balance, and continues heading towards the ditch. He finally skids to a halt, almost toppling over the ledge, and then jumps down into the hole.

"Um, Vehement? Oracle? Someone?" he calls, bouncing on his toes with anticipation. Mari and I lower ourselves into the ditch too. A flap at the back opens and the Four step out, surveying the scene then letting their eyes land on Elias.

"What's going on?" the Vehement asks.

"I think I've done it," he replies. He drops to his knees in an instant, takes off his bag and lays it on the floor. He unzips it and pulls out what looks to be a kind of small, red, plastic box. There are wires looping in and out of it, and Elias holds it up to the Four carefully. "It can blow through wood, stone, metal, concrete. I think it will work."

My body stiffens as he speaks. Is he holding up a bomb to the Four?

"So, what, it's like dynamite?" the Vehement asks, taking it off of him and inspecting it.

"Better," Elias's eyes are shining with pride at his invention. "They're totally safe right now," he says, showing them the rest of the red boxes he has in his bag. "And we don't need to light them. They can be activated from 30 feet away. See this?" he points to a black square attached to one end of the box.

"This is the receiver that picks up the signal from this remote," he fumbles through his bag and takes out a black controller. "And it's on safety now. So any accidentally pressed buttons will not set it off. There's a special sequence of buttons and a code to take it off safety. But when these go off, I guarantee it will bring the walls down wherever we put it."

He continues to list the features on his invention. The Four look between him and the devices completely enthralled. They must have asked him to do this. They're not at all caught off guard by the sudden encounter and talk of explosives. I look to Mari, wondering what she is thinking, and see the corner of her lip tugging into a smile that she is trying to hide as she listens to Elias.

"What does this mean?" I whisper to her.

"It's means we can break into the prison."

9

"Did you sleep at all?" the Vehement asks me as she awakes, sitting up to find me hunching over in my bed, legs crossed, staring at maps and books.

I look up. Her hair is messy and her sheets are twisted. She always was a messy sleeper. I look to my side and notice the light starting to shine through the window. A new day; I hadn't even realised the sun was rising; I was caught up in my work. Time got away from me.

"I guess not," I reply. I feel the Vehement's eyes still on me, but I keep my eyes down and stretch my legs out, until I feel her gaze leave me. She gets up and goes to wash, and when she comes back I am still in the same position.

"Go eat something, Olon" she tells me sternly. I shrug.

"I will soon."

"What is all this?" she asks, looking over my shoulder.

"I'm trying to find hints and clues as to where the prison could be. We're on to something now. This is where it begins."

"Have you talked to Kayin about it? Does she remember anything?"

I think the others are concerned about me. It isn't the lack of sleep. My sleep varies anyway. I think they are worried I am becoming distracted. They haven't directly told me, but I suspect it's about Kayin. I've been spending a lot of time with her, considering she's just another rogue, in theory. But she's new, and she has her own powers, that sometimes we all struggle to understand. She needs extra guiding. Or that's what I tell myself.

I shake my head and look up at her. "She doesn't like to discuss her time in the prison. And when I look back into her memories, they're faded, and they have these soft edges. She's repressing those memories. And there's a lot of blackness there, which I expect is when she would have been blindfolded and taken there," I tell her. "It's hard to pinpoint any kind of location from her memories."

"We'll get together and work on it later when we group up," she tells me, and leaves again. I sit back and stretch my arms.

I guess I don't do this with others. My words echo in my head. Why is it just her? I feel something there, some kind of connection. Whether it is just meaningful friendship, the way we work together, or something on a higher level, I don't know. It could be anything, but I feel a bond. Ever since she found me in the desert.

I think about how she appeared out of thin hair, so helpless tied to that chair, after she disappeared. I can't describe the emotion I felt when Marisol announced we had a traitor and then Kayin couldn't be found. I want to say that I'd feel like that if any rogue was kidnapped, but I don't believe that to be completely true.

Don't even get me started on how she thinks about me. At least I know I'm not alone in this. There's attraction there, but hesitation and reluctance to accept it. The denial she feels, I feel it too. Though she feels like that because she's insecure; she feels I'm too good for her. I don't know how to react to that. I give her hints as to how I feel, but I don't know how they come across exactly when I'm still unsure of my feelings. But I tense up when I hear her thinking about us. Like when she discovered my name and tested out how our names sounded together.

Having people attracted to me is not new. But I feel there's a potential to have something more with Kayin and I don't know what to think about that.

It can't happen. Us two. It's not part of the prophecy. Believe me, I know. I know what the others are thinking.

That she would get in the way, distract my thoughts. And they are probably right – I know it too. In fact, even right now I'm thinking about her, when there's work at hand. However, I have sat up all night trying to figure something out and so far nothing, so I suppose I can let myself indulge in personal thoughts for a while.

Yet, when I'm with her, I can't help reaching out and making contact, I can't help saying things that are most likely leading her on when I know I can't pursue anything, at least not until it's all over, until our generation has run its course and we're no longer the Four. I can't sacrifice the success of our rebellion just because I have a girl somewhere in the Resistance that may like me. I refuse to be the first Oracle that screws everything up. There's a lot of responsibility and pressure that comes with this role. And having generations of successes behind me, everyone looks to me to carry that torch. I will not let them down. I have to devote my mind, soul, and body - my everything to this cause. That doesn't give me time for anything, or anyone else.

When Elias had finished with his presentation of his explosives yesterday, I caught up with the Cryptic. He told me that Elias might be able to help me with my powers; the science side of it, particularly the possible teleportation power. So we arrange to get together. I woke up later than I planned to this morning, and quickly jump out of bed to get dressed. I jog out of my room and through the town so I don't waste any more time. I briefly spot the Oracle leaving his room as I jog to the other side of town. He leans against the wall and rubs his face, and I am glad to be moving fast because if I were walking he would have definitely caught me staring. Jogging only allows me a quick window to watch him run his hands over his hair, nodding to me when he looks up and I pass by.

I had trouble sleeping last night and my thoughts drifted to him. After deliberation I decided my strong feelings for him, platonic or not, only come from him being the first real contact I've had in years. I've dealt with injured ones when I was on my own, passed by the odd rogue, as it were. But they were soon gone and I didn't see them again, didn't even catch their names most of the time. The Oracle seemed to come out of nowhere. I helped him and brought him to shelter. At the time he was just a man. The idea that he was a legend agitated the spark I was already feeling. I didn't expect to see him again the next day, and be brought into this life where I see and interact with him on a daily basis. That's a good enough justification for what I'm feeling, right? It's out of my hands.

Elias ties a kind of wide plastic orange rope around my wrists and mumbles to himself as he does so. He puts another one around my head over my temples, and another across my chest over my heart. He tries to explain what the process behind this idea is and how this rope works, but it is all lost on me.

"Very long story short, I've developed this rope that, when connected to the right places, will monitor the fluctuations of your brain, the flow of your blood, the work of your muscles…basically all the things that will allow me to read and decipher your powers as and when you use them. When you try to use a power, you'll find that you can't do it, but I'll be getting all the readings on here," he says after seeing my confused face, holding up a small screen of some kind.

"Okay, I understand that, I guess. But how will we know if it's stopping me or if I'm not doing anything?"

"We'll try it both ways, and I can compare the results. If you are using your powers, I'll be able to pinpoint what you're doing and what you're using to make it happen. Then you'll know how to improve. Okay," he makes sure my wrists are secured, then makes sure the rope around my head lines up with my temples correctly, "it's on properly, so have a go."

I close my eyes and concentrated hard on the spot 5 feet to the left of myself. There is no way I'd let myself teleport into another compromising position, so it is best to try and keep it short distance and focus my thoughts. After a few moments when nothing happens, I open my eyes again, and Elias is stroking his chin, looking at the screen on the little device he has that connects with the ropes.

"There's a lot of brain activity, for sure, and something going on with your muscles," he tells me vaguely. He looks up and then decides to take off the ropes. "So something was happening in your head. Have a go now."

The ropes are off so I do the exact same thing. Concentrating on the spot not far from me, I ball my fists up and bite my lip, focusing hard. Then after a moment, I sigh because nothing is happening. I don't open my eyes yet though. I relax and for the first time wish that it were actually possible for me to teleport. When I open my eyes and see Elias standing no longer in front of me but at a new angle, I grin. Have I done it? The smile on Elias's face assures me. I've done it.

"What did I do? What'd it look like?" I ask, skipping back over to him excitedly. He laughs.

"You just disappeared, like...like gone!" he chuckles, pushing his glasses up his nose. I can tell he is itching to work on his equations and test his theories, but for now he smiles at my excitement.

After working some more on trying to teleport, varying the distance and direction, we decide to play around with my other powers. I use my bone vision on Elias, giving in to my glee at mastering the power and feeling closer to my Nana. It gets easier every time I try it. He puts the ropes back on and tells me that the results show most of the activity is coming from my brain when I use the bone vision power.

"Take this pebble and try to scratch me," I suggest, having some difficulty bending over and picking up the small stone while I have the ropes tied around me.

"Why would I do that?" he replies, shocked at the prospect of having to hurt me, clutching his device tightly.

"I want to see what my body does when it tries to use my impervious power," I explain, with a nod to the screen in his hand.

He very gently drags the pebble against my arm with one hand, glancing at his device with the other. He doesn't do it hard enough to cut me, it only leaves a red mark, but he has readings from the ropes regardless.

"The results are showing me a lot of variations in your muscles specifically. This has all been great, I've got a lot of things that I can go back and work on."

We call it a day after that because I'm not comfortable using my heart control power on him without the Four around and we've already tested everything else. I am becoming too distracted with thinking about this power and all that it means as well. I jog ahead of Elias to go find the

Four and report back to them on what we've done today.

I find them in one of the meeting rooms, where they sometimes like to group. They have papers laid out in front of them, a stack of books in the corner, clearly working, but they welcome me in and let me sit down and share my stories.

"That still leaves us with a lot of questions," the Cryptic says, when I am completely done. "So, it's definitely teleporting. But, why you? How is that possible for one of our people?"

There is a long pause, but then the Oracle stands up, and moves around the table opposite me.

"It's a good thing you came round, actually," he tells me. "There's something here you can help us with." He briefly looks to the Cryptic and back to me.

"I'd love to," I say, though there is a hint of caution in my voice.

"It will be strenuous."

"That's okay."

"I'm not really sure of the after effects it will have on you."

"What is it I need to do?" My voice is unintentionally coming across more guarded now.

When the Oracle doesn't answer straight away, the Divine stands up too.

"We're trying to locate the prison from the little knowledge we have of it. We were hoping you could help, but we don't want to make you uncomfortable."

I swallow. "It's okay. I'll try my best to talk about it. I don't know where it is but I can try to answer questions..."

"We were hoping we – or rather the Oracle – could look into your memories."

"There's not a lot I remem-"

"I think you're repressing a lot of memories," the Oracle cuts in.

I keep my mouth closed and give him a small nod. He looks at me for a moment and I hope I am keeping my mind clear so there is nothing for him to read. "It's just...your memories are hard to read. I want to try and go deeper. See if we can get something more out of the location."

"I was blindfolded when I was taken there though," I tell them. They know this already though, right?

"Let's just try. Tell me if you need me to stop," Olon says, which makes me a little nervous. He walks towards me so I sit up straight and look up at him. He lifts his hands and places two fingers from each hand against each of my temples, cups my head and tilts it back slightly. He tells me gently to close my eyes and when I do I can suddenly see it. The day they came for our town.

I am sitting in front of my house, drawing on the stone

floor with chalk. My attention is drawn to Kalu, a little boy of only 7, one of my neighbours, suddenly running by. His tanned face is red, blotchy. His eyes are puffy. He hardly glances at me, just keeps running. So I stand up, wondering why he is running. Bullies? I'll handle them for him; he's only small. But no one was running after him, so I look to where he was coming from. I see the thick smoke rising to the sky over the houses. And then a Ghost Man comes round the corner. I wasn't aware of what they were back then. He strikes fear into my heart as he strides down my street, feet thumping along the cobblestones and his cape billowing behind him. And then I can hear the screams.

"Kayin!" Gracine and my father, Mahlik come out of the house and call me back, seeing what I see. More Ghost Men appear and approach us. I turn around, desperate the get to the safety of my parents' arms. Before I can run to them one of the Ghosts materialises behind me and grabs me around the waist, hoisting me into the air.

"Mum! Dad!" I call, but they're being secured now too. The white gloved hands of the Ghosts grip onto their elbows as they lunge forward towards me but I'm being carried away and they can't move. They're violently being restrained and I'm kicking and screaming. The smoke has travelled to our street and I can feel it in my lungs as I struggle to breath under the tight grip of the Ghost. I'm taken then. I see the grey roads and streets of my home pass in front of me and as we leave the town I see all my neighbours, grouped together, being chained up. Then I'm put down roughly in the dirt and blindfolded.

"Let me in," Olon's voice breaks through my memories. I hear him breathe deeply and press his fingers against my temples slightly harder. Then my memory is reversed. I'm back in front of my house, watching my parents being constrained. No…not my parents. My mum. My dad stands beside her doing nothing, not being touched. He's got his back to me, staring at the Ghosts, but they do not fight him, they look like they're listening. My father turns back to me looking heartbroken as I'm taken farther away, and finally I see the Ghosts pulling his arms back to chain him up. But I can't see what happens after then because I'm being shaken too much over the shoulder of the Ghost as I'm carried away again.

I see the landscapes beyond our town. I'm set down next to a girl I hardly spoke to in school. She's crying. I'm chained at the ankles and wrists and my blindfold is snapped on over my eyes loosely. It doesn't end there. Usually all I can remember is the darkness until I arrive at the prison. But I remember now.

We have been walking for miles. My mouth is dry and I'm tired and I miss my parents already. My sore feet trip and stumble over each other, causing a chain reaction as the people chained in front and behind me trip too. Some of the weaker chains at the back break and I hear quick, heavy footsteps. People are running away.

"You fool!" My blindfold slips down around my neck and in my blurry vision I look up at a tree. Then a Ghost Man steps into my vision, staff raised ready to strike me for being a nuisance, and the air leaves my lungs as it lands across my stomach. He orders me to get up and an older woman in chains behind me kindly helps me get back on my feet while I struggle for breath. Tears sting in my eyes, and I can only just see the thinning grass that's transitioning to desert land beneath my shoes. It hurts when I breathe so I have to refrain from crying. The tears fall and I find myself looking at the Ghost Man in front of the tree again, my last sight before the blindfold resumes its place over my eyes.

I gasp and squirm. The pain feels too real. My eyes shoot open and Olon takes a step back. I clutch my stomach, panting, but obviously I'm uninjured, it is just a memory. I hope those people whose chains broke got away. I wonder if they're in the Resistance now.

"Anything?" they ask us.

My mouth is dry and I'm breathing heavily, but the Oracle snaps in to action.

"A tree; a big tree. With red nine-point leaves. Rare," he

says, striding to the books they have in the corner.

My head starts pounding but I try to concentrate on what Olon is doing. Why does this hurt so much? I can feel a blinding pain in the back of my head, at the nape of my neck. Orisa senses my discomfort and steps towards me. She crouches at my side and strokes my hair gently, and I smile gratefully.

"The Richlen Tree. Grows all year round and is very rare," he closes the book, "I'm sure we could find some on a map."

I feel my eyes falling closed, I am suddenly exhausted and drained, so I don't hear the rest of the conversation as I black out, sliding off the chair and into the Divine's arms as I go.

10

I lift my head slowly as I wake up. At the end of my bed, in a position I'm all too familiar seeing him in, Olon is sitting cross-legged on a chair, reading. I freeze, not wanting to disrupt him. It is such a rare sight to see him so normal, sitting comfortably on the chair with his book. After a moment he shifts, putting one of his legs down and in his movement his eyes flick up to me, an action that looks very natural. He does a double take, realising I am looking back at him, and sits up straighter, closing the book as he does so. I sit up too.

"How are you feeling?" he asks.

Is it bad that he still sometimes intimidates me? He is just such a great man, regardless of being the Oracle. Even if he wasn't and we had somehow crossed paths, I still think I would admire him like I do.

"I've got a headache," I tell him honestly, feeling the

pain in my temples as I lean back against my pillows.

"That's one of the side affects of unlocking old memories, I suspect."

"Is that to do with the tree you- we saw?" I ask, correcting myself as I point to the book in his hands. He looks down at it and strokes his thumb over the dark blue, dusty leather cover.

"No," he shakes his head and looks back up. "I found something regarding repressed memories. I was reading it to see if there was anything about bringing up those memories again and possible consequences. I don't want to hurt you," he says steadily. I try not to read too much into his words and nod briskly.

"Anything?"

"Not particularly," he says solemnly.

"But did I help? Is the tree useful information?" I ask.

He seems to perk up a bit at this. "Yes. A little. It gives us an idea of the direction. Keeping in mind you were coming from your town, and you passed that tree, we may be able to pinpoint the direction you were heading to reach the prison."

I look down and nod, my concentration fading as I get a sharp pain in the back of my mind.

"Kayin?"

"I'm fine," I say unconvincingly. I put my hand on the

back of my neck and give it a rub and look at him, smiling meekly. He looks stiffer, sitting forward and watching my movements. I try to make my smile more believable and settle my hand down again. I don't know what that pain is, just part of the headache I suppose, but I don't want Olon worrying about me, not when there are more importing things he needs to be concentrating on.

"Shall we find the others? What's the plan?" I ask, trying to distract him.

"Well, so far we've located three Richlen trees. We will head out today, while other Resistance members stay back and see if they can find any more, according to the books and maps."

"I want to come."

"Do you think that's the best-"

"I want to. Maybe I can be of help. Maybe it'll stir memories, if there are any more."

"I don't want you to strain yourself," he says.

I sigh. In all honestly I love that he is concerned about me, but I can't let him distract himself with me. I need him to believe I can be independent and I am fine, for all our sakes.

"I won't. I'll be fine. I can handle it. I handled 4 years alone without you so I can cope with a headache or two." I say, a little more bluntly than I intend. He straightens up and pauses.

"Just know that I'm here for y-"

"I don't need supervision." I cross my arms defiantly.

"Okay. You can come. We best find the others, as you suggested." He stands up and nods curtly at me, taking his book with him. I let my shoulders droop and close my eyes, sighing. I want him to sit beside me and put his arm around me and tell me I don't have to do anything and everything will be back to normal by tomorrow. But I open my eyes and reality hits me again, so I slide out of bed and get dressed.

I sit beside the Vehement. I lean down to tighten the laces on my boots, listening to Olon give the orders.

"Now Kayin has volunteered to come, you can break into pairs, and I'll go alone. Divine and Vehement, you will separate to find the tree north west of Kayin's old town. I will go east, and Kayin, you and the Cryptic will go west. Make notes of everything, I want no details left out. We need every bit of information we can get our hands on. We'll head out together to Kayin's old town and then split up."

I stand up with the rest of them, my heart beating fast. I haven't been in my old town for years, not since I was taken away. A reassuring hand pats my back and I smile as the Cryptic passes me, and follows the others. I join on to the back of the line as we file out of the door. I subconsciously feel for my slingshot, and pull my leather gloves tighter.

As nervous as I am, I am also intrigued. I don't know where my town of Woodhurst is in proximity to Wellspring, the Resistance's area. I expect us to turn left at the stream and head that way but we go right. I stay silent as I follow. We leave town and come to the point where the land drops behind the rocks and on the other side is the pool I had found before. We stride down the hill and passed the pool. They don't even give it a second look; I guess it isn't as secretive as I had thought. We continue along the side of the water, until another stream joins onto it, and we take a turn left to follow the new water.

As we keep walking, we form a bundle rather than a line. I keep glancing at Olon, but he never returns the glances. He keeps his eyes straight ahead. I hope I didn't upset him. I roll my eyes at myself at the thought. How could I upset him? As if he cares about me so much that a few stern words would trouble him. I think I'm letting his kind, strong nature get to my head. It's not just me he cares for, that's just who he is. I look across to him again. He's the furthest away from me so it's hard to get a clear look without the others blocking my view. I hope his mind reading is limited to short distance. Oh no.

The land beneath us gets moister the further we go on. It darkens a few shades under my feet so I finally pick up my eyes and look at my surroundings. We've been walking for a while and I hadn't taken a lot of notice. A lot of the sights looked the same. A bare tree. More dry land. Only now is there some variation. In front of me are the remains of a small farm we used to use. It was just a small section of land that was suitable for growing crops and vegetables and the likes. Each town has an area like this just on the outskirts. The moist, healthy soil here has dried up mostly without the proper care and there is nothing growing apart from a few weeds. It could be any towns' land. But I can't mistake the shed in corner of the patch. The bright blue paint has faded now and so has the red paint on the door. But there still hangs a bronze horseshoe upon the door, and I know it belonged my Grandpa, which means this farmland belonged to Woodhurst.

I run then, bounding up to the shed, across the old farmland. The door barely holds on to the hinges as I open it. It creaks and swings open precariously, and I walk into the dark, dust filled space. The musky smell drifts up my nose and I cough, getting a pain in my head again. My ears start ringing as I move further into the shed. I can see the dust particles floating in the light streaming in from the windows so I move into the shadows and put my hands up to my temples, the ringing getting louder and the pain in my head becoming more prominent.

"Kayin?" I sense the others catch up with me.

"What?" I struggle to hear and open my eyes. I groan in pain and feel my legs becoming weak, my knees buckling beneath me. A strong pair of hands grabs my arms and helps me stay upright. As I look up I notice a pitchfork hanging on the wall over the shoulder of the Vehement. She holds me tightly but my eyes are locked on that.

I feel myself collapse then. When I expect to hit the floor I end up just falling onto my knees. The pain is gone. The shed is brighter. I am in different clothes. I look up. There is only my Nana. Diola is standing in front of me again. I put down the doll in my hand as she comes through the shed door. One hand is clutching her stomach and she holds the pitchfork in the other.

"Nana, you're hurt!" my voice is much higher than I expect. But it isn't unusual; when I look down at myself, I am younger, thirteen years old maybe, going on 14. That means there isn't a lot of time left before we are ambushed.

"It's alright, Kay," she says with a smile, but she winces and sits down in the wooden chair, putting down the pitchfork. "Just a silly farming accident."

I feel my stomach churn as I see the blood beneath her hand and on her blouse.

"Let me show you something special," she holds my hand tightly with her clean hand, pressing her thumb into my palm so she knows I will concentrate.

She finally lifts her blood-covered hand and hovers it above her stomach. She closes her eyes and sighs.

"I'll get help," I say, but she tugs on my hand and doesn't allow me to move.

"It's part of the process," she replies and as if on cue, a golden light appears from her palm, and a streak slowly rises from her blouse and dives back in. I hear my little voice gasp, and she holds my hand tighter. Her face visibly relaxes as the gold lights continued to jump in and out of her wound. Then she smiles, settles her hand down and opens her eyes to look at me. She unbuttons the bottom of her blouse and reveals a bit of her plump stomach to me, showing me how smooth the skin is.

"How? Did you trick me?" I ask, relieved but still riding on the emotion I feel from seeing her injured.

"No, sweetheart. I was hurt, really. But I healed myself," she whispers. "I've never shown you this power before."

"Why not? Your others are so cool."

"Fortunately you've never been around when I had a patient in need of that power. Sometimes it can get messy. It heals the skin, sews up the wound, can fix severe broken bones. You may not be magical, but don't ever give up on healing people, okay?"

I don't reply, just nod eagerly; I look at her in astonishment, still feeling a little queasy. She chuckles and cups my hands, then shifts to stand up, moving gingerly regardless of whether she was healed.

"Who did that to you?" the thought suddenly hit me, but she laughs it off.

"No one, Kay, sweetie. It was honestly an accident." She hesitates, and then comes to sit back down with me.

She seems to be internally fighting with herself. Then her face falls; her eyes grow wide and she grips my shoulders protectively.

"You must know, though, Kayin. Bad people are coming. Soon. I was in a town further west helping a patient, and the bad people were there. One day I won't be here any more, I won't be here to help. But you can't let fear win, be strong, sweetheart. They're coming soon. Don't trust-"

The ringing in my ears comes back alarmingly loud with the sharp pain in the back of my head again as the scene in front of me dissipates into thin air. The grip on my shoulders that my Nana had gets lighter and lighter until she fades away. I am grasping at the air in front of me, wanting desperately to bring her back to me.

I can't hear anything over the ringing in my ears and am not aware of how loudly I am screaming until the Four materialise in front of me grimacing at the noise I am making. I am kneeling on the floor in the arms of the Vehement as she tries to keep me steady and prevent me from lashing out. When the last traces of the memory fade, the ringing and the pain stop and I collapse instantly into the Vehement. She cradles me in her arms as I cry myself into unconsciousness.

I don't know what thought to process first. What happened? What have I learnt from the flashback? What should I tell them? Which bit is most important? I look up, finally registering the four people in front of me, waiting for me to respond. The Vehement is knelt by my side, holding my head in her lap. We are outside now, in the middle of town. Before they realise that I am awake, even before I realise what I am actually doing, I am getting up on my knees and reaching for my knife. I grip it firmly in my right hand and drag it across my left arm. They all make noises of opposition at my action, leaning towards me to stop me, but it doesn't matter. The act is to no avail. The knife doesn't harm me. I sigh.

"Please explain what that just was," Orisa says. She looks at me as if I am crazy. Maybe I am. But in that flashback my Nana had shown me something special. She showed me the final healer power I need. The gold streaks that swim in and out of the patient. Mari told me she'd seen Diola do it, now I have too, and it only makes sense that this power is how she healed her stomach wound. She literally healed and closed up her cut. Which also leads me to the conclusion that she was not impervious to weapons like me. That's another non-healer power I seem to have acquired.

I explain my flashback to the Four, wanting to talk fast because of all that I want to get out, but making myself go slow because of the pain in my head, though it is fading now.

"It's unlikely you will just be able to switch on the power now that you've seen it," the Cryptic offers.

"It is also meant to be unlikely that I can teleport and be unaffected by weapons, but apparently I can and am!" I don't mean to be rude, I am just confused and borderline hysterical, which seems to happen more frequently recently, with new information and feelings. And it is a fair point, but I sigh.

"Sorry. The only way I remember finding my other healer powers is through repetition, imagining it in my head over and over. I thought maybe I could just do that but in quick time."

"You need to test your power. The sooner you learn the better it will be when the inevitable battle comes," the Oracle says. He looks me straight in the eyes and I have to look away. It isn't the soft look he gives me when we are alone; it is a hard, purposeful look of a leader in action.

Oh yes, the inevitable battle. I'm not thrilled about the

idea of people getting hurt in war, but it's all for the greater cause, and the sooner that comes the sooner we can free our people and start over, living new lives.

"I can't cut myself though, and neither can any of you. How will I practice?"

"Here," the Oracle holds up his own blade and is about to touch it down on his forearm but without thinking I step forward and grab his hand.

"I can't let you do that to yourself. I won't let you guys hurt yourselves just for me," I address the rest of them.

"We are born to save our people. This is my duty. If hurting myself to help you leads us to helping others, then it's what I must do. Besides, it's just a scratch, I can handle it," he replies, and I shut my mouth as he uses my own words against me. I let go of his hand and realise if he is going to do this, cut himself, then I have to concentrate on the power. The moment I see the first drop of blood I hover my hand over his forearm, much like my Nana had done to herself. First comes the glow of my hand, controlling his heart, but he is already calm, I just keep it steady and think hard about the cut I see, the split in his skin. I do what I think is right; I picture his skin coming together, healing, but I hear him take a sharp intake of breath through gritted teeth and I open my eyes.

The blood continues to come, and Olon has a hard

expression on his face. I know it hurts him. I drop my hand and all glowing stops. In under thirty seconds I reach for the cloth tied around my belt and have it wrapped round his arm, mumbling 'I can't do it, I'm sorry, I got it wrong', over and over as I do so.

I hold his forearm, staring at the cloth surrounding his cut, not having the strength to lift my eyes and look at them. No one says anything. I sigh, finally letting go of his arm.

"I couldn't...I..."

"You need practice," Olon interjects, but his voice is softer now so I look up and though he has a straight face, I see the kindness in his eyes, which relieves me.

I turn around and look at my surroundings. My town. This is the town square, the market place. The old stalls that once stood here are gone, scraps of wood left rotting here and there. The buildings are dusty and scarred. I look up to one of the taller buildings, instantly remembering where everything is.

"Follow me," I say, beginning to walk across the empty space to a street I knew. I want to forget about the power, what I have just done and been through, for now. Right now we need to find the Richlen Tree from my first flashback.

They follow me down a narrow alley between two buildings and then I turn right. Out of the alley there is a wide street, on either side are houses and I see the stepping stones that lead up to a door a few houses down, so head that way. Of course, the chalk drawings are long gone from the day I drew them, but I kneel down in the spot I was in the moment before I was captured, and trace my fingers along the stones, as if the drawings are still there.

"This is my house," I say to no one in particular as the others catch up and stand behind me. I can't let myself think about it too much, think about the old memories of this place, or I will become emotional. So I quickly stand up again, brushing off my knees. "If I was here when I was captured," I say, thinking out loud, looking to the spot beneath my feet, then looking up to the faces of the Four, "then that means I was lifted and taken…" I start walking back onto the street and go left, "this way. I was carried all the way down here, until we left the town and I was set down on the outskirts, then blindfolded and chained."

I keep walking, making turns and varying my pace as I remember which was I was taken by the Ghost Man, sometimes walking backwards to imitate what I would have seen as the Ghost carried me away. And the Four follow me with no questions, until finally I stop. They space out around me, looking into the open land in the opposite direction of my town.

"This is as good a time as any to split up then," the Vehement tells everyone. The Oracle nods in agreement.

"Let's go," the Cryptic says to me, gesturing to the way we should walk in hopes of finding the tree from my memory. I steal a glance back at Olon but he has already set off in the other direction.

We walk for a long time, so it seems, trying to stay on a straight path according to the Cryptic's compass. The conversation is limited. We both have our own thoughts to occupy us. But every now and then he will ask me if I am okay, or how am I holding up.

"I guess I'm kind of a mess, lately," I half laugh. I looked to my feet as I walk. I can't count the emotions I feel regarding the Resistance, the Ghosts, and the Supreme. I still think about my kidnapping. The teleportation, and my powers in general. The prisons. Our people, specifically my parents. But on top of that now is the whole 'unlocking memories' case. Now we have new information, which is good, but on the other hand it's disorientating feeling like you thought you knew all you could, but actually there are aspects to your life that you may well have forgotten completely. Not to mention the pain that comes along with opening new doors to these repressed memories. I feel I'm unreliable at the moment. A memory could come at any time, something that triggers it, anything. I get headaches and I feel achy and exhausted. But I stand by what I said to Olon; though I feel like this, I can't let myself distract any of the Four from more important issues.

"We can handle it," the Cryptic replies with a smile.

There's that word again. I wish I'd never said that to the Oracle. I was just trying to assert my independence, but actually it just came across as rude. They've all been nothing but generous to me, especially Olon, and I got blunt with him for caring. I'm such an idiot.

"I think my Nana escaped from the Ghosts once," I speak absentmindedly as we walk. The Cryptic is constantly looking across the landscape, for any sign of this tree, but he looks down at me when I say this.

"When she admitted that there was an evil coming in the flashback; she was helping a patient in a town further west, that's how she knew about the evil. Of course the Ghosts were very close at that time, we just weren't aware, and I'm surprised she made it back to Woodhurst before them. She never spoke about it again; I can't believe I didn't remember it before. About a month after that I think, she passed away, and after another month our town was attacked," I pause. "I'm glad she had already gone."

I want to defeat the Ghosts so badly. Get some pay back for all they've done to us.

With this new adrenaline I feel I suggest we move faster, but before we get very far, we faintly hear a whistle. It was that long, high pitch whistle that gets your attention and means to gather.

The Cryptic and I share a look briefly, before turning on our heels and heading back quickly in the direction of the whistle. We were told only to call back if there is information, news to tell; we are all looking for trees and any one of them could be the right one. So with my heart thumping, we pick up our pace, and finally after the journey back, plus the added journey of the Divine and Vehement, we finally see them in the distance and I sprint the rest of the way. I pull out my flask and take a big swig, as the Cryptic catches up. I look up at the tree we stand under in amazement. It is beautifully flourished, full of foliage, with such a vibrant red colour. Moments later the Oracle joins us too.

"What have you got?" Olon asks straight away, inspecting the tree to his side.

"Here," the Divine says, and walks a few steps round the large, thick trunk. We follow and look at what she is pointing at. Something is engraved on to the bark, some symbols of sorts.

"What does that mean?" Olon asks, running his thumb over the marking gently.

"At first, we weren't sure if it meant anything. It could have been anything carved into it, but to be sure, I suggested asking in the Underworld. It was the only source of information with us," the Cryptic explains, and the rest of us nod.

"So I descended, found some souls that I had crossed paths with before. They were happy to go deeper and spread the word of these markings. They found out from deceased shilo, that it's another language. It means shadow in short hand. It's basically the Ghosts marking their territory in their own language; therefore it's not obvious to us."

There is a moment of silence as we take this information in.

"So we know they came this way? This is where I must have fallen. They got me back to my feet and…do you think they continued in this straight line?"

"That's a good question," the Oracle agrees. I smile to myself. "There's only one way to find out, we'll need to explore further this way, but not now. Dusk is almost here, we should find shelter." Just before everyone disperses to do as he says, he smiles and stops us. "We're half way there."

11

"Will the rogues be okay if you are all out here tonight?"
I ask the Four. They nod.

"They're safe, and they know how to look after
themselves," the Vehement assures me.

We sit in a sort of cave, where the stone of a large rocky
wall has eroded and left a space big enough for us to lie in. I
settle down. The sooner I can fall asleep, the sooner
morning will come and we can get up and search again. We
are so close I can feel it. I am exhausted from the day,
however my eyes seem to refuse to close.

I hear the Four talking, but I just roll over and face the
cave wall, trying desperately to fall asleep. One by one the
voices fall silent, and heavy breathing replaces them, letting
me know they've drifted off. I sit up. How strange that I sit
with four of the most powerful people in this land while they

are at their most vulnerable. I scan my gaze across them, squinting my eyes in the dark, and gasp when I see Olon looking back at me. I throw my hand over my mouth to stay quiet, and regain normal breathing. One of these days that man will give me a heart attack.

"I thought you were sleeping."

"I thought you were sleeping," he replies in just the same way.

"Well, we're both not." I whisper with a sigh. I don't know what to do.

"Why are you up?" he asks.

"I can't sleep."

"Me neither," he tells me. Then it occurs to me that I seem to always catch him awake.

"Do you sleep much?" I ask.

"Not particularly."

I nod, though I'm not sure if he can see it in the dark. He pulls his knees up to his chest, and rests his arms across his knees. I look down at my hands. The moonlight cascading across his face makes him look heavenly, and the way he is looking at me makes me feel vulnerable.

"How's your head?"

"It's alright," I whisper.

"You should rest," he says firmly, in his quiet, deep voice. I don't reply. I am too tired to argue but apparently not too tired to actually fall asleep. I hear shuffling and look up as Olon tiptoes over the others towards me. He sits down next to me, on the edge of the entrance to our little cave, our arms brushing for a moment before he lifts his and hangs it around my shoulders. He stretches his legs out and lets me lean against his chest, pulling me in.

"You're no use to us if you're suffering from sleep deprivation, I don't care if you think you can handle it," his voice is soft and light-hearted in my ear. I watch the dark clouds roll across the sky in front of the stars, I take deep breaths of the clean air, and I savour the warmth of Olon beneath my cheek. I relax. And then I fall asleep.

As the sun rises in the east, shining bright through the entrance of the cave, it is as if last night didn't happen. I am lying on my side alone. I roll over and Olon is back on the other side of the cave, sitting up against the wall, slumped and still sleeping. So I rest my head a little longer, and wait for the others to wake up. When I hear stirring, I sit up again and stretch, rub my eyes, and then slowly stand up and step out of the cave. Soon enough, the others follow me out.

Once we are all out and packed up, we discuss the plan and set off. Get back to the tree and go on further from there in different directions. I pair up with the Cryptic again, though this time I'm not so distracted. I am focused and ready to put my all into searching as we head north from the

Richlen tree.

We haven't been walking for long, but I suddenly felt woozy. I take my flask out and slowly sip at the water, putting the feeling down to dehydration. I put my hand on the Cryptic's upper arm when the nausea persists, and slow down. He turns to me with worry.

"Kayin, are you okay?"

I look around. What is this? Oh, here comes another headache. There is nothing around us. Surely I'm not having another flashback episode? What could I be remembering?

But it feels different then. I feel something in my chest. My heart is beating fast, but that isn't only it. It feels like something wants to jump out of my chest. I can feel the pressure behind my ribcage, so I follow. It is as if I am being pulled along. Like a magnet.

"I don't know what's happening," I say, stumbling along the ground. I make a sharp left on the path we are headed and go that way. I just feel it's right. Like I need to go this way. This is the direction we have to go in.

"Kayin, stop, let's just rest a moment," the Cryptic says. He takes a hold of my shoulders, gently shakes me and makes me stop. "Look at me."

I look up into his eyes. He is searching mine. But I let my gaze fall again because my mind is clouded with the thoughts of whatever is in that direction. I am breathing heavily, glancing over my shoulder. I am being drawn that way. I need to go. I blink to focus my eyes, but the edge of my vision is going white and blurry. My eyelids are heavy. I try to shake my head to clear my mind, but it just hurts too much.

"I can see the prison," I tell the Cryptic, but I can't see him. The sight of me inside the prison dominates my vision.

"Where?" I hear him ask incredulously.

"Not here, in here," I reply, hoping I'm pointing at my head. I sway again and the Cryptic's arms tighten around mine. I find my footing and stand as straight as I can. This is the first time I'm having a flashback but am still aware of my surroundings.

"I can see my father too," I continue.

"Kayin, sit down and take it easy." The Cryptic attempts to lower me to the floor, but I resist, standing my ground, and even trying to take a few steps.

"The Ghosts have just been doing the dinner rounds," I explain, watching the memory play out in front of me. "The food transfer door hasn't been latched properly."

"You don't have to keep telling me what you're seeing-"

"I want to. Look, Mahlik is watching them leave too." The thumping in my chest persists and it's such a strange sensation to want to follow the direction it's pushing me, without seeing where I'm going.

"He's whispering to me. Imagine I'm outside, he's saying. Kayin, close your eyes and concentrate. He's making sure the coast is clear. He wants me to leave."

I'm surprised when I can hear a real sob come from my own mouth. "I don't want to leave you, I'm telling him. I'm looking at mum behind him but he makes me look at him."

"Kayin, your nose is bleeding. Please, stop," the Cryptic urges, more agitatedly this time, and when he shakes me again I realise I have started pulling away. I stop and touch my nose with my fingers and blood drips off of them.

"We need to go," I say, my voice is weaker than I expect it to be.

"We need to get the others." He puts his fingers up to his mouth ready to whistle, but I stop him.

"This won't get better unless we go that way," I point behind, the way this feeling in my chest tells me to go. I sound sure of myself, but really I am terrified. I wipe my nose on the back of my hand, but it is still bleeding so I just smear it over my skin. I have to pinch my nose and close my eyes. I try to slow down my erratic breathing.

Behind my closed eyes, sixteen year old me is still arguing in whispers with Mahlik.

"Cryptic. I think my father is telling me to teleport," I whine, gripping my head.

"What do you mean?" I can hear the pure intrigue in his

voice underneath the worry.

"He's saying…the latch isn't on right, he can make it look like I unlocked the doors and escaped. He'll tell the others 'she just made it passed the Ghosts before they came to lock the doors'. Thump, thump, thump in my chest, can you feel it? Wait, my father is telling me to picture the desert, run away, Kayin, he's whispering so the others in our cell don't hear. Don't stop running; just get out of here!"

"Breathe, Kayin, please," the Cryptic pleads. I suck in a lungful of air through my mouth, not realising I had stopped breathing.

"Picture the outside and go. This is your only chance. Cryptic, he knows I can do it, why does he know?" I am crying now, my head is pounding, my chest is thumping, and my nose is still slowly dripping with blood.

The Cryptic stops me then, makes me stand still until I breathe and I'm no longer on the verge of hysterics.

The crowded prison cell I'm in is unaware of my inner turmoil, Mahlik's incessant urging, telling me to leave. I close my eyes and make it happen. I'm suddenly alone, my father isn't holding me anymore, Gracine and the others I have spent the last two years in a cell with are probably up there, confused. I open my eyes; the sun warms my skin for the first time in ages. There's the prison, it's intimidating and scary and so far away, across a huge hole in the ground, yet I am on the other side. I empty the contents of my stomach onto the ground; wipe my eyes and my mouth and turn to run. All I do is run, and now I recognise the memory. It's me running, finding shelter, and running some more, away from the horrors of the prison.

"I forgot how I escaped." I cry a bit more. The ringing in my ears is quietening down, but the feeling in my chest keeps persisting. "Please can we keep moving?" I know I sound crazy, delirious even.

The Cryptic is hesitant but takes a firm grip on my upper arm and leads me along. I stumble along behind him, my vision slowly clearing up, the whiteness around the edges disappears and I can see where I'm going, grateful he is taking me the way I want.

"If anything happens to you...I swear...The others..." Abeo mumbles, not finishing his thoughts. He tugs on my arm a little more so I can keep up. He seems a little angry, but I think he is just worried.

"We're not going quick enough," I slur, trying to keep my eyes open, fully aware in my mind that I am the reason we are not going fast enough. We pass rocks and bushes and unfamiliar trees, but I know we have to keep going.

"What is happening, Kayin?" Abeo asks, after I trip again and this time fall on my knees. He stops and turns to me, crouches by side. My nose has finally stopped bleeding, but my skin is stained with the blood. I lick my dry lips and look out in front of us. There is something there.

"There," I croak.

"Kayin, I'm really worried. We're meant to be searching in the other direction. Not to mention the state of you. Are you okay, really?" He doesn't give me a chance to reply. "We need to stop and get the others."

My knees feel shaky but I stand up straight, poking my finger into his chest and clutching his shoulder with the other hand as he helps me up.

"You need to trust me. Just for the minute," I curse my shaky voice. That doesn't sound reassuring. I don't know why I'm trying to assure him of anything when I'm just as confused, but in the back of my mind, in my chest...This feels right.

"You're making that very difficult."

"There," I whisper again. I know there's something there. It's not just that I can feel it, I'm sure I can see something on the horizon.

"We'll go a bit further, but then I must call the others. Keep drinking," he tells me, thrusting his flask into my hand and pulling me along again. I try to keep up.

He keeps walking and I keep stumbling. I persist in sipping his water and we carry on passing weird rocks and bushes.

Come to me.

"What are you saying?" I ask.

"What?" Abeo slows, looking at me.

I shake my head gently. "Oh. Nothing" I rub my face. My eyes feel puffy and my lips are cracking.

Join me, my dear.

"Huh?" I mumble. *I've found you.*

The Cryptic gasps and I feel his strong arm snake around my middle, holding me up just as I fall weak. My knees buckle and my body falls slack against Abeo, so he is completely holding me up. I can't open my eyes any more; I've given up trying. I hear the Cryptic whistle, right over my head. The whistle that alerts the others, they'll be here soon. They'll know something is wrong, especially since the whistle is coming from a different area than we're meant to be in. I assume he's finally given in and whistled because he doesn't know how to handle me. I don't know how to handle myself right now.

Damn it, of course I don't. Why do I try to act tough in front of the Four? I'm nothing but a scared girl. I need help and I'm pushing them away.

The Cryptic is saying my name, trying to keep me awake. He's patting my cheek, slowly lowering me to the floor and letting me lean against his chest as he sits. He strokes my hair and keeps my head up. The feeling in my chest has died down, but I can still feel it there. Thumping. I feel like the Cryptic should be able to feel it under my skin, but he doesn't say anything. My head lulls back against his shoulder.

"Thump, thump, thump," I mumble to him. "Can you feel it? Thump, thump that way," I tell him.

"Kayin. Kayin. Stay with me," his voice is quiet and strained. "You did it," his voice cracks. "Stay with me. You did it."

But I can't focus long enough to understand what he's talking about. The Oracle's words came back to me, 'You're no use to us if you're suffering from sleep deprivation'. So I allow myself to sleep.

I feel a little dizzy when I open my heavy eyelids. I am propped up against a rock, the Cryptic sitting by my side. The Divine and Vehement are here too; I can hear them talking behind me. And as I look across the desert, I see the Oracle also making his way over to us quickly. I can't have been out long if he is just showing up.

He doesn't speak. Hardly even blinks at me as he approaches, walking up and standing beside me, looking at something behind me. What's the fuss? I try to move then, feeling terribly achy. And then the gentle thumping in my chest comes back to me. It is as if it is beating in my back now, it wants to go behind me.

"Oh, Kayin, you're up," the Cryptic says with relief and

is quick on his knees and helping my sit up straight. The Oracle tears his eyes away from whatever he is looking at and is also at my side in no time. I smile weakly at them both. I see Olon inspecting me closely.

"What happened to you?" he asks, worried.

"She had one of her episodes," the Cryptic says as way of explanation. "An awful one."

I don't want to think about my appearance right now. Not after the dizziness and puffy eyes and cracked lips, and oh, the nose bleed. I'm quite sure I started sweating pretty bad too. I must be a state.

"Did you hear the voice?" I ask the Cryptic in a haze. I definitely heard something before I had to rest.

"What voice? No, I didn't," he replies, glancing up at Olon.

The Oracle gently grips my chin and holds my face up, getting a better look at me in the light. His expression is that of concern. Then he meets my eyes and I swear I stop breathing.

"You did it," the Cryptic whispers, and I remember him telling me this before I fell asleep.

"Did what?" I ask. He nods his head in the direction behind me, and they help me turn. My body hurts, my head is still fairly cloudy, but when I get sight of the thick, tall black building, it's like I sober up. There is no mistaking the prison in front of me. It has sleek black walls and tinted windows around the top. But round the lower stories of the building there are no glass windows, just metal bars, holding in the prisoners. I remember the cold draft that came with the night, and having to huddle together with the other prisoners to stay warm in the prison, because there was no protection from the cold. No windows to shut. I involuntarily shiver. I attempt to count the windows on one wall, on one floor, but I can't focus my eyes. Olon puts his hand on my shoulder comfortingly as we stare at the building. I led the Cryptic here. I did it. I found the prison.

The one big flaw in finding the prison, is now wondering how we will get there. We are close to Ervon's Gorge at this point, but further north along the Gorge than I've ever seen, let alone been. Where we are it starts to open out into a deep canyon and in the middle of the colossal crater stand several pieces of land, rising from the bottom of the chasm. On one of these pieces of land sits the prison, tall and proud, near impossible to touch unless you're a Ghost…or you can teleport.

The thumping in my chest snaps me out of those thoughts. My chest thumps still in the direction of the prison in front of me. Oh wait, that's how I did it? My chest led me here? Whatever happened to me just now led us here? How does that work, it felt as if I was being pulled like a magnet?

As if I was attached to something. I was being drawn here. Surely I'm not attached to the prison in some way. I've experienced a lot of 'weird' in my life, especially recently, but that's too much, certainly?

"How did you do it? Why did you come in this direction?" Orisa asks me. I shrug and gently shake my head.

"I think I was led here." The odd looks on their faces in response to that makes me elaborate. I tell them the feeling I had, the pain. I tell them about the flashback and how I was still awake during and by the end of it. And through the whole thing I ended up leading the Cryptic here.

"That's very strange. You've been through a lot physically the last couple days. We need to keep an extra eye on you," the Cryptic says. I nod but don't reply, too tired, only proving him right.

"We best get out of the light before we're spotted by someone," the Vehement announces, so we all scurry (I am helped) back to a tree with a large, thick trunk and long, flexible branches full of leaves that hang down, almost to the floor, like a dome. A leafy, green dome.

They let me fall asleep again. I don't mean to, but I sit back against the trunk, with the promise that they will keep an eye out, and suddenly I find myself drifting off. I want to be fit and fine again, as soon as possible. I dream of my parents. My old friends. It doesn't hit me until I wake up with a start how close they are. How close my parents are. They are just across a big hole and behind a wall. I hope. I want to get in there. I'm desperate to see them again and I have questions.

"We better draw some kind of map out, so we can head back to base and tell the others of our discovery."

We all agree with the Cryptic as he says it. The Divine stands up and pulls a very large leaf from one of the branches and lays it out before us.

"This will do for now," she says, and marks a little X on the leaf where our Resistance is based at Wellspring and then they go about discussing how exactly we got here and which routes we took. It doesn't make sense to dwell on the sight of the prison, and waste any more time here, so they start standing up, but Olon crouches at my side.

"Are you okay to walk?" he asks, his voice soft, just for me. I smile a small smile up at him, drinking in his face through my tired eyes. I blink, closing my eyes longer than necessary, but nod.

"I'll be okay." As I stand and gather my bearings, I glance through the branches at the prison building and a thought occurs to me.

"Can I teleport?"

I softly shake my head, realising I have phrased that wrong. We have all established I can teleport, but what I was really asking is would it be okay if I teleported back in my state, knowing it would be quicker.

After a few wary looks to each other, Olon turns to me.

"Just try it out now; let's see how strong you are. I don't want you disappearing and showing up somewhere unknown where we can't help you if you're weak."

I nod and close my eyes to concentrate. Like before, I can't feel myself move but I suddenly feel an overwhelming weakness in my knees, and I open my eyes and notice that I am standing on the other side of the Four. I also notice that I am stumbling in place and the Vehement is lunging forward to catch me as I sway, but none of that matters because I can feel the pain in my head coming back so I close my eyes and take deep breaths until it goes away.

"Maybe I'll just stick with you guys, then," I concede, leaning against the Vehement. The others get themselves together and begin walking back.

"I've got her," Olon says, taking me off of the Vehement and hoisting me into his arms bridal style. The Vehement walks on and we follow behind.

"You don't have to do this," I tell Olon, but I don't sound very convincing as I put my arm around his neck for support. He only chuckles in reply.

I don't let him carry me all the way, probably further than I should have, but only until I have some of my strength back and can walk with the rest of them. As this time we know which way we are going it doesn't take us as long to get back as it did to get there. We stop only briefly twice to fill up on water, and make it back to the Resistance just after dusk. I go to bed once we are back. It is good to lie down on a flat, comfy surface, and get some undisturbed rest. I am so drained from all my recent antics. While the Four meet up with others to discuss plans and strategies they let me sleep through the night.

When I wake up, it is early morning. Probably 7am. I know others will be up and I am okay to start my day now. I have to go to the bathroom so I get out of bed, feeling better than I have in a while after such a good sleep. The stress of finding the prison is off of my shoulders; I hope the flashbacks aren't necessary any more because their purpose was just to stir memories to lead us to the prison. I'm hoping that since that's over, maybe they'll stop, and that it won't be a regular thing.

I go to the ditch after going to the bathroom. I know I will find people here. And just as I suspect, the Four are here already. Elias is with them. They are probably discussing explosives and entry tactics and all sorts, so I approach slowly.

"Oh, Kayin, we're glad you're up. How are you feeling?" the Vehement is first to greet me. The others turn and I smile at them.

"Quite good actually." I see the relief on their faces.

"Prepared for the day?"

I exhale. "I think so," I reply with a grin. The quicker we get the ball rolling then the quicker we can turn plan into action and free our people. We're doing this. We can achieve this. I know it.

"Elias?" the Cryptic says, prompting him to take over.

"Of course. Yes. Whenever you're ready, Kayin, we can continue some training, and work on your skills and powers. The better understanding we have means you can use them to their fullest potential."

"Yes, right." I look down at myself. "Well, I think I'm ready now. Let me just grab a drink."

I follow Elias out into desert land with my flask of fresh water, sipping periodically. This is near enough where we went last time. Open land, no obstacles or obstructions. He's brought his red bag of equipment with everything he needs. I don't question him much on what the bag holds inside; I just know he has what is relevant.

"Okay, well first off, I'm going to tie you up in this rope again." He holds out the rope that he had used the first time. It is the rope that stops me from using my power and records my body reactions.

"When can we practice without the rope?"

He chuckles lightly. "When we have all the possible results. Tying it around your wrists, head, and around your arms and chest allows me to get readings from it. This is how I can understand what you're doing, and you don't have to waste energy."

"So with that information…then we'll work on practicing my powers?"

"Yes, exactly." He smiles and adjusts his glasses.

"Okay," I agree, getting in position so he can put the ropes on me.

First he ties a strip around my forehead. Then ties the loops around my wrists and makes sure they're tightly secured together. He asks me to try and shake them off just to make sure they're firmly in place. And lastly, he pins my elbows against my torso and wraps a long piece around my body, so I can't lift my arms.

"What shall I do first?" I inspect my bindings and then look up at him. He's taken off his glasses and is rubbing his face. My face falls. His warm chocolate eyes have darkened, and his lips are slightly curled into the beginnings of a snarl.

"Elias?" I start to worry.

"First," he says darkly, "I'm going to tape your mouth shut, and knowing full well that you won't be able to escape this time, I'm going to take you back to the Shadow Lands."

12

I writhe against Elias's strong grip on my arms. I struggle against his hold on me but it's too tight. He's dipped me backwards and is holding me by my upper arms as he drags me across the dry land. I try to dig my heels into the dirt, trying to slow him down, but all it does is leave a trail in the sandy mud.

"Don't make me silence you by force," he leans down and whispers menacingly in my ear. I try as hard as I can to move my lips against the tape he's stuck across my mouth, but my efforts to make any kind of call or noise are in vain. I can't see where he's taking me; all I can see is the open land we were once training in moving further and further into the distance. The Resistance is far behind that, out of sight before he had even tied me up.

He drops me suddenly onto the floor on my back. Small puffs of dust dissipate around me as I hit the land. At the awkward angle I fall on the air is momentarily knocked out of my lungs. I flare my nostrils, breathing hard to get some air back into my chest, and try to roll over. In my peripheral vision I catch sight of a thick, black tyre. Then a pair of boots stop in front of me.

I feel two new pairs of hands grabbing each one of my arms and hauling me into the air so my legs are dangling, and I see the truck that I'm being lifted to. Vehicles around here aren't very common, especially nowadays. They were few and far between to begin with. This truck is a slick, shiny black; the windows are darkly tinted in the front and there are bags and some variations of briefcases sitting in the back. I dread to think what they're keeping in there.

I kick my legs to try and throw the big men holding me off balance, but they're unfazed by my weak plan. They easily throw me up and over into the back of the truck, and I hit the deck hard, unwilling to struggle any more after falling painfully. I lay still and listen while Elias tells the other two men to make no stops or detours. They must drive straight to HQ. Elias goes on to say how happy Boss will be when they arrive with me as they all pile into the front of the truck.

I'm jolted around in the back as we drive, making our way through the dry land, then over some kind of rockier terrain. If I could just get enough momentum...hitch my body up somehow, I would try and jump out. But they'd probably notice and I wouldn't be able to get far while being tied up and powerless. So I'm left to wonder how we are even supposed to get to their HQ when it's across Ervon Gorge.

My mind floats back to when I was last taken to 'HQ', or the warehouse, as I remember it. I assume it is in HQ. That vile man that makes my skin crawl. Is he the boss Elias was talking about? I'd rather not face him again, especially now they can contain my powers and there's no way that I can teleport this time. I can feel the hairs on my arm pricking up just at the thought of coming in contact with that man again.

I don't know how long we drive for. I can't see any of my surroundings. I shifted on to my back long ago and all I've been able to see are the clouds above me, slowly drifting away as we continue travelling. The only things that break up the perfect blue haze of the sky. I have nothing else to watch but the clouds, and the occasional bird that soars quickly in and out of my vision.

The truck stops at one point. There is still blue sky over me; the same blue sky wherever we go. Like it's mocking me, it's rubbing my face in the fact that I can't tell where we're going. A cloud suddenly appears above me. I furrow my eyebrows, wishing I could move my mouth. The cloud didn't float in to my line of vision, but rather literally appeared there, as if we had moved, and suddenly the truck is moving off again. No words are spoken during the break so I'm still clueless. After another while of driving, trees start to appear around us, a few at first but then they become denser. They begin blocking my view of the sky. It's colder without the sun directly on my skin, and it's darker under the trees.

I'm suddenly aware that we must be in the Shadow Land, where the Ghosts and their civilisation abide. My eyes are wide with fear and my breathing becomes heavier. How did they manage to get across the Gorge?

I hear the truck wheeze and then judder to a stop. I anticipate what happens next. The men slam their doors as they get out of the truck and come around the back to fetch me. Once again I'm hauled into the air but they decide to drag me the rest of the way. Once I can see the land again, I'm struck by how...un-desert-like it looks. The land looks healthier. In fact, it's moist. There is life growing. It's not a desert at all. I wouldn't go as far to call it grassy, but it's not the usual barren land I'm used to seeing.

A cool blast washes over me as I'm dragged inside a building. Big, heavy doors slide shut in front of me as I'm lugged backwards down a hallway. The walls are grey and long strips of light run down the middle of the walls on either side, so you can see where you're going but there's still an eerie darkness to it. It feels clean and sterile, but somehow dirty at the same time.

We turn down a corner and push through some more doors. In this room the walls are lighter. It's brighter. There are normal lights in the ceiling and they illuminate the whole room nicely...or what I can see of the room. The floor is a short, matted grey carpet. I'm left to drop again, and I grunt in response. I wish they'd stop doing that. The two men who were at my side come into my vision as they leave. One of them smiles at me as he leaves, but it's an evil smile, more of a snarl.

When nothing happens after a moment and I'm left lying there, I become frustrated. I bring my knees up and try to roll over onto them, but I can't find the momentum to roll over at all. I groan, loudly, but the groan continues and I end up letting out a muffled scream, my voice muted by the tape over my mouth. Why isn't anything happening?! My patience is wearing thin.

With this newfound energy from my anger, I roll onto my stomach. I have to lean my forehead against the scratchy carpet and lift my hips, bringing my knees up so I can kneel up. I eventually make it, and I'm panting as I finally get a look at the room.

There's a step in front of me, and on that raised floor is a huge desk. Elias is sitting silently on a chair in front of the step, to my side. We make eye contact and he looks cautiously at me. I'm sure my anger is seeping through my eyes. He looks like he could be scared, but seems to be assured by the ropes I'm tied up in. Damn right. If it wasn't for these ropes, I swear...

He looks away as the sound of a door opening in front of us is heard. Behind the desk and to the side, at the back of the room, a single door is swinging shut behind a tall, slender man. He has sharp cheekbones, and pale skin surrounding his sunken in eyes, that seem to be shining black, but I suspect they're just very dark. He runs a hand through his long, thick black hair as he surveys the room.

"It sounds like I have guests," smiling at me with a toothy grin that makes me sick. It's him. I'll never forget that voice; I hate that voice.

I try and curl my mouth into a grimace but once again the tape restricts me.

"Don't screw up your face like that, pretty girl," he addresses me. It only makes me frown more, as that's all I can do.

"Sir," Elias finally speaks, getting up from the wooden chair he was sat in and dropping to one knee, holding his arms across his chest in an X shape. He momentarily bends his head down, and then looks back up at the man looking for acceptance.

"Stand up, Elias."

Elias reacts immediately and I want to throw up. What

kind of place are they running here?

The man clasps his hands and rubs them together, watching me, like he's eyeing up the big prize at a carnival. I'm his prize to claim. He grins again, and steeples his fingers, lightly putting them up to his mouth while he thinks.

"Good work, Elias. You can leave now. You'll be rewarded for this." The man talks with less tease in his voice now, taking on his role as Elias's boss and ordering him around. He walks around his big desk as Elias nods his head again and leaves. The man slowly strolls towards me, hopping down the step and allowing his lips to curl up again once Elias is gone.

He stands in front of me, and one second I'm looking at his legs, clad in metallic silver trousers, and the next, he's crouched down, fingers pressed together and elbows resting on his knees. I can feel his breath on my face; he's so close, yet he leans closer to talk to me.

"It's good to have you back."

I growl in a response, screwing my face up more.

"Oh we can't have that. I can't hear your pretty pretty voice. Let's fix that." Without a warning, before he's barely reached the end of his sentence, he rips the tape off of my mouth, pulling my skin, and taking out a few of the little hairs on my face. I cry out and pant, trying to control myself.

"You're vile. If it wasn't for these restraints you'd be

near dead right now," I spit at him, my voice low and sinister.

"Oh there it is," he says, ignoring my insults. "Pretty pretty voice," he murmurs again, half singing the words as he stands up and circles me.

"What do you want with me?" I ask, my voice dripping with venom. He ignores me and finishes his circle, this time kneeling at my side. An appreciative moan vibrates in his throat, and I turn my head the slightest bit in his direction, not actually wanting to look at him.

"These ropes..." he trails off. His finger trails along the ones around my wrists, and he lets it slip off so he strokes my arm. I snatch my hands away as best I can while I'm restrained. "It's so good to see you tied up like this," he purrs in my ear. I involuntarily gag. He stands up slowly. "You. At my will. At my mercy," he drags the word out.

"You're disgusting. You're sick! I'm going to stop you. Everyone around here. We'll bring you down, and I'll hurt you so-"

"And how will you do that, sweetheart?!" he suddenly yells, interrupting me and takes a few paces back. He throws out his arms and looks expectantly down at me. "Hm?! Because right now it looks like I have the upper hand, and...Oh..." he cups his ear and looks to the side as if listening intently for something. "And where are your little rebel friends now?"

"They'll realise I'm gone soon. They'll find me." I'm seething. I decide it's best to say as little as possible. I try to think strategically. I don't know the situation fully. I can't put myself out there and have it thrown back in my face. I don't know their plans. Why do they want me here? Why do they want me specifically? There's an ulterior motive here, and it's occurred to me now that I can't get cocky. I should remain submissive and passive for now.

The man looks down on me, almost sympathetically. "You really believe that," he says as a statement, his voice softer again. He turns quickly and strides back to his desk, sitting in a plush leather seat behind it. He kicks up his feet and leans them on his desk, crossing his legs at his ankles. He stares me down for a moment, as if he's genuinely confused about something.

"Why are you with them anyway?" he asks, perplexed, but I'm sure he's putting it on. "The Resistance," he mocks the name, waving his hands around. "Why aren't you on our side? You could have joined us when the soldiers first took over your land. Oh, the things you can become if you join us."

The soldiers. I grimace. He means the Ghosts.

"The potential you have!" he's suddenly loud again. I can't keep up with the changes his voice makes. He speaks fast.

"The powers for one. You think you have limited powers? You think you only have healer powers? You take after the healers in your family, oh sure of course you do, that's all it's ever been, just a blood line of healer after healer after healer..." he rolls his wrist and repeats it over and over again until he's speaking so fast the words get jumbled and then he stops abruptly. "That's what you think!"

This man scares me. He unnerves me as he brings his feet down to the floor again and leans forward in his chair, resting his elbows on his desk, staring at me intensely. "Shilo practice magic and sorcery. If you have powerful potential anyway, imagine how you could prosper in our world! Imagine a pretty girl like you on our side," he teases.

My mind is reeling. What is he saying? What is he getting at? I couldn't care less about the shilo. I would never betray my people; his words are useless.

My anger returns and I'm once again frustrated, groaning at nothing and everything at once, made much easier without the tape across my mouth. And he switches topics again.

"I could make you moan like that," he's standing up and leaning, arms straight, on his desk, peering over to get a good look at me. "I could have you howling...oh, the things I would do..." he slowly climbs up onto his desk and inches over it, jumping down in front of me again. I blanch at his proximity and his words. "And you would love it…or hate it, depending on my mood."

This man. The familiar sensation of my skin crawling is back in full force. This guy is crazy. He's insane. The way he moves is like a panther, so slick and controlled, almost elegant, if he wasn't so creepy. Like a tiger stalking it's prey. But there's a sense of instability to it.

"You're crazy. And disgusting. You can never have me." I'm sickened.

"Maybe I am. And you're right. I can't have you. Not fully," he stands again. All his moving around makes me feel dizzy. "Because you have eyes for someone else, don't you, pretty girl?" He says, looking back over his shoulder as he saunters away.

I try not to give away any emotions, but I let my face fall momentarily, and he catches me do it. "Caught a nerve have I? I knew it. Let me think…I wouldn't dare say Elias, not now anyway. Although you can't deny he's gorgeous isn't he?" He winks at me, and then taps his lip in thought. "Tall, dark and handsome, perhaps? Well that narrows it down to the 'legends' you hang around with. Ooh, maybe it's the dreamy leader that has your panties in a bunch," he taunts. He knew all along where he was going with this, he's just winding me up. He's trying to get a reaction from me, but I won't give him the satisfaction.

"Cat got your tongue?" he says after I'm silent for a moment. I sneer at him.

"Oh pretty baby. You don't want a guy like him anyway. You want someone like me. Someone who will appreciate you for what you are. Worship you."

"You're bluffing. You don't know who or what I am."

"Maybe, maybe not. I won't give away the punch line. You'll find the answers you seek in your own time. Until then..." he presses a button on the intercom he has on his desk, "...Men? She's ready to be taken down to storage." He grins evilly at me and I know I'm being taken down to that desolate warehouse place again.

The doors behind me are pushed open fiercely, and I'm once more being lifted up by my upper arms. I can already picture the bruises I'll have.

"One second!" The man says, pulling something out of a drawer in his desk. His quickly strides towards me with a roll of tape, unravelling it harshly as he gets closer.

"Don't forget this," he says, but mostly to me as he sticks another length of tape over my mouth. He inches his face close to mine, and uses his teeth to rip the tape. He smooth's it across my face and cups my chin for a moment, but I shake him off viciously. He looks down at me with disgust suddenly, now we have company I suspect, and with a flick of a wrist we are permitted to leave. I feel a sharp prick in my neck. I try to speak, resisting the syringe piercing my skin but it's useless. I can feel the contents of it beginning to flow through my veins. I'm not impervious with this rope around me; otherwise they wouldn't have been able to break through my skin. Oh, and it's strong. I feel it working fast and I'm soon blacking out.

"Mari, what is it?" I ask her, seeing her worried expression as she comes gallivanting towards me.

"Oracle…it's Kayin!" she yells breathlessly before she reaches me. My muscles tense up at the tone of her voice. "I went to check on her and Elias. They're gone. I can't find them. She…There are drag marks…Like feet. And-" she's panting hard from her long run over here, I suspect. Her sentences are short as she tries to explain and she's trying to tell me what she saw by scraping her feet along the floor. "I think Kayin's been taken. They could be in danger!" she says more clearly after a big breath.

I whistle to get the attention of the Four, and start moving with Mari back to where Kayin and Elias had gone out to train, where I thought they were safe. I see what Mari is talking about immediately and quickly enough the Four appear with us, and feel the atmosphere right away. With silent communication, through a series of looks, we agree something bad has happened and we begin following the drag marks. They break off every now and then but some more will be spotted in the distance quickly. We follow them until we find tyre marks in the dirt, from a skid start where the tyres have spun before moving off, but they disappear.

"We have no idea what way to go any more," Mari says, frantically turning in a circle to find some kind of clue.

"It won't help if we start panicking," the Vehement tells her cousin. She nods and gulps and tries to calm herself. They look to me expectantly.

"What do you suggest?" the Divine speaks up, looking for some kind of leadership.

I look into the distance. For a second, while the others can't see my face, I let my expression drop and I know my forehead is creased with worry. Damn it, Kayin. Where can you be? Where have you gone?

I push my shoulders back and put on a determined face as I turn to look at the others.

"It's been long enough. We have suffered long enough and lost too much to wait any more. We know where their HQ is. We know where the prison is. And we have explosives and a powerful army." I look at each of the faces of the people in front of me. "I think we're ready. Now two of our people have gone missing, enough's enough. Now we move. We need two teams. We're going to attack."

Weapons are made; the rogues are packed up, suited up,

and ready to follow the Four into battle. They've all covered themselves in their war paint, proudly letting spectators know whom they are fighting for.

The Four are leading the first team and are heading directly to HQ. The other trusted rogues are leading the rest and they are going to take the explosives to the prison. Some of the Four will join them later for help, assuming all goes well at HQ.

The Four all have determined grimaces on their face as their army builds up behind them. With a low growl, the Oracle orders them to move, and it is only heard because their people are so silent. So filled with built up anticipation and running on adrenaline. This is what they have been waiting for. All the stories and myths that tell of this moment, it is happening.

It is a solemn march to HQ. All that can be heard is the sound of feet on the dry land. The Oracle stops them when they stand a foot away from Ervon Gorge.

The Oracle steps forward then, taking a deep breath. He is confident in his power despite it being the one he uses least. With closed eyes and an out stretched hand he summons a large boulder from the bottom of the gorge, large enough to comfortably fit three people, four at a push, but there is no use risking it at this point. The rest of the Four usher their fellow rogues onto the boulder as the

Oracle holds it hovering at the side of the gorge, easy to step onto. Three at a time, all holding on to each other. The Oracle uses his telekinesis to transport the boulder from one end of the gorge to the other, while the Four organise the rest of the task. The boulder is shaky but completely safe as it travels through the air.

The journeys are almost over. The Oracle raises a hand to his head, the power is taking a toll on him but he can handle it. He gets the Divine, Cryptic and Vehement over safely and then brings the boulder back to his side for the final journey. He steps onto the middle and has his eyes open, palms facing down as he controls the boulder beneath his feet.

He is silently congratulated with pats on the back from the Four as he steps onto the safety of the other side of the gorge. Eyes are on him with proud smiles as he walks through the crowd and takes his place at the front with his friends.

"Here's the plan," he says, turning to face them when the trees begin thickening and the menacing dark building that is HQ can be seen in the shadowy distance. "Cryptic, if you will," he motions with his arm to the army before them. The Cryptic concentrates on his power, taking into consideration the surface area and how many of them there are, and then casts his invisibility dome over them all. The

Oracle nods with a hint of a smile in gratitude.

"We're going to surround them, cover every exit. Once we expose ourselves, I refuse to let them sneak Kayin out, or anyone, for that matter. They're all going down." Olon keeps his voice low and looks at his people one by one. They all understand. They are all with him. Their loyalty makes him smile. As his lips curl up, he watches the small action reflect across the faces of the rogues.

"We can fight. We're capable of that, more than capable. We're good. But so are they. We have people to tend to wounds, but the quicker we get Kayin out the safer we'll be. We need our healer back if we intend to take them down. The Cryptic and I will go in. The Divine and Vehement, they'll be with you on the outside securing the exits. Once they're no longer an issue, you'll all join us. We'll give you the signal. Listen for it," Olon finishes. He keeps his speech short and to the point; he doesn't know what is going on inside and he doesn't want to waste any more time. He looks to his friends in this battle with him and they look back at him with reassuring nods. It is enough.

There is only so much he can say; it wouldn't change how ready they are. This is the time, they have trained and prepared and they are as ready as they'll ever be. This is no longer a time for words, but for action.

They march further forward, still concealed by their

invisibility dome, keeping their feet light in case they are heard. Once they are close they see the big front doors unguarded, but know there are Ghost Men ready to appear and defend their land.

"Oracle, I think this is for you," the Vehement pipes up, whispering to her friend. Olon gives her a knowing look and a smile. Then he exits the safety of the dome so he can be seen. As soon as he makes it close enough to the doors, just as expected, two Ghosts appear with their white staffs, ready to strike him down. Undeterred by their fighting stance, the Oracle saunters towards them, and lifts his hand to click his fingers twice. One after the other, the Ghosts relax and stand up straight, no longer threatened by the Oracle. The rogues look on with amazement, but are not surprised. They know just how powerful the Oracle can be. Only a look is needed after that to control the two Ghosts and lead them away from the doors.

The Cryptic and Vehement share a look and he gives the Vehement a nod of permission. Without missing a beat the Vehement leaps out of the dome and bounds up to where the Oracle has taken the Ghosts, and easily ploughs them both into the ground. She stomps on their heads, cracking their helmet masks, and proceeds to pound into them until they are no longer moving.

Knocked out or dead, the others don't know, but they

don't question it as the Oracle and Vehement join them back in the invisibility dome. The Oracle and the Cryptic prepare to split off from the group to enter their headquarters.

"This is when you circle the building. Make sure there are no other exits and if there are, make sure they're unusable. The Vehement and Divine will be here if anyone gets into trouble."

Once they are all agreed, the dome vanishes above them and they are visible once again. They all move quickly to dispose of any others exits and surround the building. Meanwhile, the Cryptic has erected a new small dome to just hide himself and the Oracle, and they stroll right through the front doors.

The floors and walls lined with a dull grey paint and the dim lighting instantly decrease their morale, but they push forward, inching their way through the halls so silently. They pass a few doors on either side, and slow to peer inside the windows of the wood, but the rooms look like nothing more than small classrooms or offices, and they are empty. There are joining corridors breaking off left and right, but they decide not to stray from the main hallway yet. They pass a few stairwells, but still they move straight. When they come to almost the end of the long hall, they stop where two double doors are on either side of them.

With a look and silent communication, they turn left.

Slowly, ever so discreetly, they open the doors into what looks like a small church; some kind of place of worship. There is a podium up on a step at the front on the room and pews line up on either side of them. But they aren't looking at the furniture, or the décor of dark painted walls and dark red and black cloths that seem to drape across the walls and ceiling. They aren't even paying attention to the stained glass window on the right of them that doesn't seem to help any light get into the room. What stops the Oracle and Cryptic in their tracks is the herd of Ghost Men that fill the room. Sitting completely still in the pews, looking towards the front. Gathered together at the front, hands together in silent prayer. Standing by the window and basking in the dim light. It is an eerie setting. Their white uniforms contrast to the muted colour of the room intensely.

One of the Ghosts sitting in one of the back pews slightly turns towards the door, just as it softly shuts behind the Cryptic and Oracle. They don't dare breathe in this room. They are stock still, attention on the only Ghost that seems to have noticed anything. Years seem to pass in what are actually only a few short moments, until he finally resumes his place, turning back to the front. The two of them slowly back up, waiting another few moments to survey the room so they know no one is looking in their direction, and then as slowly as they can they open up the door and back out.

The Oracle acts quickly and quietly once they are back into the bleak hallway. He takes off one of his belts and softly threads it through the handles of the doors, tying it tightly but so slowly, trying not to knock the doors in anyway that might alert the hoard of Ghost Men inside. He hopes it will be enough to stall them at least and buy them time.

At the end of the hall, there is a metal door, and as they approach it, they realise it was some kind of lift. They have nothing to lose yet, so summon the lift by pressing the button. The door opens with a gush of air and they step inside, looking at the floor options. There are eight floors above ground, and then a -1 under the ground floor. Underneath that is -2 (Warehouse). This strikes a chord in Olon, and in an instant all that fills his mind is the image of Kayin, scared and shaking after the first time she was kidnapped. She is explaining what happened to her, how she was saying that she was tied up in something that looked like a storage facility, shelves and shelves surrounding her. Almost like a warehouse...

Without another thought, Olon lets out such a high pitch whistle it will be undetectable to the Ghosts but his people surrounding area will hear it. All he knows is Kayin is close. She could be right below them for all he knew, back in that Warehouse. The invisibility dome is unneeded now they have given the signal. Within a minute the doors at the other end of the long hall are thrown open and the Divine and Vehement run in, followed by the rogues as they start filling up the area. As soon as Olon sees his partners inside, he hits the button for the Warehouse. But nothing happens other than igniting a flashing red light. He is unable to get down there without a passkey.

From the disruption the rogues cause as they enter and the whistle Olon had used to summon them, soon enough they can hear heavy feet descending the stairs and running down corridors. Their presence is known. The Cryptic and Oracle step out of the elevator to join their people, but movement in the corner of Olon's eye stops him. A man is sprinting towards him from one of the side corridors, and instinctively the Oracle kicks in and he hunches forward, ramming into the approaching man and using his momentum to lift and tip him over his shoulder, throwing him onto his back on the other side of him. Olon gets down on one knee next to the man and pins him down by his throat with one hand, uses one of his knees to hold down the man's arm, and quickly frisks him for a passkey with his other hand.

When he finds what he needs, he throws a swift punch to knock the man out, stands briskly and steps back into the elevator. He catches the Cryptic's eye before he closes the doors. He has a questioning look on his face. Why would you go alone? He is silently asking the Oracle. Olon only looks at his close friend apologetically.

"They need you out here," he tells him. He puts the passkey in the slot and presses the button for the Warehouse.

I curl my toes, wishing I could do more than that to show my disgust for this man. I've had my shoes and socks taken off of me; any jewellery I had, my belts and pouches. I've been stripped down to my jeans and tank top. I am still unable to do anything while tied up in these stupid ropes, preventing me from using my powers. And on top of that I now have normal rope tied around me keeping me pinned back onto a wooden chair. The ropes scratch my skin, but I can't stop moving, can't stop trying to writhe away from this man's advances. There isn't a lot I can do though.

He strolls round to the back of my chair, and quickly grabs hold of the top to yank it back. I am suspended mid air, if he lets go I'll fall onto my back, but that doesn't stop me from shaking my body and trying to make it hard for him to hold me up.

I stop instantly when I feel the familiar sting of leather lash across my skin. The welt slowly starts rising on my arm, and it stings more as he slowly drags the riding crop back over the wound. It is all too easy to hurt me when I don't have my impervious power and I am trussed up like this. At least this time he doesn't break skin.

"That's better. Obey me. Stay still, pretty," he coos in my ear. This is all it has been for however long I've been here now. The familiar musky smell of the storage area is the only thing to fill my nose apart from when he leans in so close I can smell his breath. My eyes can only see him, in the dim light he's placed me under. Even the shelves that I know stack up high around me fade into the shadows. The only thing I can hear is his voice and my futile screams and groans against the tape across my mouth. He is just taunting me. He'll ask me things about the Resistance; rhetorical mostly since he knows I can't reply anyway and will smack me with that dreaded crop when I don't play along the way he wants. Not to mention the incessant slurs which resemble sexual harassment.

I look away and take a deep breath to control the pain as he sets my chair back upright. I see him walk in front of me and stand slightly at my side, but he doesn't turn back to me. He faces forward. I take this chance to look up at him, but he seems to be occupied with something else; something happening elsewhere. While I calm myself, the blood rushing passed my ears subsides and I hear what he is hearing.

My heart picks up pace and starts thumping against my

chest. I try to ignore the excited butterflies in my stomach. It is faint. So faint, but I can still hear the thumping of feet, the clashing of bodies and weapons, the grunts and groans of battle. Anything but the perfect silence of HQ is unusual, but hearing these sounds only means one thing. They have come to get me. We are finally taking the Ghosts down. I want to believe the look on this man's face is something of fear or terror, anxiety maybe. But as quickly as the emotions flash across his face, he hides them again, putting his tough guy façade back up.

"Well it seems we have company, hm? Some of your little friends, perhaps?" he is smiling sarcastically at me, clasping his hands together in faux excitement. "Oh delightful, maybe we can have a tea party," his face drops, he can't even be bothered to keep up the act.

What I hear, that he didn't notice while he was talking, makes my tummy churn. The very subtle ding of the lift as it descends. I don't know whether to anticipate help coming for me or another shilo or even a Ghost Man coming. Either way we are no longer the only ones on this floor.

13

Olon hesitantly steps out of the elevator when the door opens on the lowest underground floor. While alert for any potential threat, he takes a moment to register the mere size of the warehouse. It is much bigger than the building above. It has obviously been expanded underground.

He slowly moves forward, on his toes ready for any attack. The room he is in is large enough but there are big, sturdy steel doors lining the walls around him. His movements are fuelled knowing Kayin is around here somewhere. He knows it. He is onto something, in his gut he knows he has got it right. He doesn't have time now to assess his feelings, but for her they are strong. That is all he knows. He is feeling extremely protective, and his only objective now is to get her to safety.

The first door on his right is labelled 'Freezer'. Olon shudders at the idea of Kayin being locked in there. That isn't it though, that can't be it. He keeps moving, scanning over the different labelled doors, peering into the windows. He has a strong sense that while he is alone in this big room, somewhere behind one or more of these doors, there are people. Not friendly people.

I can't hear anything else. Someone is down here, but they aren't coming in here; at least not yet.

"What are you thinking about?" the man says, standing behind me again and sliding his hands over my shoulders. He stops one after it's curled around my throat, but his right hand keeps going, sliding over my chest and skimming my cleavage. My head jerks as I gag involuntarily, but he doesn't notice and keeps his left hand in place. He grips my jaw with his right hand.

"What's going on in that pretty head of yours?" he leans his face down next to mine, his black hair falling against my skin.

I try to recoil at his proximity but he holds me in place. Everything is so futile. I can't help feeling so deflated about this situation. I have no leverage. No chance. Or do I?

I let myself relax, dropping my head back. He straightens up at my sudden movement, not used to my body being so slack. I close my eyes and try to sigh, trying my hardest to make it sound sad and full of longing.

He lets out a deep, smug chuckle. "Oh, what's this, honey?"

I open my eyes again and arch my back. He doesn't even bother to look me in the eye, instead lets his gaze wander straight to my cleavage again. He shamelessly stares at me, circling round to my side and drinking in the sight. I know I'm giving him exactly what he wants. I just hope he is too blinded by his own agenda to figure out it isn't genuine.

I try to make the change in attitude subtle. Like I have given up and have slowly decided to let him have his way. If I turn on the act too quickly and too rushed, he will suspect it.

With my head still hanging back over the chair, I roll it in his direction to look at him, taking another deep breath to show my lack of interest in trying to resist.

"Too tiring, is it?" he asks, playing right into my hands, spurring me on. I nod with heavy eyelids, letting them fall shut briefly to emphasise my fatigue. When I open them again he is licking his lips. I can't begin to fathom my disgust. At least he isn't using the crop any more, just keep that in mind.

I don't quite have a plan to follow with this, I am just sick of him trying to come on to me, taunting me, hurting me. In my mind, if I give in, he will stop trying so hard. Maybe I can get that leverage I'm hoping for. Get him doing what I want him to without him realising it.

He kneels in front of me and puts his hands on my knees. I have to resist the urge to respond with any negative actions I want to make whenever he touches me. Instead I pick my head up and look down at him softly.

"Are you excited to see your little friends?" he refers to the faint noise we can hear upstairs. I shrug my shoulders indifferently. At this action his lips curl up into an evil smile. "Have I finally broken you?" He laughs like he can't believe it.

He is getting what he wants. To him it seems I am no longer so adamant about reuniting with the Resistance. I start to cough, as best I can when I can't open my mouth. It is a dry cough that makes my chest jump up and down and my shoulders shake. I look at him with my eyebrows pulled together sadly.

"Do you need a drink?" he says, like he is talking to a small child. "Want me to get you a little something to drink?"

I want to roll my eyes at the way he is talking to me as if I am his plaything. Although, right now I guess I am.

Regardless, I give him a little nod. If I can get him out of this room to face whoever it is that is out there, I can figure out if they are a threat or a friend.

He stands up and backs away from me, smirking as he goes, then turns around and walks forward to the door. The light from outside the door illuminates the warehouse briefly and I hear his footsteps echo in the main room. Before the door has even shut again I hear skin hit skin as people attack each other. I hear a sickening thwack just as the door shuts completely. My eyes are wide and I am trying my best to listen for anything but I can't hear any movement after that.

I try to keep my heavy breathing under control as I anticipate what will happen next. It slips my mind sometimes that I have never really been in a fight or any kind of battle. I have done some training in the Resistance, but not a lot. I briefly fought that Ghost Man. I've been kidnapped, but there's a big difference between trying to stay conscious while you're pounded on and actually fighting. I am not a soldier. So far I've acted more like the damsel in distress. I just have to stay calm. I can't lose my cool.

The door opens a slither and I see a shadow sneak into the room. I bunch my hands into fists in fear. I have a dim lamp hanging over my head but in this darkness I may as well be sitting on top of a lighthouse. I'm not hard to find. So if it is a member of the Resistance why haven't they come straight for me?

Whoever it is, they are good at staying quiet. Maybe they

aren't moving at all. If I hadn't seen them slip in, I would still think I was alone.

I suddenly hear the flap of a jacket above me but I can't look up because the light is in my eyes. A body drops next to me, on their knees, after jumping from the high stack of shelves. I gasp as best I can at the shock of their appearance. They're still for a moment, then they begin to stand up.

I didn't realise how much my body was longing for Olon until I feel myself pushing towards him, all kinds of ropes digging into my skin and holding me back but I keep squirming, keep trying to wiggle towards him as he stands up until I feel my chair swaying.

He quickly catches it before it falls over and sets me straight. I just catch his concerned expression before he disappears behind me to untie the ropes. I jolt forward as I am released, pushing myself off of the chair and onto my knees, groaning in a bittersweet way at the freedom. Olon rushes towards me again, taking off the dreaded orange ropes that restrict my powers and my limbs fall free. He throws them to the side and then makes me turn to him, gently putting his finger under my chin and lifting my face up to his.

He searches my eyes; I watch his flick between mine. The sadness in his usually sparkling blue eyes makes my heart break, and then I realise that sadness is because of me.

Delicately, he begins peeling the tape off of my mouth. All my senses are on high alert and my skin is tingling from his touch, yet I can barely feel it as he takes the tape off and drops it on the floor.

Acting on emotion, I throw my arms around his neck and tackle him to the floor by accident. But he catches me just fine and I hold him tight. I won't let him move yet. I need a moment. A calm moment to get over what I have just been through, a moment to recollect myself before we go outside, and face all that is happening up there without us.

I feel his fingers dig into my skin as he holds me tighter and the moments pass by us. I feel safe briefly. As much as I can't believe I am doing this, holding him like this, it also feels right. It feels overdue. To be lying beside him while he comforts me.

I sit up slowly next him as reality sinks in.

"Is he dead?" I ask quietly, looking at the floor. I heard the crack of something against the floor, and suddenly Olon's coming in here freely? Something happened to that vile man.

"No," I look up when I hear his voice. "Just unconscious." He follows my lead and sits up next to me, still so close. His proximity is intoxicating.

"Why were you on top of the shelves?" I let a little laugh escape my lips as I say it, imagining him up there, creeping along. He smiles at me.

"I was scoping the place out. I didn't know how many people might have been in here."

It is that kind of logic that makes him a good fighter and makes me frankly quite pathetic in that field. I didn't even think of something like that.

"Kayin, did he do this to you?" he asks, now looking down at my bare skin, holding my arm in his hands. Some of the bright red marks are still fresh and still sting, and some of the older deeper ones have dried blood across the top. I nod in response, not wanting to tell him out loud. He furrows his brows in silent anger.

"Don't trust Elias," I suddenly blurt out, remembering. "The ropes he used to 'monitor' my powers; he was just figuring out how to prevent me from using them. I don't know what they're made of but those ropes stop me from using my powers. That's how he so easily captured me. He tied me up when I was willing to work with him and then he took me and these men grabbed me and threw me in the truck and we came here and I don't even know how we came here across the gorge and that guy, oh, that guy is vile. He makes my skin crawl. He said things that I just-" I have to gasp for air as I become emotional. I shiver at the memory of it. "That's why I couldn't fight back or teleport away. It was awful," I say, once I've caught my breath. My voice is a little shakier than I'd like.

Olon cups my cheek and looks at me with an expression that calms me straight away. "Let's get out of here."

He helps me up onto my shaky legs and makes sure I am steady before he takes my hand and strides towards the door. He opens it slowly, holding my hand close to his body, meaning he keeps me close. I follow him out and almost walk into the back of him when he stops suddenly in front of me. I peer around his body to what he is looking at, not expecting to see a smudged pool of blood on the floor with its owner nowhere around.

Olon instinctively grabs me and pulls me behind him, backing against the wall so I am covered and he can try to locate the man. I am blinded by his body and can't see; just trust that he knows what he is doing.

I yell as Olon suddenly screams, and his body blanches against me. For a second his hands grab me tighter, but then he lets go and his body goes limp. He drops to his knees before me, and then I see the blood drip on the floor. He falls on his side in pain, groaning as he goes down.

"Olon!" I cry, just about to go down to the floor too, but the movement in the corner of my eye catches my attention and stops me.

"Olon? First name basis with the legendary Oracle, are we? That's quite an achievement, honey." The man stands opposite me, his voice broken up by his strained breaths. He doesn't look very stable on his feet, and he has blood across his forehead. But that doesn't stop him smirking at me with bloody teeth, wiping Olon's blood off of his knife across his shirt.

"Jealous?" I ask. It is a risky game but I go for it. "I don't even know your name."

Not anticipating my answer he cocks his eyebrow and looks at me with intrigue. I flash him a smirk of my own. I step over Olon without a glance as I walk towards him. "Did you not get me my drink?" I pout my bottom lip, as I skip a little closer.

Not understanding the situation, he suddenly holds his knife up to stop me from approaching him any more. But I roll my eyes with a small laugh.

"Oh please, I'm not going to attack you." I finally make it in front of him. I stand close, happy to be out of the ropes and knowing he can't hurt me with that knife. I try to ignore Olon's moans that are pulling on my heartstrings. I want nothing more than to run to his side and cry and do all I can to heal him and hold his hand reassuringly. Maybe soon. I have to push that to the back of my mind for now.

"You have to understand," I begin slowly, looking him

up and down in what I hope is a sultry manner. "I was brought here unwillingly. I was ambushed and tied up painfully," I raise my eyebrow at him, pressing a finger against his chest as he seems to relax but is still hesitant. "You can understand my resistance, can't you?" I look him in the eye, hanging my mouth open slightly and tilting my head.

"We knew you wouldn't come willingly. We had to restrain you. And you didn't hold back when you insulted me over and over." I think he finds me intimidating, now that I am fully capable of using my powers. I have to make this believable.

"Well of course I didn't, I was furious with you." I close my eyes for a second and try to listen for Olon's heartbeat while concentrating on the creature in front of me. "I was furious. Not so much now, because I'm not tied up against my will any more." Though I am looking into his dark, dark eyes, I am thinking about Olon. I hear him gasp in pain behind me. I know he is probably catching on to what I am doing, but thankfully he doesn't give it away. I have to hurry now.

I lean up on my tiptoes to get my lips close to his ear. I press my palm flat against his chest. I can feel his heartbeat beneath my hand, fast from nerves, but still beating strong and steady. Like Olon's should be.

"Do you see where I'm coming from?" I coo into his ear just like he's done to me before. I feel him nod his head beside mine, and then he places the hand that isn't holding the knife on the small of my back. I almost have him now. "So if you want to try this again, without the assumption that I won't come willingly, maybe we can get somewhere," I am almost growling, my voice is so low as I try to seduce him. I almost break.

I hear the knife clang against the floor as he drops it and uses both hands to pull me up against him. I undo the first few buttons of his shirt while he feels me up. Not long now, please don't break now. You're a soldier; do it, do it. I slide my hand into his shirt and flatten it back against his skin above his heart. I have to distract him so he doesn't see the golden glow from my hand. With my other hand I grab a handful of his hair and yank it back, and then with a shaky breath, I cover his lips with mine. I'm working on the assumption that no matter what his original job was, he is dropping his responsibilities to pursue his personal feelings.

Thankfully he responds immediately. This is what he wants. He wants me, whether it is like this or tied up in one of his erotic fantasies, it doesn't matter, I realise. His hormones have got the best of him and he just wants me, despite whatever ulterior motives he had for getting me here in the first place. Despite whatever ulterior motives I have, I understand he just wants this opportunity. For some reason he is drawn to me.

I deepen the kiss to keep him occupied even though every bone in my body is willing me against it. He puts one of his hands on my thigh and pulls my knee up to his hip. I accidentally feel the blood that has dripped into his hair as I run my fingers through it. It makes me shiver but I try to keep my body under control. And then I go for it. You're a soldier, a soldier. Don't be a baby. Don't get emotional. I keep telling myself, feeling tears building behind my eyes as I use my power for all the wrong reasons. My hand begins glowing and before he realises what is happening I have already slowed his heart a considerable amount to make an impact. He breaks the kiss and looks straight into my eyes. His almost black irises are twinkling with the realisation of what I am doing. Just exactly what I am capable of.

"Go to hell," I whisper with a shaky breath as he releases me. He falls away from my touch but I still have him under my control. I keep my right hand up directed at him while he clutches desperately at his chest, and my other hand flies up to my mouth to stifle a sob that escapes my lips.

"You sly bitch," he coughs and splutters, gasping for air. "Though, I wouldn't expect...anything less..."

Slowly falling to his knees, I want to put him through hell before he gets there, but my conscience is too much for me and I just want to get this done. It is so wrong. But necessary, right?

I close my eyes to get it over with quickly. I feel the beat of his heart in my hand; hear it in my head. And when it finally stops I hear his slack body hit the floor. I let the tears fall, not willing to open my eyes and see him. I quickly spin on my heel and look down to Olon. He has rolled onto his back, clutching his stomach, and I see the huge gash that disgusting man has ripped across Olon's torso with his knife. The sight of Olon makes me a little less sad about killing him, and only brings on more tears.

I cry as I run towards him and fall to his side finally.

"I'm here, I'm here. I'm going to help you." My voice is quiet; it is all I could manage in this emotional state. Unsure of where to start, I rip off my tank top and hold it against his tummy. Anything to stop the bleeding. It doesn't even faze me that I am sat in my bra in front of Olon. I don't care. I reach for his hand, put it on top of the cloth and hold my hand on top of his.

"You're going to be alright, okay? Please. Be alright, for me."

I pick up on his heartbeat, my hand glowing so bright with the energy I am putting into it. It is slow and doesn't have any kind of steady rhythm, so I work hard to try and bring it back to something that sounds healthy. It seems to help him a bit; he doesn't seem to have so much trouble breathing as he just did.

He delicately lifts his other hand and puts it on top of mine on his stomach, so my hand is between both of his. He sucks in a raspy breath, catching my attention and making me look at him. He manages a small smile for me but it is full of pain and there is blood in his mouth, which only makes me feel worse.

I don't know what else to do. I could keep his heart steady forever, but it won't be any use if he runs out of blood, and his wound is soaking up my top fast.

"Oh, Olon" I whisper. I squeeze his hand and he wheezes. "My Oracle. Lead me. Tell me what to do," I can't help the sobs that escape me. It is a messy cry. The kind of cry that makes your shoulders jump up and down, makes your eyes go red and your face becomes blotchy. "Help me help you!" I almost scream at him. He blinks so slowly. I need to get out of here. This isn't the right environment to help him. I take my hand away from his and cup his cheek. I caress his face with my thumb for a second.

Then in a moment of pure desperation and emotion, I lean down and kiss him gently. Anything to get the taste of the vile man off my lips. Anything to get the taste of Olon onto my lips. The blood doesn't bother me. His lips still feel like velvet, but they are so cold. We need warmth. I cry against his lips and I know my tears are falling onto his face. He briefly kisses me back, I feel him hold his lips to mine but he is too weak. I separate from him and bury my face into the crook of his neck, taking him with me as I teleport away from this place.

I know we have moved without feeling it, but Olon doesn't realise. I feel him flinch as he feels the dirt beneath him. I have taken him back to our own headquarters, just outside of the room where all our medical things are stored. Olon groans and lifts his knee up, trying to bend his body in half from the pain. I realise I have accidentally let go of his heart as we teleported.

"Sorry." I quickly regain control and he slightly uncurls himself again as I bring it to a steady rhythm.

I stand up and run into the medical room. From my glowing hands I know I still have him under control even though I've moved away.

"Don't die, Olon! You hear me? You stay strong, you are not allowed to die!" I yell at him from inside the room, rummaging through draws and cabinets, frantically grabbing for what I need.

I run back out with an abundance of bandages and cloth and a bowl of warm water, that I spill half of on the way back, and cleaning fluids that will sting but will be nothing compared to his actual wound.

I know he is being very brave, hiding his pain. I know he is writhing in agony but he won't let it show. This is a lot worse than he is letting on. I knew it from the state of his heart before I picked the beat up again. He is dying.

"Damn it, Olon," my voice is breathy as I mumble in frustration. I take my top away from his stomach and now out in the open it occurs to me that I am still half naked. It's fine, it doesn't matter, carry on. Deep breaths.

I replace my soaking top with fresh cloth to try and wipe away the excess of blood to see just what I am working with. I dip some clean cloth into the water and try to clean around the wound. I bite my lip when I see it. His torso really is ripped open, that man really did a number on him. Where did he even come from? He jumped out of nowhere, to get Olon like that. Fresh tears spill down my cheeks. I close my eyes and try to block out Olon's moans of pain. It is getting too much for him. I can only hold onto his heart for so long until it becomes pointless. I won't be able to stitch this up in time. It is too big.

I wish my Nana were here. She could do it. She'd pull something out of her sleeve and fix the situation. It breaks my heart because I am so close to losing Olon right now. He saved me when I had no one. And I can't do the same for him. I don't have the power.

Oh.

The power. That's it. I'm missing a power. I watched my Nana use it on herself. She shut her wound up. The gold flashes that jumped in and out of her skin...How did Mari describe it? Like fish jumping in and out of a river. I need that right now.

I settle onto my knees and hover above Olon.

"This is it, okay?" I speak to him. He looks up at me with glazed eyes. I smile at him and quickly wipe my eyes on the back of my hand. "This will fix it, alright? I can do this."

As I lift my hand, Olon catches it. I look at him but he has laid his head back and shut his eyes. He is preparing himself. For death or for healing, I don't know. But he is relaxed. Still he squeezes my hand and gives me the reassurance I need before letting go. Please pull this off, I beg myself.

I don't know how to go about starting this but I decide to just lay my hands across his torso as gently as I can. I imagine it vividly in my head. I can picture the gold streaks of light weaving between his wound, stitching it up much faster than I ever could, and doing a much better job of it too. They would pull the gash together; heal the skin, leaving the faintest of scars. So much fainter than how time would heal the wound, with a thick ugly scar that would last a lifetime. These gold streaks would heal him until his skin was almost clear and flawless again.

So that's what I do. Apparently. With my eyes shut through the whole thing and unaware of what I am doing while imagining it, I have healed him. I move my hand blindly expecting to feel his wound, but it is flat. It is healed. He coughs and finds his breath and his heart beats steadily on its own. I open my eyes in shock when I feel nothing but his smooth skin, and the blood covering him, but you would never be able to guess where it came from. His chest heaves up and down with each breath he takes. For a moment he just lays there with wide eyes looking up to the sky, breathing in and out. Then he leans up and rests back on his elbows so he can get a look at the miracle in front of us.

"I did it," I whisper, and start crying with happiness.

I am so emotional. Olon sits up slowly, as if he may rip open again with any sudden movement. When he doesn't, he looks up to me and laughs. He grins at me and though his mouth is still messy with blood, the sight doesn't bother me any more because I know it is just that, just a mess. Nothing more. He is fine. He laughs some more with ecstasy. It is infectious and I can't help but giggle with him. It is all fine.

"I did it," I repeat, still in shock but so much happier.

"Oh, Kayin."

There is something about the way he says my name. It isn't sympathetic. It isn't relief, though I'm sure that is in there somewhere. It isn't as if he just remembered something. The way my name rolls off his tongue, it wipes the smile off my face. It sends a chill down my spine. It is need. He says my name with need. In which sense, I don't know. But I am happy to be here for him regardless. He picks up the water I had fetched and takes a swig from the bowl, splashes it around his mouth and then spits it out behind him. The look he is giving me makes my insides turn to mush. I wouldn't be surprised if he is reading my mind, seeing all the different emotions he makes me feel just by the simple act of saying my name.

He wipes a hand across his stomach again, without breaking eye contact with me. He takes a deep breath and smiles again, pleased with the results.

I don't have time to react as the hand he just had on his stomach reaches out to me and grips the back of my neck, pulling my face towards his. He makes sure I catch his eyes one last time before he closes them and kisses me hard. It is so different from the way I kissed him back in that warehouse. The delicate way I had lowered myself to him so as not to hurt him. The way I slowly traced his lips with mine. But this, this is fuelled with a different kind of desperation than mine. I was desperate for him to feel something, to live. Olon is just desperate for me. My libido rockets through the roof at this realisation, and I let him lay me down on the floor.

I reach up to twist my hands into his hair to keep his face close to mine as he follows me down and repositions his body so he is comfortably lying on top of me. I don't realise until it is actually happening, but this is what I've wanted all along. Those days I spent denying myself of feeling anything for him, telling myself I was just over romanticising him in my head. I pushed the thoughts away; I didn't let myself properly indulge in them. When I had inklings that maybe he cared for me, I dismissed those immediately too. It took two kidnappings and a near death experience to finally kiss each other. I could lay here forever.

He moves quickly against me. Any sign of pain from moments ago is completely gone. I have really helped him. This only spurs me on. It is like we are putting his new body to its limits. The bare skin of his torso rubs against my own, and for the first time I am glad I don't have my top on. His kisses are feverish and passionate and a soft moan escapes my throat. I circle my arms round his neck, so I can get him as close as I can. He moans as I hold him tightly, a much more guttural noise than mine, and lifts his body up, so he is on all fours above me, his hands on each side of my head and knees woven in between my legs. His head is still bowed down though because I refuse to let him get too far away even when he breaks the kiss.

I keep my eyes shut for a moment, basking in the after

glow of this feeling. When I open them and look at Olon above me he seems to be thinking things over in his mind, he looks deep in thought, troubled even. I ignore the small voice in the back of my mind that says he regrets it. I want him to stay hovering over me forever but I know we have to move. As reality sinks in I remember we are currently in the midst of a battle, but we aren't there.

"We need to go," I say quietly. Olon opens his eyes and smiles down at me, nodding his head reluctantly.

"I need a shirt," I add, and he again nods his head reluctantly with a small chuckle this time. He moves to the side and lets me sit up. I can't resist stealing a kiss before I stand up. Is this what it will be from now on? Or is it just a spur of the moment, caught up in the emotions scenario? He is the Oracle. He is a legend. As much as I think of him as Olon, my Olon, he is still the Oracle and he belongs to us all. Does he even have time for this kind of relationship? After all this is over, if we come out on top, what will life be like? We'll have to rebuild our town, our society, what will happen to us all?

My sudden deep thoughts are too much for me. I shake them from head as I jog to get a new shirt. I quickly find one in my room and shrug it over my head, and grab another pair of shoes to put on as well. Catching my reflection in a small mirror on the wall I notice how dirty I am; I still have the welts from the whip up my arms glowing red, I have a noticeable amount of blood on me, smudged across my clothes and my skin and matted in my hair. I suspect a lot of it is a mix of my own and Olon's.

I run back to him and see him standing up now. He has drying blood across his body too, and dirt and dust spread across his clothes and skin, like me. What a pair we must make. His hair is unruly, and his face is set back into the determination of the Oracle. He still looks beautiful. When he looks at me his expression doesn't change, but I see the glint in his eye as he holds his hand out for me to take. I run forward and grab it.

"Where to?"

"The prison."

14

I nod and look forward, picturing the prison in my mind until it appears in front of us, although it looks nothing like the big, strong building I remember.

My vision is blurred with dust, but beyond that I can see the structure of the building, with a huge gaping hole in the side. The brick is crumbling around it and I see a gathering of people to the side. My breath catches in my throat. They are getting out. I turn my walk into a sprint, as I am desperate to get closer to the scene in front of me.

I'm knocked to the floor before I get very close. Though winded, I try to sit up and breathe normally. I look up at the Ghost Man a few feet away from me. His staff is outstretched after knocking me down with it. Now, I'm looking properly, I see them appear everywhere. They are coming to defend the prison. To get the prisoners back and keep them locked away. But we have come too far and done too much to lose now. I have suffered too long to be knocked down by an over glorified man in a white suit and stay down. I have no wound apart from a little lack of breath, but I am fine to stand up and try again.

Before I have even made it to my knees however, he strikes me again, sending me across the floor onto my side. I grunt at the impact, and roll onto my stomach. Again I try to raise myself up but for a third time I am knocked back down.

"Stop!" I scream in frustration. I beat the floor with my fists and I swear I feel it shake beneath me. The odd feeling startles me. I look up just in time to see the Ghost Man lift his arms to strike me again, but I raise my hand and summon my power the quickest I ever have. My hand glows bright and in a moment the Ghost drops to the floor. I finally stand up again, breathing hard. I don't want this to become a common thing, using the power like this, and I am wary of how quickly I can use it like that. But as I look around and see Ghosts fighting, rogues fighting, prisoners escaping...I know this isn't the time to be soft. I am a warrior and they are the enemy.

I can feel the sweat collect on my forehead, making my fly away hairs stick to my skin. This desert heat is too much for all this fighting, especially when you can't get a clean breath because of the dust and rubble clouding the air. Across the grounds I see Mari and Selene, back-to-back and fighting the Ghost Men surrounding them. They hold hands and I see Mari knock one of them out, using her power to put them in a coma.

I intend to lift my arm and slow one of their hearts, but with anger racing through my veins, when I lift my arm it is as if I have picked up a huge shovel and knocked them out of the way. I watch one of the Ghost Men fly away from his position and get hurled across the ground, as if someone has thrown him. Looking to my hand and then looking around me, I am confused. What happened? Surely I didn't do that? I couldn't ignore the feeling in my arm though; it didn't feel like the heart controlling power. Did I do that?

The Ghost Men turn to me, thankfully leaving Mari and Selene alone, but now I have four of them to deal with.

"Supreme power," they chant in their robotic, monotone voices.

"What?!" I back up a few steps as they move forward in a line towards me.

"Kayin!" I hear my name called from somewhere. Glancing around I see the Vehement. She kicks away a Ghost and then looks at me again. "Get angry!"

That is her trick, isn't it? Getting angry. I look to the four Ghost Men in front of me. All right. Get angry.

I can feel a tight sensation in my gut; a feeling that is building and I have to let it go. Screwing my eyebrows together and setting my mouth in a firm line, I stamp down on the floor. It's what my body is telling me to do. Again, I feel the land shake beneath me, but this time there is no mistaking it. I watch the Ghosts stumble as they feel it too. The feeling in my gut isn't quite gone yet and I can feel a kind of static running up and down my arms. I ball my hands into tight fists and hold them at my sides. I stomp again and let leash the same earth shaking vibes, and then when I feel the static in my arms collect in my fist I raise my arm and throw the feeling at them, opening my hands, like I am throwing a ball. I'm shocked when I actually see what looks like a little lightning bolt escape from my fingers and hit one of the Ghosts. They stumble back and their body shakes with shock. Sparks from the attack dissipate into the dry ground and I lose my balance a bit.

"Contain her," a different Ghost Man announces, his deep, robotic voice resonating through my body. I stagger back after the weird power I released, feeling suddenly very dehydrated and tired. I hold my head, trying to clear my blurry vision and waiting for the sudden wave of nausea to pass, and can't stop myself when I fall to my knees. Before the remaining Ghosts can get any closer to me, the Vehement runs to my aid, knocking some to the ground and fighting them. I watch as Olon joins the fight, running across the land and jumping for one of them, locking his arm around their neck and dragging it down to the floor. I struggle to say anything; my mouth is so dry.

White spots dance in front of my eyes but all I can think about is getting out of the line of battle. In this state I am just in the way. Still confused by the strange way my body is acting, I try to pull myself up, my legs feeling particularly wobbly as I settle on my two feet. I sway gently, trying to stand straight, but before I can take a step I feel my feet being swept off the floor as two strong arms secure themselves around my back and under my knees. I let my arm naturally fall around Olon's neck as he carries me away with a reassuring, "Come on, let's get you out of here."

"How did they blow up the prison?" I ask meekly, seeing it in the distance as Olon moves. I am impressed at how fast he can jog along with me in his arms; just another reason to admire him.

"The explosives Elias gave us were completely fool proof. I guess while he was trying to pretend to be one of us and not a traitor, he didn't think of what an advantage the bombs would be. Maybe he thought we'd never get that far." Olon replies with a level voice. He doesn't dwell on Elias, and the conversation ends there.

His jog slows down and with each jolting step I can feel

a pounding in my head. I am so thirsty. Olon gently lowers me down and I lean against a boulder behind me. He crouches in front of me and through my unfocused eyes I can see the wrinkles on his forehead as they crease with concern. He brings one of his hands up to smooth away the hair that has fallen into my face and is sticking to my perspiring skin. His hand lingers on my cheek for a moment and his thumb gently brushes my face, consolingly. In a daze I let my head lean in to his touch.

I see him smile gently, but his smile is laced with concern and doesn't reach his eyes.

"I'm so thirsty," I tell him, my voice raspy. His eyes widen and he stands up in a second.

"Stay here, don't move." I want to tell him that I probably couldn't move if I tried but he is already running off in another direction.

I steal a glance behind the rock Olon has placed me next to, to survey my surroundings. The fighting looks far off now but the prison looks considerably closer. I wait for the uneasy feeling in my chest to return, the thumping that had lead me here the first time, but it never comes. I continue to look at the dark, menacing structure of the building and wonder why it has no effect on me this time around. Olon comes into my peripheral vision with a flask of water in his hand. He kneels by my side again and helps me steady the flask at my lips. Once I feel the fresh liquid against my tongue I can't help but chug it all. The drink is gone in a couple of gulps. With a satisfied gasp of air, I wipe my lips with the back on my hand.

I make Olon help me stand up despite the looks he is giving me that let me know he thinks I should stay down for a while. But as soon as I am up I already feel steadier on my feet, and before he can stop me, I leap into a sprint in the direction of the prison.

Olon follows close behind and makes sure I'm alright once we have slowed, but I brush him off frivolously and tell him there are more important things to worry about. I look up and smile at him gratefully, and he hesitantly smiles back, and then I spot the Cryptic and point him out to Olon. He nods knowingly and becomes all business again. I begin walking with him to the crowds of prisoners escaping across several very large trees knocked down and laid across the canyon to the land the prison stood on, no doubt the work of the Vehement. It's a smart idea. The prisoners are walking single file across the large tree trunks, some I recognise, some I don't. I am overwhelmed with various emotions suddenly.

When Olon isn't paying attention anymore I slow down. I look up at the building in awe. The memories come flooding back. I feel my fingers twitch with emotion. I have to go back inside.

I quickly glance at the Oracle and Cryptic. After so long being on my own after being in this hellhole, they saved me. I have to revisit it as my new and improved self. When I'm sure they're not looking I picture where I want to go and teleport to the prison land, just outside a large black door. I dive to my right and through the door that is left swinging wide open.

Grey. It is all grey. So dreary and lifeless. I shiver at the atmosphere. I keep walking, my steps echoing in the deserted hallway. The first seven floors are reserved for prisoners. The upper two are for our holders; not that we ever saw them; we only came in contact with the Ghosts that guarded us. The basements down below are for overflow. I'd heard rumours about the basement cells, the overcrowding, the smell, the leaks; all bad things.

Thankfully I had been locked on the second floor. My feet carry my body subconsciously round the corner and up the stairs that lead to the next floor. A few kids bound round the corner, startling me as I make it to the next level. Their eyes are wide and they look so scruffy. I can only imagine how long they've been here. They glance at me only for a second; I'm not important. They are on their way to freedom, and I couldn't be less interesting. I feel the gush of air as they run passed and I smile. The Resistance made that happen. Those kids, and all the others are out, because of them.

I push onwards, counting the doors. 1...2...3...4...5. Cell Five Level Two. This was me. The jail bars squeak as I push them open. One of the hinges is broken and the door is barely holding up. I grimace at the dirty smell. The musk of the prisoners left here to live, barely hanging on, much like the door. It truly was hell here. It is such a small room, yet they had shoved 9 of us in here.

I hear heavy footsteps above me, doors slamming, people yelling with ecstasy. A mother comes rushing down the stairs, limping behind her two children that she ushers along the corridor. She smiles briefly to me in passing, a genuine smile, and keeps leading her family outside. The flow doesn't stop.

Rogues are up on the third floor opening the cells for everyone. As the crowd coming down the stairs thickens, I can't stop the grin that spreads across my face. I turn around, looking back at the cell that once held me. I am still bitter. But it is almost a good bitter. An active bitterness that makes me productive, makes me want to do more to help, and fight.

I leave then and run down the stairs with the rest of my people, seeing them experience the freshness of being outside for the first time in who knows how long. The euphoric looks on their faces as they spread themselves out, running around in all the room they have, are beautiful. They are free. I see members of the rogues speaking to all of them, trying to make their rounds, make sure they are all okay and see if any people need assistance before they send them off along the tree bridges.

I run over to Olon and the Cryptic who are on the side of the prison now and pulling people out of the basement levels. I look down into the gaping hole in the side of the building and see mounds of people still crowded down there, helping each other up, lifting others out. I get stuck right in and start holding my hand out for people to grab as they look for something to hold onto in their journey out. By the looks of some of these people compared to those I just saw leave upstairs, it is clear that the basement prisoners had drawn the short straw. They look malnourished, dangerously pale. I barely recognise the woman who climbs out by my hand. Her once bright blue eyes are dull and almost grey, her light brown hair is dirty with grease and dust, and it is splitting hazardously at the ends. She has sunken in cheeks and chapped lips but her face still lights up and she manages a smile when her eyes lock with mine.

"Oh," she gasps affectionately, putting her hand over her mouth as if she can't quite finish the sentence. I help her get steady on her feet, and she continues to hold my hand

and look at me.

"Oh, my baby. My Kayin. Is it you?"

She looks at me like she's found her reason to live. She grips my hand and I feel the cold metal of her wedding ring. I glance down and squeeze her hand back, a tear springing to my eye. As I look back up it spills over onto my cheek. I lunge towards the woman, and feel her familiar arms wrap around me tightly, even if they are considerable thinner than I remember.

"Oh, mum."

"You did it, Kayin," my mother cries softly on my shoulder. As I hug her tighter I can feel the protruding bones in her back, her sharp shoulder blades. I become aware of how skinny and fragile her arms are as she holds me. I feel my heart drop, weighed down by the situation, and a new wave of tears spills over my cheeks.

"I'm so sorry I left. I'm sorry I didn't come for you sooner…I could have saved you sooner-"

"Oh hush, darling. Stop." She cuts me off. She lifts her head and looks me dead in the eye, holding onto my arms, rubbing them gently, reassuringly, just as a mother does. "I'm glad you left. I wanted you to get out. Don't blame yourself," she smiles through tears, her bottom lip quivering.

"You did all you could. And you came in the end. That's all that matters."

"But, mom, look-"

"Exactly, Kayin…Look," she cuts me off again and looks behind me. I follow her gaze as people continue to climb out of the basement. A new flood of people begins running out of the main doors as the fourth floor of prisoners are liberated. "Look at what you've all accomplished."

I hug her again. I squeeze her as hard as I dare to while she is in this state. When did she even get moved to the basement?

"…Dad?" I whisper. Am I expecting him to climb out too? I pull back from the hug again so I can see her face. Her eyes are shut tightly and ever so slowly I see her shake her head. So I just pull her against me again; there is no need to explain. I ignore the small part of me that is disappointed I can never ask him the questions I have after my flashback. I push my emotions to the back of my mind, until I'm ready to acknowledge them.

"Come on, let's get you some help," I tell her with a sniff, taking her hand and leading her over to the group of rogues that are offering medical attention and checking over all of the prisoners.

Though I know I can be helping others and I know

there are other tasks at hand, it doesn't stop me from kneeling down beside Gracine and checking her over.

"I have all my powers now, mum," I tell her, a little chirpier. She looks up with a small smile and wide eyes.

"I never even got a chance to talk to you about all that. We never knew if you would get them!"

She wipes the back of her hand across her forehead as she speaks, then sighs. I hand her some water and she eagerly gulps two thirds of the bottle.

"It's okay. I managed. I don't want you to regret anything, okay? Seriously, don't feel bad for anything." I tell her. She clasps my hands.

"Same to you."

I pause to smile at her. "I can also teleport," I remember. Her hands seemed to tighten around mine slightly but her smile stays constant.

"Oh really? That's intriguing…That's not usual."

"I know, but it's pretty cool. And I'm also impervious to weapons."

"Oh, my little superhero." I can tell that my mother is confused at these strange powers but she tries not to let it show.

I think about the other weird feelings I had earlier and the unusual things I seemed to be able to do. Also how strangely my body acted when I came near the prison the first time we found it. I glance round at Olon and the others and then back to my mum. "Also, actually, I-"

My thoughts are cut off when we hear an explosion not far away. Another explosive has been let off in the prison. I angle myself across my mum in a somewhat protective way when I hear bricks tumbling and crashing together and the yells of more liberated prisoners.

"Go, they need your help. Don't let me weigh you down." She says to me as we watch the building.

"You never could," I whisper with a smile, but nod gratefully and stand up to help my friends. I back away while keeping my eyes on her, grinning but biting my lip to hold back the threatening tears.

I turn and run over to the Cryptic, helping him where he is for a while. I know the Divine and Vehement are still battling the Ghosts dotted across the desert, and I have seen Olon go and join them. When I see Imara coming over to us, slightly limping, I rush to teleport away from the prison and across the gorge to meet her.

"Are you okay?" I ask, putting a hand on her arm and helping guide her to the floor. She stretches her leg out in front of her and winces as she does so.

"Yeah it's fine, don't worry."

I knew she is being brave so I quickly use my bone vision on her leg and see the fracture in her ankle. I raise an eyebrow at her.

"Kayin, there are other people who…"

"Who need you. Let me just fix it, it won't take a second." I assure her. I know it is true, I have found my last power and I feel more confident as a healer than ever before. In a few moments her ankle is fine and she hesitantly stands back up. She looks at me gratefully and while I have her alone a thought occurs to me.

"What's happening back at their HQ?"

"Our rogue army is over there, fighting. It was our mission to retrieve you and then break into the prison. Which is why we're here but our main force is over there."

"So what's our next move?" I ask.

No more fighting. Come to me. Unlock your potential.

The edges of my vision blur. I lose my balance a little which makes the Vehement reach out for me.

"What did you say?" I sway, straining to hear the wispy voice in my head. I've heard it before I'm sure.

"I haven't said anything yet," The Vehement replies. She holds me with two hands, trying to keep me upright. "Kayin, can you hear me?"

My vision clears and when I am sure the voice isn't coming back I look to Imara.

"What?"

"Kayin, what the hell was that?" Her eyes are wide with

concern.

"I'm sorry, I just…"

"Have you been drinking enough?" she asks.

"That's probably it, I haven't had a drink in a while."

She shakes her head at me but keeps an arm around me while she leads me under a tree where others are settled. She hands me a bottle and I sip at it, not really feeling thirsty.

I can feel a headache coming on. A sharp pain in my temples and the back of my head makes my hands shaky as I lift the bottle to my lips again. Oh no. This is what happens when old memories are unlocked in my head. I remember the voice then, during that weird episode I had when I unintentionally found the prison the first time.

"Whoa, steady," I hear the Vehement say, catching me as my knees buckle. She eases me to the ground and I lean against the tree trunk. "Kayin, what's going on?"

"I uh," my vision begins blurring again and the pain in my head increases. "I'm having…" I take a gulp of water midsentence to try and wet my increasingly dry mouth. "…An episode. I-" I lose my train of thought, and I let my heavy eyelids droop.

Darling we're closer than ever.

"Who?" I slur.

"What?" is the Vehement's reply.

I'm sorry for the pain. Come to me soon, darling.

"Where?"

And then I feel a thump. It takes my breath away. Pounding against my chest so hard that it winds me. It is telling me which way to go again.

"Kayin?" the Vehement's voice sounds faint now, but I can still feel her arm around me.

Another thump. It wants me to go…which way is that? South west? So I do.

"Kayin!" I hear another cry. I have only teleported a few feet away from the Vehement who sits under the tree, dumbfounded. I am thrust onto my hands and knees when I reappear and on the ground in front of me I see small drips of blood, the red contrasting against the dull yellow desert floor.

The Vehement stands up and runs to me, trying to sit me up.

"Kayin, what should I do?"

"They want to meet me?" I attempt as an explanation.

"Who, Kayin? Where are you going?"

"I need to follow my chest, the voice says we're close," I tell her dreamily, balling my hand into a fist and tapping my chest in rhythm to what I feel underneath my skin.

"Oracle!" The Vehement's chest vibrates against my face as she holds me against her. In a moment I can hear feet pounding against the floor and coming towards us, but it doesn't overpower the thumping in my chest. So I teleport again, in the hopes to calm it down. I get further than before but still not far enough. I am dangerously close to the edge of Ervon Gorge now and I know I have to make an effort to teleport further than a few feet the next time or I would fall into the chasm. I can taste the blood from my nose on my tongue, feel it drip around my mouth.

"Kayin, where are you going?"

The direction I am heading means that Olon is now closer to me from where he is coming from and reaches me before the Vehement. He clasps my face in his hands tightly, urging me to look at him, but my head lolls and my eyes are too fuzzy to focus on him.

"She's having one of her episodes. She's talking about going somewhere, to meet someone," the Vehement informs him quickly.

Olon's thumb strokes my cheek; wiping blood across my face I'm sure of it.

"Kayin. Can you hear me? Please look at me, Kayin." The worry in his voice is endearing. I find enough strength to raise my arm and put my hand over his on my face. I smile at his touch.

"She's...someone's calling me. My chest...it's thumping," I vaguely explain, once again using my free hand to mimic the thump of my heart on my chest.

"The Cryptic said this happened when they were searching for the prison. How could this be happening again? What's going on?" The Vehement questions.

The sound of weapon on weapon, the clashing of skin on skin, the talking and chatting that fills the background noise all blurs into one and I can hear my ears ringing. I am reminded of the pain in my temples. I grip my head and let myself fall limp in Olon's hold.

"Kayin, stay with me. Stay awake, stay with me!" The fear is rising in his voice but it is muted in my ears. The ringing is getting louder and blocking everything else out. I look at the people around me; I can see they are speaking but I can't hear their voices, I can only see their lips moving. My ringing ears overpower it all, until finally...it stops. For a second I think I have died. Clarity. It is so serene. I can hear no battle cries or yelling, just peace. I hear peace; I feel peace; I am peace.

My daughter, come back to me.

With what feels like a new lease of life, I open my eyes and sit up. I wipe my face, smearing blood across my arm, scanning the crowd for Gracine. Daughter? I left my mother not long ago, she is safe, where is she? What's happening? I see her. She's sitting with the others; she looks content, or as content as someone in her position can be. She is unaware of what's happening over here.

My child, I'm here.

It no longer hurts. I hear the voice clearly.

"Kayin?" Shocked by my new energy, the Vehement and Oracle watch me intently.

"She's calling me. I must go. Someone wants to see me." While talking I don't take my eyes off Gracine in the distance. I can feel the thumping, still prominent, telling me to go in the opposite direction to her. Maybe I'm going crazy; I think I'm cracking up. Yet I still glance at Olon, delicately traced his jaw with my fingers, and apologise.

"Sorry for what?" he asks. His fear is written all over his face. But I only see it for a second and then with my new burst of energy I teleport away.

15

This time I must be dead. That's it. I've finally gone and killed myself. Why is my vision blurry and green? Is that something soft beneath me? What's tickling my face?

I twitch again as I feel something soft brush against my ear again. I've found myself on the floor again after teleporting. Damn, what's wrong with me? I try and push myself up; I'm so achy. I ball my hands into fists, gripping at the floor for some leverage, but it just rips against my pull. Is that grass? With heavy eyelids, I finally open my eyes and try to clear my vision. I'm in a field. An actual field with lush grass thicker than anything we have in our towns.

I lift my head completely and see the strangest of people around me. They look enchanting and confident. They're laughing and clinking their tall, slim glasses together. Their excess of jewellery around their wrists and fingers clang and clash with each of their movements. Suddenly I'm scared. I try harder to get up quickly, scurrying back on my heels and sitting up. I'm getting a few looks; some of them have noticed me. I obviously appeared out of nowhere but I seem to be in the corner. I glance behind me at the ridiculously tall black brick wall I've backed up to.

Trying to calm my breathing, I reach for the wall behind me and use it to guide me to my feet. I can see the expanse of the field now I'm standing up. The brick wall stretches far to my sides, and I can see where the ends take a new direction and circle round. Across the field that is enclosed by the walls I can see benches, tables and chairs, large umbrellas where groups have congregated and are chatting together in the warm sun. On the far end, the complete opposite side of the field to me is a large building. A monstrous building. It's tall and black and has many windows, but it doesn't feel as daunting as other buildings I've seen owned by the Ghosts.

Surely that's where I am? Ghost territory, in the Shadow Lands? The Ghost I fought had mentioned their superior civilisation to me. That was the same moment he revealed there was a Supreme power that was above them all. And just like that I realise what the Ghost Men from the battlefield were talking about when they chanted 'Supreme Power' at me and became obsessed with 'containing' me. I don't understand what I did to evoke that from them. Thinking about how my body seems to have a mind of its own lately makes me nervous. I become self-conscious as I stand in the corner, noticing more eyes falling on me. This is the superior civilisation I've heard about. These are the shilo that Olon told me about.

They don't look so superior. They don't look real at all, to be honest. They are all too over the top, clearly way too involved in their image. They probably think they are above everything and everyone. Rolling around with the Ghost Men and dabbling in magic and sorcery probably gives them some kind of false sense of status. I see faces of intrigue, surprise, and judgement. They all look upon me differently, I just want to curl up, make myself invisible.

For a moment I am lost in thought and become shy but then I remember why I am here. It isn't an accident. Someone wants me here and I followed his or her voice. Oh God, the voice that haunts me. Were they here? I uncross my arms with new resolve and begin walking. I notice as I pass the shilo they are all tall and look broader than humans. They are all my height or taller and for once I don't feel like I stick out because of my height. No, this time I stick out because of the way I entered the land and my plain black clothes and messy body, compared to their immaculate and over dressed bodies.

Maybe I'll finally get some answers. Either that or I'm walking right into a trap. From the start I feel I've been targeted, I've been kidnapped, I have powers I can't explain, something has been revolving around me for a while and I don't understand any of it. It's all been leading up to something, though.

As I make my way through the field, I now catch everyone's attention. I stick out like a sore thumb in my black attire, dirt and blood and sweat covering my body. Everyone here looks so pristine and clinical in his or her weird and somewhat wonderful getups. Murmurs and hushed chatter surround me as I pass by.

I am biting my lip, trying to get by, and by the time I reach the building on the other side of the field I have almost bitten my lip raw. I gulp and grab hold of one of the sleek chrome handles on the huge, tinted glass door in front of me. It would be an understatement to say I have a feeling of being watched. When I glance over my shoulder to the hundreds of pairs of eyes latched on to me, scrutinising me, I've never felt so vulnerable. Regardless, I swing open the big door and walk into the cool building.

It is a relief to be out of the hot sun and the chilled air inside is liberation. I have walked in to what looks like a large lobby, or some kind of common room. The décor is the complete opposite of the outside of the building. Though black seems to be a recurring theme throughout the architecture I've seen, the Ghosts and the shilo alike seem to prefer white and metallic's. The colours and patterns and textures are contrasting and enticing and everything I'd expect them to despise. I wonder where people, like the man who kidnapped me and repulsed me, fit into this. Now that I think about it the man did wear quite outlandish outfits. Then I think of all the traitors from my own people, are they now living a life of pristine shimmering aesthetics or if not, what are they doing?

Two Ghosts appear at the back of the room as I step forward. They hold their staffs across their bodies and stand firm, blocking a door each. I stop and brace myself for a fight. I am exhausted and don't know how long I could last. But they make no movement. I slowly straighten up, wary of any tricks, but they continue to stand still in front of the doors. I could've screamed. What the hell am I meant to be doing?

"Who wants me?!" I yell, my frustration reaching its peak. I groan into the echoing silence that follows.

A door behind the Ghost Man to my right opens and he steps to the side to let the people behind him enter. A woman I have never seen before, which isn't surprising, walks in, wearing a light grey, iridescent blazer with over sized shoulder pads and matching skirt. It is odd to see, I'm not accustomed to seeing formal clothing around anymore. She has large false eyelashes that spread far across her cheeks and are lined with glitter at the base. She is followed by three other men, one of which I notice straight away. Elias solemnly trails behind this woman who saunters into the room, and he's now wearing all white attire and faint golden glitter across his cheek ones. His eyebrows have been coloured white as well and contrast greatly to his skin. White-hot rage flashes in front of my eyes instantly and without thinking I feel myself lunging towards their little group.

Elias catches my eye and I see him retract, fear in his eyes. My hands are moulded into claws, ready to gauge his eyes but before I can even touch a hair on his head the Ghost Men disappear and reappear one on each side of me, linking their arms through my elbows and securing me, lifting me from the ground naturally as they are so much taller. I kick and thrash and scream insulting things at Elias but these Ghosts who barely react to my movements, securely contain me.

"I've been told we should refrain from hurting you, but that doesn't mean we can't…accidentally break an arm or leg here and there. Please cooperate." The lady says. She has slicked back black hair tied into a neat, high ponytail. She speaks so calmly and casually that she might as well have been discussing what she was going to eat for lunch. She doesn't even look at me as she speaks, just tucks a non-existent stray hair behind her ear.

"Why should I do anything you say," I screech at her. I minimise my movement because shifting too much and being suspended like this is starting to take a toll on my muscles.

I snarl again at Elias, who is really just a coward, while the lady prepares to speak again, but before she can an ear piercing scream echoes throughout the building. The others cover their ears desperately, and I'm sure even the Ghost Men stiffen their postures, but it doesn't affect me like them. I blanche at the noise but it isn't as painful to hear like the people in front of me are having on.

"Our Supreme." The monotonous voices of the Ghost Men strike fear in me. It sends a shiver up my spine that couldn't be remedied. The reminder of the ultimate power that they answer to subdues my fury and replaces it with caution and anticipation.

The lady in front of me straightens up and eyes the Ghost Men before finally looking back to me.

"She awaits."

With a cocked eyebrow and a subtle smirk she turns on her heel and retreats through the door she and her posse had come through. They follow her willingly, and then my new bodyguards haul me through the doors behind them. I fidget and try to resist, not knowing what is waiting for me now. I feel a subtle thump in my chest and gasp. It continues gently. In my head I know that it is trying to lead me somewhere, it's what I so blindly followed to get here in the first place. I try to ignore it, wrench my eyes shut and disregard everything around me.

We come to a stop and I open my eyes to see we are in a lift. The floor drops and we begin going down. -1… -2… -3…-4. We go down. B. For basement? I'm sick of underground rooms. The doors ding and open with a gust of air and I am dragged out. The Ghosts follow the woman without a word. Even five floors down, we walk up to a wooden door and when opened I see some questionable stairs leading downwards. Where the hell are we? I tense up at the thought of what is down here and find myself thrashing in the arms of the Ghosts again.

"Let me go. Please!" I yell as we near the stairs. "What do you want from me?!"

"It's not about what we want," is the only reply the woman gives me. She steps aside and the Ghosts and I move passed her. My feet hit the floor and I am dragged through the door and down the creaky stairs. It is dark and dreary; the heels of my feet hit each step as we go. The only light comes from the open door behind us where the others stand, and then I hear the slam as they shut it on us. I am alone with the shadows and whatever lives inside them. As we reach the bottom of the stairs I see some kind of light lining the floor, dimly lighting a deep red carpet. The more I look around the more I see them, filling the room. Lining the floor and up the walls until they go so high they don't look much more than little fireflies up there. I can't even see the ceiling in the darkness.

The Ghost Men throw me down onto my knees and vaporise in an instant. They left me in this unknown place. I don't know whether to get up and try my luck at running back up to the door in an attempt of escape, or stay completely still. I am too scared to make a sound. What is down here? This is some hell of a prison if that's what is happening. That can't be it. Now I'm closer I can see the lights are some kind of small jar, filled with...electricity? Balls of sparking static that seem to pull their energy from nowhere. They spook me, but simultaneously give the room an eerie cosy feeling. One particularly bright spark in front of me entices me and slowly I move from my achy knees and stand up, moving into the field of light. I look up to the nonexistent ceiling. The floors we descended through are probably fake, to accommodate for this room.

Why put so much effort into this one place? I have to figure out a game plan if I'm going to doing anything productive. I came here for a reason, for some answers, and they all seemed to be expecting me. I wasn't attacked. They knew I was coming and prepared themselves. Prepared this room? No, this was already made up. This isn't for me. So what's it for?

The screech. Another scream rings out and shakes my bones. It doesn't just echo through the building to my ears, it is coming from in here. My mouth goes dry and my body goes rigid.

"Our Supreme," I whisper, quoting the Ghost Men. I gulp. "She awaits…"

The hairs on the back of my neck stand up, I can feel a bead of sweat form on my forehead with the anticipation and fear. After the scream I can hear movement. It is no longer silent as it had just been, and I don't know which is worse. I crane my neck, twisting my head this way and that, trying to see anything in the dimly lit room, but the further I look up, the darker it is and impossible for me to see anything.

I can teleport away. Surely. I'm safe, I'm not trapped, and I can get away. The more I repeat this to myself, the more I become confused as to why I am still standing here, waiting. There is a part of me that doesn't want to leave, I know, that wants to get whatever it is I came for, and it's the same part of me that stopped me from leaving earlier.

I can sense something else here now; there is no doubt about it. Something is lurking in the shadows around me. I can feel it closer, and closer. As if it's hanging overhead. My eyes shoot up at the feeling but again I'm met with empty darkness.

My dear.

The voice is as loud as it's ever been in my head; feels like it's coming from behind me. I twist round quickly and scream in surprise when I see two black orbs staring at me from centimetres away and suddenly two hands are clutching at my face, keeping my head in place as it looks at me. I squirm and cry out, gasping and sweating. I try to teleport but it doesn't work. I can't be concentrating enough; maybe I'm so consumed with fear that it's not working.

It must be that. I'm lashing out and holding my eyes so tightly shut that it hurts. I'm gripping at the wrists of whatever is in front of me, desperately trying to pry their hands away from my face, but it's to no avail.

I stop moving. I stop resisting, and slowly I relax myself but never let go of whatever is holding me. The pure black eyes that I only saw for a second have scared me enough to keep my eyes closed. I can't face them again. I can't. It feels like leather on my skin, the hand that's keeping me in place.

Its thumb gently strokes my cheek. I'm equally horrified and confused, enough to make me open my eyes the tiniest amount and peek. Human? Is it human? Shilo? Ghost? The pale complexion of its face so close to mine almost glows.

Lips as red as blood, and a tongue that matches, I see, when it licks its lips. I glance up at the extravagant headdress it's wearing and it distracts me from seeing the whites of its eyes slowly appear. The blackness that its eyes once swam in have shrunk to slightly larger than average pupils. If I was far enough away, I would probably mistake them for dark brown eyes, but I am too close. So intimately close that I am not fooled.

I whimper then, unintentionally. It slips out as my bottom lip begins to tremble. What am I doing? Am I about to cry? Probably. I shakily draw a breath in, watching the newly formed eyes in front of me flick to and from each of my own. Their thumb again strokes my cheek delicately, and then finally their hands pull away. I'm drained and my knees buckle as soon as it breaks contact, as if they were holding me up just by their hands, so I drop to the floor.

"Don't be scared, my sweet."

It's strange to hear a human voice come from the mouth of something that looks so…un-human. But I recognise it immediately as the voice I've been hearing inside my head recently. The one that's been telling me about my undiscovered potential, how I should come to her...calling me daughter. I bite my lip and screw up my face, scrambling backwards, away from the odd creature that seems to be getting off on being nice to me. After scaring me out of my skin first, however.

I'm not listening. I'm not here. Why am I here? Why did I think this was a good idea? I never expected this. The Supreme. The actual Supreme. A higher power that controls the Ghost Men. Since when is that anything but a myth? Since when did I step into a story my mother used to read to me?

My mother Gracine; my real mother who's safe now. She's free and she's safe. Why am I here with this thing rather than with her?

I'm shaking my head, cowering from the Supreme. But it's too silent. So I glance up. She's there, standing in front of me, head tilted to one side, standing still. So still. She takes a step towards me and I flinch.

"I'm sure you have questions."

Her voice has a weird combination of serenity, almost echoing as it purrs, and intimidation, the power behind it is not protruding but it's there, and I would not want to unleash it.

"W-who?" I manage to stammer out. She understands.

"Supreme. Ultimate being. Controller of the elements

and shadows, traveller of land and mother to one Kayin Sesay."

Hearing my name roll off her tongue like it is second nature to her strikes a chord in me. I shiver violently and shake my head, baffled.

"How is that so? Why would you say that?" My voice is gruff and raw with emotion.

"I only speak the truth. I had relations with your father two decades ago, and we had you-"

"Why would he ever be with you," I spit venom. I am surprised at my own audacity, bracing myself for the backlash. But it doesn't come.

She pauses, but doesn't seem taken aback. And without another word, her form changes. The black holes that were her eyes turn blue and sparkle. Long black hair that shimmers falls over her shoulders and glowing olive skin replaces the white canvas.

"He loved me." That was her justification. He loved her.

"H-how? How do you do that? I can't…I physically can't take this…" I groan, holding my stomach, doubling over. I don't know where to begin. Question her purpose? Her motives? Her intentions for me? Or should I push further on the mother thing she seems insistent on?

Unwillingly, my body throws me forward and I wretch across the floor. My body literally can't handle this whole situation.

"He didn't know my true form," unprovoked, she begins to explain. "I broke tradition. I was never meant to mingle with mortals, with the shilo…but I did. I grew attached to Mahlik, watching him from afar. I used my ability to change shape to form a relationship. He fell head over heels."

She paces, bare feet softly padding the floor. What I'm looking at now, is a real woman. But underneath that, I know it's not real. I wipe my mouth on the back of my hand, grimacing at the mess I've made in front of me. I scoot to the side, still holding my stomach, wishing I could block out what this creature was telling me but her voice makes it too hard not to listen and become enthralled in her words. She tricked him.

"I became pregnant. It is the worst sin of all, to become pregnant by a shilo man. They may be taller and stronger than humans but they are still unworthy of my status. My species is select and sacred. Only the highest ranked Ghost Men are put in the running. They face a series of challenges and battles and whoever comes out on top is promoted to Ghost Lord and fit to lay with the Supreme. And that's only if there's not already an heir to the title. Supreme's can rule for decades, longer even, and I was the heir at the time. It would be a long time before another pregnancy."

"Are you telling me that my father was part of the society that I saw outside this building?" I ask with my hoarse voice, once I find my breath. She nods.

"My people like false personas, alter egos, they like to dress up and let people believe what they see rather than what is actually there. It was easy to walk among them in this form. I was just another woman with something to hide."

She lets the human form fade away and I flinch when the being with black eyes and a white face materialises in front of me.

"Don't shy away from me, my sweet."

"Don't call me that." I don't sound harsh, my voice is unintentionally gentle. I am confronting too many emotions in my head to aim any at this thing. All I can do is avert my eyes while I try to process this and find something to say.

"Your father didn't cower from me."

I look up then, but I can't stop myself from dragging my knees up to my chest and trying to curl into a ball at her feet.

"When I found out I was pregnant I confronted him and showed him my true form, hoping he would flee in fear of what we had done, but he had truly fallen in love…with all of me. So we had to come up with a scheme that involved framing a Ghost Man of inappropriately laying with me by force, and of course that was considered sacrilege and he was dealt with accordingly. They're all just mindless minions, really. It was no great loss. Meanwhile Mahlik had to act clueless. When it was time for the child to be born, I told no one, and your father stole the baby and left our people. I told the Supreme at the time, my own mother, that the baby was lost and I had already buried it in an earthquake. Mahlik integrated into anther society and met your mother Gracine there…and they raised you together."

"No, no." I lay my head down on my knees and rock myself back and forth, gripping tightly at my arms.

"It was only when I came into power, meaning that my mother had died, that I could begin searching for you again. So we invaded."

"You invaded our people and started a war just to find me?" I ask incredulously.

"We don't do anything small," she tells me smugly. She does it just to flaunt the power she holds over the Ghost Men and the shilo. "Your father and I have missed you so much."

"How is that so? Last time I saw my father he was in prison, one of your prisons, and I didn't see him make it out, my mother confirmed that. How could I possibly believe you?"

"She is not your mother." She tells me with that firm, echoing voice. "And she lied to you. I have been in contact with your father. He was only in prison until I could get word to my troops to free him."

I don't want to hear any more, I want to speak to my mother. My real mother. I still believe. Even if she is telling the truth, this being will never be my mother. She didn't raise me.

"Why can't I teleport away?"

"Does that not give you a clue that you are my child?" she counters, not answering my question. "No average healer can teleport, that's a skill you inherited from me. You too can travel lands. Have you discovered your other powers? You have so much potential, my darling. You can rule."

I need so many more answers, she's covered some things but there's so much more that needs explaining. I'm too overwhelmed though, I need to process what I've heard already. I gasp when she kneels in front of me, reaching out with her hands for my face again. I flail a little, trying to avoid her grasp and flinch when she holds my cheeks, wiping away tears that I hadn't realised I'd let fall.

"I will gave you all the information you need. I can enlighten you. We…we can be great together."

16

I pull away from her touch and stand up, bracing myself.

"I am a healer. I am a Sesay." I say. I try to sound bold but I sound as if I'm trying to reassure myself rather than her.

"You are heir to the Supreme." A harsher tone takes over her voice as she stands straight and tall opposite myself. I flinch at the new emotion she's showing. "You may not be pure Shadow blood but you come from Supreme power and Shilo power. You are a mix of blood, something that's never happened. I will defend you till my death. Once you unlock your potential you can be stronger than even me, you can be one of the most powerful Supreme's there has ever been."

She lunges toward me, getting right in my face, making me look into the black pools of her eyes. I can faintly see streaks of silver swimming around deep in her orbs; flashes of power and life. She cups my face and tilts my chin up, making sure we keep eye contact.

"Think of the possibilities," she purrs. I feel a tingling sensation when she touches me, even through the leather gloves she wears. A new feeling courses through my body, making me feel light. I don't even see our surroundings moving. It doesn't register until she smiles a blood red smile at me, and I think to look away, to look down. We are surrounded by darkness, the sparks of light on the floor only emitting a dim light as they are suddenly so far away. My feet dangle in the air; we are floating. The sudden shock causes me to flail slightly but my position in the air doesn't falter. The Supreme has a secure grasp of me, and her grin doesn't waver when I met her eyes again.

"You are my child. Let me teach you." She begins drifting away from me. The panic starts setting in when she lets one hand drop from my face, seemingly holding me up by just a few fingers under my chin.

"Don't let go, please, don't let go!" I whimper. I look down and the lights on the ground are small white dots now. The lights that follow us up the walls light up her face, casting shadows across her white skin in a menacing way.

She shakes her head gently at me. "You can use your powers now. Feel it."

And then she lets go. I feel whatever was coursing through me leave my body as soon as her fingers break contact with my skin and I feel gravity hit me like a ton of bricks. I drop, air gushing by my face, flicking my hair back, I flail, throwing my arms out, but am stopped short of falling any further toward the ground when the Supreme grabs my hand again. This time there is no help. She just lets me dangle from her outstretched arm while she floats above me.

"What do you mean 'now'?" I call up to her. "I can use my powers 'now'."

"I suspended them so you couldn't leave."

"How is that possible?!"

"Whether you want to believe it or not, I am your mother. It's like a supernatural way of grounding you. I control you."

I'm looking down at the floor, and the inevitable fall if she lets go again, so that when I hear only her voice coming from above me, she almost sounds like any common mother, talking about grounding their child. Minus the powers part.

"You are heir to the Supreme. Ultimate being. Controller of the elements and shadows and traveller of land. You can do all I can, Kayin. Fly!"

Like a horse with blinkers I can't see or concentrate on anything around me, anything but trying not to fall to the ground without a fight. The way the Supreme talks is vague, she doesn't give me any set answers or instructions, so all I focus on is the feeling she ignited before, when we first ascended. I try to imagine lightness throughout my body, lifting me up. I want to recreate the tingling sensation by myself. I realise it works when the strain on my arm becomes less and I dare to open my eyes and see myself rising to eye level with the Supreme.

She smiles proudly at me. It's a bittersweet feeling. I'm overwhelmed suddenly; I can feel the hysteria rising in my chest as her black eyes watch me. I can use my powers now...

Without another thought I teleport out.

The hot, dry air hits me like a wave, and I realise then how cool the Supreme's lair was despite the sparkling balls of light everywhere. I'm still in the air. It's real; I'm flying. I need to remember that; if I teleport while flying I stay in this state when I reappear. I look down at the rogues and escaped prisoners who have yet to see me, and the shock of the height makes me falter. The weight of all I've learnt falls on my shoulders and anchors me down. I fall out of the sky; unable to get a hold of the feeling that lifts me.

My cries alert others below of my presence but it's too late by the time they notice and I hit the ground hard with a loud thud, dust blowing up at my sides from the impact.

"Kayin!"

My name is called by various voices when I land and I can't quite put the voices to the faces. My head is fuzzy and my body is weak after the fall. I try to sit up but my body disagrees with my actions and I groan with the effort before giving up.

I squint my eyes to block out the sun from the oncoming headache I can feel. Scampering feet slow down around me and I hear voices asking me questions, if I'm alright and what happened. I'm still asking myself that, and I'm too worn out to reply, until I hear one particular voice.

"Kayin," he gasps. "Clear the way."

My eyes flutter open and I watch the small crowd around me move to the side and watch Olon walk through, determinedly stepping to the front. But once his eyes settle on me they soften. He crouches by my side and cups my chin gently looking into each of my eyes. I can tell he's looking into my memories, reading my mind, trying to get answers without asking me so I don't have to exert any energy. He gives me a small, unsure smile, and as quickly as it's there, it's gone again.

"Come on," he whispers just so I can hear. He slides his arms under me and scoops me up, holding me tightly against him and I let myself fall against his chest. My eyes close again, I want to sleep, but all that fills my mind are two black eyes watching me.

Bone vision

Control of hearts

Heal wounds

Impervious to weapons

Teleport

Fly

Sitting in bed, propped up against a mound of pillows, I read the list of my powers over and over again. I debate adding the weird events that happened when I was fighting the Ghost Men. The way I seemingly pushed them over with a flick of my wrist. The rumbling of the ground when I stamped the floor. The lightning. Oh yes, the lightning that shot out of my hand. What the hell was all that about? I decide to add them to the list even though I'm not sure of it myself. I don't want to leave anything out.

Undecided:

Possible telekinesis

Control lightning

Earthquake powers.

Controller of the elements and shadows and traveller of land. I keep repeating this in my head. That's what she told me. My healer powers come from my mortal blood, right?

Traveller of land…Well that's the teleporting and flying I suppose. The elements? Like weather? Earth, lightning, air, that kind of thing? It's crazy how this is all kind of making sense and adding up in the most ludicrous kind of way.

Am I seriously considering this? That the Supreme is my mother? I'm of Shadow blood? I think I'm going to be sick again.

I lurch forward and grab the bowl that I was previously sick in after I woke up in this room the first time. Olon is all up to speed on what happened, and I didn't have to say a word. He carried me to the medical room and laid me down gently, held my hand while he looked at my memories and the rogues patched me up after the fall. He stayed by my side when they left. He told me that the prison was empty now and they were organizing a register and rooms for everyone, but that no one would be disturbing me here.

I smiled hazily as he kissed my forehead tenderly and left me to rest. I woke up with a throbbing in my head and threw up, before passing out again.

The next time I woke up the bowl had been cleaned, set a little closer. I gingerly raised my hand to pat the bandage on my head. I traced my fingers across my skin, felt the remnants of dried blood that hadn't been completely cleaned off. I grabbed some paper and a pencil and wrote my list.

And I've been contemplating my life ever since.

I wonder where Gracine is now. Have they given her a room yet? I wonder what everyone is doing, for that matter. Do we have enough room for everyone? We'll have to expand. Or was this all pre-planned?

Where the hell is my father. What's his story? I need answers from people.

Glancing around the empty room, I decide to get up. All of my movements are slow, I'm careful as I test out all my muscles. I let my legs dangle off the side of the bed and wiggle my toes. When I feel confident that I'm not going to be sick and my injuries aren't too bad, I stand up on the bed. I reach for the ceiling, narrowly missing touching it while up on the bed.

I tingled, I tingled, and I flew, I think to myself. I need to relax; working myself up and stressing about what is and isn't true won't help me figure out whether I can fly or not. I decide to sit down again and take on a position used for meditation. I cross my legs and even place my hands on my knees, palms facing up. I close my eyes and imagine the air underneath my body, lifting me; I imagine it like sitting on a cloud, or a large gust of wind picking me up and holding me up on its current. I can sense the light tingling feeling, but I dare not open my eyes yet, in case I falter.

I feel myself swaying and smile slightly. I think I'm doing it. With my growing confidence and the feel of a draft around my feet, I decide to straighten out my legs. If I am in the air they will fall straight, if I'm not then that means I'm still sitting on the bed.

To my delight I straighten my body and wiggle my toes in the air. Excitedly, I open my eyes and look down at my bed from the height of the ceiling. Many moments pass while I'm up like this, barely feeling my injuries anymore, just enjoying the weightlessness. I don't let the thought of where this power comes from slip into my mind. When I am feeling more confident I lay horizontal in the air, rocking myself on a breeze as if I'm in a crib.

"Kayin."

The deep solemn voice is calm and collected, but it shocks me as it slices through the silence. I drop in the air a few feet but catch myself, proud of myself, until I look down into Olon's eyes.

"You look like an angel flying," he says softly, expressionless, and despite the kind words I can't work out what he is feeling at first glance, and that makes me hesitant as I lower myself to the floor.

I let him look at me, his eyes flicking over my body several times. He is inspecting me. I know I am a mess. I never seem to let any of my wounds even slightly heal before I go off and get a new one. Fellow rogues have only cleaned me briefly when they have to clean me to patch me up, so I can only imagine the remnants of dirt and blood that are still clinging to me. When he smiles slightly I feel myself exhale heavily, deflating like a balloon. He steps towards me and holds my chin lightly between his thumb and forefinger. For a second I think he was going to kiss me, but with just a hint of smile left, he sighs and drops his hand.

"We need to talk."

Oh no. He's breaking up with me and we're not even an item to break up. He gestures to the bed for me to sit down and as always he takes up the space on the chair by the bed.

"You scared the hell out of all of us, do you know that?" he asks, almost forcefully. "You were experiencing one of your episodes, and you were hearing voices, then you're suddenly fine, and then you disappear? You were a mess, Kayin, and you left."

"I was in a weird place." I reply shyly. I have no real justification for my actions, it's like I was in a trance.

"And then…when I heard the yells…I felt the thump, when you hit the ground. The gasps and cries as people crowded you. I don't think you understand what that was like."

He goes silent for a moment. I feel guilty, I truly do.

"Olon, talk to me." I urge quietly.

"Olon. When did you start referring to me by my first name."

He isn't mad, not reprimanding me anymore, he is just asking, but phrases it more as a sentence. I'm confused; I have to think about it.

"I, I'm not-"

"No one does that. Not commonly, at least. But I opened up to you and didn't stop you when you started. I let you get close to me…I let myself get close to you. I've never done that."

Half way through talking it appears he is no longer speaking to me but to himself.

"Now…I'm sorry to say, but I don't know who, or what, you are."

I am taken aback. "Olon, you know me."

"I owe you a lot. You saved my life, and what happened after that was…intense." He keeps a straight face through all of this, his voice even.

"But I'm born of legacy. I'm the Oracle."

"Apparently I was also born into quite a high ranking family." I speak confidently at first, defensively even, with his sudden changed feelings, but the realisation of what I was saying kicks in and I am almost whispering by the end of the sentence.

He stands then. "I just wanted to make this quick. I just feel until we're sure about our situation, all aspects of it, we should keep this professional. I have responsibilities."

He turns ready to leave, but I call for him. "Olon, wait. Oracle."

I see his shoulders tense, but then he relaxes and slowly turns back to me.

As he stands tall and strong in front of me, looking like the Oracle of legend, as he says, I put my hurt feelings aside and nod. He crosses his arms, waiting, and I realise I'm not sure what I want to say. He has a point too, I refer to him as Olon a lot, considering when I first met him I called him Oracle and felt star struck around him almost 24/7. He was mythical, he was a legend, and he was the one they tell stories about. He is that one. I once told him I didn't need supervision in an attempt to deter him from feeling anything for me, because I knew I would only be a distraction. After getting a taste of him…it went to my head. I wanted him for myself. I've let the thought of the prisoners being free fool me into thinking this war is over. It's far from done. And all the Four need to be on top form. I can handle my problems on my own; I can figure my life out by myself.

I've taken to fiddling with the bed sheets between my fingers while thinking of what to say, the right words. I look up at him again and begin my sentence, but with a small smile he cuts me off.

"I try to pick a time and place to read minds, remember."

I smile at his back as he finally walks out, remembering when he said that the first time, when we shared a moment in the Chapel, and he told me he usually reads my mind when I'm alone, with him. I sigh with mixed emotions; glad I was able to say all I wanted, without actually saying a word.

I've lost track of days. Day and night blend into one and days of the week mean nothing anymore.

I find myself walking towards the room my mother has been assigned with a new found resolve. I've had time to think and put things into perspective, and especially after the brief talk with Olon, or the Oracle, I feel like I've figured out my place again. I'm trying to train myself into calling him Oracle again. Olon is too personal and it allows me to indulge too much on our personal relationship rather than a professional one, as he put it.

If creating some space and distancing ourselves means our special friendship suffers, I may have to rethink things. Ever since I found him alone and injured, I feel a deeper connection to him than the others. I'm confident after recent events in feeling this, compared to when I first met him and was too insecure to believe it. I want that connection to remain; we just need to focus on our priorities.

Which leads me to now, as I knock on the door and

Gracine's voice calls out for me to enter.

She's up and gushing over me as soon as she spots me at the door.

"How are you darling, how are you feeling? Come sit down and rest. Oh gosh look at your poor head," she refers to the large plaster on the side of my forehead. "My, I am just so shocked every time I look at you. You're so grown, so strong, look at what you're doing!"

I flinch at her words, knowing she missed 4 years of me growing up, the crucial years as it were. And it just reminds me of why I'm here.

"Mum, I'm not yours, am I?" My words are particularly slow as I speak, and I can see each reaction as they sink in for her.

"What have you heard? You are my daughter no matter what." She tries to smile but she looks fearful.

"And you are my mother no matter what!" I hug her quickly so she knows I'm sincere and I hear her exhale.

"I love you," she mumbles into my shoulder.

"Me too." I pause and let go. "But mum, please tell me the truth. I've got a lot on my mind and a lot of stuff to figure out. I need the facts." I try to speak as gently as I can, but my mind is running on hyper drive with all the things on my mental to do list, and my emotions are the last thing on my mind right now.

Her bottom lip trembles, but she keeps up a strong stance. I sit down and she takes my hand in hers, settling down on the bed next to me.

"Your father came to our town one night when it was dark and cold. I was by the stream at the time, not doing a lot, I think maybe I was just reading in the moonlight. I wouldn't have paid any attention to him if I hadn't heard the cry of a baby. I looked up and there you were, barely visible however, wrapped in a blanket. So brand new, so tiny. He looked at me with desperation, so I helped him that night. We spent a lot of time together, while I helped him get to grips with this new baby he had. I had a lot of experience babysitting for our neighbours, and wanting to help comes naturally to our family, as you know. Spending so much time with him, we fell for each other. I knew it was a lot to take on. Rarely new relationships come with a baby, but I had also been spending time with you, bonding with you. You had come to trust me too. So I was all in. Mahlik and I got together, and we raised you. "

Mum is shedding a few light tears while she speaks.

"Oh, mum" I hug her again. She cries onto my shoulder. I want to stay in that moment and share it with my mother, but now my mind is occupied with thoughts of my father. So the Supreme may be telling the truth? So I'm of Shadow Blood and mortal blood? My mission is to get to the bottom of who I am and what I'm capable of.

"So if I came with dad, why do I have your name?" I ask, just for the knowledge. I am still a Sesay through and through.

"Your father didn't like to talk about his past, I still know very little of his life before he came to our town, but he was running away. And to leave his life behind he decided to take our name," she explains, wiping her eyes.

"And what of dad now?" I ask delicately.

My mother takes a shaky breath in, and nods like she was expecting this follow up question. "About a month after you had left, he was taken. I was asleep with some of the others in our cell and suddenly we woke up to kicking and yelling. I just opened my eyes as the cell door was slammed shut again. Oh my, it was awful, honey. Of course, I'm grateful you weren't there to witness it, but at the time I didn't know where you were or if you were okay by yourself, and selfishly all I wanted was for you to be there, back in the prison with me. So I wasn't so alone. Mahlik caught my eye as he was dragged away, he smiled reassuringly, but..." she sniffs loudly. "But I never saw him again." Her voice cracks, she is barely audible. "My angel," she whispers.

"He was just dragged out? After being in there two years? So you think...they killed him?" I ask tenderly.

Mum nods, pinching her eyes shut tightly, no doubt

probably reliving the horrific moment. I hate to see her so upset. Another hug. She holds me tightly and we don't say anything else. To my dismay it is all making sense. Gracine is innocent in all this.

I'm not biologically hers. The Supreme said my father was only in the prison until she got word to her troops to get him out. Perhaps it was just coincidence that I had escaped before that happened. Or maybe she planned that? But surely that can't be, since she's been trying so hard to contact me lately, she could have just had my father and I together. No, it couldn't have been part of her plan to retrieve him alone. Maybe it genuinely did just take two years to get word to her troops and I was lucky enough to get out before that. My father must have not known he was going to be taken out when he insisted on me running away.

My mother urges me to stay for lighter chat and a drink, but I tell her I have things to do. She nods understandingly but still looks sad.

"It's hard adjusting to all this. You're part of a greater scheme, not just my little girl. I love you," she tells me.

"I love you," I reply, walking out. 'A greater scheme' doesn't even cover half of it.

Walking from the town to the pit feels surreal. I feel like this is all new again, with new faces wandering around, new voices, and new situations. It's like joining the Resistance all over again. Though I've been through so much and learnt so much more. I'm a different person. I have my mother back and earned a new one. I lost my father and found out he's not actually dead; that's if I can believe what the Supreme says. Unfortunately though, everything she's said so far has been vaguely proven right, I have yet to come across a lie.

The rebels believe they have won the battle.

A deep voice booms across the grounds and I instinctively reach for my slingshot that I've recently become reacquainted with, even though I know my powers are stronger than this small weapon. It's a home comfort.

The war is far from over. We will accomplish what we set out to do.

The defiant voice echoes over our land, and I see people around me started to squirm and panic. I look to the sky and all around for some kind of source but I see nothing.

Their bravery is bold but will be in vain.

Who is that talking? It's a male voice. I watch people looking for cover, trying to block their ears, but I am too interested in hearing what is being said. The audacity of the voice, the confidence. I have a new mindset and mission and this is only intriguing to me now.

Do not let your trust in us falter. We will be victorious.

I begin sprinting to the pit. Those who have been in the Resistance for a long time are standing by, also listening. The new members, fresh out of the prison have scattered and hidden, still fragile and traumatized.

"What was that?" I call to nobody in particular; just hoping someone might have a clue.

Usually the sight of the Oracle in any instance makes me feel something, but in this moment I am undeterred as he steps forward. It's strange how quickly my attitude and feelings have done a 180 in the last day. I feel power surging through me with every new piece of information about my past and my abilities, and my confidence is growing. I am okay by myself.

"They're broadcasting from HQ. One of them, probably one of the higher ups is letting their people know they should not be afraid and it's under control. And by extending the broadcast across the land in the hopes it will reach us, is their way of calling to the weaker ones, hoping they can create a fear which will turn them over to their side." He looks determined and mad as he speaks, letting his deep voice carry over the pit as everyone listens intently. "This is not the end."

"I think it might be the Ghost Lord," I suggest. All eyes are on me. "What have they set out to do? What is their ambition? Surely imprisoning us and controlling us was their initial intent?"

"You would think, but I believe there's more to it than

gaining a few more workers and putting a whole society in prison. They want something specifically," the Divine offers.

Her words burst through my naivety and modesty and suddenly I realise what they want. If they're all working for the Supreme, then it makes sense to think about what she wants. What she's missing...

"I've got to go," I announce, while they are all thinking and reflecting, and then I vanish.

17

I am in the bright lobby of the shilo building with the Supreme's lair below it.

"I want to talk to someone in charge," I tell the Ghost Men when they appear to guard the doors again, as I expected they would. My request is met by silence. I walk across the furry chrome colour rug, traipsing mud and dirt over it with my boots, and stand in front of the empty desk. I slap my palm against the light marble surface trying to alert someone of my presence.

It is a bold move to so confidently come into this shilo society and yell my demands when, apart from the fact they look slightly human, I actually have no knowledge of what they are like. The Supreme said they like alter egos and false personas, and when she changed shape she said she was just another woman with something to hide. What are all the rest hiding? She also said they were generally taller and stronger than humans, does that mean they could be more violent in an asserting-their-dominance kind of way?

I walk around the desk to one of the Ghosts.

"Can you talk to me?" Silence. I didn't expect much. I'm startled slightly when it steps to the side. The door behind him is opening and the familiar face of the woman I met here last time walks through. The slight falter in her step as she sees me standing in front of her tells me she wasn't expecting me to be here this time, that it is just a coincidence she had come out here, but she doesn't let it show any more than that. This time she is wearing a deep plunging black trouser suit, with chunky transparent heels that put her more than a few inches taller than me. Her dark hair is slicked back again but left down, flowing behind her back.

Without so much as glancing at me as she walks behind the large marble desk and leans over to open a draw of files, she says to me, "what is it this time?"

"I want to talk to you. You seem in charge here. I want answers," I demand. She straightens up and briefly checks me over, her eyes scanning me top to bottom. She is clearly unpleased with what she sees. She looks back down to the files in front of her.

"What makes you think I'll talk to you," she says with disinterest. I can't think of a reason right away until I remember who is just a few floors below us, lurking away in the shadows.

"You're obviously aware of the Supreme," I begin. She slows her movements but doesn't completely stop flicking through the papers; nevertheless I know she is listening. "I'm guessing you're in contact with her. So if she's interested in me, shouldn't you be too? Are you aware of who I am?"

I am letting a hint of smugness creep into my voice, but I try to keep it at bay. Maybe here it is worthy of bragging that I know the Supreme, but I know truly that I shouldn't be proud of it.

"Ten minutes," she states. She grabs her selected files and shuts the draw harshly, turning to me. She raises her neatly sculpted eyebrow as she walks passed me, curling her finger in a gesture that tells me to follow her. I trail behind her back through the door she originally came through and look back as it is shutting to see the Ghost take his place in front of it, and through the small window of the door I see him disappear.

We are now in a wide corridor that has brightly painted white walls with a light grey horizontal strip along the length of it. I can't believe the contrast the inside of this building has compared to the soul sucking black and dark grey dull designs that every other shilo or Ghost building I have seen uses. Even on the outside of this very building is nothing like this. Inside is truly shilo culture.

The woman in front of me briskly enters a room to her left and I follow her in. The floor is white marble and is immaculately clean, I almost feel bad about walking on it with my dirty boots until I remember where I am, and how they treated me last time I was here. She is obviously thinking the same thing about my boots; I catch her grimacing at my footwear as she sits down behind a mirrored desk in front of me. She puts down the files she has been carrying and then puts her hands together, locking her fingers, which I notice now are adorning large pointy fake black nails with a small diamante on the base of each one.

"Sit," she commands, looking very briefly to the soft touch deep grey armchair to the side of me. Again, I am wary of how dirty I am, but forget all about it when I sink into the comfortable chair. There's such a pristine atmosphere and aesthetic around here; not a lot of colour but much lighter than the Ghosts.

"You are wrong," she begins, so I lift my head up and concentrate on what she says. "I may know about the Supreme, but I'm not in contact with her. I can only talk to the Ghost Lord." She talks confidently but there is an edge to her voice, she is defensive.

"You speak to the Ghost Lord?" I ask to confirm.

She pauses for a moment and watches me. Then cocks

her head to the side, looking at her hands. "He speaks to me."

Oh, I get it. She has no authority; she's just summoned when they need her.

"How do you know she's real? Have you ever seen her?"

She looks at me as if I am stupid, but she sits up straighter and reclaims her passive expression. "I'm part of a strict religion that believes in the Supreme. To others she is just a myth; to us she is a God. I have recently been appointed to Head of the Religion, and I have been trusted with the knowledge of the Supreme. I suppose I have you to thank for that," she says with no real gratitude in her voice.

I am confused. "What have I done?"

"After your escapades with Aren, he had to be replaced, and I was next in line for that position."

"Aren?"

"He was the man who supervised you while you were in our care. An order was given to retrieve you. Ailin was sent for you. She crossed the gorge with a Ghost and when she had you the Ghost brought you both back over it. Aren was the one in charge of the mission and was supposed to bring you to the Supreme after questioning, but he fell into some…problems."

"I escaped," I recall.

"Indeed," she replies curtly. "Aren then had to make a

call to one of our longstanding employees."

"Elias," I whisper to myself, suppressing my anger. She doesn't hear me.

"You were securely contained with his help, but again…Things didn't go to plan for Aren."

"I think he forgot his original intentions," I scoff, bile rising in my throat as I remember the vile man and how he 'supervised' me. "So you weren't aware of any of this until you were put in this role?"

"No. Everyone in this building and the gardens are members of our religion. But the rest of the shilo do not support the idea and believe the highest power in our society is the Ghost Lord. I was just merely a follower in the belief the Supreme existed," she hesitates, probably wondering if she is giving away too much information.

"As Head of the Religion, you earn the right to know the truth and become the go-to shilo for the Ghost Lord when he needs our people to carry out tasks. Aren was aware of all the facts. The Supreme wanted you for some reason and that was our task. When he lost focus and unfortunately met his end, I took his place. Fortunately for me there was no need to plan a kidnapping because I had word from the Ghost Lord that the Supreme had successfully made contact with you and you were willingly coming over. It made me look very good."

"And what of the rest of your people? What are they like? What do they believe?"

She sighs. "They believe in sorcery and spells and magic. Shilo are well known for dabbling in the supernatural. There are some who are capable of teaching themselves powers; not strong ones, but mixed with the right spells and knowledge, they are quite powerful within our society. The Supreme to them is just a myth, an aspiration that will never be achieved with their pathetic magic."

I think about this. So some shilo do have powers? Like some humans. But we don't associate with sorcery and magic.

"So do you understand who I am?" I ask after a silent moment. I'm the Supreme's sin. Technically that makes me the Supreme heir, but she doesn't seem aware of this. The Supreme was meticulous about making sure those around her didn't know I was still alive, so I can't imagine the secret has come out yet.

Her strong façade wavers for a moment at the question.

"You understand that I am wanted by the Supreme? Clearly she doesn't want me dead or I wouldn't be here now, so what does that tell you? You think it's wise to be treating me like dirt when you don't know my relationship with the Supreme?" I am becoming brave again.

"You're just a human!" She snaps and slaps her hands

against her reflective desk. In a second she retracts and covers her mouth with the tips of her fingers, pushing her shoulders back and calming herself.

I stand up sharply. I take a step towards her desk but think better of it and instead just wipe my shoe on the chair behind me spitefully. Her mouth falls open in shock but she doesn't say a word.

"You're lucky I've got better things to be doing," and with that I leave.

"Why did it hurt?"

The Supreme shifts in the shadows. She floats down to me, still hovering above my head, and looks at me with her shiny black eyes.

"Why did it hurt when you called for me? That was you, right? All those times I heard voices in my head. When I was dizzy and in pain and had nosebleeds. Why?"

Her blood red lips creep into a smile and she drops gracefully to the floor. When she takes a step closer to me I flinch. I have just appeared back in her lair, after teleporting from the room with the woman. I am desperate to get some more answers from the Supreme after the Ghost Lord's broadcast we heard. I have someone on the inside I can talk to. I feel the Supreme won't maliciously hurt me if I'm her daughter but I'm still wary of her. She is an ultimate being after all; I don't even know half of what she's capable of. When I got here, that was the first question that came to mind.

"I knew you'd come back to your mother."

"Why." I demand, albeit not as forcefully as I wish I had the confidence to do.

"That was just me working out what frequency you were on." She turns away as she explains, then peers over her shoulder at me and looks pleased to see I am confused. She comes rushing back up to my face in a blur of darkness.

"See here," she begins, lifting her fingers and creating little shadow silhouettes, which stand on top of her other hand. "These are my people. Shilo." White and silver mix with the black shadows to distinguish the costumes and jewellery her people wear. "They're on a different frequency to you. Though they look human, they are still a different species." The shadows move and dance as her people interact. She waves her hand and they dissipate.

Another finger wiggle and larger, bolder shadows appear in front of my face. "These are my loyal Ghost Men." She grins as they stand tall and still on her palm. "They're on another frequency with which I can communicate to them. That's why the little whistles you and your friends use go unheard to my men. But not me," she giggles as if she thought we were so small and stupid. I blanche at her grim smile. She has been aware all along.

A wave of her hand and a final wiggle of fingers and it's me, standing on her palm, bigger than the other shadows she had previously made. Silver flickers through my shadow replica, much like the way I saw it flicker in her eyes when I was so close previously.

"Then there's you," she says almost giddily, elongating the last word. Her voice is gruff. "Can you guess what I'm going to say?" The light of the sparks around us reflect in her eyes as she looks at me.

With a grimace, I reply, "I have a difference frequency?"

She is falsely ecstatic. She jumps into the air and spins around, picking up pace in the way she speaks. "Yes! Those humans have a whole new frequency, one that I've never had to use before! Of course! I'd never needed or wanted to interact with vermin."

"Those are my people you're talking about! I'm one of them." I reply, instinctively rising a few inches into the air with my new flying power I am still becoming accustomed to.

She meets me half way as I rise and grabs my face tightly with her leather glove clad hands. I freeze, wondering if I have been too outspoken. With a blank face, she stares at me a moment before speaking softly, making my skin crawl.

"But you…look at you. You're different. You're not all human, remember. You're half Shadow blood, part shilo and part human on your father's side. The mortals of my civilisation and human mortals have been mingling for centuries, disgusting; but it's not surprising that you have human blood in you somewhere. Which is why it took a few tries for me to find the correct frequency. Not human, not shilo, not Shadow, just a specific frequency, set only for you. The Kayin frequency."

I had forgot, or not realised until that point, that I am not actually human. My father is not of my people. My mother, well, she floats in front of me right now, my biological mother. So it was just a coincidence that I had human blood in me at all? Every time I come here I get new information that just overwhelms me. I underestimate how messed up this all is every time.

"You were gone by the time I could reach your father in prison." She tells me. "He was terrified for years my Ghosts would find out who you truly were and destroy you. How was he to know I was so close to finding you both?" As I suspected.

"You kept yourself hidden very well for a long time. I had yet to meet you grown up but I was already impressed. The Resistance; I keep them under close watch. They don't know it. They never even suspected that I was anything more than a myth. So when you joined the rogues I finally got wind of your existence and where you might be."

She drops her hands from my face and I fall, forgetting to hold myself up; still not used to this power. I stay on the floor, just listening. I want as much information as possible that I could relay back to the Resistance, even if she knows I will.

"I had barely interacted with the Ghost Men and my civilisation until then. I told that Ghost Man you fought with; remember that fight? I told him to mention me, and that got the rumours spreading once you told the others of what he had said. When you were trying to find the prison, I tried to contact you, hoping I could reach you before you found anything. But by opening that link between us, it opened old memories and feelings, which had already been kick started when your little Oracle unlocked repressed memories. The dizziness, nosebleed, whatever else, that was all me, using the wrong frequency. The beating your heart did, showing you the direction to go, was all you and your healer powers, subconsciously controlling your own heart according to your emotions and new memories."

She is no longer looking at me. She is pacing in the air above me as she explained everything and blowing out sparks only to see them relight a second later with a flick of her wrist as she shoots a mini bolt of lightning from her finger. I watched her, amazed, finally seeing this power in use. As I try to figure out what to say, and form a response in my head, she shoots up into the darkness high above. The white dress she wears fades into the shadows and my eyes play tricks on me, thinking I can see her up there moving but I don't believe I can. Her voice echoes from above, menacingly. I flinch, looking all around trying to locate her, just like the first time I came here.

"Has that alone not caused doubt of the life you've known since you found out I was your mother?!"

"What are you talking about?" I call into the distance. I consider flying up there, but the darkness is so intimidating I decide to stay on the floor where I can see my surroundings.

"Healer?!" She cackles loudly and it ricochets around me, confusing me as I try to pinpoint where she could be. "You're no real healer!"

"I am! There's one in every Sesay generation!" I argue. Lips pursed and eyebrows furrowed in frustration, I think of what else I can do to find where she is. In an instant my eyes flash and I use my bone vision on the space above me. I see her body directly above me. It is so small I can only infer that she is very far away.

"In what family? Your fake mother Gracine is a Sesay, and her mother, Diola. But you are not related to them my dear child. Can you not see what an extraordinary being you are? How magical and powerful you are because of your mixed blood? You were taught by your so-called Nana about how to be a good healer and care for others; it wasn't until you joined the Resistance you began to discover you had powers. That was only because you heard from another human about the powers your Nana had. I am aware of all of this. You never truly inherited those powers, you taught yourself them. You didn't even know it, but I did."

"That can't be true!" I say, unconvincingly as I realise it is in fact true. I'm not actually related to my mother's mother, or anyone on that side of the family. I begin recalling all the times I discovered my powers. All my apparent healer powers came about after much deliberation in my mind. Repeating memories, thinking about how it should work. Also working under great pressure, forcing my hand. My other powers came about by chance, naturally. It makes sense. I am sick of everything making sense.

"Think of all the other things you could teach yourself just from belief." I see her descending slowly; it is so ominous, the slow descent out of the shadows that she controls.

I am so upset. I can feel pressure building behind my eyes but I can't cry. I get frustrated. And then I get mad. And then I remember the advice the Vehement gave me and I get angry. I feel the feeling of static running up and down my arms, the feeling I have only felt once before. The tight feeling in my gut urging me to stamp comes back too, but I focus on the electricity coursing through my body. I can feel my mouth becoming dry, and as I watch the Supreme lower herself towards me, so smugly, the energy in my arms fly to my hands and I shoot them up. A flash of lightning briefly lights up the room and I see the yellow streaks heading right towards her.

But she sees it coming. As if in slow motion, I watch her deflect them with her own burst of blue lightning from one hand in an instant. As the shots fizzle away in the air with a loud crack, she looks down on me with a bittersweet smile. My eyes are wide as she comes ever closer and I am scared then, regretting my impulsive actions.

She is so calm and in control, and I am so panicky, desperate to protect myself in case I have angered her. I lift my arms, my hands glow and I try my best to slow her heart, make her falter, show her I'm not weak. Why do I want to impress her? Though I can feel her heart slow slightly, it doesn't bother her, and with a flick of her wrist I feel a large current of air grip hold of me and throw my body across the room into the wall. I grunt loudly as I fall in a heap on the floor. I want to flee, teleport away, but another part of me wants to stay and fight back. Show her what I can do.

I try not to think too much or doubt my abilities, and to

trust that what I think I can do, I probably can. In this instance I know it would be futile to shake the ground because she is flying, and we are underground; the whole building could come down on us, but I remember knocking over the Ghost Men much like she had just thrown me, so I try to do it back to her. With all my effort I rise to my knees and combine my powers. My hand glows as I sync myself with her heart and I wave my arm up and across, succeeding in my plan to slow her heart and knock her off her feet. While she is momentarily vulnerable as she is tossed across the air, I kick up the power behind my heart control and use two hands, hoping to affect her before she is able to get up and stop me. She gasps and screeches that unbearable scream of hers.

Instinctively I go to cover my ears, it hurts more than the last time I heard it, and before I can react she has me pinned up high against the wall.

She is breathing deeply, and her black eyes look wider than usual. I am silently pleased I have affected her.

"Don't even think about it." She says, just as I have it in my mind to teleport. Her voice is different than her usual tone. It is deep and powerful and it sends chills up my spine. I realise then that I couldn't teleport even if I wanted to; she has suspended my powers.

It seems like forever that she holds me up against the

wall, standing below me on the floor. My fear is creeping on hysteria before she finally smiles. A grim smile showing all her bright white teeth.

"Now imagine a scenario where we work together with our powers." She isn't speaking. She is talking to me through my special frequency; her voice is running around my head, invading my thoughts. "We could do great things together."

She slides me down the wall. My back scrapes against the concrete bricks and scratches my bare shoulders. She puts me down on the floor but keeps me flat against the wall as she approaches, grabbing my chin in a way I'm getting all too familiar with and forcefully holds my face to look at her.

"I'll see you soon, daughter." She lets go finally and I teleport away.

I hear a gentle yell.

I look down.

"Oh, damn," I whisper to myself. I forgot to tell anyone I had come back.

I have teleported back into the open desert. Still reeling from my encounter and full of adrenaline, I decided I was going to practice my powers right away. Tumbleweeds and rocks became my victims as I practiced manipulating the air currents and moving things. Not just flinging things across the dry land, but picking them up gently too, holding them in the air, moving them.

Then I shot up into the air. That was easy, I had already got the taking off part down, it was the actual moving and flying, and as it seems, the landing, I have to work on. I don't know how long I was up there before I decided to have a break and let myself float on my back, looking up at the blue sky. It is extraordinary to be at this height and see it fill my vision. Though I hadn't realised how high I had gone, and when I turn over and look down, I see people wandering beneath me, looking around, and looking very small to me.

"Oh, god," I curse to myself again and slowly begin descending. As I get closer I hear the gentle yells are not so gentle and they are calling my name.

I drop down behind the Cryptic and the small group of rogues he has with him looking. I make sure to concentrate on my landing, and touch down with only a small thump, but it is good.

"I'm so sorry," I say to catch his attention. He spins on his heel and looks relieved to see me, then a little worried. He comes up to me, cupping my face and starts checking me over.

"Are you okay? Where did you go? Kayin, you must stop disappearing like that." When he is sure I am okay apart from the minor bumps and scratches, he steps back.

"I know, I guess my emotions got the better of me." I assume he is up to date on all my escapades, so I continue as the four other rogues run over after spotting us. "I was with the Supreme."

The Cryptic's eyes grow wide. "What happened? Did she do this to you?" he asks, delicately holding my arm and pointing to the red mark around my elbow that was slowly starting to bruise.

I hesitate. "Yes."

"Kay-"

"Listen, I'm okay! Can we go back now?" I look around. "Whereabouts are we?"

"It's a straight path back to the pit. Why are you all the way out here anyway?" He looks behind him and gestures to the others, who are waiting patiently, that we are heading back.

"I'm not sure, this is just where my head told me to take me when she let me go."

He gives me a wary look at the phrase 'let me go', but I ignore it, and we all head back.

I tell the Four I am feeling tired and though they look hesitant to let me go, they allow me to retreat to my room alone. I have new information that I want to reflect on by myself, and new plans to make.

I am starting to create a hierarchy in my head now, so I

grab some paper and a pencil and started scribbling. At the top is the Supreme, and under her is the Ghost Lord. The Ghost Lord has control over the rest of the Ghost army, and is also in contact with the Head of the Supreme religion. The Head of this religion is of course the higher power of the religion, which are all shilo and just believe in the Supreme. And then you have the other shilo who do not believe in the Supreme and to these, the Ghost lord is the highest power in their society.

Now what could the Supreme be up to? If the plan was to take over humans, what was the end goal? And now we've dismantled the prison and released the prisoners, what next? Should they not be targeting us harder to control us again? Something doesn't add up here. The Supreme told me, after all, that she ordered the invasion to find me.

When Orisa, wise as ever as the Divine, said 'they want something specifically', it struck something in me. The Supreme was searching for me for years, but that can't be all, can it? She's found me. So what now? She obviously doesn't want to kill me, because she would have done that by now. I've willingly walked in to her lair; she's had every opportunity to do it if she wanted. Though I hate to admit it, I think the Supreme cares for me in a crazy kind of way. I'm her heir.

So what is our next move? Our game plan is something I

should really be discussing with the Four, who are the beacons of leadership that the rest of us look to. But if this situation has been created just because of my messed up family connections and me, then surely there's something I can do?

I lay on my back, staring up at the ceiling, knowing what I am thinking is probably dangerous and possibly irresponsible but also...it can work in my favour.

Every time I've gone to see the Supreme, I've come back with more knowledge and the motivation to perfect my powers. If I keep going back to her and training, I could really hone my powers, and surely that will only benefit us all in the long run? Especially if there's a fight looming. I want to do all I can. Not that I could even guess when or if that will happen. The actions of the Ghosts and the shilo and the Supreme all just baffle me. I'm just so determined to be the best I can be now; I think this is something I've got to try.

My chest feels heavy and I sigh deeply, sinking into my bed and closing my eyes. Clearing my mind for a second allows me to realise how much my body is aching. I feel deflated in body and mind. Despite it all, despite everything that's happened in my life I try to keep a positive outlook on it all, and I don't think this a lot, but I wish just for a moment, I wasn't me. That all our problems didn't link back to me, I still had a family, we still had our town, and I wasn't expected to do anything or be anyone. I could live a different life, even if I was just a nobody in the Resistance. A face in the background. What might she be like, I wonder? What would she look like? Not as tired as I look, I bet.

"Oh, sorry, didn't mean to interrupt."

A voice at the door disrupts my thoughts and I sit up and see Marisol at the door.

"That's okay," I smile at her. It is nice to see her.

"I thought my friend was in here, is all."

I am confused then. I am her friend, aren't I?

"Mari?"

"Yep, that's me." She stops herself walking out and turns back to me. "I don't think we've met yet."

"Mari, it's me? Are you okay?"

She inches forward, looking at me carefully now, but shakes her head gently.

"I'm sorry, I don't recognise you, really."

Just by chance I glance down at myself and jump in surprise when I see much darker skin that isn't cut and scratched. I see cleaner clothes without holes and tears. And in a second it changes before my eyes, back to my own skin and dirty clothes.

"Kay!" Marisol cries. Her mouth is so wide in shock her jaw is almost touching the floor. "How did you do that?!" The shock of what she has seen turns to amazement, it is displayed on her face. She is fascinated.

"Do what? What happened?" I stand up off the bed not able to look away from my hands. They are still mine. They move when I tell them to, they look like my own.

"I honestly didn't know it was you! That was impressive. What kind of trick is that?"

When I look at Marisol there must be something on my face to tell her that this is new to me too, because her grin fades a little and she furrows her eyebrows. I watch her face change and see her conflicted emotions. She doesn't know who I am, what I am capable of. I shouldn't be ashamed because I know I'm fighting on the good side, but I don't want to scare her. Especially as I'm not feeling my bravest right now. I make a quick decision.

I grin and laugh, relaxing my body. Mari is soon laughing with me.

"It was a trick!"

"I knew it!" She exhales with relief. "How did you do that? I was so oblivious."

"I can't reveal my secrets," I reply coyly. She laughs and steps forward to hug me, and when she can't see my face I let my smile drop.

"I feel like I haven't seen you in ages. What's been happening with you? It's been absolutely manic trying to get all the prisoners settled and help them adjust...but I can't stop grinning about it."

We pull out of the hug and sit down on my bed. It is hard to explain what I have been doing without revealing the Supreme and everything else I've learnt. She asks me about the episode I had the day we broke out the prisoners and I blamed it on the lack of water and all the fighting. I tell her I'd been spending a lot of time catching up with my mother. Which isn't a total lie. In fact it is the truth in two ways. There is a comfortable silence in our conversation, then Mari leans across to hold my hand.

"You seem troubled."

"Aren't we all?" I reply with a forced laugh. She gives me a small smile.

"Just remember what you're capable of. Remember who you are. We can get through this."

She tells me she has to go and I follow her to the door and wave as she leaves. When my door is shut I lean my back against it and let myself slump to the floor. Remember who I am. How could I forget?

18

I try to figure out how I had achieved changing my appearance after Mari leaves. It thrills me to have discovered a new power but also disheartens me when I realised it must be the shape shifting power the Supreme used to seduce my father all that time ago. This is the power that caused all of our problems.

I have talents I could have never dreamed of, I should be elated, but just knowing the origin of them, why I have them, puts a dampener on the whole experience.

It has been an extremely long day and I'm not up for long figuring this out before I drop onto my bed and fall asleep as soon as my head hits the pillow. Waking up naturally when your body is so physically exhausted does not make for a very productive day. The sun is high and shining brightly when I finally open my eyes in the early afternoon.

My problem is not knowing what we have planned next. I don't know what people are expecting from me, what I should be doing. Should I be doing anything? I feel at this point I've had such a prominent position in our plans of action that I'm not sure if that's still my place, now our goal of breaking our people free is complete.

I kick my blanket off of me but stay on my bed. I lift my hands to examine them. I want them to look shiny, like gold, I think to myself. I concentrate hard on what that should look like but nothing happens. Okay, let's start basic. I want my hands to look pale, a creamy white. Nothing. I groan. Do something! I want to be blonde? How about that? I grab the tips of my hair and pull them up to my face to see if I succeeded. I did not.

I sit up, knowing getting frustrated when I've just woken up isn't going to help me one bit. Maybe I need more of an emotional motive for shifting until I'm better at it. Last time I was wishing to be someone else. I'll have to work on it.

I decide to take a stroll down to the small rock pool just outside of our dwellings so I can soak my body in the water. I strip down and dunk my head under the cool water as I slip in. It feels amazing to have my sore body float weightlessly without the fear of falling out the air like when I'm flying. I want to spend the rest of the day here and wash away my woes but I know I have work to do, so I pull myself up onto the bank and put on my clothes, which are still scuffed and dusty. Feeling slightly more refreshed I'm ready to go find some human contact.

I can just see the door to my room in the distance as I make my way back and beyond that four distinct figures walking in a line towards me. It's the Vehement who notices me first and I see her tell the others. They all stop outside my room and I'm suddenly nervous as I walk over to meet them. What's happened or what have I done to deserve a visit from the Four?

"You've got a letter."

The Vehement's voice is even as she tells me. I can sense the anticipation they're all feeling. The Oracle hands over a white envelope, slightly bent at the corners. No address of course, just my name in a thick, messy scrawl. I'm hesitant to open it but I'm aware of them watching me so I jab my thumb into the flap and rip the top.

I hope this reaches you. I hope it doesn't take too long.

I am alive and well and I am desperate to see you my princess. Please meet me. I love you so much.

I know you've heard and found out a lot recently. All the more reason I hope you'll see me soon, so I can explain. You know whom to contact.

All my love, Dad. X

"It's from my father."

I can't take my eyes off the letter. He used to call me princess all the time and it's the same messy handwriting I remember. Yet it feels like a completely different man trying to contact me than the man in my memories. I have to go see the Supreme; she'll get me in touch with him. See you soon, daughter. Her farewell words from yesterday echo around my head. I don't want to have to see her again. Not like this, not to get answers from my father. I want to see her on my terms.

"Don't you dare disappear."

The Oracle's stern voice brings me back to reality. He is being firm; he is serious. He is reading my mind and warning me not to teleport away, as has become my bad habit apparently.

"I have to see him."

"Can we see the letter?" the Divine asks me, on behalf of the non-mind-readers in front of me. Olon's eyes are still on me, unwavering as I pass the letter over to Orisa who holds it up for the others to read.

I look to the floor and concentrate on hiding my memories of my last encounter with the Supreme, which I have yet to tell the Four about, and my newly discovered powers, hoping the Oracle isn't trying to see into my mind.

"We know the Supreme claims to be your mother,"

Abeo speaks up. "The Oracle told us." The others nod. That was after my first meeting with her. They don't know the rest.

"He wants me to go see her, to see him. That's kind of the last confirmation I needed," I reply. The Supreme has told me, Gracine has told me, Mahlik has told me; the Supreme is my mother.

"Remember who you are, Kayin," the Cryptic tells me with all the best intentions, just as Mari had said it. I know it means I should believe in myself, stick to my roots, but it just reminds me that I am the heir to the Supreme. I'm…Am I actually a princess? A sick, twisted kind of princess, but am I? Sudden flashbacks of every time my father has called me princess, fully aware of my bloodline, come to mind. It knocks me back physically so abruptly I step back unbalanced for a second.

Do I belong here at all? I'm barely human. I want to fight for them but I am not one of them, not really. I'll fight for the side of good, but I can't keep fooling myself like this.

"Are you okay?"

"Yes, sorry. It's just a lot to process," I tell them after a moment.

Let me go, I think, looking straight at Olon and making sure he's paying attention. His jaw tenses in thought, I can almost imagine him grinding his teeth, but his face is fixed when he speaks.

"We need a plan, come with us."

He turns on his heel and the three others follow him, unaware of the mental indecision he just had. I follow behind with heavy feet, unwillingly. I could just leave right now, why am I following? Because I know I would never intentionally disobey his orders. Why can't he let me go and figure this out? It's my father, not technically a problem to be solved. He says he wants to keep this professional but I refuse to believe there's not a certain amount of emotion behind this decision.

I follow them through our town and to the ditch where the Oracle heads towards a disguised flap at the back and moves to lift it. This is the place I first saw them emerge from. My first time in the ditch. Imara had told me I wasn't allowed in this room, it was like their 'office', and I have yet to step foot in there. Until now.

It is hardly magnificent; a dug out room a little taller than us, but it is still quite large. In my mind I picture this as where they started, when they first created the Resistance, before they were safely able to expand to the abandoned town, which is now a thriving community of rebels. There is a slightly unstable looking brown table in the middle with four matching chairs circling it. There are mounds of files and papers at the back of the room, and just as many overlapping and pinned to the dirt walls, with writing and scribbles all over them.

"It could be a trap," Olon begins speaking, straight to business, the flap of the room has barely closed shut. Eager to get going if I can, I reply.

"And what would be their end goal?"

"You've been kidnapped twice already and been targeted in other ways. They want something from you."

"They want me. She wants me," I tell him. I'm trying to keep my voice even in a mature way because I can't help feeling like I'm being treated like a child. I'm not the helpless loner that he first came across alone in the desert all that time ago. I'm an heir of great power.

"Kayin, we're just thinking of you," the Cryptic tells me.

"But it's my father. I think the best way to handle this is directly. He wouldn't hurt me and I need answers." I'm aware suddenly of my use of 'I' instead of we, knowing I've subconsciously counted them out in my mind. This is for me.

"The Supreme is dangerous." Olon states.

"I'm dangerous," I say, without missing a beat, slightly surprising myself. The Vehement and the Cryptic are sitting at the table now, I'm standing closest to the entrance, staring at Olon who stands opposite me, and the Divine just behind him to the side by the table. I see Abeo and Imara faintly glance at each other, but I don't look their way.

"Until recently she was a myth of unthinkable power. We know you, Kayin." It is the Divine's turn to talk. A calm voice.

"We need to tread carefully around the Supreme," the Oracle says, never breaking eye contact with me. I can see him becoming more frustrated as our talk goes on, but so am I. I have been so confused and hurt and lost but brave and strong and independent for so long, despite everything that's happening. We were doing so well, we had a bond. And then Olon pushed me away because he said he wasn't sure of 'who I am' anymore. I bet he didn't tell the others of his worries; they haven't lost any faith in me. But Olon needs to keep this professional? Yet he seems to be tightening the leash on me. I can't help the emotions I feel building in me. Does he feel like he needs to tread carefully around me?

"Don't you trust me? Why aren't you letting me do this?"

"Because I'm the Oracle! It's been prophesised that I will lead the Resistance to victory. I need to know what everyone is doing!" For the first time Olon is beginning to raise his voice. I understand that he has a lot of pressure on him in his position, but this is something I think none of us could see coming. This is something unlike the stories we used to be told.

The shuffling of the other three reminds me of their presence. I glance at them but they aren't looking at me, they're sharing looks with each other. I know they're in the same position too; they are part of this prophecy and they're also looking to the Oracle for leadership. But there's more to all of this, our circumstances, this argument...and they know it.

"I'm the Supreme's daughter. I'm her heir! Do you know what it feels like to be so closely linked to the wrong side of the prophecy?!" I cry, my voice threatening to break. I didn't realise actually how much this idea was weighing on me.

"Kayin, we know you're on our side. Like Orisa says, we know you!" Olon steps towards me, and in a rush of emotion and frustration I know in an instant that I've done it. I haven't failed this time. There are shocked faces all round and Olon takes two steps back.

I know I have a new face, new hair, and new skin. I don't know what I look like but I know I've successfully shape shifted.

"Do you really know me?" my voice is softer again now. I can feel how much energy I burnt up to use this new power I'm not used to. I'm aware that this new revelation for them probably doesn't build the argument that they should trust me. My wavering emotions cause my new façade to fade and I'm back to myself. There's a silence. They're processing what they've seen. Until finally Olon speaks again, his voice still firm, but slightly shaky with frustration, or is that anger, that he's try to repress.

"This is the kind of thing…that I, that we should know about."

I can't tell if he's just shocked at this power, mad at me for not sharing this new power with them, or wondering whether he can trust me. I thought I could understand where he was coming from when we had our conversation before. About having so many people depending on him, he is a legend after all and he can't be distracted. But now I'm just hung up on his words. I'm sorry to say, but I don't know who, or what, you are. I feel betrayed; feel like this is the root of his frustration. He doesn't know how to lead me, how to control me.

"The Supreme has powers we can't even begin to fathom right now," he adds. In another life I wouldn't let my emotions control me so easily, but I'm at a loss because I feel like he's saying these things to keep me away from her, from the outside; keep me detained rather than tackle it head on.

"So…Do…I!" I really try to stop it but the familiar static feeling I've been practicing lately shoots through my arms and sparks and cracks at my fingers, waiting for a target.

"Woah!" Abeo is up out of his chair in an instant. He's the one who said it all along, the power and potential I have. But even he wasn't aware of the extent of it. The room around us rumbles softly. Several looks are aimed at the Vehement, but she's staring at me. The first time I used these powers was during the fight the day of the prison break, after Imara told me to get angry. I wasn't sure until this point whether she had ever seen me use these powers. I think it's safe to say by the look on her face that she, like the others, was unaware of these abilities. The only reason she is looking at me is because she knows she wasn't the one to cause the rumble.

The last time I used these powers other than when I've been practicing to use them safely, was the fight I had with mother dearest, the Supreme. And I know they don't know about that.

"Let's step outside, shall we?" Imara is saying delicately. She's definitely aware of the fact that we're in an underground room and she knows small earthquakes will not benefit us.

I turn quickly on the spot and flick my wrist at the door. The flap roughly lifts up like in a gust of wind and stays open for us to exit. I head out first because I need the air now, and I know they're wary of standing anywhere near me. As soon as I can see the open sky above me I leap into the air, causing another small rumble as I push myself off the ground. I float not so far above them in the sky as they exit the room and step out into the ditch.

"You want me to be careful? Is that what you're really worried about? That I'll get hurt?" I call down to them. The static in my arms is getting intense now so I shoot a bolt of lightning out of both arms to my left and watch it crackle across the desert and scorch a mark in the ground as it lands. I want the truth but I'm almost scared to hear the answer to the question that hasn't left my lips yet.

"Or are you scared of me?"

"Kayin, please come down," Abeo urges me.

I suddenly feel my body lowering to the ground. It isn't obeying my mind. The static in my arms leaves and I don't have the earthquake causing sensation in my gut. My feet land softly on the ground and I walk calmly over to the Four against my will. I know then that the Oracle is controlling me, using his mind control powers. I've always been amazed and frightened of this skill, but never would I have thought he would be using it on me. I saw the Divine once break free of this control and use her own powers so he couldn't do this to her. But she's so strong.

"Be careful," Orisa says, but I'm not sure whom she's aiming it to.

My mind is telling me to lift my arm but I can't do it. I

put everything I can into summoning my power even though all my body can do is walk towards the Four. I can almost feel my hand glowing; it is so intense as I fight against the Oracle's power. I feel the constriction of his mind powers tighten around me, and as I look to him I see his face falter. I definitely have control of his heart. I hear his heartbeat faintly in my head behind the rest of my mental struggle but I concentrate on it as much as I can. I watch him as I do so. With the careful slowing of his heart, he shouldn't be in pain but it should be harder for him to use his powers now, as he gets weaker. I am close enough that I can see his fists shaking by his sides as he tries to repel my power and amplify his own. I am breaking a sweat pushing against him.

Finally he falls back a few steps and grasps at his chest, and as soon as his power is released I also stumble back without the help of him keeping me up. My hand stops glowing immediately and we both stand back, hunched, shocked at the interaction and trying to catch our breath. I feel ashamed. I had taught myself those healer powers with the intention to do some good. It emotionally hurt me when I used it maliciously against a Ghost. Now I've just willingly used it against the Oracle to weaken him? What's wrong with me? Who am I becoming?

I can't bring myself to lift my eyes from the ground and look at the Four, who have subtly edged towards Olon, but still stand in the middle ground. I am so conflicted with so many emotions, too much pride.

I lift my head and feel a cool breeze pass over the wet trail marks that a few delicate tears have left on my cheeks. My knees buckle beneath me and I let myself fall to the ground. At my movement they look towards me and I meet their eyes; mixtures of shock, of worry, hesitance, concern. They are right to feel guarded around me, but I don't deserve their feelings of concern.

"I'm a liability," I say sadly, just realising this myself, barely audible but they hear me. This is something I have to do alone. I have to go see the Supreme and Mahlik and get answers and keep my people safe. My people, humans, with whom I grew up with and lived with. Always.

"Let's talk about this calmly," the Divine says, always the voice of reason, walking towards me slowly. I know I won't have another outburst of power, but she doesn't know that and she comes towards me anyway. They're all so kind. I must keep them safe.

"I'm so sorry. I owe you all everything."

And at last, it is probably overdue, I teleport away.

I don't go straight to her lair, I teleport just to the other side of Ervon Gorge, on Shadow territory. I turn and look back across Dead Man's Desert, knowing beyond that barren land the rebels are living freely, scheming and plotting. For now.

I walk away from the Gorge and towards the land hidden in shadow by large trees and ominous buildings. I am entering the Shadow Lands by foot. The dry land beneath me gradually forms into concrete and grass and merges into pathways to walk down. It takes me a moment to adjust my eyes to the darker surroundings. It is strange almost to see such a built up city when in the last 6 years I've swapped from a small, crowded prison cell, to the remains of an unfamiliar town barely surviving it's damage.

I only vaguely know which way I'm going. I keep looking to the sky to see if I recognise anything from being kidnapped in the truck and taken here before, but of course I don't. I'm scared to run into anyone suddenly. The shilo I saw in the garden when I first teleported to see the Supreme are on another level of living and looked down on me the minute they saw me. I don't fit in and if I'm spotted by anyone they'll know I don't belong here.

Not confident in my shape shifting ability, I kick off into the air and fly up in the trees. I stay high in the branches and shadows as I move along the paths. The air is colder here in the shadows than in the direct desert sun as I'm used to. While making my way flying from one tree to another, I finally come across a street of houses and see their inhabitants, and they're everything I remember.

They sit in their pristine gardens; overly green grass sits below their extravagant outdoor furniture. There are ornate black iron tables and intricately designed chairs to match in a few of the gardens. I see the shilo dressed up in light and metallic clothing, laughing together, with their family or friends.

I decide to fly higher now. I can't imagine my father ever living like this. It just doesn't make sense with the man I think I know, but I guess I never really knew him at all. It just reminds me of why I'm here and I'm again eager to get my answers, so I rise above the trees and fly across their tops.

The sun is warm on my back again and the views of this forest from above are beautiful. In any other situation I would love to slow down and appreciate my surroundings, but there's no time. The tip of the large black building I know the Supreme lurks underneath of breaks through the top of the trees ahead of me and I know where I have to go. I land on the roof gently, and then walk to the edge to peer over. It's a long way down, and I know under the ground there are at least 6 floors of nothingness where the Supreme resides. I wonder if my father is in there with her right now.

The view in front of me is the large garden bordered by

the black walls where I found myself the first time. I float down to the floor, watching the shilo in the garden area. There aren't as many as there were last time, but still enough of them to make me feel uneasy. I go unnoticed as I scale down the side of the building and land in front of the tinted glass doors. I quickly slip inside and feel the same cool air as before, then take a deep breath in, knowing how close I am now. The doors that we went through last time are ahead of me and I walk towards them carefully, aware that the Ghosts might appear to guard them. I am right.

The Ghosts materialise before me and make no signs of moving. It's a risky move but I call upon my lightning and let it spark at my fingers, holding my hand up in view of the Ghost Men.

"Let me through," I demand, but my voice isn't as threatening as I intend. It doesn't matter though; the Ghosts spot my hand and shift their staffs across their body, ready to strike.

"Supreme power." They chant in that menacing way like before, holding their staffs stiffly. "Contain her."

A sudden wave of panic washes over me. I can't fight two of them, can I? I steel myself and prepare for what I may have to do, when that oh so familiar scream reverberates around the building, but it doesn't hurt me at all anymore. The Ghosts halt what they are about to do and step back, holding their staffs back at their sides. They've been given orders. I've got my guard up and I watch them for a moment, and then slowly step towards them. They don't move at all, so I take another step. And another. It's like I'm not even there as I reach for the handle of the doors behind them and sneak through.

Before the doors behind me have properly shut, the door in front of me on my left opens, and the woman I encountered before steps out. She looks the other way down the corridor and then towards me. Her eyes widen slightly at the sight of me but she doesn't react other than that.

"I wondered what the noise was about," she tells me indifferently, smoothing down a few stray hairs of her much more casual hairstyle today. It's sleek and runs effortlessly down her back in waves, tucked behind her ears. I know then she heard the screech of the Supreme too and it affected her much more than me.

"I'm going downstairs," I tell her, propping my shoulders back and standing straight.

"What authority do you have?"

It is becoming a favourite trick of mine, so I summon the lightning back to my fingers.

"I said so."

Visibly gulping, the woman doesn't try to hide her fear now. She thought I was just a human but I'm so much more than that, and I think she's finally realising my role in all this.

"You'll need a key card," she tells me meekly. I don't reply, just merely raise my eyebrow at her and lower my hand slowly. She scurries back into her office and returns after a few moments with her own key card. She turns down the hallway towards the lift that we went down in last time without even looking at me. Her thin black heels tap loudly on the floor as she walks briskly in front of me. My boots make a much duller thump as I follow behind her.

She steps into the lift when the doors open and waits for me to get in beside her, and then I watch her slot her card into the keypad. The newly available buttons light up with the rest of them and she presses B, like before.

"You can leave now," I tell her, keeping my eyes forward. I don't need her chaperoning me down to the Supreme's lair again. I don't want any company on this trip.

"My key card is still in the slot," she replies, in a bid to make me let her stay in there.

"Yes, thank you for that," I brush off her comment. She gets the hint and steps out of the lift. I press the button to close the doors and see her walking away from me as the doors shut. She looks over her shoulder just briefly before the doors close completely.

I breathe a sigh of relief that I got through okay, and then remember where I'm heading. I don't know what I'm expecting to be in her lair. Will she call my father once I'm there? Will I have to arrange another meeting? There's only one way to find out, I think as the chime of the lift tells me it's as low as it can go. The doors slide open and I see the familiar wooden door ahead of me, that doesn't fit the modern stylings of the rest of the building, which I was forcefully pushed through last time.

The stairs are just as dark and creaky as I remember. Step by step I'm lowered into the dark abyss until finally the light of the bottled sparks in her lair glow at the bottom. I'm scanning the room as soon as I'm at the bottom for the Supreme, but what I'm not expecting to see is my father, standing there waiting for me.

I can't help running to him then. He grins as he spots me and opens his arms wide. He catches me easily in his big arms that I remember so well. He barely looks like he's aged, which makes me wonder then if shilo have the same life span as humans. They must be similar, right? As I nuzzle my face into his neck and he holds me tightly, I'm aware that he doesn't smell the same, and suddenly I feel uneasy. The pure nostalgia and relief of him being alive I felt when my eyes first landed on him has quickly dissipated and everything that's happened comes flooding back.

I separate myself from him and properly look at his face. Signs of aging are subtle and his sharp features are accentuated in the light of the sparks coming in at different angles. His wide, brown eyes are looking at me, searching my face for something, and the way his forehead is creased is telling me he can't find what he's searching for.

I don't know whether to be mad, or scared, or hurt or happy. My confusion makes me take another step back.

"Look at us," her voice cuts through the silence like a blade slicing skin. She steps out of the shadows behind my father in all her shape-shifted glory. "All together again."

"Change back right now," I'm seething. Her big doe eyes, sparkling blue, look at me with innocence.

"This is who I am."

She rests her tanned hands on Mahlik's shoulder and he naturally puts his arm around her waist, only briefly glancing at me, but looking at her as he does so.

"I am still myself no matter what form I am in."

I'm clenching my jaw so hard I'm scared it will break, looking at the two of them together, when she looks like that.

"Show your true self now or I am leaving."

She giggles and rolls her eyes playfully, looking up at my father. He smiles at her with nothing but love behind it, it's like I'm not even here. Her form changes back into the creature I know, but the loving look between them doesn't falter and I feel sick to my stomach. I know I'm visibly grimacing at them when my father finally looks back to me and almost looks hurt.

"Let's discuss some things, shall we?" he says with a hopeful smile.

"Don't act so innocent," I sneer.

"Surely you can understand my choices, Kay? You know what we've been through, right?" His arm around the Supreme tightens.

Those are my parents…

"You deceived my mother. Did you ever really love her?" I'm so defensive on behalf of the mother who raised me suddenly, that no matter how happy I am to see my father alive, it doesn't make me any less mad at him.

"She was a wonderful woman, Kayin. Of course, I loved her."

"But not like you love…her." I can barely get the words out.

I am their child…

"It's different. Can't you understand that?"

"Can't you understand that the people who raised me, the people you entrusted me with, are suffering because of you both?! The only life I've ever known is under threat and you want me to 'understand' why it doesn't matter to you?"

I am raging. The Supreme's blood red lips are set in a straight line and her large black eyes are blank, but there is more emotion on my father's face.

"Do you know how it feels to watch them all barely make it by because of everything you've done…all because of me?"

My father finally steps out of their embrace slightly, comes a little closer to me.

"I admit I may have been quick to put those feelings aside. I never had the same connection you have because my objective was always to get back to where I belong."

"I belong with them." I tell them boldly. Looking at them, my flesh and blood, I feel out of place. I can't believe this is where I come from. In our dimly lit surroundings, I take in the impassive look on my father's face, and the pure myth of my mother. This doesn't feel like family.

"Don't you see how they've held you back?" The Supreme finally makes herself heard again. "You're at a place now where you can hone in on your powers. The humans…They don't understand what you are. Who you are. All you can be. But we do!" Her raspy voice is starting to sound excited and she leaves my father's side to step closer to me. As inch after inch between us diminishes, I'm forced to look at her. I try to keep up my strong front but I can feel my face contorting in disgust as I truly look at her. She is my mother and I can't bear the sight of this creature.

"Here, with us, with the Ghosts and the shilo, you can

live like a God. You'll be worshipped for the beautiful, powerful being you are."

She is so close to me now. I think she is going to reach out and touch me. Before I can reply, my mouth shaping into a snarl as she grins at me, Mahlik leaps forward and with a more caring, calmer voice, takes my hand tightly.

"Listen, Princess." The nickname that used to thrill me now makes me cringe. "Your mother is right." He is right to pause here; the way he so easily calls her my mother riles me up. "Those humans you've been staying with, yes, yes they're good people, who think they have good intentions! But they're not truly good for you. You deserve the world. We want to give it to you. Those Four, the 'legendary' ones. What do they know, really? This is so much bigger than them."

"They're characters of a prophecy," I argue back lamely, momentarily subdued by my father's familiar voice. I have missed his voice so much.

"So are you. You're not a Sesay. You're a Supreme. Are you telling me you've never felt like an outsider when you're with them?"

"We're all outsiders. All outcasts."

"But there was always something special in you. We see it as special, as magnificent. But they're afraid of it, unsure of you. I can bet you've felt looked down on there."

I don't answer. I don't want to admit it. It started off so well, all the support they gave me in the Resistance. But the minute Olon started getting doubts, the uncertainty behind his eyes when he realised I was much more than a Healer, it hurt me.

In the short silence that follows, my father peers over his shoulder to the Supreme, like he is looking for confirmation. She nods subtly.

"We don't want you to live the traditional life of a Supreme. We want so much more for you, as any parents want for their child."

He reaches back and the Supreme eagerly takes his hand, watching me. "We can work with you, my sweet. Make sure you live to your full potential. Your mixed blood is a gift."

The facts are I'm their child and they are my parents. But to think of it from their point of view is bewildering. To think the Supreme has any kind of maternal instinct and love for me; I can barely imagine the idea of her having emotions. But it doesn't stop me from feeling a certain rush of relief course through me to hear such accepting words.

They know who I am and all I can be and they support me unconditionally. It's a messed up situation and I have my reservations, due to the fact of the unlawful imprisonment of all humans just to find me, but to be selfish just for a moment and let myself feel comfortable in my own body, is remarkable.

"Let us prove to you this is where you belong."

19

"Do you have all your powers yet?" The Supreme asks me eagerly.

I shrug, eyes down, too many thoughts of where I belong and where I feel comfortable clogging my mind.

"What powers should I have?" I reply half-heartedly, forgetting whom I'm talking to for a moment.

"You can fly and teleport?"

I nod and float a few inches in to the air. I look down and wiggle my feet confirming they are indeed off the ground, and then I teleport behind them. They turn and spot me. My father audibly gasps and clutches his chest in what can only be pride by the look on his face. I drop back to the floor and despite my forlorn thoughts about who I am bringing me down, the corners of my mouth twitch upwards.

"Can you shape shift yet?" The Supreme steps towards me with a devilish smile. I'm almost bashful as I reply.

"I've very recently discovered that one." She grins at me and before I can stop it she's in front of me and grasping my hand.

"Can you show us?"

I look over her shoulder at my father and he nods gently, eyes wide in awe. I'm aware then that he's been waiting for this moment my whole life. He's known the whole time what I've been capable of. This isn't just a reunion after years of separation for him; this is finally a time of no lies, cards on the table, finally sharing the truth with me. Very briefly, I feel a flash of pity for him. From a non-objective position, he's been living in hiding, nothing but secrets between those he loves, and watching a daughter live below her potential. So I want to show him now.

"I'm not sure I can," I admit.

"I'll do it with you, shall I?" she says, like a regular mother teaching her child to ride a bike. The thought of the Supreme shape shifting still makes me queasy because it's the reason we ever got into this mess, so I shake my head quickly.

"I'll try."

She drops my hand and I clench my fists and concentrate. I'm unsure of how to summon this power. I don't want to strain too hard, but I close my eyes and think of someone else, anyone else. When I open my eyes my father looks like he's suppressing a laugh but looks proud nonetheless. I look down but nothing has changed, so I reach up and feel thick curls sticking out of my head. I pull a strand in front of my face while the Supreme chuckles in that low voice of hers and see that I've given myself a head of red curly hair but nothing else.

"I'm not very good at it," I say, feeling embarrassed and a little mad that they find this amusing. I can feel my normal hair fall back against my shoulders without me willing it to, and just as quick the Supreme is jumping forward again. She pushes into the air and above my head, picking up handfuls of my hair and stroking it gently.

"We'll work on it, my sweetness. Don't be down."

I tense and swallow hard, but the irritation I just felt disappears and I don't feel as embarrassed.

"I know firsthand of your telekinesis and lightning," the Supreme continues. She lowers herself back to the floor behind me and I get a tingling sensation on the back of my neck. "Earthquakes? What about weapons?" she coos into my ear.

"I can create earthquakes. Weapons can't hurt me." My voice is shaky.

Her hands clasp my shoulders and she squeezes them momentarily. They then slither down my arms, and she rubs my skin with her cold hands.

"She's the full package, darling."

I can't see her face but ahead of me Mahlik's eyes light up and he claps his hands together with a grin. He is looking past me and over my shoulder and shares a look with the Supreme that I can't decipher which makes me uncomfortable, so I force myself out of her grasp and stand between them.

"Do you see how happy this makes us, princess?"

"Do your other friends encourage you like this?"

"That's not fair," I quip back, turning my head to both of them back and forth.

"And what of your others powers? Your self-taught healer powers? Do they know they're self-taught?" The Supreme continues.

"I don't think I've mentioned it to them-"

"Those powers were deemed acceptable, weren't they?"

I turn to face the Supreme fully. "Those powers are used for good, they're not threatening."

"For good?!" she cries. She laughs sharply. "You killed my Ghosts. You used those powers to fight me. They're not threatening, you say?"

I open my mouth to argue back but I'm silenced temporarily.

"It's just because they knew where those powers came from," I reply a lot less confidently.

"But they didn't really," the Supreme is quick to respond.

"However," I carry on, "my inherited powers were unexpected and strange and hard to control. The Four were just...scared." I sigh. "Oh god, they were scared and confused and I kept getting mad when they couldn't understand it right away. Even though I couldn't understand it either."

"Honey, don't blame yourself. No one is to blame here. But it just shows that you don't belong with them."

My father closes the gap between us and holds my shoulders, making me look at him.

"You need to be surrounded by people you can look up to and people who can teach you, not people you always have to be proving yourself to and educating. Stay with your family. Stay with us."

The Supreme swoops in beside us.

"We just want what's best for our daughter," she says in a singsong voice, resting her chin on Mahlik's shoulders. He tilts his head towards her affectionately. This action confuses me; I want to be disgusted by it, but my father truly loves her, which in itself baffles me, however he is happy with her.

I exhale deeply. I used to think he was happy with the mother who raised me. I imagine her then, in her room in the middle of the Resistance, trying to adjust, believing her husband is dead. But he's here with another woman. Not woman, creature. And she is the one behind enslaving the humans. I shake my head. No matter what they say and how accepted they make me feel, I could never stay here. This is not where I belong. Not how I've been raised.

"I can't trust you."

My father's face drops and his hands fall from my shoulders. The Supreme screeches and backs away.

"You must stay here and train! You must!" she cries.

"Dad…" I try to reason with him, my eyes are pleading.

"Kay…Please." He looks back at the Supreme who has her hands in front of her face, like she inches away from clawing her eyes out. He turns back to me, desperate. "Give us a try."

To him this is normal; it's all he knows. But to me this request is absurd. He looks at the Supreme and wants to work with her through this frustration; I look at the Supreme and see a creature on the edge of breaking point. I'm scared of her and I'm wary of losing him completely if I leave. But I have to choose between the only life I've known and the life in front of me.

"I want to stay with Gracine," I say delicately, just to him, feeling myself break into pieces the more hurt my father looks. He's not the man I thought I knew but I care for him deeply.

Just then a sharp ringing in my ears and an unbearable sting in my temples forces me to the floor in agony. The Supreme is screaming and she's not using the 'Kayin frequency', as she calls it. The wretched noise pierces through me and I let out my own scream of pain. Looking up to my father through watery eyes, I can see he's affected but he only seems to be wincing. He looks more pained to see me like this.

"I'm your mother!" Comes her powerful, booming voice. I find relief when she stops screeching but can't bring myself to move. The Supreme kicks off into the shadows with a frustrated cry. My father watches her fly up above us and into the darkness with a worried look.

"Honey?"

If I didn't know any better I could almost mistake his tone for fear. With a fleeting look to me in my crumpled position on the floor, he calls up to her again, begs her to come down.

"She cannot be convinced," her menacing voice cascades down on us. I'm staring at my father, waiting for him to make a move, to shine a light on why the Supreme is taking this so hard.

"Kayin. You're our child. She loves you, honest she does. Take a chance on us. Let us train you," he's back to pleading.

There's that word again; train. Why do they want to train me? I get they want me to be all I can be, but why phrase it like that so persistently?

"I don't need to be here. I don't need you two." With every word I can feel myself becoming less brave, less bold to be speaking back when the Supreme is dangerously mad right now. Suddenly a blue bolt of lightning illuminates the space around us and crackles loudly as it collides with the floor right beside me. My drained body jumps out of the way, and I look back to the black scorch mark just next to where I was lying.

Above me I see the Supreme's white cloak emerging from the shadows and descending upon us. She floats above our heads and with outstretched arms, palms facing the sky she looks down on me with deadly, black eyes.

"You may have all my powers but you are weak."

Terror has got me in a chokehold and I'm frozen. This being in front of me is the kind of Supreme I feared unleashing when I first met her.

"If you do not stay with us by choice I will make you stay." There is a scary tranquillity in her voice; a tone you would expect of someone who was so angry they surpassed the exploding rage phase. She is beyond calming down.

Against my will, my body rises from the ground and into an upright position. The Supreme is picking me up with her telekinesis and I can't do anything to stop her. My feet scrape along the floor and my arms hang stiffly at my sides until I'm finally pushed back against a wall and a few inches above the ground, forcing me to look at her.

"I have kept my distance. I have let you have your fun with the humans." Her voice echoes with power. "We need you. Here. Create a future with us, or I will destroy everything you know."

"What more is there to destroy?" my voice is strained as I think about our deserted towns and ruined buildings.

"I will level the human lands and there will be no survivors," she promises me, and I'm sorry I asked. She replies so quick I'm sure this isn't a spur of the moment decision. She's been waiting for this all along, for the opportunity to do just that. I'm disgusted, with her, with myself for ever considering staying here with them by choice, with Mahlik for loving such a creature. She's talking about genocide, but I bet this won't deter him. What do the humans matter to him, anyway? He's a shilo.

But they matter a lot to me. I don't for a second believe the Supreme wouldn't follow through on this threat, and I can't let any harm come to those I know and love. I care about them too much.

With the weight of my choice hanging heavy on my shoulders, but knowing the destruction of my people would be too much to bear, I breathe in deeply through my nose and will the tears not to fall.

"I'll stay."

A sudden wind blows past my face and the sparks around us flicker in the breeze. I know it's the Supreme causing this draft and she grins proudly when I look at her.

"You have to tell them."

My father's voice is so level and calm I almost don't hear it over the wind whistling past my ears.

"What do you mean?"

It's a shock to my system when the Supreme releases her hold on me and I drop to my knees involuntarily. She cackles, knowing what my father is talking about.

"What a spectacle, won't that be something?"

"What are you talking about?" I get to my feet and stand straight again on my own finally.

"You'll have to tell your precious humans that you're never going to see them again!" The Supreme is giddy with this idea; it makes my blood boil.

My father, trying to keep the peace with what little mortal power he has, speaks up again, with a kinder voice.

"You'll have to tell them you're doing this willingly, staying here. Or they'll come for us, they'll try and take you back."

I want to remind him I'm not doing this willingly, but I

keep that thought to myself. He's right. The Four will come looking for me, and I know they will be prepared for a fight.

In the heavy silence that follows as I digest my choices, the Supreme finally returns to the ground and Mahlik goes to her side, stroking her pale arm comfortingly. She's a myth and he's a shilo. I've been accumulating odd and potentially scary powers and fighting with Olon and appearing to be flying off the rails. Especially after my latest argument with the Four, and disappearing how I did…If I go back and announce now that I'm leaving them, staying with Mahlik and the Supreme in the Shadow Lands…Everyone is going to think I've gone to the dark side, so to speak. They're going to believe I've betrayed them, after everything we've been through. Gracine, oh no. She'll find out that my father is alive after all and doesn't want to be with her, and now I'm leaving too. She's going to be heartbroken.

I sniff audibly, overwhelmed with emotion, and earn back their attention. They look towards me, but I'm still caught up in thoughts of my mother. She hasn't got any other family there. What will she do? Will she cope? I can only hope the rogues will look after her.

I angrily wipe at the tears that are silently running down my cheeks. I'll never get to explain to them why I'm leaving, not really.

My father steps towards me, closes the distance and puts

his arms out like he's going to hug me, but I jerk away and he hesitates.

"Don't…please."

He lowers his arms with no reply.

"When do I tell them?"

"As soon as possible!"

Once again I'm disgusted at the Supreme's joy in all this.

"Now that I have my heir back, we can come out of hiding, darling!" The Supreme clutches at Mahlik. He holds her tightly.

"Now we have her back we can do many things, my love." They share a mischievous look that tells me there's something they're hiding, and I'm not surprised. Of course there's something more to this than just parental instinct. The Supreme turns back to me.

"Now you're rightfully by my side we can show the people just who's in charge. It'll be fun to take our place on the throne again," she grins at me as if I'm going to return her excitement.

"What throne?"

"Metaphorically, princess," my father chips in, and the irony of that nickname hits me like a tonne of bricks.

"Why were you in hiding at all?"

The Supreme sighs melodramatically and rolls her eyes.

"The Supreme blood line used to rule all these lands, until my mother. She wasn't big on the theatrics and over the years her presence became less and less, kept me inside with her. We live for a long time, you see, and eventually she was forgotten, and all eyes were on her sidekick, the Ghost Lord. Our existence became nothing more than a rumour. She died years after you were born and I had made you disappear," she floats gracefully in one step over to me, cups my face before I have a chance to reject her touch.

"I was distraught about losing my heir. My flesh and blood." She squishes my face and shakes my head a little, in what I assume is in an affectionate way. "The Ghost Lord thought you were a product of abuse against me and had no remorse when you 'didn't survive', but gave me the space I needed to grieve. I had no interest in returning to the public eye without my daughter by my side. And I finally can!"

She glances back towards my father, and when I look at his face he looks a little sad. The Supreme lets her gaze linger on him before turning slowly back to me. She is so close I see the glints of silver swimming in her black eyes again.

"You and I, Kayin. We can do wonders."

"And dad, too?" I ask, hoping to get some understanding into their forlorn looks shared a moment ago.

"Hopefully soon," she replies, as cryptic as ever. In a

sudden change of atmosphere, she spins on her heel, leaving me dazed. She leaps into the air with a new resolve.

"Shall we get started then? It'll be absolute bliss to feel the sun on my skin again."

Her words cause my stomach to do flips as I remember what I have to do.

"I'll meet you upstairs?" I say meekly, and before they can reply I teleport up to the ground floor, back into the hallway, just outside of the lift. The carriage has returned back to this floor and I quickly poke my head in and take out the key card the woman had inserted before I went downstairs. As snobbish and self-righteous as she is, I owe her a warning at least; she has been helpful after all. I jog back up the hallway and knock on her door. But before I can even reach the third knock, the Supreme's ear piercing scream reverberates through the walls and I see the silhouette of the woman approaching her office door through the blurred glass.

She flinches when she sees me, and she already looks somewhat rattled from the Supreme's calling. I hand her key card back to her and she slowly reaches for it, sceptically.

"I don't know what's about to happen now…" I begin. She watches me carefully. "Okay, I sort of know what's about to happen now. Rejoice, for your Supreme rises!" I say, with a weak smile, lifting my arms noncommittally with a shrug in celebration.

Her eyes go wide and she drops the key card she'd just taken off of me.

"What do you mean?" Her voice is apprehensive and shaky.

"She's coming out of hiding and we're going to take over the world," I say quickly with only a hint of sarcasm, hurrying to get my words in as the Supreme screams again.

The appearance of the two guarding Ghosts through the windows in the door to my left catches my eye and we both look in that direction. Suddenly we can hear gasps and yells and the clatter of plates. The Ghosts begin walking away from the doors so without thinking I follow them, pushing the doors open and stepping quickly out into the lobby, the woman following closely behind me. The Ghosts are heading towards the large tinted doors that lead into the garden. Instead of opening them, they teleport onto the other side in sync and continue on.

The commotion outside launches my stomach into its acrobatic flips again and I feel nervous to go out there. The woman overtakes me and goes a few steps ahead, but she stops and looks back. Something in her eyes, the way she is no longer confident in her role, the familiar screeching call I can hear outside, it all set my insides on fire. I shut my eyes tightly, ball my fists up, can almost feel the Supreme heritage in my blood as it pumps through my veins. I can't deny the sudden power surge that I feel.

"Your eyes…"

Her voice is small and she points a shaky finger at me.

"They're black. You really are…" She can't finish her sentence.

The only difference it makes to my sight is a faint black shadow around my field of vision, but it directly affects my ego. I tilt my head at the woman and she slightly bows, dropping her gaze to the floor.

"Supreme," she whispers.

"The heir of," I reply. She raises her head, still in her bent position and smiles submissively.

With my nerves eradicated, I stride towards the doors and use my power to push them open before I reach them, so I don't break my stride as I exit.

Shilo all around the green garden are down on their knees, picnic tables have been pushed over, plates smashed to pieces in the grass. They are all facing the Supreme, who's floating proudly in the air, my father also kneeling to her side below.

"Daughter! My sweet!" she cries, spotting me. "You look enchanting. Join me!"

Without a thought I kick into the sky and float opposite her.

"Your ruler is back!" She addresses our audience. She twirls so she can see them all around her. "Thank you for staying loyal. Believing. It will not go unnoticed."

A hushed murmuring follows as the shilo turn to each other with smiles on their faces.

"It is time to take back my rightful place as your Supreme, with my true heir by my side." She gestures to me passionately, grinning with all her white teeth on show.

The Ghosts that have joined us in the garden stiffen, clutching their staffs across their chest.

"Stand down!" The Supreme calls menacingly, the smile wiped from her face. I look over my shoulder to them, wondering what brought on their sudden change of stance. I float to the Supreme's side, wary when they don't lower their staffs right away, like they are running through their options. I realise, when they put their weapons straight by their sides again but their gaze stays locked in my general direction, that I am their problem. I gulp and blink and as I do so the blackness around my vision disappears and I know my eyes have returned to normal.

It is easy to take my place next to the Supreme with all the confidence and self assurance in the world when I float above the shilo who have believed they are above myself and humans for so long, but my strong bravado falters when I remember I shouldn't exist. All the Ghosts, they believe I am an illegitimate heir and had died when I was a baby. I shouldn't be standing, well flying, here right now. The Ghosts have always targeted me and wanted to 'detain' me whenever I showed any of my Supreme powers, it's what they believe they should do.

"There's a lot we have to accomplish." The Supreme is close to my face now, speaking to only me. "Don't worry," with a fleeting look of disinterest to the shilo she takes my hand. "We'll get you trained."

A feeling of dread takes over me, unsure of what the second half of her plan is, and whether I will ever truly find out.

The Supreme shoots further into the air then, with a theatrical gust of wind that blows a few shilo off of their knees below. She flies so high I have to shield my eyes from the sun to look up at her. She screams and it echoes powerfully across the land. I turn my gaze down to my father who is looking up like the rest of the shilo, but he doesn't look astonished or fearful, he looks proud. He gives me a subtle nod, which I know means 'go with her'. Some more pieces of the puzzle come together in my mind. Just like I shouldn't exist, no one can know the Supreme had any kind of relation with a shilo man. Mahlik hides behind the lie that a Ghost laid with the Supreme forcefully and who since has been 'dealt with'. With this revelation I realise I can't have any open relation with him either if we are taking this into the public eye. My emotions are conflicted. True, he isn't the father I thought I knew but he is still my family, and I spent so long waiting to be reunited with him, just to now have to hide our kinship.

I know I can't linger any longer and the Supreme is waiting for me, so I also fly higher into the air to join her, with less of a flourish as she had. Below us the shilo stand up, jumping in place, waving and cheering and whistling as we leave their presence. Never believing in anything myself, I try to imagine the feelings they must have. A God like figure of their religion revealing herself on a normal day like any other. It must be extraordinary.

20

"She's probably just cooling off, which is what you should be doing," the Vehement tells the Oracle. He is still pacing around the ditch.

After Kayin disappeared, once again, Olon had got up and searched around the town, calling for her, hoping for the slightest chance that she hadn't gone to see the Supreme. The Four had collected back in the ditch, and the other three are still trying to calm down a high-strung Oracle.

"She's not cooling off. She's with the Supreme. And maybe her father." The Oracle turns towards Imara and finally stops pacing. "Don't you see? I've wound her up, put all kinds of thoughts into her head, and she's gone straight to her. I handled that all wrong."

"Don't blame yourself. We were all there," the Cryptic

tells him. He can sense Olon is near breaking point. He puts so much on himself. A short silence follows and Olon turns away from them, rubbing his face with his dirty hands.

"She means a lot to you, doesn't she?"

The Divine's voice is small, delicate, much like Orisa herself. It isn't forceful, or accusing, and the calmness of it relaxes Olon, despite everything he is feeling. They all se his tensed shoulders droop and his arms fall back to his sides. With a sigh, he faces them once more. His eyes meet Orisa's; he looks defeated.

"You've always had a close connection with her," Orisa continues.

Olon doesn't reply. Again, he lifts his hand and rubs his forehead, over thinking as usual, now having to face facts.

"Is it possible this has been affecting your decisions? Wanting her to follow your rules so closely?"

The Vehement and Cryptic watch this exchange with intrigue, sharing looks. They all had their suspicions that there may have been more to it, more going on between them, and the Divine has finally brought it to light.

"I've been so controlling. It was going well…between us." Olon becomes nervous now, talking openly about it when he has been trying to keep it under wraps for so long. "I'll admit I got a bit scared when she started developing all these new powers. It was confusing and I knew she felt the same. She was unsure of herself. I realised maybe it was best, for us all, if I retook the role of the Oracle to her, rather than Olon."

Looks are shared, and eyebrows are raised, at the new information that they were on a first name basis.

"I wanted to show her I was in control. Not of her, but of the situation. I wanted her to know that it didn't matter if she was unsure or scared, because I had it under control." He sighs again. The sun is lower in the sky now but still hot, and it beats down on his shoulders while he speaks.

"I definitely went about that the wrong way. She became hostile and I think she felt hurt. But the more she distanced herself, the more I wanted to know what was going on, help her, have some kind of power over the situation."

He groans loudly and kicks up some dirt, frustrated. It almost fees cathartic, being able to admit this all out loud and express his emotions to his friends.

"I should not have used my powers on her. That just came across as belligerent. I just wanted her to calm down." He finally meets the eyes of the Four, hesitantly. "She's strong. Even if she doesn't fully know how to use all her powers. She can only get stronger and I don't want the Supreme to take advantage of her."

His final words sit heavily in the air, while they all process what that could mean. Unbeknownst to them, they were about to find out.

Their thoughts are soon interrupted by an echoing screech that has them clawing at their ears, looking for some relief to the noise. Fear and worry etch across all their faces as they look at each other and straighten up; no words are needed before they all make a move to jump out of the ditch and find the source of the noise.

They run out into open desert, looking around for anything that could give them a clue. The earth beneath them begins rumbling. A curt shake of the head from the Vehement tells them all it was not her doing. They struggle to stay upright as their bodies shake roughly. A loud crack is heard not that far away from them, and they all sink to their knees for support as they watch the dusty desert floor fracture and split from the earthquake. When the shaking finally stops and dust fills the air around them, they all hear a loud cackling laugh coming from the West. Apprehension takes them all by the throat but it doesn't stop Olon jumping back to his feet and running towards the noise. The other three are quickly up and following him, coughing on the dust that is filling their eyes and lungs. They kick debris out of their way as they run.

The dust settles and the air becomes clear as they run towards Ervon Gorge, and in the distance, above the great canyon, a large blue light is floating, sparking even. When they get close enough to see what it is they all halt. Standing together in a line they look up at the Supreme with wide eyes. Olon had seen her when he looked into Kayin's memories, and he'd described her to the others, but none of that prepared them for her in real life.

Too busy ogling at the Supreme, as she laughs and works up a hard wind around them, they don't see Kayin standing by herself on the other side of the Gorge. But as she moves ever so slightly closer, it catches Olon's eye and he looks down away from the sky. She is watching him, wringing her hands nervously. He tries to read her mind, find out what she is thinking, what is happening, but she is too far away and the small twister the Supreme is whipping up distracts him. He can't hear anything but the faint crow of the Supreme's laugh and the wind in his ears.

"Kayin!" he yells, his voice still muffled by his surroundings. He lunges forward but Abeo sticks his arm out and grabs his shirt, stopping him from going any further, worried about what the Supreme might do if she sees him making a move towards her daughter.

Dark clouds gather together above them and block the sun out. The Supreme is looking towards the sky with her arms up, and the blue electricity that engulfs her being buzzes around her as she shoots a bolt of lightning into the clouds, illuminating them briefly.

"Legends!" She cries, finally acknowledging the Four as they stand below, dumbfounded.

"Your services are no longer required!" The Supreme roars with laughter once more. "My heir has been returned to me and she no longer needs you!" With this not so subtle cue, Kayin steps into the air effortlessly and floats up towards the Supreme, hovering by her side.

"Congratulations! You have fulfilled your prophecy."

The Four are unsure how to react to her words. Yes, they have freed their people from the prison, but the Supreme still reigns, the leader of the evil they are fighting, so surely it isn't over? And Kayin is not safely by their sides, where she belongs. They can't end it now.

"What do we do?" The Vehement whispers yells to the others, bracing herself from the wind.

"We need to talk to Kayin." The Oracle is worried this sounds like a bias answer now that new information about the two of them has been discussed, but he is happy to see his friends nod in agreement.

The Cryptic closes his eyes and erects a dome of invisibility over the four of them. This would give them time to regroup in private.

The Supreme screeches at their disappearance and Kayin becomes worried. What are they up to?

The Supreme strikes the ground where the Four once

stood with a bolt of lightning but it just fizzles out into the ground. The Four have moved.

"We need to bring her down," the Vehement says from inside the dome, bringing their attention back to the plan and away from the scorched land where they were just standing.

The Cryptic lifts his hands and circles them around each other, and between them a small fire starts blazing until he is holding a large fireball ready to throw. A nod from the others puts them all on the same page.

The Supreme is desperately scanning the ground for any sign of where the Four might be.

"Why are you doing this?" Kayin speaks quietly to the Supreme.

"They should know who's in charge and their duty is over. You're in our care now."

"I was never in their care," Kayin replies stubbornly. "They were my friends."

"You don't need them anymore."

The Supreme is barely able to finish her sentence when a fireball comes hurtling towards her out of nowhere. Kayin swoops out of the way instantly, and the fireball hits the Supreme in the chest. She screams loudly and clutches at her clothing, being pushed back a few feet in the air. It isn't the heat that affects her, as she can withstand the heat of lightning, but the force of the impact on her stomach catches her off guard.

With her defences momentarily down, the Oracle steps out of the invisibility dome and lifts his arms towards the Supreme, his hands shaped like claws, trying to tap into the Supreme's mind and control her. It isn't like controlling another human, or even a Ghost. When he does that, it is like he imagines themselves in their brain, can see their thoughts, their instincts and manipulate them. Controlling the Supreme, if he closes his eyes, he can see an empty room, hear echoing footsteps seemingly coming from nowhere. While the Supreme in front of him is lowering herself to the ground, inside his head he can hear her voice. Her coarse whispers lap at his subconscious.

"You think you're strong?"

"You think you can save Kayin? She doesn't need saving."

"How long can you keep this up?"

"You're getting tired now, aren't you?"

"I'm too strong for you."

Her voice taunts him, over and over. He tries to shake his head, get her voice away from his ears. It is so close.

The Supreme is hanging over the Gorge now, but Olon is losing his controlling grip. Her blank expression lights up, and she begins smiling threateningly. She forcibly lifts her arms against his powers, and summons a bolt of lightning. The blue energy sparks out of her fingers and just as she is about to shoot it, the Divine jumps in front of the Oracle and controls the light particles around her, emitting a blinding light that shakes the Supreme and makes her recoil. The Four collect together, anticipating her next move when the Supreme regains her composure. The snarl of her face makes them all shiver.

"Enough!" Kayin balls her glowing hand into a fist in the direction of the Supreme, and she gasps and splutters. Kayin has stopped her heart completely in an instant, just for a moment so she can take control of the situation. She wouldn't have been able to hold it for much longer anyway; the Supreme is too strong. The ever growing windstorm settles down but the clouds stayed in place.

The Four look hopefully up to Kayin, their friend, despite the display of strong powers she is showing. She looks sadly down at them, as the Supreme joins her and floats mere inches behind her. She rests a hand on Kayin's shoulder, still recovering from Kayin's move.

"Enough." Kayin says a little less forcibly. "It's true. You can go back to your lives. Rebuild yourselves. Promise not to bother us and we will not bother you. Our war is over."

The Four are shocked, mumbling their dismay as she

speaks.

"Kayin. Come down here, please," Abeo begs her. She almost caves, looking down into his friendly eyes. The man that always saw the best in her, always saw the potential. She is going to miss him.

"You belong with us!" Olon cries, stepping forward, his emotions not as under control as the others have theirs, but they don't stop him. He looks heartbroken, but keeps up a strong stance, barely. Kayin can see through it, and it melts her. But she thinks of the greater good. If she separates from them now, they get to live their lives freely. If she puts up any fight, the Supreme will level their civilisation. It's a no brainer; she just wishes she could have the opportunity to explain it to them.

"I'm staying with the Supreme, and my father." She wants so badly to leave a message for Gracine, for them to give to her, but she knows if she gets emotions involved it will only hurt her more, and Kayin might crumble.

"Please," her voice almost breaks. "Leave us be." A second longer and she might start crying; Kayin knows she has to leave right now, so she teleports out of sight. The Supreme screeches one last time and with a wave of her hand knocks the Four over with a gust of wind, before disappearing herself. A faint echo of her laugh and aching bodies are all they are left with.

"That wasn't her talking! They've forced her to say that!"

Olon is furious as the Four make their way back to the ditch, battered and bruised.

"This is what I was afraid of. This is my fault."

"Olon, come on." The Vehement grabs his arm, making him look at her. "You said it yourself, Kayin is strong, and she can only get stronger. If you truly think this isn't her choice-"

"Of course it's not!" Olon cuts in. "You all know Kayin. She was good. She is good. There is no reason for her to join them."

"Her father is over there," the Divine suggests.

"Her mother is here!" Registering his friends' faces, Olon amends his statement, a little softer. "Her mother, Gracine, who raised her is here. Kayin wouldn't leave her by choice. Family is important to her."

"As I was saying," Imara continues, bringing Olon's attention back to her. "If you truly think this isn't her choice, then our main problem is the Supreme. We all know Kayin is good at heart. It's not her we need to worry about."

"What do you suggest?" the Cryptic asks the Vehement.

"We should attack, surely?" she replies, always thinking on the offensive.

"Maybe we should think up more of a plan before we

jump into anything?" the Divine interjects.

Olon thinks about it. "You're both right. I think we should attack but we need a game plan. Is it a case of bringing Kayin back? Attacking the Supreme directly? Are they going to be expecting us to attack or did they think we would back off, and how does this affect how we go forward?" He pauses, a heavy silence hangs over them. "We've got a lot to think about but we have to do it quickly."

"I thought I was just going to tell them I was leaving!" I am fuming when we return to the Supreme's lair. I wish I had something to throw or punch.

"They had to know-"

"Yes! They had to know who was in charge!" I cut her off. "I get it!"

I halt my pacing and turn to face her angrily. "Why do you have to destroy everything around you?" I'm seething; I can feel the emotion dripping from my words. My conscience is in turmoil, questioning how I could have ever agreed to work with this monster, despite knowing the other option would mean destruction for the humans.

The Supreme's eyes are as black and emotionless as ever, like looking into a void. She comes towards me but I throw my hand up in protest and stop her from coming any closer by blowing a gust of air against her.

"Don't touch me," I spit.

"Oh temper, temper," she says with a hint of amusement, in the patronising tone she uses that has become too familiar. "What will your father think of this tantrum?"

I ball my hands into fists and throw them down at my sides with a loud groan, and involuntarily release another blast of air that kicks up some dust and blows the sparks out around us. As the sparks relight themselves in their little containers there is a silence between us.

I concentrate on relaxing my muscles and unclenching my hands, pushing the Supreme out of my mind. After a moment when I've regained control of my breathing I look to her but she is not there. I spin quickly on the spot but she's nowhere around me. Then I feel a shiver run down my back in dread and I look slowly upwards into the darkness that looms above me. Her favourite place to go, a place that fills me with anxiety.

"I must destroy everything around me…" her voice echoes. She talks slowly and deeply on purpose because she knows how it affects me. "Because I plan to dismantle traditions that are centuries old."

She lowers herself enough that I can faintly see her shape in the shadows.

"The Supreme species have lived by the same rules and

regulations for a long time, and I am taking it upon myself to change the outdated regime."

"Why?" I stammer. "Why you? Why now?"

"It doesn't work."

"It seems to have worked for a long time." I counter.

"It seems to have survived for a long time. It does not work for us, it is not beneficial to us."

Her emphasis brings another question to mind.

"Who is 'us'?"

A pause. I'm not sure if she doesn't know the answer or if she doesn't want to tell me. I am ever apprehensive as she lowers herself back to my level gracefully. With barely a sound as her feet touch the floor, she sighs.

"What are you prepared to do for love?"

Her question throws me off. She says it softly, simply asking rather than accusing, but my eyebrows crease in confusion and my mouth opens but nothing comes out. My guard is up even though I'm not under attack.

"I'm not sure what you mean."

"For love," she states again. "I am prepared to tear apart the only life I have ever lived by…Ever known, for love."

The solemn tone and sadness in her voice makes it easy to realise what she's talking about. Mahlik. She can't live with my father, because it's sacrilege as far as the Ghosts are concerned, despite what the Supreme might want. My father would be killed if this secret ever came to light.

"But you, you're an ultimate being, powers beyond belief…" I'm trying to process these new thoughts and insights as quickly as I can.

"But they are an army." She takes on a harsher tone again now. "A strong army whose loyalties lie between the Supreme and our traditions. If I break those traditions, with whom do the Ghosts side? You saw them in the garden earlier. They had their sights set on you, my little abomination, they were conflicted."

I let her approach me now. She cups my face as she always does, with a firm grip. She changes her eyes and gives me something human to look at. It's hard to focus on anything else, when she does this; acts human. Relates to my emotions. I'm reminded again how controversial I am within their society. A baby born of a defiled Supreme. Born at the wrong time. The criminal Ghost was killed and I didn't survive birth. I shouldn't exist in every sense of the phrase.

"That's our little secret," she confides. "Mahlik and I have been waiting for this day to come. With you by my side, with your mixed blood and potential, together we can take them down. Create new rules. There may be backlash in the shilo community but they mean nothing in the bigger picture."

I flinch slightly with the reminder that she considers

anyone beneath her to be collateral damage, and the mortality of everyone I love rears its ugly head in my mind again.

"We have a better chance to change the way things are if we do this together."

I wonder if this has been their plan all along for the benefit of us as a family or them as a couple. Am I just a pawn in her plan to live happily ever after with my father or does she want this new life for us all. I'm silent throughout all of this, scared to voice my thoughts.

"Can you imagine what it feels like to not be able to be with the one you love, because people want to keep you apart?" The Supreme's voice is soft again, and her face is so close to mine her words fill my ears and without meaning to my mind finds Olon. I realise I know exactly what it feels like to not be with the one you love because of other people's interference.

I focus back on the Supreme. I know what she wants from me. She wants me to join her in her war so she can love freely, all the while not realising she's not letting me love freely. I weigh up my options. I can run back to the humans, and back to Olon, anger the Supreme, disappoint my father and risk death and destruction. Or, I can join her, dismantle the Supreme regime and fight the Ghosts, help my mother and father be together, and when they're happy and settled…I can return to Olon with the knowledge that the Supreme no longer needs me.

The choice seems obvious.

"What do you need me to do?"

21

Three days after I officially started training with the Supreme, I decided to write another list of my powers and abilities.

Bone vision

Ability to heal wounds

Heart control

Impervious to weapons

Earthquakes

Lightning

Telekinesis

Shapeshift

Teleport

Fly

Black eyes

The Supreme and I refer back to this list and strategise.

In the last two weeks we have been assessing what

powers I need extra practice with. Looking at which ones would come in most handy in hypothetical situations. We try to think of every possibility. My father comes by sometimes, it's nice to have him around. If I ignore the rest of my surroundings, it's almost like being a kid and I get that same feeling I used to get when he came home from work. If I ignore the fact that I'm planning a war with the Supreme rather than helping Gracine wash up when he walks through the door. Yeah, almost like it used to be.

I don't leave the lair as much as she does. She regularly goes upstairs, outside to her people. I can't imagine the commotion that must be going on up there. The Supreme has returned. How are the shilo possibly reacting to that? Her followers celebrate, but what about the others? I can't be sure, not until I see it for myself, but I have my sights set on only one thing and that's making the Supreme's goals become reality.

I've had a chance to venture further into the lair than just the main room at the bottom of the stairs. It's much more than that one room and it's all underground. There's a room with a bed that I can only assume my father sleeps in. I can't imagine the Supreme going to bed and I'm not wholly sure she sleeps at all. But I make that my temporary dwellings, as I do need sleep. It's not the most comfortable mattress I've ever slept on; I can feel the hard springs poking into my back as I lay staring at the darkness above me at night. But it doesn't keep me from falling asleep; my body feels so spent at the end of each day from working hard to improve my powers.

The lack of natural light down in the lair and all the sparks of artificial light have messed with my sense of time, so I'm not sure what time I wake up, whether it's even morning or not, but I slide myself out of bed and quickly make it over, before wandering out into what I now think of as the main room. Sometimes the Supreme is already in here, sometimes she's lurking above me or sometimes she'll be out gallivanting around outside, enjoying time with her worshipers I suspect. This is one of those mornings, it's empty and the lights of the contained sparks illuminate a tray of breakfast waiting for me.

I know it's for me because this has happened every morning. I'm not sure who makes it or who brings it down here, but it must be an order from the Supreme. I sit on the floor next to the wooden tray and glance over what I have today. A large glass of orange juice that I eagerly pick up and start gulping down to relieve my dry mouth. There are two slices of dry toast and an apple sitting beside them, and what I assume is peanut butter in a small pot next to that. There's a moist towel sitting on a little plate in the corner too.

I spread the peanut butter across my toast as best I can

with my finger and after every bite of that I take a bite of the apple, for the juice. It's been like this most mornings, random pieces of food thrown together, but I make do. I don't think about it too hard, I just eat and keep my thoughts on the day ahead and my plan.

I'm mid using the towel to rub my face and my armpits as I do every morning, and jump when the door at the top of the stairs opens suddenly, partly out of embarrassment that I was washing my armpits and partly out of alarm. The Supreme never uses the door for obvious reasons so I'm curious to see who is coming down.

Heavy footsteps come quickly down the stairs and then I see my father step into the light. I never asked him how he gets in an out of here, but I assume he must have his own key card to make it down to the basement through the lift. I wonder what the woman upstairs in her office thinks of that.

"Hello," I say, not as warm with him as I once was. Things have changed.

"Kayin, your mother wants you outside."

"And she sent you to get me? Why didn't she call me herself?" I am confused.

"She's busy." He looks a little flustered. His hair is messy and has specs of dirt in it, his brows are furrowed together, in fact his whole person looks a little windswept and anxious.

"What's going on?" I ask him, taking a step forward.

"The rebels are advancing. They're sneaky but someone spotted one of them and your mother is trying to track them down before they infiltrate us."

I hold my breath. Oh, what are they doing? This isn't part of the plan. Despite not wanting them here, I have to bite my lip to suppress a smile at the thought of whatever they have planned. I am one of them after all, no matter what anyone else thinks, and the legion has probably already infiltrated further than my father or anyone else thinks.

"Will you come upstairs and survey things with her?" my father says after a silence. I nod slowly then grab his hand with the intention of teleporting us outside. Teleporting with someone else is a skill I've mastered recently with the help of the Supreme; I know how to do it safely. When I teleported with Olon after he was stabbed, and then when I took him to the prison, it was a fluke and the Supreme later told me I could have done some serious damage to his body or mind.

My father snatches his hands away. "No, I have to take the stairs. If someone sees us appear together, they'll start asking questions." He raises his hand to stroke my cheek with his fingers more affectionately. "You go ahead. I'll see you soon."

Of course he knows it could be days before I see him again and his subtly sad smile assures me of that. I feel a little twist in my heart but I still feel a detachment to him. I've compartmentalised the father I grew up with, and the father who stands in front of me now. I nod and step back and teleport up to the garden.

It's eerie to see the large field so empty. I don't think I've ever seen it like this. I thought there would be someone out here who could send me in the right direction. With my senses on high alert I walk across the grass towards the building again, and with a final look over my shoulder to the deserted garden, I open the doors and step into the air-conditioned lobby. No one sits at the desk in front of me, and there are no Ghosts guarding the doors but I'm sure they'd be ready to appear if someone tried to get through. I'm not keen on facing them without the Supreme ordering them to stand down, especially now as they know who I am, whereas before they just thought I was a rebel.

I consider going upstairs, but I know that somewhere outside the rogues are lurking and the Supreme is hunting them, so I decide I have to find the front door to this building. Or back door. Whatever door leads me out to the other side.

On the far side of the desk I see a corridor I'd never noticed before, never needed to notice. Whenever I was in here I was usually preoccupied with the doors to the right of the desk, where the lift is which ultimately leads down to the lair.

My steps echo softly as I walk around the desk. Still confused as to the lack of shilo around, I hesitantly peer round the wall and up the hallway but not surprisingly that too is deserted. As I walk I collect my hair together and pulled it into a secure ponytail. At the end of the hall looks to be a dead end but I keep going. Several doors appear on each of my sides but glancing through the windows of the doors I can only see what looks to be normal office spaces. Once I am closer to the end I can see that the corridor turns right, so I pick up my pace to a jog to get there quicker. Another careful peek around the corner, and I can see I am definitely at a dead end now, but there is also a large black door. I'm not sure what is on the other side of the door, I am struggling to picture my location in my head and I'm not familiar with the Shadow Lands at the best of times, but that doesn't stop me from pushing the bar across the door, flinching at the creaking metal noise as it opens and stepping out into the shadows.

I am standing on a barely used path in the woods, stretching far to my left and right. Greenery grows on either side of the narrow muddy path, and trees stand tall all around, blocking the sun. It smells fresh and clean, but dirty and muddy all at once. I step onto the path and decide to go to my right, crunching over twigs and sticks as I go. Every time I hear a noise, a rustle of leaves or a snap of a branch, I can't help but dart my head around. What am I scared of? Shilo? They are of no threat to me with my powers, and if they are a follower of the Supreme then they would be allies to me. Ghosts? They wouldn't be in the trees, but I am concerned of their whereabouts. No matter how small the threat is to me I have trouble blocking out the same fear I felt when I was kidnapped. Twice. How vulnerable I was. But I'm stronger now, beyond my wildest dreams. I'm okay.

It still startles me when I hear a loud clamour above me. When I look up, there is nothing but leaves fluttering in the breeze and I sigh and roll my eyes at myself. With a small chuckle I look back in front of me and take a step, but it is cut short as a large hand clamps over my mouth and a strong arm catches me around the shoulders. Instinctively I send a pulse of electricity through me, just like I have practiced with the Supreme, for moments just like this. It shocks the enemy enough to stun them and throw them off guard so I can make a counter move. I spin on my heel ready to use my telekinesis to push whoever it was away but their moan of pain registers in my head and stops me dead, and I turn face to face with Olon.

I gasp with a grin and feel guilty when I see his look of shock and physical hurt, but when he lifts his gaze to my face and his light eyes meet mine I can't help myself when I lunge forward into a hug. Since I have met him I have never spent so long away from him and it is a relief to see him, though I wish it wasn't here. Just like that, why we were here comes rushing back to me, our last conversation, how I had left, on such bad terms. Though he squeezes me back I jump away and look at the ground, ashamed and embarrassed.

"Kayin," his voice is flooded with emotion, it forces me to look at him. He closes the space I have just created between us and cups my face tightly. I can't tell what he is feeling; he seems to be fighting himself with which emotion to deal with first.

"I'm so sorry, Kayin."

I am momentarily taken aback at his apology. Surely it should be me apologising? He takes my silence as a bad sign.

"Please forgive me."

"There's nothing you have to apologise for," I reply, keeping my voice low. "I'm the one who's sorry."

"I tried to control your every move and I ruined everything between us." He begins stroking my cheek with his thumb gently as he speaks, and I realise how much I have missed this simple gesture that I have come to love so much.

"I tried to take things into my own hands. You had every right as the Oracle to question my motives and worry about the situation."

He sighs with visible relief and manages a small smile.

"I was worried about you," he tells me with a soft shake of his head. I raise my hands up to his, covering them and lean my head into his touch.

"I've missed you," I whisper, and it is then how much I had actually missed him hits me, filling me with the feeling. It is one thing to have him in mind when I am training and living mostly isolated in the lair for over two weeks, but to have him here now, knowing that he shouldn't be, that it's not part of my plan and he'll have to leave again soon is a whole other kind of hurt.

I feel him tug my head up, so I look up to his beautiful face that is inching ever closer to mine, like in slow motion. The loose tendrils of my hair blow around my face as a breeze picks up around us, and I close my eyes as the leaves on the floor rustle and bluster. By chance, I open my eyes and glance up at him again and as I do I notice he is looking over my shoulder, something else has caught his eye. Then the slow motion feeling stops and all at once time rushes to catch up, and the gentle breeze blowing around us hit us like a wrecking ball and knocks us off our feet. The strong gale whips up dust and breaks branches that fall on top and around us while we shield our eyes from the oncoming windstorm.

When I am able to, I raise my arm away from my eyes and squint through my eyelashes to see down the pathway.

The narrow path and arching trees have acted like some kind of wind tunnel, funnelling the gust straight towards us, and behind leaves and dirt flying around, at the end of the pathway, I can see the source of the not so natural onslaught. White gown billowing around her, arms out and palms facing up, hanging in the air so still like she is on a hook despite the storm she is conjuring up, is the Supreme.

"Am I proud that my daughter caught one of the humans or do I feel betrayed that she didn't call me right away?" Her voice comes booming down the lane to us, full of emotion to let us know that she is definitely feeling betrayed. I glance across at Olon as best as I can and he too is struggling to sit up. The wind begins circling around us, throwing our limbs around until finally it stops all together and we both drop heavily to the ground.

The Supreme floats effortlessly towards us as we catch our breath, coughing and scrambling to our feet. Olon still looks a little dumbstruck as he watches her, close up, and it reminds me of the look he had when I had displayed all of my powers. Except the Supreme is a myth come to life from his perspective and I can tell his clever brain is working overtime to process the new information and what this means for him and his strategies. It's just another problem to be solved.

"Well, well, well. This is the legendary Oracle?" the

Supreme sings tauntingly. "A little bit scrawny. Look, Kayin, I can pick him up with one hand." She shoots her right arm forward and Olon is lifted in an instant, coughing and grasping his throat like invisible hands are choking him.

"Stop it!" I cry, jumping forward as if being in between them would block her control over him. She rolls her eyes and with a flick of her wrist, chucks Olon a few feet back and leaves him to skid across the floor.

"Remember whose side you're on," the Supreme warns me while Olon is out of earshot. I remember my plan and stand dutifully closer to the Supreme.

"Where are the others?" I call to Olon. I want them to go back and stay safe. I want to tell them I know what I'm doing and I'll be back one day, but I need the Supreme to believe I'm on her side and that I won't desert her later on. In fact, I want to believe that I'll be alive after the war she's planning to have a chance to desert her, but I haven't been acknowledging that fear.

"We're everywhere," he tells me, standing straight again now, dirt smeared across his clothes and face. He begins walking back towards us and I'm tense as he does, hyper aware of any movements the Supreme makes. When Olon notices my new stance by her side his steps slow. He stops completely as the Supreme clenches her fists. I can see her scowling in the corner of my eye. Olon's face hardens and I see his jaw clench.

He raises his fingers to his lips in an instant and whistles loudly and sharply. My eyes widen in fear and anticipation. What has he just done?

The Supreme lowers herself out of the air and touches her bare feet down on the ground. She pulls her shoulders back and takes a menacing step towards Olon as her fingers spark with lightning, but her attention is stolen by a loud crackling noise and bang very close by, followed the obvious sounds of brick crumbling and falling. We all turn our heads behind us and watch the back wall of the building I hadn't long ago exited get blown apart. Bricks shoot across the pathway and into the trees beyond. Some shrapnel bounces down the lane to us, and in an instant Olon and I are moving away, running further down the path to avoid being collateral damage. Even the Supreme hops into the air and moves backwards away from the blow. There's a distinct moaning sound as the internal structures of the building concave and collapse. Trees surrounding the building aren't safe and come down with it, causing a domino effect down the lane.

Olon stands a step in front of me, trying to shield me with his body as we watch the destruction. I wonder how this will affect the lair and can only be thankful the building was practically deserted from what I could see, and then I wonder if that was the rogues' doing. I feel a sting of emotion in my chest, hoping my father left the lair as soon as I had and is somewhere else, safe.

The Supreme screams, making Olon grip his ears in pain, and while he is off balance she once again hurls his body through the air with an impressive gust of wind, sending him a fair distance closer to the falling building. Most of the damage has been done but it is still crumbling and collapsing slowly into a pile of debris.

"Bring him to HQ." The Supreme demands and then soars into the air. I wait until I can't see her past the trees looming above me and only then do I sprint to Olon's side. His body is slumped against a tree and he is out cold. I quickly use my bone vision on his body, recalling a time when this skill was new and untamed I had to think about every little thought and movement to use it. The Supreme has broken the bottom two ribs on Olon's right side with the force of the throw, but fortunately there are no other bone injuries, and the breaks haven't damaged any other organs. He has some extensive gashes and scrapes across his broad back, from where he skid across the rough ground on impact, that make me wince when I lift up his torn, black t-shirt.

Knowing time is of the essence I get to work healing his wounds as much as I can. Golden streams of light jump out of his torso and dive right back in, like thread would if you were sewing with sunshine. My hands glow a matching honey colour from my palms as I maintain a comfortable heartbeat for him after it spiked when I began healing him, and I think how good it feels to use these powers for the right reasons, rather than against my enemies, but I can't dwell on this for long.

My eyes are closed as I focus on calling the chondroblast cells to the breaks and speed up the healing process so a hard callous forms around the point of breakage. My father has been teaching me the science side of using my powers. He worked as an assistant healer when I was growing up, and learnt all about injuries and manual healing from my mother and Nana. Then carried on with this profession back here in the Shadow Lands. He says he enjoys it a lot more than his old job as an apothecary shop owner for shilo, but this makes me sad when I think of the way Gracine improved his life and he gives her no credit for it.

Regardless, it makes it a lot easier for me to use these powers, and makes them more precise and effective when I can imagine what is happening to my patient. In the same way as I heal, it makes it a lot easier to use these powers for evil, and I dread the day I'll have to.

Gently as I can, I roll Olon onto his side while the breaks are still rapidly healing even without my touch. It takes longer for the Osteoblast cells to create new bone, but I can leave it to do that independently.

I begin healing as many of his back scratches as I can before I hear yelling and the distinct sounds of two sides colliding in the distance, and I know I must move Olon to a safer place. I sit back on my heels and lay him flat. Drawing in a deep breath, I now summon the powers I've been working with the Supreme to harness and perfect. I hover my right hand over him, palm facing down, and use my telekinesis to raise his body into the air. I use my left hand to steady the currents of air I'm balancing him on, and keep them consistent underneath him so his body doesn't flop.

I know I can teleport with him to HQ if I want to, but this is an opportunity to test my new skills. Telekinesis is much more than throwing people across the ground as the Supreme demonstrates. The better I know how to use my power in little ways, the more distinctively and effectively I'll be able to utilise it later.

I softly take off and rise into the air with Olon by my side, and now I'm really testing my multitasking and concentration. Every little chance I get to better myself means I'm one step closer to being powerful enough to dismantle the Supreme traditions. I glance down at Olon's face, his features soft and serene as he remains unconscious, and I remind myself that I'm one step closer to returning to him.

If I look forward, all I can see are green trees below me and all blue sky above. The air is dry up here but fresh and I inhale as much as I can get in one breath. I want to float on my back and watch the clouds roll by, with Olon here too, untroubled. But that's just a fantasy, and I'm brutally reminded of reality as the ominous black building that reaches above the trees that I know is HQ rears its ugly head. I drape a protective arm over Olon and straighten myself up, slowing my flight.

HQ is where I was held hostage, abused physically and verbally in the basement. Where I first…killed someone. I'll never truly clean my hands of that blood spilled. It's also where Olon almost died, but I saved him. I keep that in mind now, gripping a fistful of his shirt in my hand. The thought of losing him urged me to be better, forced me to teleport and find the strength within myself to discover my final healing power. Having him around makes me stronger, always.

I touch down and head inside with Olon propped up against me. I'm not too familiar with HQ, the last time I was here I dragged backwards through the lobby and down a hallway to the office of Aren. I stand in the lobby now, and I see the doors ahead that I know section off the hallway from this room, but I look to my right where there are large double doors, and through the windows in the doors I can see black leather couches. I head that way. I push the doors open with a small gust of air before I get to them and stride through, keeping Olon close. The décor is drab; it lowers my mood instantly. The dreary dark grey walls, blacks seats, dim lighting above. It makes me miss the gleaming and light colours of the shilo building that has just been blown to bits. But this will do.

I set Olon down, hoping he will be safe here for a while. His body touches either end of the three-seat sofa, but he just fits. He looks okay. I know this isn't what the Supreme intended for him when she ordered me to bring him here, but I don't want to send him into one of the office rooms, or worse, down into the basement. I'm hesitant to leave, hoping he wakes up before I go, but he doesn't and I know I should get outside and find the other rogues before something awful happens that I can't fix. I know he'll wake up soon enough without me and hopefully by then he'll be healed fully.

22

Meet me on the battlefield.

I hear the Supreme's voice gently echo around my head. Though she sounds calm I can only imagine the chaos ensuing if she's already established a 'battlefield'.

I exit HQ and jump into the air, higher and higher, way above the tops of the trees. The sun is hot and blazing, the air is thinner, and I look down around me to try and locate where everyone is. I can hear so many noises coming from every way, but all I need is to just spot something specific. A dense group of people, the reflection of sun off metal, anything to catch my eye. And then I notice it, across the vast forests beneath me, in the distance a couple of particular bulky trees are blown to their side, unnaturally far for such a strong kind, and I know it's the Supreme's doing.

I rush through the air and dive lower, stopping when

I'm in the trees but out of sight so I can survey the situation undetected. We're at the edge of dense forest now on the outskirts of the Shadow Lands, and though there are trees scattered around still, the ground is dusty from the sand blown across from the desert land. The large clearing is covered with humans and shilo and Ghosts, all fighting one another.

I can see my friends, battling better than I've previously seen them train. It occurs to me then, deeply, that they've been training without me, just like I have without them. It's probable that I have missed so much, and they may have learnt things that I wasn't there to witness. Who knows how long they've all been aware of the situation. I wonder when the four must have told them the true circumstances of the situation, and wonder if they've left any details out. Have the Resistance been training for a week? Two? Or for the almost full three weeks since the Supreme confronted the Four. I wonder how they are all dealing with the new information of an ultimate being that they have to fight.

The Ghosts are interspersed between the many fighting groups but there's a particularly crowded group of them that I notice to my right. I turn my body slightly and rustle a few leaves as I do so but not enough to catch anyone's attention, and above the Ghosts I can see the Supreme looming above the arena. She's far enough away that I can't hear her above the clangs and grunts of fighting but I can see her blood red lips open and moving as she orchestrates her army and laughs or yells, I'm not sure which.

She begins to roll her hands around the air, summoning a ball of wind between them, and then throws it across to the other side of the clearing where I finally spot Orisa, Abeo and Imara standing back to back to fight off the approaching Ghosts. The gust of wind hits them head on and knocks them all across the ground, destroying their formation. I gasp as the Ghosts take this opportunity to lurch towards them while they're down, but I don't let them get close enough and swing my arm from the confines of the trees, and direct my powers towards them. They fly off their feet and struggle to get up elsewhere far away, while my three friends bounce back to their feet and are unaware of my intervening.

I spot some armed shilo marching towards a group of rogues closer to where I am and send a subtle but effective bolt of lightning towards their feet. They flinch and jump to the sides. I do it again and again, sending small shocks down to where they stand until they have jumped far enough off their designated path to hurt my people. I don't want to hurt the shilo but I know for whom I truly fight.

Where are you, daughter?

I ignore the question from the Supreme, glancing up to

where she was only a few moments ago and not seeing her there. I tense and dart my eyes around, looking for her whereabouts and see her directly in front of me but much further away. She's hovering over the edge of the battle and people are following, stretching the battle land further into the desert.

I make out a wounded human lying face down on the dusty floor and push my power to its limit to heal the gash across her back from so far away. Many people run through my line of sight and disrupt my work but I smile with relief as she twitches and slowly pushes up onto her hands and knees. A fellow rogue sees her then and rushes over to take her out of danger.

It has been so long since I have seen so many people in one place. Not counting the Ghosts or the fighting shilo, but humans alone are such a larger number than I'm used to. It's not only the rogues, but the escaped prisoners too, all come together to fight who wronged them. I'm surprised to see so many shilo fighting with the Ghosts too, and I wonder if they're fighting for loyalty to the Supreme, or out of fear. Who here fighting was already a member of the religion which worships the Supreme?

Come fight with your mother.

I can hear the growing frustration even as she talks to me through my mind, but I daren't show myself. I want to fight for the humans and end this, but I told the Supreme I'd work with her and I fear making her mad if I disappoint her. I'm aware of my cowardice at not wanting to reveal myself too because I don't want to appear as if I've picked a side without being able to explain my reasoning.

More bodies join the fight every minute. A sudden commotion draws my attention to below me. Out of the trees, Olon strides into the battlefield. He looks stronger than ever but my heart lurches as he's noticed and enemies run towards him. I shift and swing down to a lower branch so I can see him better and keep an eye on him. He's got a determined grimace on his face and doesn't flinch as Ghosts circle him. Without breaking stride he raises his arm and within a second the Ghosts halt. They stand in position until Olon walks through the group of them and then they fall into step behind him. I've seen this talent in action before, I've had it used on myself, but I've never seen Olon use it with this much ferocity and power behind it. Olon continues to march further into the fighting and as a new wave of enemies approach him, he and the Ghosts under his control begin to attack.

For a moment I am stuck staring at the Oracle in awe. When I finally drag my eyes away from him I can see other people who need my help so I continue as I was doing, using my powers to aid them, all the while glancing back to Olon and the rest of the Four to make sure they are okay.

A deafening scream that I know all too well pierces through the sounds of battle and pauses the fighting. Humans and shilo alike hold their ears and grit their teeth at the unforgiving sound, as even the Ghosts twitch in pain. I look up in fear and far across the land I can see the Supreme's saturated black eyes staring back at me. I have been spotted and this can only get worse.

I can hear a loud crack and then feel the tree beneath me swaying. It begins to fall forward and I hear the cries of people below who see it coming and are running out of the way. I jump into flight and dodge the branches falling towards me to rise above the danger and while I'm preoccupied avoiding this one hazard, I feel a tightness surround my neck. Like an invisible hand digging its fingers deeper into my skin, I cough and splutter and through my watering eyes I see the Supreme using her powers to strangle me. I can't fight back as my body is taken from my own control and held in the air by her force.

"How dare you!" She screams. I know I've messed up completely, I wasn't subtle enough, I shouldn't have even tried, I should have hidden better. Thoughts run through my mind at a record-breaking speed while I watch, paralysed as white spots start to dance in my vision. Have I put everyone else in danger now?

She drags my body slowly towards her through the air and I'm aware of the quietness around us. The fighting is on hold as everyone stares dumbstruck into the sky. I hear the crackle of her lightning before I see it sparking around her body, and my whole world slows down as one of the thickest bolts I've seen leaves her body and heads straight towards me. The icy blue of the electric current hisses and fizzles, and all at once the sound around us comes back. I hear gasps of shock and awe, cries of fear, groans of anticipation.

It can't kill me, it won't kill me…She wouldn't kill me, would she? She needs me, I desperately think to myself.

The Cryptic was already juggling a large fireball between his hands before the Supreme's lightning ever left her hand. The Oracle charges towards the Vehement and jumps as high as he can. His feet fall into her open and waiting hands and she uses this momentum to propel the Oracle into the air at the same time as the Cryptic launches his ball of fire. Soaring side by side with the fire for a moment, the Oracle takes a moment to find his target. He could steer this fire right at the Supreme, knock her down, if only momentarily; it could give them an advantage. But the lightning bolt would still be hurtling straight towards Kayin. He makes up his mind.

Using his telekinesis to control the fire without touching it, he twists his body as his jump finds its peak, and he begins descending again. Time is moving slowly around him as the Oracle works as quick as he can to push the powerful fireball between the oncoming bolt and Kayin.

The right moment comes and he thrusts the fireball into place. Reality speeds up as the burning red sphere collides spectacularly with the blue lightning and a bright purple light bursts into the air. A fiery explosion follows and a wave of heat erupts from the smash of the two fiery objects. It hits Olon first, closest to the explosion as he's still falling from his jump, and pushes him backwards through the air. His skin stings and sizzles with the massive heat blast until finally he hits the floor and rolls across the sandy ground, extinguishing him as much as it can.

The tightness around my throat is gone suddenly and I feel gravity weigh on me heavily. I cry out in pain as I fall, my retinas are burning from the sudden burst of light and explosion of heat. I'm not fully aware of what's happened and I fall to the ground so hard on my back it knocks the air out of my lungs. As I struggle for breath and make an effort to clear my vision, I let my head fall to the side to try and see what divine intervention interrupted my near death experience.

I recognise his body in an instant. Slumped on his back, still as can be. Just like the first time I saw him. It hurts to move, my body argues fervently to stay still, to rest, but I keep pushing onto my side. And then up onto my knees. The scream of the Supreme piercing my ears does not stop my motion as I start crawling across the ground until I have enough force to pull myself up onto my feet and make something of a pathetically slow run towards Olon.

Around me humans are lying on the floor; some are kneeling, some are supporting others. Shilo are doing the same, all trying to make sense of what just happened and helping their friends and family. Ghosts are also on the floor I see, scrambling to their feet to stand guard as quickly as they can. I can feel eyes on me, there are so many people watching me when I finally make it to the Oracle's side.

"Olon," I grab his face and use my bone vision on him quickly, before gently shaking him so I know I'm not doing any more damage. "Olon, open your eyes, please."

He twitches as I slide my arm underneath his neck and pull him into my lap. I've never heard so much silence from so many people in one space before. You can hear my shallow, strained breathing across all the occupied land.

"What did you do?" I whine, suppressing my weeping in front of all these people but I can't stop the shaking of my voice. I question his actions but what I really want to ask is 'was I worth it?' Am I worth losing his life? Saving me, is that worth any of these people's lives? I realise I couldn't love him more for his actions, for wanting to protect me until death, but I condemn them. Going to war, for the Supreme's heir? Fighting the Supreme to take her daughter away from her? That's a fool's mission, but I love him anyway. Olon's body shudders under my touch, so I take his heart in my mind and slow it to a comfortable place so he's not in much pain.

I'm ready to spend the next decade sitting like this if it means I make sure he recovers, but reality rears its ugly head again all too soon and the Supreme screeches once more and people begin yelling and bodies begin moving and I can feel my own being taken from my control again.

I'm ripped away from Olon and my power is disconnected. His heart speeds up again too quickly and he's jolted awake, only to see me soar into the air above and away from him. He's out cold before I can share a look of remorse; so unbeknownst to him I leave him against my will.

Tell them to call off the battle. Tell them to stop. Fix this mess or I will make good of my threat.

I have to go through with my plan for the safety of my people. The ones I love. This fight should have never taken place; the Four should have heeded my warning the first time, though I don't blame them for not believing me. They have to this time, or I'll never get to finish my mission, fulfil the Supreme's wish and finally go home in peace.

"This must stop!" My voice booms across the land as I

project it to every pair of ears that need to hear me. I sound deceivingly authoritative and strong for someone who was on the brink of tears that everyone saw, mere moments ago.

"Humans, listen to me! Go home. Back to your towns and your villages. To your family and friends. Live in peace and leave this land alone. Fighting is no use. Look at your leader!"

I dare not glance down at Olon lying unconscious beneath me as I mention him in my speech, for fear that I won't be able to keep up my false confidence. I circle in the air to look at everyone on the battlefield; I make sure they're all listening. I see the rogues dotted all around. I keep talking.

"Take this as your first and final warning. To take us on is futile, so leave now and do not engage us again. Do not defy this order, or you might find yourselves without a home to go back to next time."

It sounds like my own threat, but truly I am warning them of the Supreme's intentions if they don't listen this time. I don't look down but I see bodies moving below me. I turn my attention to the Supreme, who's staring me down with an ugly smile. Her usual flawless milk white skin is scuffed and dirty, but her black eyes gleam and swim with power as always. I can't tell what she's thinking. I'm unsure if she's still mad or happy to have seen me so blatantly pick a side in front of all my friends. I can't imagine what they must think of me anymore, so I push the thought from my mind.

I'm aware of the Ghosts who have aligned themselves in front of the trees to make sure no humans walk back into shilo territory. They stand so fierce with their staffs across their bodies ready to swing, that I notice even some shilo are hesitant to go back home passed them.

Abeo, Imara and Orisa are below me, with Olon's body. I finally look down, aware that the Supreme still watches me, so I'm careful I don't make any show of emotions. Orisa hovers over Olon, connecting with his spirit. His soul would be safe with her if he were to pass over. I stop myself short of finishing that thought. Then I spin my body so my back is facing the Supreme so she can't see the way I screw my face up and hold back tears at the idea of Olon dying. He'll be fine. I have to believe he is going to be okay.

I cast my gaze back over my shoulder and down to the people who befriended me, protected me, and mentored me. They must sense me watching and all three of them glance up. I can't read their faces, and it hurts me deeply to not know what they are thinking and that I may have lost their trust. I hope one day I can earn that, and their friendship, back. I take comfort in the idea that they worked together to stop the Supreme's bolt from hitting me. They care, or cared, for me, of course. But they are good people who would risk themselves to save anyone, and I know that. I know I definitely lost respect in their eyes when I told them to leave and never come back; such a harsh way to indirectly tell them I'm not going back with them.

They look away from me and I know they won't look back. Imara picks up Olon's body and carries him against her chest, and I watch them leave with the rest of the rogues and ex-prisoners. Wishing so much that I could follow them, and knowing if I watch too long I might give in to that whim, I spin back around and fly a few paces closer to the Supreme, and she flies towards me.

As the chaos below cools down and the crowds of both sides disperse, the weight of my body and the intensity of my injuries are heightened now the adrenaline has worn off. I can feel my eyes rolling back into my head as exhaustion overtakes me and the effort of keeping my broken body aloft is too much, so my flight falters and I drop towards the ground with every other breath, but the Supreme still flies strong and she swoops towards me and catches me in her arms as I finally fall.

"Shh, my sweet princess." She strokes my hair with her gloved hand and I murmur something that I'm not sure is objection or content.

"My darling daughter, rest. Close your eyes. Your mother has big plans."

ACKNOWLEDGMENTS

A massive thank you to my wonderful family and friends. My Mumma who was my sounding board when I wanted to rant about characters and plot and problems and life, and show all my scribbles and doodles to. My gal Paige Swift who was the first person to ever read this story. Much love to all my buddies who got excited with me when I hit 50,000 words, and then when I finished it. My dad, and Spencer. Susannah, Greg, Alexis, Hannah, Sabrina, Charlotte. Heart eyes emoji to you all.

Printed in Great Britain
by Amazon

37832712R00249